Martin Archer Shee

# The Life of Sir Martin Archer Shee

President of the Royal Academy, F.R.S., D.C.L. Vol. 2

Martin Archer Shee

**The Life of Sir Martin Archer Shee**
*President of the Royal Academy, F.R.S., D.C.L. Vol. 2*

ISBN/EAN: 9783744721424

Printed in Europe, USA, Canada, Australia, Japan

Cover: Foto ©Raphael Reischuk / pixelio.de

More available books at **www.hansebooks.com**

# THE LIFE

OF

# SIR MARTIN ARCHER SHEE,

PRESIDENT OF THE ROYAL ACADEMY, F.R.S., D.C.L.

BY HIS SON

## MARTIN ARCHER SHEE,

OF THE MIDDLE TEMPLE, ESQ., BARRISTER-AT-LAW.

In Two Volumes.

VOL. II

LONDON

LONGMAN, GREEN, LONGMAN, AND ROBERTS

1860

# CONTENTS

OF

## THE SECOND VOLUME.

---

## CHAPTER XVII.

### 1839—1846.




## CHAPTER XVIII.

### 1846—1850.

## APPENDICES.

# LIFE

## OF

# SIR MARTIN ARCHER SHEE.

## CHAPTER XII.

### 1831—1834.



THE second year of Sir Martin's presidency witnessed the revival of a practice, the discontinuance of which, during the rule of his immediate predecessor, had deprived one of the most important observances of the Academy of its full effect in stimulating the efforts of youthful talent, among the students of the institution.

The biennial distribution of prizes, when the gold

medal is awarded to the most successful competitors in historical painting, historical or poetical sculpture, and architectural design, is an occasion which it seems highly desirable to invest with all the *éclat* compatible with the nature of the ceremonial. The value of an honorary reward as a tribute to success, in a struggle of competitive emulation with rival energies, cannot fail to be estimated, to a certain extent, in reference to the degree of notoriety attending the contest, and the more or less of publicity which marks and dignifies the result. Whatever serves to attract the attention of society to the occasion on which such rewards are conferred, has a natural tendency to forward the legitimate object of their institution.

Upon this principle, the early practice of the Academy had recognised the expediency of inviting a certain number of distinguished visitors, not professionally connected with the arts, to be present at the distribution of the higher class of medals,—a ceremony which occurs only once in two years. The prizes bestowed in the intermediate years are of inferior value and importance, being awarded merely to the most successful examples of careful imitation and diligent study, in the Plaster Academy, the Life Academy, and the Painting School.

One of the earliest and most striking academical reminiscences on which Sir Martin loved to dwell, referred to the first occasion on which he was present at the distribution of prizes ; when he saw the late amiable and accomplished secretary of the Academy, Henry Howard, then a youthful student of the institution—in after years, his attached and highly-valued friend and colleague,—receive the gold medal for historical painting from the hands of the President, Sir Joshua Reynolds, in the presence of Edmund Burke and many others of the *élite* of the literary and social world. "*I thought him*," Sir Martin would say, when adverting to this gratifying circumstance of Mr. Howard's distinguished and honourable career,—"*I thought him the most enviable man in existence.*"

Perhaps the high reputation achieved by Sir Joshua's didactic efforts, in connection with these biennial displays, had some share in producing in the mind of his immediate successor, an unwillingness to encounter the same amount of publicity, while undertaking a task rendered doubly arduous by the remembrance of his success.

The custom of inviting the attendance of strangers, however limited in number, to do honour to the successful candidates on the proclamation of their triumph, had certainly been abandoned long before the death of Mr. West; and his distinguished successor, Sir Thomas Lawrence, took no steps to restore it. But it so happened that on the last of these solemnities at which he was destined to preside, and but a very few weeks before his lamented death,—viz., on the 10th December 1829,—he had been induced to extend his address to the students beyond the usual limits, in order to pay a just and graceful tribute to the genius and memory of Flaxman, whose loss the Academy and the arts had been recently called on to deplore. The task thus imposed upon him by sincere admiration for the genius of that great artist and most amiable man, was performed with so much eloquence and effect, that an unanimous request from the Academy obliged him to consent to the printing of the address in question ;—a production which left no doubt on the minds of those who heard or perused it, that the hand of its gifted author could hold and guide the pen, with no small share of that graceful and forcible talent which it never failed to display when wielding the pencil.

Had Sir Thomas's life been prolonged until the next biennial distribution, he would in all likelihood have consented, in deference to the wishes of the most influential among his academic colleagues, to revive a practice so well calculated to give· impressive effect to the ceremonial in question, by summoning around him, on the occasion, some of his eminent contemporaries in the kindred pursuits of science and literature, and a few of the most conspicuous personages in social, political, and official life, whose feelings towards the art and the Academy would have led them to view with friendly interest and curiosity, the proceedings of the day.

Sir Martin had, on more than one occasion, strongly urged on him the expediency of this return to the traditional policy of the institution; and when himself unexpectedly placed in circumstances where its adoption or rejection depended on the verdict of his own judgment, the new President felt himself in a manner pledged to the adoption of that course which he had so earnestly recommended to his distinguished predecessor, as a duty incumbent on the occupant of the academic chair. Lawrence, as a man unpractised in literary composition, might be pardoned for exhibiting that diffidence of his own powers, which, however ill founded, was unquestionably sincere. But in one so well skilled as Sir Martin in the use of his pen, and already conspicuous for its successful efforts in the cause of the art, it would have been simply affectation to allege a feeling of incompetency, as an excuse for following the more recent precedents bearing upon the subject of this biennial solemnity.

He therefore determined on restoring the original practice of the Academy, and accompanying the distribution of the gold medals by a carefully studied, and written discourse on the principles, practice, or history of the art, giving at the same time a greater amount of publicity and *éclat* to the triumph of the successful candidates, by inviting the attendance of a number of eminent persons not professionally connected with the art, at a ceremonial which he justly regarded as one of the most important within the range of academic functions. To this practice he strictly adhered during the remainder of his active career as President; nor was it discontinued until the failure of his bodily health and strength had utterly disqualified him for the mental and physical exertion involved in the performance of the interesting duties connected with the occasion.

It need hardly be observed that the altered customs of our day, as regards the time of year fixed for the commencement of the parliamentary session, make it impossible to secure for any public ceremonial, unassociated with feelings of political or religious excitement, anything more than a very scanty attendance of persons belonging to the *élite* of society, when such ceremonial takes place in London, in the month of December. But though "the world," *par excellence*, are scattered about in regions far remote from the influence of metropolitan attractions, no small section of the aristocracy of talent, may, at that dreary season, be still found within the bills of mortality. In addition to the chief dignitaries of the Law, and the principal functionaries of the various scientific and literary communities whose head-quarters are in London, the most eminent men in every department of active professional life are all within hail, and contribute, with the minor luminaries of the official and *bureaucratic* world, to enliven the gloom of the social system, and rescue the western division of the great city from the horrors of total desertion.

Thus, although it was a hopeless task to summon round the academic display of the 10th of December, 1831, an assemblage such as that which graced the delivery of Sir Joshua's discourses, the auditory collected to witness Sir Martin's first performance of the ceremony in question, was sufficiently distinguished in rank, station, and talent, to render the scene more interesting and impressive in the eyes of the students, than any distribution of academic prizes that had taken place within the memory of the then existing generation.

The subject which the President selected for this, his first discourse, was legitimately supplied by the genius and career of his immediate predecessor ; and never, perhaps, was the language of panegyric employed with greater sincerity than in the glowing tribute of admiration paid by Sir Martin to the memory of that great artist. His peculiar merits, as a painter of graceful and characteristic portraits, were indeed such as could not be too earnestly impressed on the attention of the student about to devote himself to that branch of the art; while his wonderful mastery of effect, as regards *chiar'oscuro* and arrangement of colour and form, in appropriate accessories, was calculated to supply the most instructive examples for the imitation of all. Among his contemporaries, no one could have been found more anxious to do justice to his claims, or more competent to explain and develop their peculiar characteristics than Sir Martin ; and the manner in which he acquitted himself of the duty thus undertaken was felt to be worthy of the theme and the occasion. His academic colleagues testified their approval of the performance by an unanimous vote of thanks, and a resolution that the address to the students should be printed. I may here mention that a similar compliment was paid to the President, on every succeeding occasion, when the delivery of the gold medals was accompanied or succeeded by a didactic discourse from his pen.

The political changes that marked the end of the year 1830 were not without interest for the arts and the Academy. If the break up of the Wellington administration involved the resignation of Mr. Peel, whose liberal patronage of the arts afforded a satisfactory guarantee of his readiness, as a minister, to promote every reasonable scheme for their encouragement that could be fairly urged on his attention,—on the other hand, the reform cabinet, although mainly composed of politicians too much engrossed by the stirring questions of constitutional science, to bestow much thought on the less obtrusive topics of art or literature, could boast among its numbers some of those who, in the higher ranks of London society, were most conspicuous for their just appreciation of the claims of genius, and their enlightened sympathy with its exertions, in every department of intellectual labour. The names of Grey, Lansdowne, and Holland, were not less familiarly associated with the literary and social, than with the parliamentary triumphs of the time; and there was good ground for hope that, whenever the excitement of political agitation, inseparable from the discussion of the Reform Bill, should have sufficiently subsided to allow of some share of administrative attention being directed to the interests of learning or taste, these interests would not be treated with indifference, or meet with less encouragement from a cabinet presided over by Earl Grey, than would have been awarded to them under the sway of his immediate predecessors.

Nor was it long before circumstances arose which were calculated to test the disposition of the ministry, in reference to a subject of great importance to the future prospects of the art in this country. The noble collection of pictures, purchased many years previously for the nation, from the representatives of the late Mr. Angerstein, in order to form the nucleus of a National Gallery, and subsequently enriched, from time to time, by the addition of a few choice specimens of the old masters, were still adorning the walls of the house in Pall Mall, which had been the private residence of the original collector, and which, like most London residences of a moderate size, was inadequate in point of space, and unsuited in point of lighting, to the effective exhibition of a large number of pictures, comprising many of the most celebrated productions of the pencil to be found throughout Europe.

To provide a more suitable locality for this collection, had long been an object of urgent importance, in the view of those who could appreciate its claims upon public attention, and were consequently fully alive to the deficiencies of its temporary position. The question of erecting a building sufficiently capacious in size, and dignified in appearance, for the display of the national pictures, had been frequently mooted in public and in private,—in the columns of the daily press, and in the desultory discussions which so often encumber, but occasionally enliven, the merely formal business of the House of Commons, at an early hour of its sittings.

But a salutary fear of increasing the grand total of an already formidable annual budget, and an ill-founded distrust of the liberality of Parliament, where national objects are at stake, had long operated as a check on the favourable dispositions of more than one previous cabinet, in dealing with matters of this description; and it was not to be wondered at, if the reform ministry, with whom "*retrenchment*" was a prominent and plausible watch-word, were affected with a similar financial timidity, as regards the interest of taste, in presence of the radical majority of the newly-constituted House of Commons.

In the mean time, however, sundry metropolitan improvement acts, passed in recent years for the embellishment of the courtly quarter of London, had, by clearing away the vast masses of dingy brickwork formerly covering the space now occupied by Pall Mall East and Trafalgar Square, thrown open the finest site in England for the erection of a public building, partially filled up by the King's Mews, an edifice of slight architectural pretensions, but not wholly devoid of such decorative attractions, as were suitable to its unpretending style of brickwork massively coped with stone, —and presenting a façade sufficiently striking for the unobtrusive locality in which it originally stood.

Such as it was, it appeared to a high architectural authority to possess capabilities not unworthy of consideration, in dealing with the question of a fitting *local* for the National Gallery; and these capabilities were brought under the notice of the Government, in connection with a proposal for effecting, at a comparatively moderate expense, the object of providing the requisite accommodation for the national pictures, and a more fitting domicile for the Royal Academy.

This proposal emanated from Mr. Wilkins, an architect of great eminence, and one of the royal academicians.   It suggested the facility of converting the existing building of the King's Mews into a set of apartments applicable to the desired purposes, and of adding to the space, so provided, by the erection of a corresponding portion or wing, to be built of the same material and in strict conformity with the outward design of the original building, with such alterations and additions to the façade of the whole, as might impart a more dignified and ornamental character to the architecture of the entire edifice, when completed and adapted to its new destination.   Mr. Wilkins laid before the Government elaborate elevations of the building, as intended to be improved and enlarged, and careful estimates of the expense involved in the design, which he offered to execute for, I think, the sum of 35,000*l.*

The plan thus submitted to the Treasury was approved and, in the first instance, adopted by Government.   But in the progress of the discussions and deliberations that took place, on the subject, between Mr. Wilkins and the authorities, the latter came to the conclusion that it would be but a paltry economy, and an inconvenient restriction of the powers and judgment of the architect, to confine him to the exact plan and dimensions of the existing building, in the additional structure which he was about to erect; and that, if rather more expensive, it would, at any rate, be a far more judicious course—in reference to the adaptation of the edifice to its intended purpose,—if the King's Mews were to be pulled down, and the whole space made available for the construction of a new brick building, in the erection of which the architect might have free scope for the development of his own ideas, as to external elevation and internal distribution, subject to the judgment of those on whom the placing of the pictures would depend, as to certain details of lighting and general arrangement. This amended project,—involving of course some considerable additional outlay,—was accordingly adopted by the Treasury. But ere the inventive genius of Mr. Wilkins had been called upon to develop itself in the subdued aspect, and modest architectural pretensions of a brickwork palace, another change came o'er the spirit of the ministerial dream; and with increasing reliance on the enlightened liberality of the national representatives, the Treasury resolved to apply for a grant sufficient in amount to justify the employment of a more costly material, in the erection of a building destined to purposes of great public interest, and capable of being rendered a conspicuous ornament of the British metropolis.

The notion of a brick building was accordingly discarded; and the architect was empowered to proceed with his plans on the understanding that an edifice of stone, in every way suited to the importance of the object in view, and the dignity of the nation at whose cost it was to be erected, was required at his hands. From the adoption of his first proposal, therefore, Mr. Wilkins's original designs and elevations were subjected to two successive modifications, of so sweeping a character as to involve all but a total change of plan and system of construction. He had now, however, as it appeared, ample space and verge enough; and although the dread of offending the austere virtue of parsimonious radicalism, in its stern guardianship of the public purse, had necessarily induced him to pare down his estimates to the lowest figure compatible with the production of a creditable monument of national taste, and a commodious asylum for the highest interests of the art,—he had at least a site to work upon which Wren might have envied, while designing St. Paul's.   He had shaken off the trammels by which his fancy had been incumbered in the earlier stages of the business ; and all now would be clear for the unfettered exercise of his genius.

In due course of time, his plans were matured,—his elevations submitted to, and approved by the Government.   The design, or at least the general line, of the façade was made known to the public.   A storm of opposition immediately burst forth.   The space presented by the north side of what is now Trafalgar Square, was ample, as regarded the extent of the frontage or width of the intended building.   But in order to secure the requisite depth, from front to rear,—where the barracks of the Foot Guards presented a boundary line, between which and the new building, a commodious thoroughfare was to be retained,—it had been considered necessary to bring forward the line of the façade to a point, at the eastern extremity, where the angle of the building would partly conceal the portico of St. Martin's church, from the spectator approaching it from Pall Mall East, or contemplating its glories from the steps of the Union Club.

Up to that critical period, the London public had been somewhat indifferent, if not wholly insensible, to the architectural claims of this respectable ecclesiastical structure, and its now famous portico.   True it is, that until the sweeping away of sundry streets and alleys had laid it open to the more distant gaze of Charing Cross and Cockspur Street, it was not so circumstanced as to challenge very general notice from the *dilettante* saunterer, or foreign tourist.   Even now that it was

well seen from many points, in all its *integrity*, there
were not wanting those who,—in rash disregard of the
new-born enthusiasm created by the recent manifestation of its beauties,—ventured to criticise its details, and
to suggest that the pediment of the portico was open to
serious animadversion, if judged according to the rules
of outline and proportion to be collected from the most
admired precedents supplied by the remains of ancient
Greek and Roman architecture.   The metropolitan
mind, however, was attacked by one of those violent fits
of the *picturesque*, which occasionally, and at rare intervals, disturb the apathetic equanimity of its usual
state of feeling, where " high art " is concerned ; and
the aspect and necessities of the new building were
universally held as of no account, and magnanimously
treated as dust in the balance, when sought to be put
in competition with the paramount object of displaying,
in prominent relief, this *chef-d'œuvre* of metropolitan
architecture.

Newspapers thundered, — parochial meetings petitioned,—tory and radical *virtuosi* assailed the Treasury
bench in a tone of indignant reproof.   The ministry
trembled and gave way.   Mr. Wilkins was directed to
throw back the line of his façade so as to admit the
portico.   Vainly did he object that the proximity of
the barracks in the rear, made this change in the line
of his building impossible, if his plans and elevations
were to be retained.   The truth of the objection was
undeniable.   It was then timidly suggested by some
conciliatory spirits that the particular locality in which
a few companies of the Guards were to be housed, was
not a question of great importance, as regarded the
discipline and efficiency of the army, and that perhaps
it might be advisable to solve the difficulty by pulling

down the barracks,—a range of buildings of the meanest aspect and construction,—and erecting new ones elsewhere. The ministry, it was thought, might have been brought to acquiesce in this view. But an insurmountable obstacle presented itself in the highest quarter. The retention of the barracks in that place, was insisted upon by an august personage. The idea was of course abandoned.

In the meantime the unfortunate architect and his plans were somewhat in the position of the ancient and unwarlike Britons, at the time of their piteous appeal to " Ætius, thrice consul." The barbarian votaries of St. Martin's drove them back on the barracks ; and the barracks drove them forward on the barbarians. There was no help for it. The building must be subjected to a *procrustean* operation. The intended outline must be sacrificed. If the whole line of the edifice could not be thrown back,—which was manifestly the case,—a thick slice or two must be scooped or carved out of the frontage at the eastern end; an expedient involving, of course, a corresponding and equally unmeaning indentation at the extremity of the other wing. True, a quantity of space available to, and valuable for the purposes of the building would be lost ;—to say nothing of the interference with the architectural elevation, as originally designed and approved of. But the full revelation of St. Martin's portico to the gaze of an admiring posterity would be secured ; and the practical inconvenience that might be experienced from the necessary curtailment of internal accommodation, would fall, in the first instance, only on a body to whom a considerable section of the public were much disposed to grudge the share likely to be allotted to them in the projected edifice, viz., the Royal Academy.

The details, above recorded, of the origin and history of the building in question, are familiar to all those who, like the writer of this biography, had peculiar opportunities of observing the progress of the negotiations and discussions connected with its erection, and indeed to many whose knowledge of the facts is derived merely from contemporary rumour, and the information supplied, from time to time, by the columns of the daily press. But the generation which has sprung up since the period when the site of the projected building was matter of public and parliamentary discussion,—while perhaps sharing in the feeling of critical discontent so general among the public of five-and-twenty years back, in contemplating the architectural result of a great national commission, — are probably but little aware how much of the inadequacy of that result is chargeable on ministerial timidity and vacillation, parliamentary caprice, and cockney sentimentality, rather than on the shortcomings of the architect himself, who,—straitened in expenditure, cramped in space, and thwarted in the development of the very plans which the Government had sanctioned and adopted, — had to complete his arduous task amidst a tempest of hostile criticism and conflicting objections, involving a degree of annoyance and vexation, the continual pressure of which, during several years devoted to the work, seriously impaired his health, and, in all reasonable probability, accelerated his premature decease.

The idea of uniting under one roof the two distinct establishments of the National Gallery and the Royal Academy, had early formed part of the schemes which were, from time to time, submitted to the Government, for the transfer of the Angerstein collection to a more suitable domicile. The plans originally suggested by

Mr. Wilkins were prepared, I believe, on the assumption
that such an arrangement would be adopted; and, from
the first, the suggestion was favourably entertained
by the ministry, who could not but concur with those
who recognised the just claims of the Academy, or did
not view that body with malignant and unreasoning
hostility, in anticipating substantial benefit to the art,
from the close juxtaposition of the two institutions.

The Government, indeed, had a strong inducement to
the adoption of this view, in their anxiety to obtain
possession of the apartments in Somerset House, then
occupied by the Royal Academy, which,—in common
with the corresponding rooms on the other side of the
archway, tenanted by the Royal Society,—were much
coveted for the increased accommodation of some of the
many public offices to which the greater part of the
building had long been devoted.  On the other hand,
many reasons combined to recommend to the favourable
consideration of the Royal Academy, any project of
removal which might secure for them, on the same
terms of independent and undisturbed occupancy, a
suitable set of apartments, more convenient as to locality,
more spacious in area, and more accessible in ascent,
than their rooms in Somerset House.  These apartments
were now very inadequate, in size and extent, to the increased requirements of the institution ; more especially
as regarded the rooms devoted to the annual exhibition,
from which, every year, hundreds of meritorious works
were excluded by reason of want of space ; while of those
which covered the walls, a large proportion were necessarily placed at a height too great to allow the spectator
to judge of their merits,—and where, however attractive
might be the display, its enjoyments were beyond the
reach of all whom age or accidental infirmity incapaci-

tated, or deterred, from undertaking the tedious ascent of a spiral stone staircase, the length and steepness of which appeared somewhat formidable, after a walk of moderate extent, even to the soundest in wind and limb, among the crowds of pedestrian visitors that annually thronged the exhibition.

There was also an obvious advantage to be anticipated for the students of the Royal Academy, in the close proximity of the schools of the institution, to the gallery which would permanently contain the national treasures of art,—thus affording them the daily and hourly opportunity of usefully applying the lessons of theory, by the studious contemplation of the happiest results of practice, and sustaining their emulative ardour, by placing before them the brightest examples of excellence in every department of the art.

Among those who were most powerfully impressed with the notion of benefit to be derived to the Academy, and consequently to the arts, from the suggested change of locality, no one was more anxious for the satisfactory accomplishment of this object than the President; and from an early stage of the official discussions to which the architectural question was subjected, he took occasion to urge, in the strongest manner, on the attention of the prime minister, Earl Grey, the claims of the Royal Academy to share in the advantages intended to be secured to the arts by such parliamentary grant as might be voted for the erection of a National Gallery; and at the same time he never failed to insist, as a matter of strict justice, on the right of the Academy to occupy their intended share of the new building, on precisely the same footing, as regards the crown and the country, on which they had been originally admitted to, and had continued in, the enjoyment of their *locus standi* in Somerset House.

However desirable, on the grounds above mentioned, the transfer of the academic domicile might appear to those who were interested in the prosperity of the institution, Sir Martin was well aware that no change of locality could, in the long run, be really beneficial, or indeed otherwise than disastrous to the Academy, unless, in their new abode, the same independence of ministerial control and parliamentary interference, which they had up to that time ever enjoyed, were practically guaranteed to them,—and unless the peculiar, and perhaps exceptional tenure by which they occupied their apartments in a building erected at the public cost, and devoted to national purposes, were to be the rule and standard of their " tenant right " in their portion of any national edifice to which they might be transferred.

This was a point of which he never lost sight in his frequent communications with the head of the Government, during the somewhat protracted period over which the discussions, official and parliamentary, that preceded the final settlement of the ministerial plans in reference to the projected building, were necessarily extended: and whatever may have been the views of a portion of the ministry,—whose tone, from time to time, in the House of Commons, was such as to create considerable distrust in the minds of the Academy, as to the sincerity of their professions of good will towards that body,—it is certain that, from the first, the academic interests, as urged and enforced by the energetic advocacy of the President, experienced the readiest attention and the most cordial sympathy on the part of Earl Grey; from whom the Academy eventually received every satisfactory assurance of the permanent recognition of their claim of " fixity of tenure," which the nature of his authority, and the limits of his ministerial responsibility, could enable or allow him to give.

At a period like the present,—when the Academy are threatened with ejection from their apartments in Trafalgar Square, under circumstances which entitle them to characterise the intended proceeding as an act of deliberate spoliation,— it cannot be considered immaterial to the subject of this biography, to recal the memory of facts bearing so directly on the question of those rights of which the late President was the strenuous and able asserter,—and tending to exhibit, in a correct point of view, the exact relative position of the Government and the Academy, when the latter,— in full reliance on national justice and ministerial good faith,—were induced to exchange the vantage-ground of their secure position in Somerset House, for the delusive benefits of a dwelling, to which, notwithstanding the substantial value of the equivalent given for it, in their vacated apartments, they would now appear to have obtained but a phantom title.

I have said that they gave a substantial consideration for the benefits held out to them by the proposed change: and a bare statement of the facts connected with their first occupation of the apartments so long enjoyed by them in Somerset House, will suffice to show that their position in that building was virtually, if not technically, a permanent tenure, in no manner exposed to the chances of dispossession or disturbance, from ministerial caprice or radical hostility,—and that, in fact, the title by which they held, being derived from the personal will and pleasure of the sovereign, could not have been arbitrarily interfered with by the ministry or the Parliament, without an unseemly disregard of rights conferred by the august founder of the Academy, in respect of property over which his Majesty had, under a parliamentary arrangement, reserved to himself a disposing power, equivalent to that conferred by individual ownership.

The Royal Academy was established on the 10th of December, 1768, by the sole authority and act of King George III.,—not incorporated by charter, but constituted by royal sign manual of that date, as a body wholly emanating from, and dependent on, the royal pleasure, to be governed according to the rules and forms of proceeding which his Majesty laid down for their observance. It is of the very essence of their constitution to be subject, in all things, to the personal will and control of the sovereign for the time being, with whom they enjoy the right of direct communication through their President and officers; and in their collective or official (for they have not in strictness any corporate) capacity, they acknowledge no responsibility to any other authority in the state.

By the favour of the king, the Academy were first accommodated with rooms in a house in Pall Mall, being the property of the crown; and here they met for the first time on the 14th of December, 1768.

On the 7th of January, 1771, they were, by a similar act of royal favour, transferred to and duly installed in a set of apartments allotted to them by the king in old Somerset House; at that time one of his Majesty's palaces, and as such, available for such purposes as to his Majesty seemed fit.

In this position, it cannot be pretended that the Royal Academy were liable to be disturbed in their occupation of the apartments so allotted to them, by any authority, public or private, save that of the sovereign himself, at whose will and pleasure they held. Ministerial control and parliamentary interference, as affecting their tenure, while Somerset House remained the property of the crown and the palace of the sovereign, were clearly out of the question.

In the year 1775, however (15th Geo. III.), an Act of Parliament was passed "to convert and consign Somerset House to the uses therein mentioned," viz., for the purpose of erecting on the site of the palace so devoted to national objects, certain public buildings and offices specified in the Act "and such other public offices and buildings as shall be thought fit by his Majesty, his heirs and successors, convenient to erect and establish there."

The king, in assenting to a measure which diverted his own royal palace from the uses pertaining to it, as one of the private residences of the Crown, thus reserved to himself a right of direction and control over the disposition of the building, so far as the purposes to which in its new character it was to be devoted, were not distinctly specified in the Act ; and in the exercise of this right, his Majesty was pleased to give instructions for the appropriation of a suitable portion of the building about to be erected, to the use, and for the permanent residence of his Academy, in substitution for the apartments which, by virtue of his grant and authority, they continued to occupy in his former palace, until the period of its demolition under the provisions of the Act.

In pursuance of these instructions, the internal distribution and details of the new building,—so far as they related to that portion of it which was to be occupied by the Royal Academy,—were arranged and decided upon in strict reference to the convenience and necessary accommodation of that body.

On the 4th of October, 1776, the architect of the new building, Sir William Chambers, who was also a royal academician, presented to the council of that body, the plans of the intended new Royal Academy, to be erected as part of the new building of Somerset House; and those plans were approved and signed by the President and council, the keeper and the secretary.

On the 11th of April, 1780, a letter was addressed, on behalf of the Lords Commissioners of his Majesty's Treasury, to Sir William Chambers, directing him to "deliver up into the hands of the treasurer of the Royal Academy, who is by virtue of his office to have the inspection and care both of the buildings and all other his Majesty's effects employed in that institution, all the apartments allotted to his Majesty's said academy in the new buildings at Somerset House, which are to be appropriated to the uses specified in the several plans of the same, heretofore settled."

Thus had the Royal Academy, for a period of upwards of fifty years, enjoyed an uninterrupted and undisturbed occupancy of their apartments in Somerset House;— apartments erected expressly for their reception and accommodation, in obedience to the royal command, and of which they obtained possession by the authority of the sovereign, given in strict pursuance of the terms of an Act of Parliament reserving to him and his successors the requisite right of appropriation.

If this state of things did not constitute an inde- feasible title to the apartments so occupied, it virtually secured the position of the Academy in these apart- ments from any chance of disturbance, as long as their peculiar relations with the sovereign, in virtue of which alone they could be said to exist in a definite or quasi-corporate form, should continue in their original force and integrity. The rooms, being allotted to them by the sovereign, avowedly in substitution for those which he had placed at their disposal in his own palace, were not, in any sense, a gift or boon from the liberality of the nation, or held by any tenure which afforded a pretext for parliamentary interference with their concerns.

But the contemplated transfer of their *penates* to the new building in Trafalgar Square, if effected without a distinct understanding between the Government and the Academy, as to the security and permanency of their position, would have been a step of very doubtful prudence on the part of that body, at a period when jealousy of their pre-eminence, and hostility to their rights, entered so largely into the feelings of those who assumed to guide public opinion, on the subject of the arts, in the columns of the daily press.

The anti-academic spirit, fostered by a few discontented individuals, whose overweening estimate of their own merits induced them to resent, as the grossest injustice, their non-admission into the ranks of the favoured body, had begun to find an echo in the House of Commons among a small *clique* of parliamentary *doctrinaires*, to whom the slight honorary distinction, and slender privileges connected with the designation and character of an R.A., were alike odious, as repugnant to the principle of social equality,—so dear to their republican sympathies,—and incompatible with the true theory of free trade, and the eternal maxims of utilitarian wisdom. With this party, or section of a party (whose general competency to deal with the concerns of taste, may be estimated from the fact that their chief organ and mouthpiece in Parliament was the late Mr. Joseph Hume), the main object, during the discussions relating to the new building, was to exclude the Royal Academy from all participation in the benefit of the sums to be voted for its erection ; while, if this result should prove unattainable, the next *desideratum*, in their view, was to avail themselves of the pretext which would be afforded by the application of a portion of the sums so voted, to the purposes of the Academy, in order to control and harass that body in the exercise of their existing rights, and if possible, ultimately subvert their privileges, destroying at once their connection with the Crown, and their *prestige* with the public.

While, therefore, it was considered by the Academy a matter of great importance to secure the advantages of an improved locality and increased accommodation, by the cession of their existing apartments in exchange for that portion of the new building which the Government proposed to place at their disposal, great caution and vigilance were requisite on their part, to provide against the possible result of a change that might, under no improbable combination of circumstances, afford great facilities for their serious annoyance.  To this object Sir Martin devoted himself, with untiring energy and perseverance, in all his communications with the Government, on the subject of the new building and its ultimate appropriation.  And if the success that attended his exertions should, after the lapse of a quarter of a century, prove not to be of so substantial and enduring a character as it appeared to be on the day when, as President, he publicly received the keys of the newly-erected building devoted to the Royal Academy from the hands of the King in person, such a result will certainly not be attributable to the neglect, on his part, of any means which a judicious forethought could employ, to secure for the body over whom he presided, the permanent enjoyment of those rights of which his fearless advocacy obtained the full recognition from contemporary power; — rights often threatened, indeed, from various quarters, during the remainder of his official career, but never effectively assailed, while *he* lived to do battle in their defence.

It must not be supposed, from what I have here stated, that in his zeal for the honour and security of the Royal Academy, he lost sight of what he owed to the kindred interests with which he was also officially connected, or that he was insensible to the claims of the National Gallery, as regarded the plan and distribution of the new building.

Even those uncompromising enthusiasts, whose devotion to the cause of " high art " impels them to agitate for the unconditional and uncompensated removal of the Royal Academy from their present habitation,— in order to obtain for the National Gallery the undivided possession of the highly-prized locality now occupied by both institutions,—owe a debt of gratitude to the memory of Sir Martin, for the successful efforts made by him to confirm a wavering Government in their half-abandoned intention of appropriating the admirable site in question for the erection of a national building, to be devoted to the most beneficial purposes and highest interests of the art.

The subjoined correspondence, which took place between the President and the head of the administration, at a rather critical period of affairs in the history of the national edifice, will afford some evidence in support of this assertion, by exhibiting at once the freedom and vigour with which Sir Martin urged his views on the attention of the prime minister, and the importance attached by that eminent statesman to the President's opinions, as justly entitled to influence the decision of Government on the point in issue.

It should here be mentioned that as early as the month of August 1832, the plan of locating the National Gallery and Royal Academy in one building, to be erected in Trafalgar Square, was so far settled, that the Commissioners of Woods and Forests had directed the architect to submit his plans to a committee of the Royal Academy, appointed expressly for the purpose of considering the adaptation of a certain portion of the intended edifice, to the purposes of that body; and some official correspondence had taken place between the Board of Commissioners and the Academy, on the subject of the apartments to be allotted to the use of the latter, which proceeded on the assumption that the design was to be carried into effect, and that the details, and not the principle, of the project, constituted the sole ground of discussion between the Government and the intended occupants of the new edifice.

It was therefore with no little surprise that, in the latter part of the session of 1833, the Academy found the organs of the administration, in the House of Commons, not merely hesitating to propose the additional vote of money which the extended design and consequently enlarged estimate of Mr. Wilkins had rendered necessary for the purposes of the projected building, but, to some extent, appearing to favour the notion of applying the sum of 50,000*l.*,—already voted towards the erection of a National Gallery,—in a manner totally inconsistent with the retention of the plans provisionally sanctioned by the Government, and formally approved of by the authorities of the two institutions for whose benefit they were intended.

Alarmed by the appearance of vacillation exhibited by the Government on this point, in some incidental parliamentary discussion on the subject of the intended structure, Sir Martin had sought an interview with Lord Grey, for the purpose of strongly urging on his lordship, as prime minister, the expediency of adhering to the original decision, as to the locality and destination of the new building.   What passed at that interview,—which took place on the 14th August, 1833,—may be collected from the following letter, addressed to Lord Grey by the President, on the 15th of the same month, in consequence, as it would appear, of Sir Martin having learnt from the newspaper report of the previous night's debate in the House of Commons, that the Chief Commissioner of the Woods and Forests, Lord Duncannon, had thrown out, for the consideration of the House, a suggestion that the Banqueting House in Whitehall might be judiciously converted to the purposes of a National Gallery.

" Cavendish Square,<br>"Thursday, 15th Aug., 1833.

" MY LORD,

" With the greatest reluctance I yield to the sense of duty which impels me again to trespass on your lordship's valuable time.  But the importance of the occasion to those interests which I am pledged to promote, by every effort in my power, will, I trust, excuse, at least, if not justify, my present address.

" Of your lordship's liberal disposition to protect the fine arts, I am fully convinced; and in the interview with which you honoured me yesterday, your sentiments in their favour were illustrated by the expression of your regret, that circumstances should exist which would probably prevent the execution of the plan which, after so much deliberation and discussion, had been formed for their advantage, and from the completion of which, under your lordship's auspices, you were pleased to say you would have derived so much gratification.

" The principal difficulty your lordship stated to arise from the increase which appears in the last estimate, submitted by Mr. Wilkins, and the consequent dissatisfaction which your lordship conceived would be excited among the members of the House of Commons, on the ground of expense. Of this increase, or the causes which have been assigned for it, I am unqualified to judge. The proposed structure has been approved of, as calculated to answer the purposes for which it was intended, by the committee appointed by the Lords of the Treasury, by the trustees of the National Gallery, and by the committee of the Royal Academy selected to consider its adaptation to the peculiar objects of that institution ; and fifty thousand pounds had been voted most readily by Parliament for its erection. What reception the increased estimate might have met with from the House of Commons, if brought forward, as surely there was some reason to expect, with the countenance, at least, if not the recommendation of Government, I can judge of only by the sentiments generally expressed last night by the members, when the subject was alluded to : and if the parliamentary reports are to be depended on, the weight of opinion seemed rather in favour of the proposed building, than against it, and certainly appeared by no means to patronise the new project introduced to the House by the Chief Commissioner of Woods and Forests.

" I confess I cannot avoid lamenting here, that the weight of official influence should appear to have been withdrawn from a plan which had been · approved by the parties appointed and competent to judge of it, and which had been partially sanctioned by a vote of Parliament, and that it should seem to be transferred to a project, on the propriety of which no competent authority appears to have been consulted, and of which, in my humble opinion, no competent authority can approve.

" Though very unqualified to form a judgment of what may be the sense of the House of Commons, on any subject, and offering my opinions with great diffidence on the present occasion, I cannot, I confess, bring myself to believe that with the growing sentiment of liberality towards the Arts which has appeared among the members, the plan for the building in Trafalgar Square would have been effectually resisted, if the estimate had been officially recommended or even proposed.

" On the manner in which the interests of the arts, as far as the Royal Academy is concerned, have been overlooked in the proposition of the noble lord who presides over the Woods and Forests, I shall make no observation. Your lordship is aware of the just claims of the Royal Academy to some consideration in an arrangement of this kind; and I am sure you would be the last person to countenance any proceeding in which these claims might appear to be disregarded.

" Most earnestly would I entreat your lordship for a reconsideration of this matter,.while there is yet time. The interests of the arts,—the credit of the country and, may I not add, my lord,—to a certain extent, the credit of the Government, are involved in it. Let not an undertaking be lightly abandoned which was so nearly matured, and to which there appears no decisive Parliamentary opposition. Your lordship will, I am convinced, never allow a great public object of national utility and ornament to be sacrificed to a speculation of trifling pecuniary advantage, or to considerations which, if closely investigated by those who incautiously allow themselves to be influenced by them, might perhaps be found to originate in private interest, professional rivalry, or personal opposition, rather than any just principle of public economy, or rational view of the public advantage.

" If I appear over ardent on this theme, your lordship will, I am sure, extend to me your kind indulgence. I should consider myself as violating a most serious duty,—as deserting the cause of the arts, the cause of the Royal Academy, the cause of the National Gallery, and, as far as these interests are concerned, the cause of the country,—if, in the station in which I am placed, I should hesitate for a moment most respectfully but most earnestly to represent to your lordship, even with the force of a remonstrance, that if the plan for providing for the National Gallery and Royal Academy should now be abandoned, so favourable an opportunity for their accommodation cannot reasonably be expected to present itself again.

" And especially, my lord, as a trustee of the National Gallery, I should beg most respectfully, but most earnestly, to remonstrate against devoting the Banqueting Room in Whitehall to an object for which it is wholly inadequate, and its application to which can only lead to a wasteful, because injudicious, expenditure, and to a result but little creditable to the taste or the liberality of the country.

" As an humble individual, my lord, I am well aware that no man can have less pretension than I have to be attended to on this occasion; and nothing but an honest, though perhaps imprudent, desire to fulfil to the best of my power the duties which attach to me in the relation in which I stand to the National Gallery and the Royal Academy, could induce me to trouble your lordship with a representation which I have little reason to flatter myself will be effectual, and which I have much reason to fear may be considered officious.

" Grateful for the many instances of your lordship's polite attention which I have experienced, and with the most profound respect, I have the honour to subscribe myself,

     " My Lord,

        " Your Lordship's most faithful

          " and obedient humble Servant,

            " MARTIN ARCHER SHEE.

" The Right Hon. the Earl Grey, K.G.

    " &c. &c. &c."

To this letter Lord Grey returned the following answer: —

          " (Private.)

             " Downing Street, 10th Aug., 1833.

" DEAR SIR MARTIN,

    " I had the pleasure of receiving your letter yesterday. It required no apology. Your anxiety for whatever might promote the improvement of the fine arts was natural; and fully partaking in that feeling, I could not but receive with all the attention that was due to them, the suggestions of a person whose authority, on such matters, must justly be considered as the highest.

"I lost no time in communicating your letter to Lord Duncannon, and have this morning received from him the enclosed, which I send for your information, and will thank you to return.

"I trust it will not be altogether unsatisfactory to you, as affording proof of a sincere desire to assist the object which you have so much at heart. I had observed with pleasure what had passed in the House of Commons, and am sanguine in my expectations that we shall be enabled to recur to the plan for fixing the establishment of the Royal Academy, and of the National Gallery, in Trafalgar Square.

"But I entirely agree with Lord Duncannon, that nothing will tend more to defeat this hope, than any endeavour to press this question further at present.

"I am, with great regard,<br>"Dear Sir Martin,<br>"Yours most faithfully,<br>"GREY.

"Sir M. A. Shee, P.R.A."

In returning, as requested, the note from Lord Duncannon, enclosed in the foregoing, the President recurred to the subject as follows:

"Cavendish Square, 17th Aug.; 1833.

"MY LORD,

"The kind and prompt notice with which you have honoured my application, notwithstanding the many important objects which necessarily press upon your attention, affords a new proof of the interest your lordship takes in the cause of the arts, and demands my most grateful acknowledgments. My Lord Duncannon's note to your lordship, which I return enclosed, again revives a hope. No man can doubt for a moment, that his lordship is actuated on this occasion by the most anxious desire to consult the true interest of the public. This sentiment, operating on a liberal and enlightened spirit, will induce him to listen with some distrust to suggestions which may not perhaps originate from so pure a source ; but I confess, when I saw him not only *not* advocating a measure to which the arts and, let me add, the country had been led to look forward with so much confidence,—when I saw his lordship not only *not* extending his official protection to a project upon which so much time and thought had been employed,—but actually proposing another, in which the best interests of a National Gallery must be sacrificed, and the just claims of the Royal Academy would be entirely disregarded,—I was reduced to despair. So many concurring circumstances as appear at this juncture to unite in favour of an object important alike to the honour and interest of the nation, it will be vain to expect again in the course of a century.

"With respect to the public notice which has been taken of this subject, either in or out of Parliament, I can truly assert that the Academy have not, in any degree whatever, occasioned it. They have never moved but in compliance with the official communication from the Commissioners of Woods and Forests; and, as to myself, from the first moment when I took the liberty of mentioning the subject to your lordship at Dulwich, my reliance has been so entirely placed upon your lordship's liberal feelings towards the arts, that I have never entertained an idea of resorting to the operation of any other influence.

"Personally, no man can be much less interested in this matter than I am; and I assure your lordship there cannot be a purer gratification than that which I should feel in seeing your lordship not only the patriot Minister, but the Mæcenas of your age,—the protector at once of the arts and the liberties of your country.

"I have the honour to be, with the most sincere respect,

"My Lord,

"Your Lordship's, &c.

"MARTIN ARCHER SHEE.

"The Right Hon. Earl Grey, K.G.
  "&c. &c. &c."

That these energetic remonstrances on the part of the President had a considerable share in fixing the wavering intentions of the ministry, with respect to the locality and appropriation of the intended structure, can, I think, hardly be called in question, when it is remembered that within the short space of one month from the date of this correspondence, to which the unsettled plans and hesitating policy of the government had given rise, *the new building in Trafalgar Square was actually commenced.*

From the commencement of his Majesty's reign, the King had, on all public and private occasions, when brought into communication with Sir Martin, been uniformly gracious and affable in his demeanour towards the President, on whose part his Majesty ever encouraged that open and frank expression of his wishes, and avowal of his opinions, on the subject of the arts and their relation to the state, which no one knew better than Sir Martin how to combine with the respectful and loyal deference due to the person and character of the sovereign. The privilege of personal access to his Majesty on all matters connected with the Academy, where the royal pleasure was to be ascertained for their guidance, — or the royal sanction obtained to their proceedings, — was freely and fully conceded to the President, with a considerate promptness in granting the solicited audience, which could hardly be exceeded in the case of those high functionaries of state, whose right to such an honourable distinction is constitutionally indisputable. But, however satisfactory may have been this recognition of his claims, in his administrative or official character, he had not, down to the autumn of the year 1833, been honoured by any mark of personal favour on the part of the court, or called upon to exercise his pencil in obedience to the royal command.

The hospitalities of the palace too, which had taken a very liberal range, in compliment to intellectual and professional eminence of various kinds, even apart from the consideration of what might be due to official station, had never been extended to the President of his Majesty's Academy.   And it was not without some show of reason that Sir Martin, when contrasting this apparent neglect on the part of the court, with the flattering attentions vouchsafed to others not more conspicuous for social and professional claims, — and far less distinguished in official station than himself, — inclined towards the belief that there were personal influences at work in the royal circle, which sought to withhold from him that degree of observance properly belonging to his position, to which he felt himself entitled,—not on his own account,—but as a mark of respect for the body at whose head he had been placed by the unsolicited votes of his professional brethren and rivals, with the hearty and openly expressed approval of his Majesty, who had, when Duke of Clarence, on more than one public occasion, borne the most flattering testimony to the merits of the new President.

How far Sir Martin was or was not warranted, in point of fact, in suspecting the existence of a hostile feeling against him in some of those who had opportunities of approaching the throne, it is not now worth while to inquire.   The subsequent history of his relations with the court will, at any rate, show that if any efforts, open or disguised, were at any time made to influence the mind of his late Majesty, in a sense unfavourable to the personal claims of the President,—

such efforts were far from being permanently successful, and were indeed, in the long run, singularly abortive.

Be this as it may, the circumstances which first brought him into professional contact, and consequently more familiar personal communication, with the court, were not the result of any spontaneous act of favour on the part of his Majesty; still less were they attributable to any personal effort or *démarche* on the part of the President himself. This will sufficiently appear by the subjoined extract from Sir Martin's correspondence with Miss Tunno.

It should be mentioned that the most conspicuous work among his contributions to the annual exhibition of the Royal Academy, in the year 1833, was a large whole-length portrait of the Marquess Wellesley, in the robes of the Order of the Garter. This distinguished statesman and accomplished scholar, whose brilliant career exhibits so remarkable a display of successful talent and energy, in the exercise of the highest functions of many various departments of public official life, was now about to assume, for the second time, the important post of Lord Lieutenant of Ireland. On vacating, in consequence, the office of Lord Steward of his Majesty's household, he had requested permission to present to the king the portrait in question — an animated and characteristic likeness of the noble marquis, which represented him with his white wand of office, as in the performance of his courtly duties as Lord Steward.

Sir Martin had long enjoyed the respect and esteem of the marquess, as an Irishman whose talents conferred credit on their common country; and of late years a good deal of social as well as professional intercourse between them had expanded these dispositions into a feeling of warm personal regard, combined with a very high degree of admiration for his great mental powers, and manly dignity of character. His lordship had, on more than one occasion, exhibited a friendly desire to be of service to the President, by interesting himself in the advancement of one of the junior members of Sir Martin's family, whose views were turned towards an official or diplomatic career; and it is beyond a doubt that he frequently, and quite spontaneously, availed himself of his opportunities of personal communication with the king, to speak in terms of the highest commendation of Sir Martin's character and acquirements; nor could his Majesty fail to be impressed by the favourable report of one so well qualified by his own rare abilities and attainments, to appreciate intellectual superiority in others. These details are not immaterial in reference to the tone and contents of the following letter:

*To Miss Tunno.*

"London, 19th Sept., 1833.

.        .        .        .        .

"I thought your zealous friendship would have prompted some sanguine anticipations from the appointment of Lord Wellesley to the Government of Ireland; but poor . ,. . . is, I fear, not much more lucky than his father. You do us no more than justice in believing that you would not be the *last* to hear, if anything favourable had occurred; but though Lord W—— is, I believe, well disposed, we have little or no hope from that quarter. He assured me that it would give him great pleasure to be of use; but under present circumstances,—the necessity of retrenchment, — and the reduction of all the establishments, it would be only deluding me if he were to make a promise on the subject;—that after he had been some time in Ireland, it was *possible* that an opportunity might arise, and he would keep the matter in view. Lord Wellesley has certainly behaved in every respect to me, like a gentleman, and, wholly unsolicited on my part, has shown every desire to sustain my interests in high quarters. I had a note from him some little time ago to say that his portrait was to be sent to the King, who had assigned a place to it in Windsor Castle, and that his Majesty '*agreed in the public admiration which had been expressed of that happy production of art.*' I had last week another communication from him to say that the King had promised to sit to me for his portrait, to be sent to Lord Wellesley in Ireland,—that his Majesty would sit at *Brighton*, where he was to go in October. Whatever may be the result of this, Lord Wellesley's part in it has been most friendly; and I have reason to feel the more grateful, because I had never dropped even a hint to him on the subject. Yet notwithstanding all this, my dear Miss Tunno, I have a shrewd suspicion that my countrymen are not destined to be *gratified* by an *effigy* of our gracious sovereign from *my hand*. I think I have some friends about the court who will save me the trouble and expense of a trip to Brighton for this purpose, and turn the royal countenance in a different direction.

    .        .        .        .        .        .

You have seen by the papers that the building for the National Gallery and the Royal Academy has been at last commenced in Trafalgar Square. Not having cares *enough* of my own I have had a good deal of trouble on this subject. But the intriguers have been foiled. This letter you will admit is like a wet summer's day in the country, (everywhere but at Taplow Lodge) long and dull . . . . Since writing the foregoing, Seguier has called on me from the King, about Lord Wellesley's picture. His Majesty told him he was going to sit to me, and appeared as if pleased to do so. This gives the matter a somewhat more serious air."

In conformity with the intimation which he had received from Lord Wellesley, under the circumstances detailed in the foregoing letter, Sir Martin was honoured by the King's commands to attend his Majesty at Brighton, soon after the removal of the court to that place for the winter, in order that the King might give the necessary sittings for a state whole-length portrait of his Majesty, to be sent to Lord Wellesley in Ireland.   He accordingly proceeded to Brighton on the 7th November, and within two or three days of his arrival was enabled to commence the portrait.   The very confined space afforded by the Pavilion for the requirements of a royal residence, was greatly insufficient for the accommodation of the court, comprising, as it did at that time, a double royal household; and not merely inferior functionaries, but some of the high officers of state in attendance on their Majesties, were, from want of suitable private apartments in the palace, obliged to distribute themselves among the lodging-houses of the adjoining Steyne.   It was not therefore to be expected that the President should be lodged under the royal roof during the progress of his operations at the Pavilion ;   where, however, one of the most splendid among the state apartments was placed at his disposal as a painting-room, on the days appointed by his Majesty for the royal sittings.

It may be collected from the tone of his observations addressed to Miss Tunno, in the foregoing letter, that he entered on the performance of his task, with some misgivings as to the personal feelings entertained towards him in those " high latitudes," in the midst of which he was about to exercise his pencil on a work, the subject and occasion of which appeared to justify a more than ordinary degree of anxiety for its successful completion.   His impression of the restraints and exactions of courtly *étiquette*, as he had heard them described by some of the surviving *habitués* of the palace during the two preceding reigns, led him also to anticipate a large share of annoyance during the progress of his labours.   Never, certainly, were the prognostics of evil or discomfort in which he was constitutionally prone to indulge, more signally falsified by the event, than in this instance. His career at court was, from the first, a social, as well as a professional triumph. If, in the exercise of his academic functions, his sound judgment and straightforward character had established an amount of influence with the King, on subjects connected with the Academy or the art in general, highly calculated to facilitate the satisfactory discharge of his duties as President, the more intimate experience of his moral and intellectual qualities, which the progress of the portrait in question afforded, not only to his Majesty, but to the brilliant and distinguished personages who formed the ordinary *matériel* of the court circle, soon secured for him the highest degree of popularity, and, as regards the King, heightened the feeling of mere official confidence and approval, to a sentiment of warm personal regard, which continued, in undiminished force, during the remainder of his Majesty's reign. A few extracts from Sir Martin's domestic correspondence during his stay at Brighton, upon this occasion, will tend to show the rapidity and extent of his success in *acclimatising* himself in the courtly atmosphere by which he was surrounded.

*To Lady Archer Shee.*

"November 10th, 1833.

.    .    .    .    .    .    .    .

"The King sat to-day for an hour and half; I worked at the rate of a steam engine of forty-horse power, and had the whole court circle in admiration of the progress I had made. The King's favourite daughter, Lady Sidney*, came in during the sitting, and exclaimed that it was very like already. At the close, Lord

* Lady Sophia Sidney.

and Lady Errol, Lord and Lady Brownlow, and several others whose names I did not catch, poured in, saying that lady gave such an account of the picture, that they were desirous to see it; and they were *all pleased.* The King was gracious; and we exchanged anecdotes, with ease on my part, and affability on his. So far, my dearest Mary, so good. But we must not be too sanguine. Though they are so much pleased at *first,* they may be difficult to please at *last.*"

To the same.

" November 19th, 1833.

"My Dearest Mary,

"Although I did not intend to write to you again during my abode at Brighton, yet I *feel* that there are some events and circumstances, the details of which, as I before observed, must be more satisfactory when received at the first hand; and as the air of *the court* has not *as yet* so far disturbed my uxorious tendencies as to render me indifferent to your gratification, I am willing again to submit to the task of narration. I am perfectly aware, however, that M—— is a much more lively and entertaining historian than I am, at least to any lady *but you.*

" Everything goes on at the Pavilion, *couleur de rose.* Even M—— is content, for I have been *asked* to *dinner;* a compliment which, certainly, considering the extent to which it has been carried, implies no great distinction; but not to have received it would, in my case, have been exceedingly unpleasant in every point of view. It would have been in the eyes of the Academy an affront to the arts, — and in the eyes of the world, a mark of personal discredit or professional slight.

" Certainly, if the King delayed the honour, he conferred it handsomely at last; for I was asked to the most magnificent dinner given this season at this place. The cabinet ministers had all come down to hold a council; and all the splendour of the Pavilion was put in requisition to entertain them. I found my Lord Grey cordial and friendly. He said he was delighted to see me there; it was what he often wished, and what ought to have taken place before. I was also particularly noticed by

Lord Lansdowne, Lord Ripon, Lord John Russell, Sir James Graham, and others. . . . . The Lord Chief Justice was there, and particularly friendly. In the drawing-room before dinner, the Queen, in noticing the *principal guests*, did not forget *me*. She crossed the room to speak to me; and in the strongest manner expressed her approbation of the picture; declared it was the best by far that had ever been painted of the King, and repeated her commendations before me to Lord Grey, who told her Majesty that the pictures of the Lord Chief Justice and *another judge*, and Lord Wellesley, were the finest portraits in the last exhibition. . The *other* judge I found was Sir Gilbert Blane.*   The Queen drew some comparisons between my portrait of his Majesty and others that have been painted, which would not have sounded pleasantly in the ears of the *officials*. The Princess Augusta, also, with whom I had not previously had any communication respecting the picture, came up to me, and in the most gracious manner expressed her *delight*, and asked me if I did not think that the King bore a strong resemblance both to his father and mother. In short, my dear Mary, I have heard nothing but praise of the picture from the first sitting: not a single criticism of any kind; and if I could like it myself but half as well as it is approved by others, I should be content. But I hope to make it a respect-able picture. . . . . . At dinner I sat between Lord Mount Edgcumbe and Sir James Graham, opposite the Recorder and Lord Falkland. The King sat at the middle of the table,— the Queen opposite between the Chancellor and the Marquis of Lansdowne. The King sent twice to ask me to take wine with him. My Lord Mount Edgcumbe and I are become *cronies*.

" The King was to have sat to-day; but my Lord Grey re-mained with him on business; and they have the *bad taste* to give precedence to state affairs. I am in great hopes of finishing the head this week; for the King does not appear to dislike the operation. He regularly says: ' Well, Sir Martin, I will sit to you *to-morrow*, if public business does not prevent me.' "

* Sir Martin had that year contributed portraits of the Lord Chief Justice Denman and Sir Gilbert Blane, o  he exhibition of the Royal Academy.

Sir Martin was not left in doubt as to the sincerity of the praises thus graciously bestowed by the Queen on the result of his labours. At the request of her Majesty, re-echoed by the unanimous voice of the court, the King decided that the portrait should be completed as a commission from himself, and placed in Windsor Castle as part of the royal collection; his Majesty promising, at the same time, to sit to Sir Martin for another portrait of the same size and class, to be sent to Lord Wellesley in Ireland, in substitution for the work thus diverted from its original destination. It need hardly be said that Lord Wellesley, to whom this evidence of the President's courtly success afforded the sincerest gratification, promptly acquiesced in an arrangement so complimentary to the talent of which he was a sincere admirer.

Throughout the period during which Sir Martin was engaged in this arduous operation at the Pavilion, and on all subsequent occasions when official or professional duty, or the gracious command of the King, brought him within the range of the social atmosphere of the palace, he invariably experienced from every member of the royal circle, an amount of friendly cordiality and considerate attention, which rendered his visits to these courtly regions as agreeable to himself, as they appeared acceptable to those around him.

Among those whom he found in waiting at the Pavilion there were not a few with whom he was already acquainted; while to most of the principal functionaries in attendance on their Majesties he was personally as well as officially known. All vied with each other in welcoming him as a valuable addition to their society; and the rapid progress which, from the first, he evidently made in the royal favour, was viewed with universal satisfaction, and became a source of much good-humoured raillery at his expense, on the part of some of the *habitués*, who declared his success to be something marvellous, and such as only the most skilful and accomplished of courtiers could have achieved within the time.

The portrait thus commenced and completed under such flattering circumstances, was exhibited at the Royal Academy in the annual display of the ensuing year, 1834. It represents his Majesty in the robes of the Garter. It was subsequently engraved by that eminent artist, Mr. Samuel Cousins; but the engraving, which was on a rather small scale, in reference to the nature and character of the picture, is, I think, but little known. The picture was ultimately placed in the throne room at Windsor Castle, where it remained, I believe, down to the end of his Majesty's reign. I know not whether it still retains that position.

# CHAPTER III.

## 1834.

The Anti-Academic Party. — Their Supporters in the House of Commons. — Apathy of the Ministry. — Remonstrances of the President. — Interview with Earl Grey. — The first Parliamentary Move against the Academy. — Mr. Ewart's Motion. — Its Object defeated. — The President takes his Majesty's Pleasure on the subject. — The Returns made *in obedience to Royal Authority*, — and through the Home Office. — Installation of the Duke of Wellington as Chancellor of the University of Oxford. — Hon. Degree of D.C.L. conferred on Sir Martin. — Mr. Raikes's Diary. — Revival of an absurd and unfounded Story. — The King, the President, and the Admiral.

THE parliamentary session of 1834 was not allowed to pass over without an attempt on the part of the *doctrinaire*-radical coterie, to prepare the way for future assaults upon the position and independence of the Royal Academy.

The commencement and regular progress of the building in Trafalgar Square, according to plans approved by the Government, which were well known to include a suitable amount of accommodation for the Royal Academy, precluded all hope that the ministry could now be prevailed on to withhold from that institution its acknowledged right to participate in the advantages of the rising structure. But this very participation in the benefits of a grant of public money might, it was at once seen, afford a pretext for bringing the machinery of parliamentary interference, and perhaps legislation, to bear upon their concerns, in a manner sufficiently effectual for all purposes of annoyance, even if it should be found impracticable to displace the Academy from their honourable position in reference to the Crown, or to despoil them of the titular distinctions and scanty social privileges, which excited so much envious rancour among some of those who had long coveted, without being able to obtain them.

It is of little moment to trace the rise and progress of an agitation as pitiful in its origin and apparent motives, as it was clearly uncandid and unscrupulous in its systematic pursuit of the object it had in view.

To assert that it arose from any widely spread discontent among the great body of artists, occasioned by the injustice or partiality with which the affairs of the Academy were administered, would be manifestly contrary to the fact. Of those who, at the period in question, were pursuing their profession with more or less of success in the metropolis, without having yet attained the academic rank of associate, probably by far the greater number were indebted to the liberality of the Royal Academy for the perfectly gratuitous and effective course of instruction which the schools of that institution supply for the benefit of the student in art. It would be an unpardonable libel on the great mass of artists so circumstanced, to represent them as sharing in those feelings of malignity towards their professional benefactors and guides, which distinguished the language, and dictated the proceedings, of some who were foremost in their active hostility to the interests of the Royal Academy.

No doubt, among those who, conceiving themselves entitled to academic distinctions, saw the period of their admission into the privileged body indefinitely postponed, — there were some who viewed with dissatisfaction, not unmixed with resentment, the preference annually shown, in the elections, to claims which they rated as inferior to their own.   But to men actuated by a love of fair play, and forming that common-sense estimate of human affairs so characteristic of the national mind, feelings of personal disappointment, however acute for the time, are not sufficient in matters of intellectual competition, — the decision of which is subject to the caprices of individual judgment, — to excite that degree of envious animosity, which, in rancorous disgust at its own failure, seeks to deprive success in others, of its legitimate results.

In such cases the best men are generally content to " bide their time," which seldom fails to come round, except in the instance of the few whose overweening vanity, exasperated at the delay which occurs in the public recognition of their superiority, prompts them to sacrifice their future chances to their resentment, and declare open war against those privileges of which they cannot command the immediate enjoyment; affecting, like the fox in the fable, to depreciate the advantages which they have ineffectually sought to obtain.

The open assailants of the Academy, among the members of the profession, were so few in number, and, with two or three exceptions, so insignificant in point of social or moral influence, that it is difficult to understand by what means they contrived to enlist in their service the energies of several conspicuous members of the House of Commons, and gradually work up an anti-Academic agitation in Parliament, developing itself in that singular feeling of hostility to the Academy, which marked the proceedings of the Committee of 1836 on the subject of the fine arts, and was so discreditably exhibited in their report, — to the contents of which I shall hereafter have occasion to advert.

The members of the House of Commons who were foremost in their opposition to what they stigmatised as the academic monopoly, belonged, I need hardly say, to the extreme radical section of the House, and were chiefly found among those in whom democratic tendencies,—not easily distinguished from theoretic republicanism—and a strong bias in favour of the *Benthamite* heresy, combined to develop the most offensive form of utilitarian dogmatism, in all matters of political or administrative discussion.

In the eyes of these gentlemen, the Academy was a royal or aristocratic institution to attack,—an exclusive and privileged body to destroy. Its existence was an offence against commercial freedom and social equality. Its avowed object, its legitimate functions, and its acknowledged services, they were neither solicitous to examine nor qualified to appreciate. Of the few who affected to interest themselves in the question of its organisation and conduct, no one was even so much as suspected of the slightest familiarity with the principles of taste, or the most elementary smattering of the theory or practice of art. Respectable as are the parliamentary traditions connected with the names of Hume, Warburton, and Co., in matters relating to economic science, it must be conceded that, on subjects appealing in any degree to the imaginative or ideal element in the human mind, their authority was of little more weight than that which attaches to the discriminative judgment of a blind man, when exercised on colours.

Their æsthetic deficiencies, however, were more than compensated by a superabundance of zeal in a cause, the true merits of which were, indeed, far beyond the scope of their intellectual sympathies, but which challenged their support on grounds referable to those commercial and social theories, that constitute the chief articles of the utilitarian creed.

In any movement directed against an institution, associated in the minds of men with the ideas of courtly privilege and royal favour, these *doctrinaire-dilettanti* could, as a matter of course, command the active assistance, or, at any rate, the silent co-operation of all that was most determined among their brother radicals of the English, Irish, and Scotch representation.

In the month of April 1834, Sir Martin had occasion to observe, with a degree of surprise not unmixed with indignation, that, although attacks of the most illiberal character, founded on accusations equally absurd and groundless, were frequently made upon the Royal Academy, in the House of Commons, by certain of the radical party,—whose purpose it suited to become the mouthpiece of anti-Academic malignity, as represented by half a dozen disappointed artists,—no member of the Government thought it worth his while to say an effective word in defence of the institution, or to discourage, in any degree, the view sedulously put forward in these incidental discussions by the assailants of the Academy, that their occupancy of the apartments destined for them in the new building, was to be merely on sufferance, and that they were liable to ejection therefrom, at any time, and at the shortest notice, at the mere pleasure or caprice of the Government.

The President was the more annoyed at observing this pusillanimous reserve or ungracious apathy on the part of the Treasury bench,—during these assaults on a body whose merits and claims were fully recognised by the noble head of the administration, and which could boast so honourable a connection with the crown,—because he had, as early as the month of February 1833, at the request of the Secretary of the Treasury, Mr. Spring Rice (now Lord Monteagle), furnished that gentleman with an elaborate and detailed statement respecting the origin, constitution, and career of the Royal Academy, drawn up with the express object of enabling the Government to vindicate that body from the frivolous and unfounded charges so frequently made against them, by ignorant or malevolent hostility.

In reference to some remarks which had been made on the subject of the Royal Academy, in a recent debate, Sir Martin, on the 15th of April, 1834, addressed to Mr. Spring Rice the following letter, referring, as it will be seen, to the circumstances above mentioned, and recalling his attention to the contents of the document in question.

(Private.)<br>"Cavendish Square, 15th April, 1834.

"MY DEAR SIR,—I have seen, with equal surprise and regret, the observations on the Royal Academy which were made in the House last night. From the spirit which seems to actuate some of the honourable members, there is reason to believe that such remarks will be shortly renewed. Founded, as the accusations against the Academy are, upon the grossest ignorance of the nature of that institution, as well as the most rancorous misrepresentations of interested parties, they would be matter only of ridicule and contempt if brought forward in any other place than the British senate.

"It is most unfortunate, however, that the interests of an establishment which certainly deserves the respect, and let me add, that it is not too much to say, the gratitude of the country, should find so few disposed, and none sufficiently informed, to defend them.

" I had hoped that I had enabled you to be an exception to the latter part of this observation; and the motive for my troubling you at present is to draw your attention to the statement of a few facts respecting the claims and constitution of the Academy, which, at your own request, I some time since placed in your hands, to be used, as I understood, upon any occasion when the concerns of that body should be called in question.

" Occasions of this sort appear to me to have often occurred; but the pressure of more important affairs has no doubt occupied you too much, to allow of your bestowing any attention on the paper to which I allude.

" As the present position of the Royal Academy, however, both with respect to the National Gallery and the general interests of the arts, appears to be extraordinary, and was certainly unforeseen by that body, you will perhaps excuse my recalling to your notice the statement in question.

" Should you consider it inexpedient to refer to it, you will, I am sure, agree with me that a just regard to the interests and reputation of the Royal Academy requires that such use may be made of its substance, as the discretion of that body may deem most proper to refute the false and calumnious imputations to which they have been subjected.

" I remain, my dear Sir,

" With much respect,

" Very faithfully yours,

" MARTIN ARCHER SHEE."

" To the Right Hon. Thomas Spring Rice, &c. &c. &c."

The document to which the above letter refers, may, I think, be not inappropriately introduced in this place; as it contains a short statement of facts relating to the Royal Academy, the knowledge of which is essential to the full understanding of the nature, character, and position of that body, and places in a striking point of view those gratuitous and disinterested services which it had continuously rendered to the arts from the period of its foundation,—services which it was the object of the assailants of that institution, not merely to disparage or depreciate, but, if possible, wholly to keep out of view, in discussing the claims of the Academy to the favour and respect of the public.

"Cavendish Square, 7th Feb. 1833.

"MY DEAR SIR,—In compliance with a wish that you were so good as to express, when I had the pleasure of an interview with you at the Treasury, I take the liberty of troubling you with the statement of a few particulars concerning the Royal Academy, the knowledge of which, you seemed to think, might be useful in the event of any discussion arising in the House of Commons on the merits or interests of that institution.

" The multiplied misrepresentations which have gone forth to the world, from time to time, through the medium of the daily press, on the subject of the Royal Academy, have seldom been considered worthy of notice by the members of that body. A formal refutation, however triumphant and conclusive, of such absurd misstatements, would serve but to give an undue importance to a species of attack contemptible in itself, and most probably as little regarded by the public at large, as by those against whom it is directed.

" The same accusations, however, which may appear harmless or insignificant when proceeding from the pen of an anonymous writer, and confined to the columns of a newspaper, assume a serious character when uttered within the walls of Parliament; and as it is possible that, in the absence of more authentic information, some members of the House of Commons may have received very erroneous impressions concerning the Royal Academy, from the misstatements of ignorance or malevolence, it is of essential importance that the means of refutation should be supplied to those who are officially employed to carry into effect the liberal measures of Government in favour of the arts and the Academy.

" At a period also, when Parliament has been called upon to vote a sum of money for the promotion of objects in which the interests of the Royal Academy are materially concerned, it may appear desirable that the House should be enabled to judge of the manner in which that body has fulfilled, and continues to fulfil, its duties towards the arts and the public—duties, on the conscientious discharge of which they must depend for the recognition of their claims on the liberality of the legislature, and the confidence of the country.

"The Royal Academy was founded by his Majesty King George III. on the 10th of December, 1768, for the promotion of the arts of painting, sculpture, and architecture, to which its establishment may be said to afford a twofold mode of encouragement, at once assisting the efforts of rising genius, by providing the amplest means of study and improvement to the students in art, and supplying a reward to the exertions of more matured talent, by the academical distinctions conferred on a certain number of eminent professors.

"It may here be remarked, that it is chiefly with reference to the last-mentioned division of its functions, that the Academy comes under the notice of the public, to a great portion of whom it is known merely as a body of forty artists, distinguished by the title of Royal Academicians, and deriving a considerable income from the proceeds of their annual exhibition.  The exemplary and disinterested manner in which they apply the funds so obtained (funds, be it remembered, produced by their own exertions) to the support of a national school of art, and to the many other creditable and benevolent objects of the institution, is little noticed, and perhaps little known.

"In the infancy of the Academy, when but little taste for the arts existed in any portion of the public, it was not to be expected that the unassisted efforts of the artists themselves, should suffice to support the establishment in such a manner as to render it available for the purposes of its institution.  Accordingly, during the first eleven years of its existence, some deficiency of its means was supplied by the royal founder, to the amount of 5,116l.  From the year 1779, however, the Academy has depended entirely on the income derived from its exhibitions; and with the exception of their apartments in Somerset House, which they are allowed free of expense, except in the article of taxation, they have never received any farther assistance, either from government or from the contributions of lovers of the art.

"Thus, during a period of fifty-three years, the Royal Academy have supported, entirely at their own cost, a national school for the cultivation of painting, sculpture, and architecture; having disbursed for that purpose, and in the necessary expenses of the establishment, upwards of 240,000*l.* Of this sum no less than 26,000*l.* have been devoted to the relief of distressed artists and their families, the far greater proportion of whom have been unconnected, in any way, with the members of the Academy. Amongst these may be found the widows of two men who have done honour to their country—Hogarth and Woollet.

"From a principle of liberality which is not, I believe, exemplified in any other profession, the course of study in the schools of the Royal Academy is perfectly gratuitous; and admission to participate in the advantages which they afford, is not, and *cannot be* the result of favour or interest. The only qualifications which the Academy require are a good moral character, and the production of such a drawing or model as may, in the opinion of the council, exhibit that degree of elementary knowledge without which the student would not be competent to derive any benefit from the opportunities of study which the institution supplies. The works of the candidates for admission are, at stated periods, laid before the council, who receive or reject them by vote, according to their merits; the name of the candidate not being declared until the decision has taken place.

"Once admitted as a student of the Royal Academy, the young artist finds every facility for the prosecution of his studies. The schools of the Academy supply him with the most perfect casts from the antique, the best living models, male and female, that can be procured, and choice specimens of the old masters, selected by the council for his study and imitation. Distinguished professors are appointed to superintend the schools, and to deliver lectures on the different branches of the art; and the library of the Royal Academy affords the student abundant sources of information, on the theory and practice of his profession.   There is also an annual distribution of prizes, which are adjudged by ballot, and delivered before the general assembly of academicians:

" Thus, during eight months of the year, the student has the means of unremitting application at the Academy; the regular course of study being interrupted only by the necessity of devoting all the apartments to the use of the annual exhibition, to which, however, every student has free access during the period that it is open to the public.

" All artists, without exception, are allowed to exhibit with the Royal Academy, and may send as many of their works for that purpose as the members of the body.

" Those students who obtain a certain class of prizes are entitled for life to the above-mentioned privileges; others retain them for ten years only, but are re-admissible by application to the committee from year to year.

"From amongst the students who have obtained the gold medal, a painter, a sculptor, and an architect are selected by rotation, to be sent to Italy for the prosecution of their studies, at the expense of the Academy, who allot a suitable stipend for their maintenance abroad during three years, together with a sum sufficient to defray their travelling expenses to and from Rome.

" It is impossible, in a communication of this description, to enter into all the details of the government and administration of the Academy; and I fear to trespass too far upon your valuable time.   But the above statement will, I trust, suffice to prove that the Royal Academy are not chargeable with any neglect of their duty towards the rising generation of art.   It will also satisfactorily account for the application of those funds which they derive from their annual exhibition, and which would, indeed, be insufficient to meet the heavy expenses inseparable from so extensive an establishment, if a system of economy, unexampled in any other public institution, did not prevail in all its departments, and if the distinguished artists engaged in its official duties,—such as the keeper, secretary, treasurer, &c.—did not submit to a rate of remuneration wholly disproportioned to the time which they devote to the service of the Academy, and inadequate to their support, unassisted by professional exertion.

"The ordinary business of the Academy is managed by a council, consisting of the president and eight academicians, who serve by rotation. All elections of academicians and officers take place, and all laws are passed, in the general assembly of members, and require the sanction of his Majesty. The council and the general assembly, including the president, perform their duties gratuitously.*

"The scrupulous forbearance with which the Academy abstain from the exercise of any privilege which might seem to sacrifice, in the smallest degree, the interests of the institution, to the personal convenience of the members, may be judged of by the fact, that no free admission to the annual exhibition has ever been allowed to the families of the academicians, from every individual of which the entrance-money is as rigidly exacted, as from any other person who visits the exhibition.

"As to any charges which have been, or may be, brought against the Academy, with respect to the selection of the artists on whom they have bestowed the honours of the institution, they resolve themselves into matters of criticism; and, as such, it is obvious that they are not susceptible either of proof or refutation. The distinctions which the Academy confers are open to all artists of character and talent; and few of this description fail to attain them in due succession, according to the maturity of their claims, and their estimation with the public. Upon all such points, however, the Academy must be content to appeal from individual censure to the tribunal of public opinion; but the memory of the many eminent artists who have been enrolled in the ranks of the Academy may be not unsuccessfully invoked in testimony of the impartiality and judgment with which its elective functions have been heretofore

---

* The sum of five shillings is allowed to every member who attends a meeting of the council or the general assembly, in order to defray the expenses of his conveyance to and from the Academy. But this cannot, I apprehend, be considered inconsistent with the above observation.

exercised; while the mass of distinguished professional talent existing in the Academy at the present day may, it is hoped, be appealed to scarcely less triumphantly, in proof of their continued adherence to the original principles and objects of the establishment, and of their faithful and disinterested guardianship of the important interests committed to their charge.

" To the honour of the Academy, it may be here observed, that no instance can be adduced of their elections being swayed, as in other societies, by any interference of the great, or any influence foreign to their own body.

" From the foregoing observations, it appears that a national institution for the cultivation of the fine arts — an institution which in all other civilised countries is considered of such public utility, as to be allowed an establishment at the expense of the state — has been in this country supported for fifty-three years, by the unaided exertions of a body of artists associated under the title of the Royal Academy : —

" That while uncheered themselves by that necessary patronage of the state, which sound policy as well as taste might have been expected to extend towards them, and with few of those flattering hopes of distinction, or prospects even of independence, which stimulate exertion in other avocations, — neither more useful nor important, — as agents of moral or social good, — the members of the Royal Academy have, during this period, disbursed, for the support of this institution, upwards of 240,000*l.*, derived from the annual exhibition of their works — a species of fund which must be confessed to be their own undisputed property, and which every other society of artists in the metropolis appropriates to the individual advantage of its members : —

" That, during this period, between fifteen hundred and two thousand students have been gratuitously educated in the Royal Academy, many of whom have distinguished themselves in the highest departments of the arts, to the honour and advantage of their country, while those who have failed to attain the nobler objects of their ambition have all contributed, through the various channels of exertion in which their humble powers have found the means of operation, to refine the general taste and improve all the products of national industry.

" Although, from the acknowledged importance of those
interests which the members of the Academy so zealously
sustain, they might reasonably expect a liberal and enlightened
Government to co-operate with them, by the contribution of an
annual fund available to the purposes in question,—and though
the present depressed state of the arts, in all their departments,
might well prompt and justify an earnest application in their
behalf to those who regard them as worthy of public favour and
patronage,—yet the members of the Royal Academy have advanced no such claim.  They are willing to continue for the
future, as they have in the past, their exertions in the great
cause of public taste; and in soliciting a more commodious
habitation for the arts, they feel that they are uninfluenced by
personal considerations,—that they ask nothing connected with
their individual interests, and seek only a means of rendering
those exertions more efficacious for the attainment of an object in
which the interest, as well as the fame of the nation is materially
involved.

" I fear, my dear Sir, that, in this long trespass on your
attention, you will think my zeal has outrun my discretion.
I will therefore add to my prolixity no farther than by the
assurance that, with full confidence in your friendly disposition
towards the object of this address,

 " I remain, with the greatest respect,
  " Your much obliged and faithful humble servant,

      " MARTIN ARCHER SHEE.'

" The Right Hon. Thomas Spring Rice, &c. &c. &c."


Not content with this endeavour to recal the attention of his official friends, to the contents of the statement on which he had vainly relied for an effective
ministerial defence against the parliamentary assaults
of Mr. Hume and his party, Sir Martin sought an
interview with the prime minister, for the purpose of
expressing his surprise and uneasiness at the turn
which the affairs of the Academy, as connected with

its interest in the new building, appeared to be taking in the House of Commons; and in order, if possible, to ascertain distinctly the intentions of the Government, on the subject of the apartments which were to be allotted to the use of that institution.

Sir Martin has left, in his own handwriting, a detailed memorandum, drawn up at the time, of what passed at that interview, which took place at the Treasury, on the 17th of April, 1834. For the scrupulous accuracy of this report, his well-known character for straightforward truthfulness would be a sufficient guarantee, even without the internal evidence of authenticity which the document itself supplies. As his motive for thus perpetuating the memory of what passed between Lord Grey and himself on this occasion, was evidently a desire to place on record the sentiments expressed by that eminent statesman, — as the head of the administration, — in reference to the claims of the Royal Academy to a permanent and suitable domicile, to be provided at the public expense, — I conceive that I am doing no more than complying with what I must assume to have been his deliberate wish and intention, in laying the contents of this paper, verbatim and *in extenso*, before the reader.

*" Statement of a Conversation with Lord Grey,*
*17th April,* 1834.

" I observed on my entrance that, confiding in his lordship's kindness, I resorted to him in all cases of embarrassment or difficulty respecting the arts. With some expressions of civility, he inquired what was the difficulty to which I alluded. I said that if his lordship had seen the observations made in Parliament on the subject of the Royal Academy, in the recent debate, he could not be surprised that the members of that institution were impressed with some anxiety and alarm, at the position in which it appeared to be intended to place it. The Academy had expected that in the new building to be erected under his lordship's auspices, they were to find a permanent establishment, in which they might consider themselves as having rights of residence similar to those which they now enjoyed in Somerset House, and in which the arts might possess a home which they might use and enjoy without the danger of molestation or ejection. His lordship here observed that this was always his view of the arrangement, and that he thought we ought not to attach too much importance to such observations as those which seemed to attract our attention. I observed that the observation which surprised and concerned the members of the Academy, proceeded from a member of the Government, Mr. Spring Rice, from whose statement it appeared that instead of the fixed and appropriated residence which the Academy had reason to expect, that institution was to be admitted only to occupy a part of the building of the National Gallery, during pleasure, and subject to be ejected from it whenever the trustees of the latter establishment might think fit to require it for the accommodation of the national pictures. His lordship observed, that he had not particularly attended to the statement made by Mr. Spring Rice; but he repeated that his impression always was that the National Gallery and the Royal Academy should be united for the benefit of the arts, which he considered would be benefited by such union in the proposed building, and that the Academy should be accommodated in it with an appropriate and permanent residence:—that he was sure if any occasion arose which would render it advisable to remove the Academy, they would not object to such a proceeding, if it was for the advantage of the arts, and when care would be taken to provide them with an equally convenient residence. I replied that such a contingency was what we had reason to dread; for that to supply us with an equally convenient residence would not be in the power of the Government:—that his lordship was aware that the existence of the Academy depended on the shillings received from the public; however disgraceful Mr. Ewart and such persons might think it in the Academy to receive them; that the position or standing in which the Academy was to receive them was of the utmost consequence, and that there was no other spot in the metropolis, except that in Trafalgar Square, which would justify the Academy in removing from Somerset House — that if his lordship could give us St. James's Palace or Buckingham House, it would be the ruin of the Academy to be lodged there. His lordship said he thought we allowed this matter to impress us too strongly — that we must be aware of the disposition of the administration to be favourable to the arts and the Academy, and that nothing could be intended which could militate against their interests. I observed that we had the utmost possible confidence in his lordship's kindness and liberality, and that nothing injurious could take place under his influence; but that administrations were unfortunately mortal as well as men, and there was no saying what might occur under such an unsettled position of the Academy. His lordship here observed that the mortality of administrations was true with regard to him in a double sense; but that the person who would be naturally looked to in such an event, Sir Robert Peel, was equally well disposed to the Academy.

" I said the Academy had the fullest confidence in the kindly sentiments of Sir Robert Peel towards that institution, and that he was one of the most liberal patrons of the arts. I was sorry to perceive that Sir Robert had advanced a position which, with every respect for him, I could not but feel disposed to dissent from. He had stated the right of the Government to deprive the Academy of their apartments in Somerset House. I was not well qualified to give an opinion on the subject; but I was led to believe the apartments were a grant from the king; that we have an undisputed possession for more than half a century.

" His lordship here observed that, strictly speaking, he believed the right existed; but he should be very sorry to see it exercised.

" I observed that the Academy could not but feel considerable mortification at the position in which they were placed before the public in this matter. The objects and interests of that institution appeared to be disregarded, and, I might say, contemned, when viewed in connection with the National Gallery.

But in any rational or patriotic consideration of their different claims, the Academy was by far the more important establishment of the two. The gallery was a national decoration, useful certainly, as well as ornamental, but bearing no proportion of utility which can be compared to an institution upon which the actual existence of the arts depends — an institution which is the only school for the education of artists—an institution which has maintained and fostered the arts of this country, for more than half a century, and cultivated and diffused the principles of taste through all the channels in which they can be supposed to operate, through the unaided exertions of the artists who composed it, and without a farthing expense to the Government. In any just view of their operations, it must be confessed they had some claim to respect, and had laid their country under some obligations. I believed there did not exist, and I believe there could not exist, a more disinterested establishment—one conducted with more integrity, or where the individual interests of its members were less attended to,—where those artists, who had themselves painfully attained to eminence and distinction, regularly devoted their means and their exertions for the education and professional accomplishment of those, who must become their rivals, and might supersede them in public estimation.

" His lordship acknowledged the merits and just claims of the Royal Academy, of which he declared no man could be more sensible then he was, or could be more desirous to promote the interests of the arts; and he thought that no administration could be justified in disturbing or would attempt to disturb the Academy in the new building about to [be] prepared for them.

" I observed that however that might be, I thought it was matter for the ·serious consideration of the Academy, how far they may be justified in relinquishing a residence in which they have long enjoyed, and are led to believe that they possess, undisputed claims of occupancy, to remove to a position in which they are expressly told they have no right—where they are to be placed merely on sufferance, as the temporary occupants of the apartments of the National Gallery, and subject to removal whenever the interests of that institution might appear to require it.

" His lordship here observed that the Royal Academy had long complained of want of accommodation in Somerset House, and had anxiously sought to effect the transfer of their residence to the new building. I said it was perfectly true that the Academy had long suffered from the restricted accommodation of their present residence, and were anxious to obtain the advantages of a more commodious establishment, inthe building to be erected under his lordship's auspices: but the Academy were certainly not aware of the kind of tenure under which these advantages were to be held.

" Here his lordship, appearing desirous to close the conversation, observed, that he thought the Academy ought not to be too jealous or particular in their consideration of these matters; that he would, however, make it a point to see Mr. Spring Rice and Lord Althorpe, and communicate with me further on the subject.

" I apologised to his lordship for trespassing on his time— trusted he would excuse the earnestness which I had manifested in the discussion, for I was not only interested in it from the position in which my brother artists had placed me ;—but from the active interference which his lordship's kindness had allowed me to use in promoting it, I felt that I was doubly responsible for the result.

" His lordship readily allowed that it was just and natural that I should be anxious and zealous on the occasion; and without further observation I took my leave."

Mr. Ewart, at that time member of Parliament for Liverpool, whose name occurs in the above memorandum, was, I need hardly state, among the most active of the anti-academic partisans in the House of Commons.   He had, about this time, been put forward as the *pro-pugnator* of the party, and, as it appears from the following letter of Sir Martin to Mr. Spring Rice, had opened the trenches by an inquiry addressed to that gentleman, as an organ of the Government, touching the feasibility of successfully moving in the House for the production of certain returns relating to the Royal Academy, and the internal administration of that body.

"Cavendish Square, 18th April, 1834.

" My dear Sir,—Your letter, with the enclosure, which I return herewith, was sent to me last night to the Royal Academy, where I was detained by business too late to admit of my sending you an earlier reply. It seems to me doubtful whether Mr. Ewart's question respecting a motion for ' a return of the rules and bye-laws of the Royal Academy' relates to a ministerial or an academic ' objection.' By his addressing the question to you, I should suppose he referred to the former, but by your referring his inquiry to me, and desiring to know what answer you should give to it, I must infer that you think he alludes to the latter; and as you are so good as to undertake the task of reply, I shall, in compliance with your desire, state the principles by which, according to the best of my judgment, the Royal Academy should be governed in replying to such a query.

" As far as the interests, the objects, and the wishes of the members of the Royal Academy are concerned, they can have no possible objection to the fullest disclosure of their laws, regulations and proceedings, in any place or for any proper purpose. As the Royal Academy, however, is not a chartered body, and is not endowed with any corporate privilege or capacity,—as it is a private institution under the patronage and protection of the king, existing by his will and pleasure, communicating *immediately* with his Majesty, submitting all its laws and proceedings to his sanction, and responsible only to his Majesty for the manner in which its concerns are administered,—the members of the Academy, I conceive, cannot with propriety, recognise in Mr. Ewart a right of inquiry into their proceedings; nor can they, I apprehend, be authorised to furnish a return of their laws and regulations for any public or parliamentary purpose, without the knowlege and express permission of his Majesty.

" For this permission I am confident the members of the Royal Academy will be always ready to apply on a proper occasion; and so far are they from desiring to withhold from the public or Mr. Ewart, a full and complete knowledge of their laws, regulations, and proceedings, which, in my humble opinion, it must always be to their credit to promulgate, that should Mr. Ewart, as a private gentleman, require any information on the subject, whenever he thinks proper to apply, in that character, to the Secretary of the Royal Academy, at Somerset House, an authentic copy of the laws and regulations of the Royal Academy, now in force, shall be placed at his disposal.

     " I remain, my dear Sir,

        " With much respect,

          " Very faithfully yours,

            "MARTIN ARCHER SHEE.

"The Right Hon. Thomas Spring Rice, &c. &c. &c."

I am unable to state how far the substance or details of this letter may have been communicated to Mr. Ewart, or whether he availed himself of the channel of correct information, as to the constitution of the Royal Academy, which the President pointed out to him. But about ten days later Sir Martin received from him the following note :—

         " House of Commons, 1st May, 1834.

" Mr. Ewart presents his compliments to Sir Martin Archer Shee, and encloses a copy of some returns which he is desirous of moving for relative to the Royal Academy.

" Lord Howick has stated to Mr. Ewart that the Government has no objection to the production of the information required.

" But Mr. Ewart wishes first to submit the returns to Sir M. A. Shee for his consideration.

" At the same time, he will feel obliged by an early reply."

The returns sought for were, according to the memorandum enclosed in the above note, as follows :—

" Return of the number of exhibitors at the Royal Academy, in each of the last ten years, distinguishing the number of exhibitors, members of the Academy, from the number of other exhibitors.

"Of the number of works of art exhibited at the Royal Academy in each of the last ten years, distinguishing for each year the number of historical works, landscapes, portraits, busts, and architectural drawings respectively contributed by members of the Royal Academy, from the historical works, landscapes, portraits, busts, and architectural drawings contributed by other artists.

"Also, a return of the number of professors in the Royal Academy; of the number of lectures required by the rules of the Academy to be annually delivered by each professor; and of the number of lectures which have been annually delivered by each professor during the last ten years."

To this application Sir Martin returned the following answer. The delay that appears to have occurred between the receipt of Mr. Ewart's note and the transmission of the reply, was no doubt occasioned by the necessity that existed of taking the sense of his academic colleagues, on the question of the course to be pursued in reference to the subject of this correspondence. From the spirit which animated the members, and which ever prevailed in their councils, while he continued to preside over the deliberations of the body, Sir Martin could not entertain a doubt that the view of their position, so emphatically enunciated in the last letter to Mr. Spring Rice which has been laid before the reader, would be unhesitatingly adopted by the Academy, in dealing with this first formal move of their parliamentary enemies.

"Cavendish Square, 9th May, 1834.

"Sir,—In answer to your letter of the 1st instant, enclosing for my consideration copies of some returns respecting the Royal Academy, which you are desirous to move for in the House of Commons, I beg leave to refer you to the accompanying copy of a letter to Mr. Spring Rice, which was written to him on an occasion which the letter itself will explain.*

" I take the liberty to refer you to this letter, because it contains a statement of some circumstances respecting the Royal Academy, of which you are probably not aware, and because it appears to me to be applicable to the communication with which you have honoured me.

" In addition, I have only to observe that, should you still deem it expedient to move for the returns in question, the respect which the members of the Royal Academy entertain for the House of Commons, and the anxious desire they feel to communicate any information respecting the Academy which may, even by possibility, be rendered available for any useful purpose, would, I am confident, prompt them to solicit his Majesty's permission to supply the returns required, as far as they have the means of doing so.

" I have the honour to be, Sir,<br>
" With great respect,<br>
" Your obedient humble servant,<br>
" MARTIN ARCHER SHEE."

" William Ewart, Esq., M.P., &c. &c. &c."

The course thus taken by the Royal Academy, in sheltering themselves under the prerogative of the Crown, and repudiating all direct responsibility to the House of Commons, was probably productive of some little embarrassment to the ministry, who, fearful of offending their radical supporters by adopting a firm tone in defence of the Academy, could not but feel that the position assumed by that body was one which they were in strictness entitled to occupy, and on which they were fully justified in insisting. Some further communication appears to have taken place between the President and Mr. Spring Rice, on the subject of

---

* This was no doubt the letter of the 18th April, 1834, given above.

the returns in question, and the mode in which they were to be furnished; the Secretary to the Treasury being somewhat averse to the view which would represent the matter as wholly beyond the competency of the House of Commons,—while the President, on behalf of the Academy, was fully determined that the returns, if supplied at all, should be granted in such a form as would render it manifest that *obedience to the will of the King*, and not *acquiescence in the right of the House to demand the required information*, was the *vis motrix* of the proceeding.

In accordance with this view, the President, in the early part of the month of June, sought and obtained the honour of an interview with the King, for the purpose of ascertaining his Majesty's pleasure in the matter, for the guidance of the Royal Academy. In this interview, Sir Martin stated to the King that the Royal Academy were far from wishing to withhold the particulars in question from the knowledge of the House or the public; being sensible that the fullest investigation of their conduct and affairs could only redound to their credit; but that having the honour to be dependent in all things on the good pleasure of his Majesty, and responsible to him alone, for their proceedings, they did not conceive themselves at liberty to supply the returns sought for by Mr. Ewart, either to the House of Commons, or to any person demanding them on behalf of that assembly, without the express sanction and authority of his Majesty, previously obtained. The King, fully assenting to the propriety of the course adopted by the Academy, and satisfied that no objection existed, on their part, to the production of the returns in question, was graciously pleased to signify his Majesty's permission and desire that the required information should be supplied for the benefit of the House of Commons.

The returns were accordingly made out, and transmitted, not directly to the officers of the House, but to the Principal Secretary of State for the Home Department, to be by him laid on the table of the House.

It will be seen from the foregoing details, that throughout the whole of this transaction, the President, acting on behalf of the Academy, carefully and successfully avoided the adoption of any course which could, even in point of form, be construed as the recognition of a parliamentary claim of interference in the concerns of that body,—and while freely supplying the returns which formed the subject, and afforded the pretext for Mr. Ewart's motion,—contrived, in great measure, to defeat its real purpose, by maintaining, unimpaired, that principle of exclusive responsibility to the sovereign, on which the Academy wisely relied as the most effectual safeguard of their legitimate interests and rights.

It is hardly necessary to observe, that the motion was devised chiefly with a view to the formal assertion and practical exercise of that very right of interference, which the Academy so resolutely denied and successfully resisted.

The result of the returns sought, was so obviously attainable by any one willing to avail himself of easily attainable sources of information, that there could be no reasonable pretext for bringing the peremptory terrors of an order of the House of Commons, to bear on the momentous inquiry.

As to the first and second points in reference to which the returns were sought, the exhibition catalogue of the Academy, for the previous ten years,—copies of which were doubtless forthcoming from the custody of many individuals of the "high art" fraternity, by whom they had been carefully treasured up, as glaring records of academic delinquency,—would at once have supplied the information required, at a very small cost of arithmetical exertion.  To the reader, whom I may fairly assume to be tolerably familiar with the form and system of arrangement observed in that widely circulated *manual*, it will be evident that a very slight effort of those powers of calculation and analysis, for which Mr Hume and his parliamentary followers were so conspicuous when dealing with the statistics of *oligarchical misgovernment*, would have sufficed, as regards the academic display of any one given year, to eliminate the *scanty cockle* of *privileged imbecility*, from the *golden harvest* of extra-*academical genius*.

The object of the intended revelation was unmistakeable.  It was to show that the non-academical exhibitors greatly outnumbered, in every year, the members of the body, who contributed to the exhibition; and a triumphant conclusion was, I presume, to be drawn from that fact, to the effect that those who furnished the majority of the works, from the display of which the Academy derived its pecuniary resources, should be admitted to share in the management of funds which they had assisted to create, and in the general control of an institution which they helped to sustain..

This view of the subject could not be supposed to involve a very correct estimate of the comparative amount of merit, displayed by the two classes into which the exhibitors were about to be arranged.  The degree in which the works of members of the Academy contributed to make up the attraction of the annual display, was a point not exactly ascertainable by reference to

the superficial extent of canvas over which the result
of their labours might happen to be spread: and even
assuming the academic, to be in the proportion of not
more than 10 or 11 per cent. to the non-academic, element, in the calculation, the least imaginative of Scotch
economists could hardly have relied upon that fact, as
affording the accurate measure of comparative benefit
secured to the academic treasury, by the works subjected
to so rigid a process of arithmetical criticism.

Taking, however, the computation of numbers for
what it may be worth, in such an investigation, it is
quite clear, that had the object been, not merely to make
out a plausible case against the Academy, but to afford
the public an opportunity of fairly appreciating the
claims and services of that body, another inquiry would
have been added, in the motion for the returns, to those
so astutely framed, viz. — *what proportion of the unprivi-
leged exhibitors, who would so greatly outnumber the R.A.'s
and A.R.A's in the required list, consisted of those who
were, or had been, students of the Royal Academy, and, as
such, indebted for their most effective professional education, to the perfectly gratuitous bounty of that institution?*
But the result of such an inquiry was calculated to
interfere inconveniently with the working of the principle on which the anti-academic party, in and out of
Parliament, systematically acted,—that of bringing pro-
minently forward every specious charge that could be
suggested against the Royal Academy, while carefully
suppressing whatever might redound to its credit, or
tend to vindicate the integrity of its career.

The Academy, however, having decided on granting
the returns, were careful not to fall into the trap which
had been laid for them. In furnishing the required
details, they took care to supply also, to some extent,

the information so essential to a fair view of their case, which the notice of motion discreetly abstained from seeking. The returns divided the annual lists of exhibitors not into two classes merely, viz., members and non-members,—as the motion suggested, but into three, viz., *members, students,* and *others:* the same classification being observed in the tabular statement of the different classes of works, exhibited in each year of the period over which the inquiry extended. This process, without taking into account such of the " other " exhibitors as had formerly been included among the students of the Academy, but, from effluxion of time, had ceased to fill that character, exhibited, in its average result, a proportion of about 40 per cent. of the academic, to the non-academic element, in the *matériel* of the exhibition.

I must not, however, omit to notice the third point to which the parliamentary questions were directed,—the staff of professors attached to the institution, and the number of lectures delivered by them within the previous ten years. Here, too, the exhibition catalogue supplied a portion of the information required, viz., the number and names of the professors; while the nature and measure of the duties imposed upon them, were at once ascertainable from the printed copy of the laws and regulations of the Academy which, as we have seen, had been placed at the disposal of Mr. Ewart. There had been, however, as was well known to the parties promoting this system of inquiry, some shortcomings in the efficiency of the branch of this academic machinery, under circumstances somewhat embarrassing to the institution,—regard being had to the position and services of those to whom the neglect was attributable.

The public teaching of the Academy comprised a certain amount of *vivâ voce* instruction in painting, sculpture, architecture, superficial anatomy, and perspective;—in each of which departments a professor of eminence was appointed by election of the general assembly, subject to the approval of the crown, to deliver a course of six lectures during the year. How efficiently these chairs had, for the most part, been filled, as regards the qualifications of the eminent men who had, from time to time, been induced to undertake the duties involved in these appointments, may be inferred from the fact that the chair of painting had been successively occupied by Barry, Opie, Fuseli, and Phillips; while, from the first establishment of a professorship of sculpture,—a measure not contemplated by the original arrangements of the Academy, but adopted at a comparatively recent period, at the instance and through the exertions of Sir Martin himself,—the chair in question had been connected with the name and adorned by the genius of the most illustrious artist, in that department of the art, that has ever graced the annals of the British school; a sculptor in European celebrity and estimation, second only to Canova,—John Flaxman;—on whose death a few years back, an able and appropriate successor had been found in the person of Mr. (afterwards Sir Richard) Westmacott, who at the period of Mr. Ewart's motion, still retained the appointment. The chair of anatomy, also, — a post much coveted by many eminent members of the surgical profession who combined a taste for art with the severer studies of their noble and beneficent science, —had from the first been effectively filled; and indeed with regard to these three important branches of academical tuition, the instruction had been, throughout, as regular as it was efficient.

The post of professor of architecture had been for

many years held by Sir John Soane, who had long performed its duties in a manner that evinced a more than ordinary amount of enthusiasm, in the cause of the art in which he was so distinguished a proficient, and a liberal zeal in the development of its principles, of which there are probably but rare examples to be found in the annals of didactic exertion. Those who, like the writer, have enjoyed the privilege of being occasionally present, although in early boyhood, at the architectural lectures delivered by Sir John Soane in the great room of the Royal Academy at Somerset House, will not easily forget the interest communicated to the subject, and the pointed and practical application given to theory and precept, by the numerous, extensive, and beautifully-executed illustrations, which, at every step of his course, accompanied and elucidated his observations. To say that the mere pecuniary outlay involved in the production and exhibition of this vast and ever-varying series of architectural drawings,— showing, on a large scale, and with finished accuracy, the beauties, defects, and characteristics of the most celebrated buildings of ancient and modern Europe,— must have practically reduced to an absolute nullity, the very moderate remuneration attached to the performance of his duties as academical professor, would be greatly to understate the case, as regards Sir John Soane's disinterested and generous exertions in favour of the students in architecture. It is probable that, at the end of every annual course of lectures, he was greatly out of pocket; and it is, at any rate, certain, that in discharging, as he did, *con amore*, the functions of his office, he throughout exhibited a liberal disregard of all considerations of expense, which might have reasonably impeded the full and costly development of his views.

That such unusual devotion to his duties should be duly appreciated and gratefully remembered by his academic colleagues, cannot be matter of surprise; and when a few years previously to the parliamentary outbreak of anti-academic hostility, the partial failure of his eye-sight occasioned an interruption in the regular performance of those duties, it was no wonder that the Academy exhibited an indulgent forbearance towards their accomplished professor, in submitting patiently to the evil resulting from the discontinuance of his lectures, so long as there remained a hope that he might, at no remote period, be enabled to resume their delivery; and if, when this expectation had vanished, they still hesitated, in the absence of his voluntary resignation, to supersede him by an act *in invitum*,—which, however justifiable in principle and even expedient in theory, could not fail to be highly offensive, in form and substance, to one whose advanced age, eminent talents, and distinguished services invested him with strong claims on the respectful consideration of the body,—perhaps they might not unreasonably urge in extenuation of their culpable lenity, the difficulties, in point of feeling, which suggested themselves in the adoption of this course.

The blot, however,—and one that was very easy to hit,—was to be found in the department of perspective: the chair of which science had long been nominally filled by a distinguished royal academician, who, without apology or pretext of any kind, had for several years, left the duties of the appointment wholly undischarged and unnoticed.

It was therefore to be expected that the flagrant departure from academic propriety, involved in this wilful and wayward neglect on the part of the professor, and the apathetic acquiescence of his brother members, would figure conspicuously among the facts of the case which Messrs. Ewart and his friends were industriously getting up against the Royal Academy.

Accordingly, the point did not fail to be duly noticed in the course of the formidable impeachment of the body, comprised in the voluminous evidence given during the session of 1836, before that memorable parliamentary tribunal which, under the name and pretence of a "Select Committee on Arts of Design," was chiefly employed in seeking out plausible pretexts for a public censure on the character and conduct of the Royal Academy, and furthering, as far as possible, the designs of private animosity, at the bidding of the professional assailants of that institution.

As to the charge in question, it was certainly not capable of being met by any effectual plea in justification; and all that could be urged in extenuation is, I fancy, comprised in the answer given by the President when under examination before the "Select Committee," to the following question: "Has the School of Perspective been conducted in an entirely unexceptionable manner by the Royal Academy?"

"*Answer.* The professor of perspective has not recently delivered his lectures; and, as far as relates to the non-performance of his duty, the course of instruction in the schools must be confessed to be incomplete. The Academy have forborne to press on the professor of perspective the execution of his duties as strongly as they might perhaps be expected to do, partly because many of the members consider the process of lecturing as ill-calculated to explain the science of perspective, and partly from a delicacy which cannot perhaps be perfectly justified, but which arises from the respect they feel for one of the greatest artists of the age in which we live. He, of course,

receives no emolument during the cessation of his lectures."—
*Minutes of Evidence before Select, Committee on Arts and Prin-
ciples of Design, 15th July, 1836.*

The defaulting professor, so justly described by Sir
Martin as " one of the greatest artists of the age " was
the late James Mallard William Turner.

Probably the *éclat* of so great a name, in connection
with circumstances intrinsically deserving of animadversion, had ultimately some effect on the members of
the committee, in inducing them to emulate the lenient
forbearance of Sterne's " Recording Angel," as regards
this particular illustration of academic perversity.
For although, in their report, they have duly registered
a censure on the Royal Academy, obviously grounded
on the two great facts, — or assumed facts, — now
" damned to everlasting fame " — on the strength of
which the Nemesis of high art was supposed to demand the suppression of the Royal Academy, — viz.,
the withholding from Mr. Haydon's picture of " Dentatus," in the exhibition of 1809, a position " *quæsitam
meritis*," — and the accidental spilling of some varnish,
a few years later, over a work of Mr. Martin's which
had been sent for exhibition at Somerset House,—that
remarkable document failed to denounce, in adequate
terms of reprobation, the didactic delinquency to which
the President had, on behalf of the Academy, virtually
pleaded guilty, as we have seen, while boldly asserting,
— as we shall hereafter have occasion to see, — the
merits and integrity of the Academy, on all other points
where the conduct of that body was impugned.

But I am here anticipating the discussion of matters
which will come more regularly under our notice, as we
proceed.

In the summer of 1834, the installation of the Duke of Wellington, as Chancellor of the University of Oxford,—a dignity to which His Grace had been unanimously elected on the death of Lord Grenville,—took place amid an unprecedented display of academical splendours, and an attentive interest on the part of the public, naturally created by a ceremonial in which the great captain of the age was the chief actor, and that ancient and venerable seat of learning, the scene of the celebration.

The imposing solemnity in question afforded to the authorities of " Alma Mater " a graceful opportunity of conferring on a number of eminent persons, selected from the ranks of science, art, literature, and politics, the honorary degree of Doctor of Civil Law.  This complimentary distinction,—in the bestowal of which prescriptive custom appears to recognise the claim of official rank, as well as of conspicuous talent,—had been enjoyed by two, at least, of Sir Martin's predecessors in the chair of the Royal Academy ;  and I am perhaps justified in asserting that it could not have  been decorously withheld from the existing occupant of that chair, at  a time when the distribution of the degree was about to take a very extensive range, — including many individuals whose title to such a mark of respect from the university, had been established in fields of exertion similar to, and, in some instances, identical with those in which the President had achieved his professional and literary triumphs.  His name was accordingly placed on the list of those who were to be graced with the degree of D.C.L., on the auspicious occasion to which I have referred.

By some unaccountable, and certainly rather discourteous, negligence on the part of the university officials, however, he was not apprised of the honour intended for him, which, as in the case of the other persons selected to receive it, was to be publicly conferred in full convocation, in presence of the newly-installed chancellor, and the imposing array of collegiate dignitaries and distinguished visitors who were to grace the theatre, on the day of the installation.   The result was that, at the appointed time, when each embryo doctor, who had received due notice of the day's proceedings, was in attendance to hear the announcement of his name from the mouth of the public orator, and be in due form presented by that functionary to the electoral body as a fit recipient of the " *doctoratus*," — some surprise was excited among the assembled spectators, by the fact that when Dr. Phillimore, in going through his list, had arrived at Sir Martin's name, and, in " very choice" Latin, proceeded to announce it in connection with the impending degree, — the formal " Placet" of the Senate was not followed by the appearance of the *doctor designatus*, to receive the gown which he should then and there have reverently assumed.  The unexplained absence, on such an occasion, of one on whom the university were conferring this much-coveted mark of academical favour, was ingeniously accounted for by the special correspondent of one of the leading London journals, — in his detail of the day's incidents,—on the hypothesis that some religious obstacle, arising out of the President's well-known adhesion to the Catholic communion, had impeded the assumption of the gown.  But as no subscription involving any principle of orthodoxy is, or ever has been, required as a qualification for the degree of D.C.L., and no dogmatic test of any kind is applied to ascertain the fitness of the candidate for an honour

which has, if I mistake not, been conferred, in some instances, on Mahommedan celebrities, — this conjecture
was manifestly insufficient, and to those who had the
*carte du pays*, carried its own refutation on the face of it.

The names of those about to be honoured with the
degree had, — whether from official sources or otherwise, — appeared in the morning papers on or previously to the day fixed for the ceremonial; but this
announcement had escaped Sir Martin.  It happened
that on the day in question, he was engaged to dine
with Lord Darnley; and the first intimation he received
of his being included in the list, was in answer to his
inquiry as to the meaning of the general exclamation of
surprise, which greeted the announcement of his name,
as he entered the drawing-room of his noble host, in
the midst of a discussion as to the probability of his
keeping his engagement to dine in Berkeley Square, on
a day when he was clearly bound, by every principle of
*étiquette* and propriety, to be in attendance on the
magnates of the university, and engaged in swelling the
triumph of the new Chancellor at Oxford.

While dealing with the events or recollections of the
year 1834, as connected with the subject of this
biography, I cannot avoid noticing an absurd and
malignant fiction, equally injurious to the memory of
the late king, offensive to the feelings of a gallant and
highly-distinguished admiral, and annoying to Sir Martin himself; which—current for a week or two, and
soon forgotten as a " lie of the day "—in the summer of
that year—has been, at a comparatively recent period,
reproduced in print under circumstances which might
possibly impart to it, in the minds of the majority
of readers, a plausible character of authenticity.  I
allude to a rumour industriously circulated in society,

shortly after the opening of the Royal Academy exhibition in the year 1834, which represented the King as having, on the occasion of the accustomed visit of their Majesties to Somerset House, on the morning of the day devoted to the private view of the exhibition, rebuked the President, in terms of gross and insulting scurrility, for pointing out to his Majesty a portrait of Admiral Napier;—a rebuke, accompanied, it was said, by the most violent abuse of that gallant admiral himself. This alleged outburst of the royal displeasure was supposed to have reference to the part so successfully taken by Admiral Napier, in the contest at that time still undecided between the two rival branches of the royal House of Braganza for the crown of Portugal.

The object of those with whom this stupid and libellous *canard* originated,—and of some at least who contributed to accredit it in the public mind,—was apparently to create an impression that the private feelings of the Sovereign were diametrically opposed to the views entertained by his existing ministry, on the subject of continental politics; while not a few were prompt to believe, and eager to circulate it, as affording evidence that the state of the royal mind and intellect was such as must speedily disqualify his Majesty for the performance of the constitutional duties attached to his exalted station.

It will be in the recollection of many who are old enough to have witnessed the various phases and manifestations of party spirit, in those days of unusual political excitement, that among a certain class of politicians, feelings of disappointment, produced by the protracted exclusion from office of the party with which they sought to identify themselves, found vent, at intervals, in spiteful reports on the subject of the King's language and demeanour, evidently framed with a view of exciting misgivings as to the mental sanity of the sovereign.　In the present instance, it is impossible to attribute to any source but the most unscrupulous political malignity, the dissemination of a rumour so well calculated to give colour to these alarming insinuations. The reader who, in the amusing journal of Mr. Thomas Raikes, may have found, under the date of the 13th June, 1834 (that gentleman being then resident at Paris or Versailles), an entry containing a version of the story, on the authority of a letter from London, stated to have been shown to him by a lady, whom the context of the passage seems to identify with the Hon. Mrs. Lionel Dawson Damer,—a letter which, as quoted by Mr. Raikes, purports to have been written by one of the party who accompanied their Majesties in their visit to the Royal Academy on the occasion in question,—would be naturally led to conclude that a narrative, presenting itself with so circumstantial a show of authenticity, must at any rate have more or less of a foundation in fact.

Mr. Raikes's statement, indeed, bears internal evidence of error or misapprehension in dealing with the subject; since, as reported by him, the startling scene is represented as occurring between the King and the President of the Royal *Society*,—which office was then held by his Royal Highness the Duke of Sussex; a fact of which no one among the distinguished persons in attendance on their Majesties, during the royal visit to Somerset House, can well have been in ignorance. But whatever may have been the actual contents of the letter which formed the groundwork of the entry in Mr. Raikes's journal,—whether the writer did really, as that gentleman seems to have understood, represent himself as forming part of the royal *cortège* on the occasion ; or, which is far more probable, merely state that he was at the *private view* of the exhibition on the day when the royal visit was paid, a privilege which he may have enjoyed, in common with the *élite* of the *connoisseur* world, who on those occasions were admitted by tickets, not during the stay, but immediately after the departure of their Majesties and suite,— it is absolutely certain that the story so circumstantially recorded is, in *substance* as in *detail*, a *pure fiction*, and that the royal visit in question was unmarked by any incident which could afford the slightest pretext for so preposterous a report, or to which it could, through the utmost ingenuity of distortion, be traced with any degree of plausibility. No portrait of Admiral Napier was pointed out to the King by the President; nor did any observation relating to or connected with the name or services of that gallant officer, fall from the royal lips, either in conversation with, or in the hearing of Sir Martin, during the royal visit, throughout which his Majesty was in excellent spirits, and uniformly gracious and affable in his demeanour towards the President.

I make these assertions on the express authority of Sir Martin's own statement, distinctly made, in my presence, a few days after the opening of the exhibition; when the report reached his ears for the first time, to his surprise, and not a little to his amusement, on the return home of a member of his family after a dinner party, where the story had been ventilated as the newest gossip of the day.

As the ingenious fiction, though freely circulated in private, did not find its way into the newspapers, no public notice could properly be taken of it at the time ;

and Sir Martin contented himself with such opportunities of denial as the conversational chances of society afforded. The matter was, or seemed to be, speedily forgotten. But, some years later, the subject was once more brought to the President's notice, when on a visit at Leigh Park, the hospitable mansion of his friend, Sir George Staunton, by Sir Charles Napier himself, on the occasion of their meeting for the first time at Sir George's table ; when, in answer to an inquiry from the gallant admiral as to the amount of credit due to a story concocted, apparently, with at least a collateral view to his personal annoyance, Sir Martin had the satisfaction of assuring him that the ill-natured report was destitute of the slightest foundation.

As the entertaining work in which this ephemeral *méchanceté* is accidentally resuscitated, has met with an extensive circulation among those readers who take an interest in the social and political annals of the last quarter of a century, it has become a duty incumbent on Sir Martin's biographer to notice a misstatement so plausibly endorsed, which, if left uncontradicted, would tend to affix on the memory of King William IV. an imputation of unfeeling, insolent, and brutal vulgarity, such as the bitterness of party hate could alone have dared to ascribe to one of the most amiable and kind-hearted monarchs that ever sat on the throne of these realms.

# CHAPTER XIV.

## 1835—1836.

Progress of Anti-Academic Agitation.—Changes of Ministry.—Secure position of the Academy in the Favour of the King.—Social Popularity of the President.—Portrait of Queen Adelaide.—Death of Mrs. Dillon.—Parliamentary Committee on the subject of the Fine Arts.—Its Proceedings in 1835.—Professor Waagen.—Singular Change in the *matériel* of the Committee, as constituted in 1836.—Open Hostility to the Royal Academy.—Witnesses examined.—Messrs. G. Rennie, Foggo, Martin, Haydon, Clint, &c.—Examination of the President and Officers of the Royal Academy.—"Lame and Impotent Conclusion" of the affair.

THE course of political events in the years 1834 and 1835 had but a slight bearing on the prospects of the arts and the Academy. But as far as the influence of ministerial changes could be felt in reference to matters so insignificant in public estimation, as compared with the great struggles of constitutional or parliamentary warfare, that influence was not favourable to any of the interests which the Royal Academy assumed to represent, and which, according to the sincere and profound convictions of the President, were inseparably linked with the prosperity of that institution.

It was fortunate for the views of those who desired to see the noble *emplacement* in Trafalgar Square devoted to the erection of a building capable of suitably accommodating the national pictures, and at the same time supplying an appropriate domicile for the king's Academy, that Sir Martin's earnest and energetic remonstrances had, as we have seen, confirmed the wavering ministry in their original intention, which they had all but abandoned in deference to the suggestions of a pitiful economy, ostensibly put forward to conceal the true motive of the threatened opposition, viz., a desire to exclude the Royal Academy from any participation in the benefits of the parliamentary grant.

The result of the President's earnest appeal to Lord Grey, against Lord Duncannon's project for converting the Banqueting House at Whitehall into a National Gallery, has been seen in the commencement of the new building in Trafalgar Square within a very short period of the discussion in which Sir Martin played so important a part. Had Lord Grey's retirement from office occurred a year earlier, the President would in vain have appealed to feelings and ideas which found no responsive echo in the heart or mind of that accomplished nobleman's immediate successor in the post of prime minister; and the pusillanimity which the uncertain tenure of power renders all but inevitable in the head of a rickety cabinet, would have combined with his avowed indifference to the interests at stake in the discussion, to secure a willing acquiescence in any modification of the government projects, which might serve to deprecate radical hostility, or obtain *doctrinaire* support.

The foundations of the new building, however, were laid, and the structure was gradually rising under the critical gaze of the public, when Lord Grey seceded from the Government; and any attempt to interfere with a plan which had proceeded so far towards completion, was felt to be a hopeless task, so far as the locality and destination of the edifice were concerned. As we have seen, therefore, the anti-academic agitation, though by no means softened or subdued, in the degree of its hostility, experienced some change in the nature and direction of its attacks; and under the auspices of an administration presided over by Lord Melbourne, a fairer prospect of success presented itself to the assailants of the Royal Academy, than could have been hoped for while the presiding genius of Downing Street exhibited those kindly sympathies with the objects and views of the institution, which characterised the conduct of Lord Grey throughout the official negotiations and proceedings connected with its projected removal to Trafalgar Square.

The break-up of Lord Melbourne's first cabinet, occasioned by the death of Earl Spencer, and the consequent removal to the House of Lords of the respected nobleman, whose honest frankness of character and personal popularity had supplied such effective support to the falling fortunes of the administration in the post of Chancellor of the Exchequer, gave promise of brighter times for the arts, in the accession to power of their steady, generous, and enlightened friend and patron, Sir Robert Peel. The events, however, of the short ministerial campaign, which ended in the resignation of the Peel cabinet and the return of Lord Melbourne to office, were of too engrossing a nature, to leave much time or opportunity for the discussion of matters extrinsic to the interests that supply the ordinary battle-field of party warfare.

The state of things in Downing Street, on the reconstruction of the Liberal administration was, to say the least of it, quite as unpropitious to the just claims of the Academy, as it had been previous to the Conservative *interregnum;* but the frank and cordial support on which they could rely at the hands of their august patron and protector, far more than counterbalanced the dangers by which they were threatened, from the combined operations of ministerial apathy and radical dogmatism, in the House of Commons.

The session of 1835 passed off without any violent demonstration of anti-academic hostility in debate, of sufficient consequence, as regarded either its author or its abettors, to call for active opposition or official protest, on the part of the President, in his communications with the Government.

In the mean time he continued to enjoy, in an eminent degree, the favour and regard of the King, who ever encouraged on his part the free expression of opinion on all matters connected with the interests of the arts, and the welfare and conduct of the body over which he presided, and readily afforded him every opportunity of personal communication with his Majesty, which the somewhat exceptional state of the academic affairs rendered desirable,—apart from the more strictly official occasions, on which the privilege of access to the royal presence was claimed in the ordinary course of academic business.

Nor was his Majesty backward in exhibiting his respect for the professional talents of the President; as from the days of his courtly success in the execution of the state portrait, originally intended for Lord Wellesley, the King called into frequent exercise the powers of Sir Martin's pencil, during the few years which intervened between that period and the lamented death of his Majesty.

His social popularity among all that was distinguished in rank, station, and intellect among his contemporaries, naturally increased in the same *ratio* in which the proprieties of his official position, multiplied the occasions when he was, in a manner, compelled to mix in the most brilliant circles of the London world, and encounter the flattering homage which it was his fortune to meet with, from those in whose estimation the claims of conspicuous station were greatly enhanced by varied intellectual acquirements, conversational brilliancy, and a charm of manner and address, as rare as it was attractive.

No one who witnessed the happy flow of his eloquence, and the impressive grace of his delivery and demeanour, when presiding at the great social anniversary of the Academy, or responding to the complimentary *banalités* inseparable from the proposal of his health at some public dinner connected with the interests of art, science, or literature, could fail to recognise the existence of qualities not less calculated to enliven the intercourse of private society, than to impart an unwonted and exciting interest to the stereotyped formalities of symposial oratory. Nor were those who, acting on this assumption, sought to attract him within the circle of social intimacy, doomed to experience the species of disappointment which sometimes attends that peculiar manifestation of hero-worship, familiarly characterised as *lion-hunting*.

In a preceding chapter I have mentioned his restoration of the practice sanctioned by early precedent in the case of Sir Joshua, with regard to the biennial award and delivery of the gold medals, &c., to the students of the Royal Academy, viz., that of inviting a number of distinguished visitors to be present at the ceremonial. The following extract from a letter addressed by him to Miss Tunno, at the close of the year 1835, contains some reference to the recent distribution of prizes on the 10th December in that year, by which it will be seen that the attempt to supply the ambition of the students with the additional stimulus derivable from the eminent or dignified character of the guests who were summoned to the ceremony, had not been wholly unsuccessful.

Dec. 25th, 1835.

.    .    .    .    .    .    .

" I am not surprised that you did not see any account of the academic proceedings in print. . . . . None of the *press-gang*, as Fanny ·Kemble calls them, are ever admitted on these occasions. An official statement of the names of the successful candidates is sent to the daily papers by the secretary, who merely mentions that, after the distribution, the President delivered an address. On the recent occasion, however, a flourishing account of the ceremonial appeared in the *Morning Herald,* which was written by a student of the Academy, who, it appears, has some access to that paper. There was a tolerable show of *grandees* on the occasion, considering that at this time of the year everybody that is anybody is out of town: Lord Abinger, Lord Lyndhurst, the Bishop of London, one of the Lords Commissioners of the Great Seal, the Vice-Chancellor, the Chancellor of the Exchequer, the Chief Judge of the Admiralty, Sir John Nicholl, and many minor luminaries of science, literature, and the arts. As I had to invite the guests and provide the entertainment, you may suppose there was some expense of time, thought and trouble. It was but homely fare, I am afraid ; but as it is to be hashed up in print by desire of the Academy, you shall have an opportunity of judging of my cookery on the occasion.

"Your last letter contains three capital puns—a large proportion of wit for one epistle. Had you sparkled so brightly in a letter to Wilkie, he would have cudgelled his brains for a week to rival you. But such an effort would be quite hopeless on my part. My fancy begins to feel the frost of age. But the heart is not easily chilled to those we love ; and the warmth you have excited there must glow while sense remains."

In the month of May 1836, Sir Martin received the King's commands to attend at Windsor Castle for the purpose of commencing a whole length portrait of her Majesty the Queen, to be placed in the hall of the Goldsmiths' Company; and it was intimated to him that, with that view, he must be in attendance at Windsor from the 14th of the month, the day which had been fixed for the arrival of their Majesties at the Castle for the summer season.

On the day in question he accordingly proceeded to Windsor; and not having been apprised of the fact that he was to be accommodated in the Castle, as the guest of their Majesties, during the continuance of his professional attendance, he dispatched the necessary *matériel* for his operations in the painting-room, to the Castle, to be placed under the care of the page to whose department the requisite arrangements belonged; and after reporting himself in due form to the Master of the Household, he took up his abode at the Castle Hotel ; his arrival at Windsor having preceded that of the court by some hours.  The next morning, however, he was waited upon at his hotel by an officer of the household, conveying the King's commands that he should take up his residence at the Castle, and form part of the royal circle during his stay at Windsor ; an apartment in the Round Tower having been provided for his reception, to which accordingly he was required to remove without delay.

These details, of little intrinsic importance, are necessary for the purpose of enabling the reader to understand one or two of the allusions in the subjoined letter; —a document too characteristic of the writer's domestic and affectionate feelings, to require any apology for its insertion in a biography which seeks to illustrate his moral and social individuality, as well as to record the main incidents of his official and professional career.

### To Lady Archer Shee.

"Windsor, Wednesday, 18th March, 1836.

"MY DEAR MARY,—As M—— has no doubt given you in person all the necessary details up to the period of his departure, I may safely restrict myself to the narrative of subsequent events. My *compagnon de voyage* was so pleased to be relieved from duty, on what had certainly every appearance of proving a forlorn hope, as far, at least, as amusement was concerned, that he seemed but little sensible of my distress, on being *left alone*, I may say, and delivered up, bound hand and foot, to the Philistines. He has, I dare say, *amused* the domestic circle with a lively picture of my consternation, on receiving the royal sentence of imprisonment in the Round Tower for an indefinite period. I am willing to admit that it must have appeared a rather ludicrous *embarras* in the eyes of most reasonable people — but I never set up for a very reasonable person; and where my feelings, propensities, and peculiar habits are concerned, I consider myself as gradually merging the character of an old man, to which time has entitled me, into that of an old woman, to which I am rapidly succeeding in *my own right*. I consider it, therefore, no breach of duty, affection, or even decorum, to be laughed at by my family in all cases where they have some reason to suppose that *my foibles* lean to *their side*, that is, to *virtue's side*. You see I am desirous of putting the best face upon my folly. With respect to *you all*, my selfishness is certainly social; and if I am causelessly unhappy abroad, it is because I am so long accustomed to be made happy at home. *There*, my dear Mary, you are the principal culprit; and if you had indulged me with a few *matrimonial varieties*, and communicated an occasional gloom to the domestic horizon, I might have found as much pleasure as other people in changing the *atmosphere*. The nearer the time of our final separation approaches, the more I feel any temporary interruption that arises, to the little that remains for us to enjoy of each other's society. But you are beginning to be tired of all this prosing, and would prefer an account of my proceedings to a parade of my reflections. I must tell you, therefore, that I have just returned to my nest in the Tower after a second sitting. As yet, I have met with high approbation; to an extent, indeed, that considering the state of the picture, seems almost ridiculous: all parties, from the King himself downwards, prognosticating a most agreeable likeness. I must tell you, however, that I do not at all share in this confidence. The difficulties arising from the nature of the subject are beyond anything I could have anticipated. In my opinion, Beechey has done wonders. Her Majesty gave me but a short sitting to-day,—one hour and twenty minutes,—but promises a better to-morrow. She is very gracious, expressed surprise that I could do so much in so short a time, and particularly requests that the picture may not be flattered. I remained until near four, endeavouring to forward the work, and shall spend the remainder of as fine a day as ever shone, in my room, till the hour of going to dine in state. We sat last night till half-past eleven. Lady De Lisle very agreeable, and Lord Frederick Fitzclarence very chatty. The Queen's band playing the finest music all the time, and nobody listening."

It is perhaps not wholly unworthy of remark, that the portrait of her Majesty Queen Adelaide, to which the foregoing letter refers, was honoured by a complimentary mark of royal approbation, precisely similar to that already recorded as having been bestowed on the portrait of the King originally intended for Lord Wellesley. The destination of the Queen's portrait was, as we have seen, the hall of the Goldsmiths' Company. But the likeness was so successful, and the composition and execution of the picture were so satisfactory to the King that, on its completion, his Majesty intimated to Sir Martin his intention of retaining it in his own possession; and it was accordingly arranged that the President should paint another whole length of her Majesty, for the worshipful corporation in question.

The spring of the year 1836 was marked by an event, which, although reasonably to be anticipated in the natural course of things, was fraught with painful interest and affectionate regret to Sir Martin. This was the death in Dublin of his venerable and admirable relative, Mrs. Dillon, at the advanced age of ninety-two. Her vigorous intellect had remained unimpaired until within a few weeks of her death; and her warm and generous feelings, ever alive to what concerned the happiness and well-being of those with whom she was connected, had experienced no detriment from the chilling effects of age. The long period—upwards of thirty years—which had elapsed since she had seen her favourite and beloved nephew, had produced no diminution of interest, on her part, in his fame or his fortunes; and to the last, every detail of his public career,—every evidence of his social or official popularity, was sought for with avidity, and dwelt on with exultation, by her enduring affection and unselfish spirit. The sacred trust which, on the premature death of her only sister, she had spontaneously undertaken, viz., that of supplying a mother's place to her orphan nephews, was, in the case of Sir Martin, performed throughout with such scrupulous care and devoted solicitude of affection, that her name requires to be conspicuously recorded among those to whom he was indebted for moral and material benefits, that exercised the most salutary influence over his long and honourable life:—and her memory, which must ever be held in veneration by his descendants, may well claim to be associated, in the pages of his biographer, with the brightest reminiscences of a career, pursued under the guidance of principles, and marked by the practical exhibition of virtues, which she had sedulously inculcated by precept, and signally enforced by example.

The parliamentary session of 1836 witnessed the further development of that spirit of hostility to the Royal Academy, which pervaded a small section of the House of Commons, in the singular proceedings of the select committee on arts and manufactures. This body, which professed to continue and prosecute the inquiry into such branches of the subject as had not been fully investigated by the labours of the committee appointed, with the same avowed objects, in the previous session, (1835) had been,—by what process of parliamentary packing or compression it is needless to inquire,—reduced to less than a third of the members of which the original committee was composed. But to whatever cause this change in the organisation of the tribunal may have been attributable, the result exhibited a remarkable exclusion from its ranks, of several members of the committee of 1835, whom public opinion would have pointed out as peculiarly qualified to deal with questions affecting the highest interests of art, literature, or science,—and a corresponding concentration of anti-academic venom in the *matériel* of the committee.

The committee of 1835 numbered among its members, Mr. Bernal, the late Lord Colborne (then Mr. Ridley Colborne), the late Earl of Ellesmere (then Lord Francis Egerton), the late Sir Robert Peel, Lord Monteagle (then Mr. Spring Rice, and Chancellor of the Exchequer), Lord John Russell, the late Sir Robert Inglis, Sir Edward Bulwer Lytton (then Mr. E. L. Bulwer), Mr. (now Sir Henry) Lytton Bulwer, the present Earl Stanhope (then Lord Mahon), and the late Lord Sudeley (then Mr. Hanbury Tracy).

It is evident that of these distinguished *celebrities* of the political, literary, and social world, few, if any, could have been found willing to co-operate in gratifying the

personal spite and disappointed vanity of a small body
of discontented artists, by converting the committee,—
ostensibly appointed to inquire into the statistics of art,
with a view to its promotion and development,—into a
kind of Star Chamber or high commission court, before
which the Royal Academy were to be arraigned on the
most frivolous pretexts, and on evidence as ridiculous
as it was contemptible, on a charge of high treason
against those interests which for upwards of half a
century they alone had earnestly, perseveringly, and
effectively sustained.

The inquiries of the committee of 1835 took a wide
range over questions relating to the connection of the
arts with the progress of manufactures.

The great majority of the witnesses examined before
it, were persons more or less practically acquainted with
the details of those branches of industry which are in
their nature subject to the influences of art, and consequently affected by, and reacting on, the state of public
taste and knowledge in matters of design.

The proceedings were indeed inaugurated by the evidence of Professor Waagen, whose position as director
of the royal galleries at Berlin, entitled him, no doubt,
to the respectful attention of the committee, on points
connected with the statistics of German art; while the
vague impression of his social and critical importance
in the regions of Teutonic taste, imparted much additional weight to his official authority. It would, however, be perhaps difficult to discover on what grounds
the committee of 1836 were so eager to recognise in the
opinions of this highly respectable and accomplished
functionary, that peculiar character of oracular wisdom,
before which the authoritative claims of talent, experience, and high official station, in the persons of emi-

nent British artists, were expected to yield, in deferential acquiescence and conscious inferiority.

The value of Professor Waagen's testimony, in the eyes of those who organised the committee, and skil-fully controlled its proceedings, consisted obviously in his avowed hostility to academies established under royal or imperial patronage, and invested with honorary distinctions or social privileges, as a means of fostering and promoting the true interests of art in its higher departments; and having at the commencement of the proceedings secured this valuable authority, as an auxiliary force in their contemplated proceedings against the Royal Academy, they were content to keep it in reserve for the period when the position and demerits of that body could be more conveniently brought under dis-cussion, before a committee of greatly reduced numbers, from whose ranks every name in any degree suggestive of sympathy with the views, or respect for the services, of the institution, should be carefully excluded.

Thus the committee of 1835, which included the many eminent persons whom I have mentioned above, were allowed to range over the extensive field presented for their labours by the *artistico-industrial* question, without openly directing their inquiries to matters connected with the conduct or administration of the Academy, or *touting*, like their successors in 1836, for statements inculpatory of that body.

At the close of the session of 1835, and the approach of the prorogation which was about to put an end to their collective existence, the committee not having exhausted the subjects referred to them by the House, abstained from making any practical or partial report, founded upon the voluminous evidence which had been brought before them—leaving to those on whom might devolve the resumption of their duties in the succeeding session, the task of deducing from the facts and opinions already recorded, such results as they might fairly suggest, when viewed in connection with the additional materials to be supplied in the further progress of the investigation.

They, however, stated the nature of their labours, and specified the portions of the subject to which their inquiries had been limited, as follows:—

" The Select Committee appointed to inquire into the best means of extending a knowledge of the arts, and of the principles of design among the people (especially the manufacturing population) of the country; also to inquire into the constitution, management, and effects of institutions connected with the arts; and to whom the petitions of artists and admirers of the fine arts, and of several members of the Society of British Artists, were severally referred; and who were empowered to report the minutes of the evidence taken before them to the House:—Have examined the matters to them referred, and have agreed to the following report :—

" The Committee began its labours by dividing the subject of inquiry into the following parts :

" The state of art in this country and in other countries, as manifested in their different manufactures.

" The best means of extending among the people, especially the manufacturing classes, a knowledge of, and taste for, art.

" The state of the higher branches of art, and the best mode of advancing them.

" The investigations of the Committee have been principally confined to the first and second subdivisions of the subject. The Committee lay the evidence hitherto taken before the House, and recommend the resumption of the inquiry early in the next session of Parliament.—*Report*, September 1835.

Thus it will be seen that the statistical and commercial aspects of the subject had chiefly engaged the attention of the committee of 1835, while they had left untouched those higher topics of investigation, requiring for their satisfactory development a large amount of discriminative knowledge on the part of those who were to conduct the inquiry, and an extensive acquaintance with the theory, practice, and true objects of art, in those whose opinions were to be collected and compared, for the effectual guidance of the committee, in working out the practical result of their labours.

A bare enumeration of the names composing the *expurgated* committee of 1836, may probably enable the reader to judge how far these requirements were answered, in the constitution of a tribunal empowered to decide authoritatively on the highest interests of taste; while the course adopted by them in the selection and examination of witnesses, will certainly supply the measure of their earnestness and sincerity, in the ostensible prosecution of an inquiry, in reference to which they sought no information but such as could, *per fas aut nefas*, conduce to the result which the promoters of this parliamentary *mystification*, had already decided on, as a " foregone conclusion."

The committee, as appointed in 1835, consisted of the following members :—

| | |
|---|---|
| Mr. Ewart. | Mr. Heathcoate. |
| Mr. Morrison. | Mr. Strutt. |
| The Lord Advocate. | Mr. Hutt. |
| Mr. Pusey. | Mr. Brotherton. |
| Mr. John Parker. | Mr. Scholefield. |
| Mr. Wyse. | Mr. David Lewis. |
| Mr. Henry Thomas Hope. | Mr. Davenport. |
| Dr. Bowring. | |

To intrust a committee so constituted with the task of investigating " *the state of the higher branches of the*

*art, and the best mode of advancing them,"* was an act
the palpable absurdity of which requires no comment.
As regards that small section of the public which attached any importance to the inquiries involved, and,
with arcadian simplicity, relied on the *bona fides* of the
transaction, it was, to borrow the phrase of an illustrious
judge, when characterising certain eccentricities of Irish
legal procedure,—"*a delusion, a mockery, and a snare.*"

It affords, however, a happy illustration of the system prevalent in the appointment of " select committees," on subjects of little or no general interest :—
those convenient safety-valves of legislative mediocrity
and pretension, destined to carry off the superfluous
vapour of parliamentary activity, in rambling and
gossiping inquiries, terminating in bulky and valueless
reports.   In cases where the ostensible points of inquiry are matters of utter indifference to nine-tenths of
the House, it is no wonder that we find the construction
of the tribunal before which the sham investigation is
to be carried on, readily confided to those who, having
already determined on the verdict, are solely bent on
obtaining and recording such one-sided evidence, as may
afford a plausible groundwork for conclusions arrived
at long previously to its delivery, and in no degree
affected by its purport.

Never, assuredly, was this natural result of the *poco-
curante* spirit pervading the House, in the appointment
of committees on scientific or speculative questions,
more forcibly exemplified than in the proceedings of
Mr. Ewart's committee of 1836.

Apart from any consideration of its *matériel*, it will
hardly be disputed that a committee, no matter how
constituted, and however personally competent to be
oracular on the subjects referred to them, are still, if

avowedly entrusted with the duty of inquiry, under some moral obligation to consult those sources of information which the voice of public opinion, and all but unanimous professional assent, unite in recognising as authoritative. *Cuilibet in arte suâ perito credendum*, is a venerable maxim,—not perhaps of invariable application,—but certainly one to which the experience of men of business and the common sense of mankind at large, have long yielded a ready practical acquiescence. The studious disregard of the principle it involves, must ever cast a certain amount of suspicion on the proceedings and motives of those publicly engaged in the investigation of facts or theories connected with the development of any branch of art, science, or industry.

It was therefore not too much to expect that the committee, when inquiring into " *the state of the higher branches of art, and the best mode of advancing them*," should take the necessary steps to obtain the opinions of the most eminent professors of British art, in each of its various departments, in aid of their own not wholly infallible judgment, in deciding on questions of so comprehensive a range. Nor would it have seemed unreasonable to anticipate that, as there existed in the country a body of artists, associated together under the immediate patronage and direct control of the crown, for the avowed purpose of promoting the interests involved in the subject of the inquiry,—and whose official organisation, system, and proceedings were obvious and legitimate matters of careful and dispassionate investigation, as closely connected with the question of the advancement of art,—the principal officers, functionaries, and professors of that body would be applied to, in the first instance, and in a spirit of decent if not respectful courtesy, for those statements and explanations which were essential to the full understanding of the nature and objects of the institution, and a fair appreciation of its past and present claims on the confidence of Parliament and the public. The undoubted and undeniable fact that the body in question included within its ranks, an immense majority of the conspicuous names that adorned the records of living genius, in every department of the art, might in itself have been sufficient to protect it from the studied and insolent discourtesy which throughout marked the proceedings of the committee in their regard.

During the period over which the labours of the committee of 1836 extended, the Royal Academy consisted of the following members, exclusive of five associate engravers:—

ACADEMICIANS.

| | |
|---|---|
| William Allan. | Edwin Landseer. |
| Sir Wm. Beechey. | William Mulready. |
| Edward Hodges Baily. | Thomas Phillips. |
| Henry Perronet Briggs. | Henry Wm. Pickersgill. |
| Augustus W. Callcott. | Charles Rossi. |
| Alfred E. Chalon. | R. R. Reinagle. |
| Sir Francis Chantrey. | Robert Smirke. |
| Abraham Cooper. | Sir M. Archer Shee, *Pres.* |
| William Collins. | Sir John Soane. |
| Richard Cook. | Sir Robert Smirke. |
| R. Constable. | Clarkson Stanfield. |
| Thomas Daniell. | J. M. W. Turner. |
| Wm. Daniell. | Henry Thomson. |
| William Etty. | Richard Westall. |
| Charles Lock Eastlake. | Sir David Wilkie. |
| Wm. Hilton. | James Ward. |
| Henry Howard, *Sec.* | Richard Westmacott. |
| Geo. Jones. | Sir Jeffry Wyatville. |
| Charles Robert Leslie. | W. Wilkins. |

Charles Robert Cockerell, } R.A.<br>John Gibson, } Elect.

ASSOCIATES.

| | |
|---|---|
| Joseph Gandy. | John James Chalon. |
| Archer James Oliver. | W. F. Witherington. |
| Samuel Drummond. | William Wyon. |
| George Arnald. | Andrew Geddes. |
| William Westall. | Thomas Uwins. |
| George Francis Joseph. | Frederick Richard Lee. |
| Washington Allston. | Daniel Maclise. |
| Francis Danby. | Solomon Alexander Hart. |
| John Peter Deering. | |

Not one of these eminent persons, however, was called upon for a statement of his views or opinions, on the important subject which the committee were professing to investigate. Messrs. Howard and Hilton, indeed, in their characters of Secretary and Keeper of the Royal Academy, were summoned before this *impartial* tribunal, for the purpose of supplying official details connected with the institution, which their genius and acquirements so signally graced and adorned. But although these gentlemen were confessedly among the most earnest and successful votaries of historic and poetic art, the committee studiously refrained from putting to them any question which could seem to imply a recognition of their professional or personal claims, or a desire to seek the benefit of their judgment and experience, on the question ostensibly under consideration, viz.: " The state of the higher branches of the art, and the best mode of advancing them."

The committee, indeed, took little pains to disguise the hostile *animus* which actuated their proceedings, wherever the Royal Academy was concerned. The official representatives of that body were not called before them, until they had exhausted the evidence of those whose rancour against the institution was displayed in vague and unscrupulous accusation, and

sometimes in gross and all but scurrilous abuse, to which
the committee lent a complacent and encouraging attention.   It was not from the official sources of information, but from men openly hostile to the very
existence of the institution, and, in every case but one,
avowedly labouring under feelings of personal resentment, and attacking the Academy on private grounds of
complaint,—that details of the nature, constitution, and
government of the body, were in the first instance sought.
The eagerness with which the committee welcomed
every disparaging observation on academics in general,
and on the Royal Academy in particular,—sometimes
even suggesting, by the form of their questions, the very
terms of the censure or accusation which, yet unpro-
nounced by the witness, they were bent on recording as
part of his evidence,—would be simply ludicrous, if it
were not a subject of grave regret, to see a tribunal entrusted by a legislative assembly with the task of a
solemn inquiry into matters of assumed public interest
and importance, thus merging the character of the judge
in the partisanship of the advocate,—soliciting the
manifestations of individual spite, and willing to render
their judicial proceedings subservient to the views of
private malevolence.*

* The following are a few amusing instances of the *leading question* system
adopted by the committee, in order to elicit from the witness under examination the precise answer which would suit the colour of the intended report.

Mr. George Rennie is asked, Q. 641 : " Do you imagine that it would be to a
great extent as absurd to encourage the pursuit of poetry by institutions or
fixed rules, as to encourage the arts of sculpture and painting ? "   Of course
Mr. Rennie answers, " I do."—*Min. of Ev.*, 21st June, 1836.

Mr. Martin is asked, Q. 800 : "Have you ever exhibited in the Royal
Academy ? " to which he answers, " Yes."   The next question (810) is as
follows :

" Have the circumstances attending your exhibitions led you to complain
of the manner in which works are exhibited there ? "

Further on, Mr. Ewart puts the following question (830) :   " Have you had

In addition to the President, Keeper, and Secretary, who were among the five or six witnesses last called before the committee, — the only royal academicians examined were Messrs. Reinagle, Wilkins, and Cockerell. The examination of the first of these gentlemen turned entirely on the subject of the relation between geometry and the beautiful forms of the antique;—and his evidence consisted exclusively of a short lecture, illustrated by diagrams, on the interesting subject referred to. Not a single question was addressed to him respecting the Academy, — its history, constitution, or management.

Mr. Wilkins's examination, as might be expected, was wholly confined to matters relating to the erection, internal distribution, and present or future appropriation of the new building of which he was the architect.

Mr. Cockerell, the eminent architect, was examined on the subject of "competition among artists, in the design and execution of public works."

The committee sought no information or opinion from him on the subject of the Academy. As he was a very recently-elected academician,—his diploma being yet unsigned by the king,— he was probably at that time but

reason to complain that your historical paintings have been jostled out of an appropriate place for them, by the intrusion of some petty portraits ? "

Q. 835. " Is it or not, not only injustice to an artist, but to the nation, to let them see in a most conspicuous place the easiest of all styles, the portrait ? "—*Min. of Ev.*, 24th June, 1836.

How far Mr. Ewart's personal experience may have enabled him to decide that "the portrait" is "the easiest of all styles," it is not for me to conjecture; but to an admirer of Vandyke and Reynolds, the *petitio principii* cannot but appear of doubtful admissibility.

In Mr. Haydon's examination, he is asked (Q. 1064): " Do you think that it (the Royal Academy) is a system which involves undue patronage on the part of some, and induces self-abasement and dependence on the part of others ? " As might be expected, the eager reply is, " Certainly; I think the moral character of English artists is dreadfully affected," &c.

Q. 1066. "Have you suffered in your reputation and emoluments by the injustice of the Academy ?"—*Min. of Ev.*, 28th June, 1836.

little conversant with questions relating to the internal
management or administration of the body.

Who, then, were the artists selected as the most competent, not only to enlighten the committee as to "the
state of the higher branches of the art, and the best
mode of advancing them," but also to speak, with conclusive authority, on the subject of the Royal Academy,
and the proper estimate to be formed of the claims and
services of that institution? — Messrs. George Rennie,
Foggo, Haydon, Martin, Hurlstone, Hofland, and Clint.

The first of these gentlemen,—who bore a name more
familiarly associated in the public mind with the
triumphs of engineering science, than with the history
or practice of those branches of art for the promotion
of which the Royal Academy was instituted, — was at
that time engaged in the profession of a sculptor,
which he, not many years after, relinquished for the
pursuit of politics, and the dignified labours of official
life, as governor of one of the colonial dependencies of
the crown.   He had spent some years on the continent,
in the course of his professional studies, and was, or
was assumed to be, on that account, peculiarly qualified
to speak authoritatively on the merits and demerits of
academies in general, and the Royal Academy in particular.   There was this distinction to be noted between
his evidence and that of the six other "promoters" of
the inquiry, — that in his case, the origin of his hostility
to the Royal Academy did not transpire; — and when
the presiding genius of the committee, with eager solicitude, endeavoured by leading questions to put him on
the track of personal complaint, and extract from him
individual instances of academic delinquency, he discreetly shrank from accepting the challenge, preferring
to rest his case on vague generalities of charge, which,

as they were undefined in meaning and extent, did not admit of positive or distinct refutation. It did not appear that he had ever been a student of the Academy, or in any way personally conversant with the details of its management or administration. His evidence, therefore, carried with it no greater weight in condemnation of the Academy, than is generally attached to loose assertion, unauthorised inference, and wholesale censure, when directed against public establishments by those who, whilst imperfectly acquainted with their proceedings, are earnestly bent on disparaging their claims.

But if the readers of the evidence, and probably some members of the committee itself, were left in ignorance alike of the grounds of Mr. Rennie's enmity to the Royal Academy, and the motives which suggested his examination as the first formal witness against that institution, — they could be in no doubt as to the *vis motrix* which operated in the instance of each of the other six gentlemen who were selected for the purpose of establishing the anti-academic case. Messrs. Foggo, Haydon, Martin, and Clint had each a personal grievance, on which he expatiated with indignant eloquence. Messrs. Hurlstone and Hofland were the president and secretary of the Society of British Artists, — a body of gentlemen associated together for very legitimate objects of private advantage,—neither performing nor affecting to perform any public duties connected with the cultivation or promotion of the arts,—but simply seeking to sell their works and divide amongst themselves the profits of their exhibition. These gentlemen, in the interest of their rival institution, were loud and vehement in their complaints of the unjust preference shown by the crown and the government, for the Royal Academy, in conceding to them the important privileges

attached to the character of an R.A., — and providing
for them a local habitation, in return for their public
services in the maintenance of a national and efficient
school of art, out of their own resources, and by the
application of funds which, according to the principle
acted upon with unimpeachable propriety by the Society
of British Artists, — the Academy would have been
perfectly justified in appropriating for the personal advantage of its members.

Messrs. Foggo, Martin, Haydon, and Clint, however,
as I have already intimated, openly based their accusations on personal grounds of complaint against the
Royal Academy; and these real or imaginary grievances
so completely gave the tone and colour to their evidence,
that any tribunal with the slightest pretensions to impartiality, would have received their general statements
with distrust, and attached but little weight to their
eagerly expressed opinions,—warped and embittered, as
they evidently were, by feelings solely referable to
worldly disappointment or wounded self-love.   Had the
personal complaints in question been such as necessarily involved the fact of any dereliction of duty on
the part of the Academy, as a body,—the committee
would doubtless have been fully justified in taking
those complaints into consideration, when about to report on the history and conduct of that institution.   In
no one instance, however, was the alleged grievance of a
nature to be dealt with as a palpable or obvious devia-
tion from any administrative principle to which the
Academy were bound to adhere, — or even as raising a
strong presumption of injustice or unfairness, in their
treatment of the complaining party.

In Mr. Foggo's case,—the first that was paraded
before the sympathising hostility of the committee,—the

Academy was made answerable for the failure of that gentleman's ambitious hopes as a votary of " high art," and represented as blighting all his prospects in life,— on the strength of statements which, if assumed to be strictly true, would prove nothing more than a want of due regard for the convenience of a brother artist, on the part of an individual member of the body.

The circumstances under which the complaint originated were as follows :—

The Government, with a creditable deference to the interests of art, had for some years past established and acted on a rule,—I believe still in force,—in conformity with which all works and materials of art, imported from the continent by artists, for their own use and improvement, were allowed to pass, duty free, at the custom-house.   But as such an indulgence, unless carefully restricted within the limits of its ostensible and legitimate object, might easily open a door to serious abuses and frauds, it was clogged with the provision that no works or articles of the description referred to, should be exempted from duty on the above-mentioned ground, except on the authority of two royal academicians who, from personal inspection and inquiry, should certify to the Treasury, their belief that the case was one which came fairly within the principle of the regulation.   This was, no doubt, a wise and reasonable precaution against the tricks and devices of professional picture-dealers; but the effect, as regarded the Royal Academy, was to require from the members of that body, the gratuitous performance of a very troublesome duty, involving occasionally a serious sacrifice of time.

By arrangement among the academicians themselves, this duty was undertaken by the different members in turn, upon a principle of rotation;—two of the forty being each year named or agreed upon as the members who were, when occasion required, to be employed on this special service. In undertaking the task, however, they could not be supposed to pledge themselves for its performance, in every instance, at a moment's notice, — at the request of any artist who might require the benefit of their certificate ; and a reasonable consideration for the convenience of gentlemen engaged in professional labours of an engrossing character,—who were called upon to interrupt, simultaneously, their ordinary avocations, and sacrifice the whole or the greater part of a professional day, in doing the unpaid work of custom-house officers, for the security of the revenue, and the personal benefit of those who might be perfect strangers to them, — was necessarily involved in the arrangements to be made, from time to time, for these official inspections of imported *virtù*.

Mr. Foggo's complaint was, that some sixteen or eighteen years previously, on his return to England from a residence on the continent, his property and pictures had been detained at the custom-house, for want of the academic certificate, until the departure from London of Madame de Boigne, daughter of the French ambassador, the Marquis d'Osmond, — a lady who interested herself in the professional success of Mr. Foggo, and through whose influence that gentleman had reckoned on introducing a picture, executed by him abroad, to the notice of the great world in London. He alleged that one of the two academicians whose services were due by rotation in the matter of passing works through the custom-house, had, in his case, refused, or delayed for an unreasonable time, to attend to the duty in question, — and had thus deprived him of the opportunity, which had never again presented itself, of making his *début* as an artist under high diplomatic and aristocratic auspices.

How far the sanguine anticipations of rapid and brilliant success entertained by Mr. Foggo, in reference to Madame de Boigne's patronage, would have been realised by the event, had he been able to secure such an introduction for the works thus unfortunately detained *in transitu*, it is unnecessary to conjecture. But, while giving him the full benefit of the doubt, and regretting that delay should have occurred in the extrication of his works from the stern grasp of fiscal rapacity, to which he ascribed such disastrous consequences, we may fairly assert that the circumstance, however unfortunate in itself, afforded but scanty grounds for a sentence of general proscription against the Academy, and could hardly justify the rancorous feelings exhibited by Mr. Foggo towards an institution to whose patriotic liberality he was indebted, as a student, for the gratuitous enjoyment of ample means of study, and abundant opportunities of improvement, in the art to which he was devoted.

The case of Mr. Clint may be dismissed in a very few words. At one period of his career, the Royal Academy had thought so highly of his talents as to elect him an associate of their body,—the preliminary grade of distinction necessary to be attained, before a candidate for academic honours could be eligible for the rank of R.A.; the vacancies among "the forty" being, in pursuance of a fundamental law of the institution, recruited from the class of associates, whose number is restricted to twenty. In this intermediate category, Mr. Clint was fated to remain for a considerable number of years, during which he saw many subsequently appointed associates promoted, over his head, to the higher academic rank.  Combining a high, and, no doubt, very just estimate of his own powers, with a less equitable appreciation of the talents of his more fortunate competitors for academic favour, he came to the conclusion that a body which exhibited so culpable an insensibility to his claims, could not be deserving of public confidence or national support.  He therefore resigned his rank of associate, and joined the anti-academic agitation, with all the zeal of a convert, and somewhat of the rancour of a renegade.  Unfortunately, however, his evidence afforded so patent an illustration of a venerable fable,—conspicuous in the pages of Æsop, and every subsequent expositor of that peculiar form of human wit or wisdom,—that it lost in authority, more than it gained in earnestness, from the too transparent personal feelings to which it owed its peculiar colouring; and however conscientiously Mr. Clint sought to impress the committee with a sense of the injustice involved in the preference of other artists over himself, in the distribution of academic honours, they failed, in their report, to take judicial notice of the fact of that gentleman's superiority over the competitors whose promotion constituted " the head and front " of his grievance against the Academy.

But it was in the evidence of Messrs. Martin and Haydon, that the anti-academic *animus* was exhibited in its most remarkable development, under the influence of undisguised feelings of personal pique, arising, in the case of each of these gentlemen, from the fact that at the outset of his career, the Academy had not been sufficiently prompt in the recognition of his claims, when dealing with his works in the arrangement of the annual exhibition:—while, as regards Mr. Haydon, there was the additional grievance, gravely brought forward as a justification of a continued system of implacable hostility towards an institution, as to which he himself admitted that he had "derived the greater part of his knowledge studying there"—that when he put down his name as a candidate for the rank of associate, in the year 1810, he did not obtain a single vote at the election that ensued.[*]

In recalling the circumstances of a parliamentary inquiry, curiously illustrative of the history of the arts in this country, and too intimately connected with the reminiscences of Sir Martin's official career, to be passed over in silence, or lightly touched upon by his biographer, I unwillingly ·recur to details, calculated, perhaps, to cast some slight degree of ridicule on the memory of two eminent men, whose jealous susceptibility, on the score of their own merits, arrayed them in opposition to the Academy on grounds which a dispassionate estimate of the facts, would fail to recognise as a legitimate cause of permanent offence.  The proceedings of the committee, however, constitute a significant passage in the history of the anti-academic intrigue, which it was the President's fortune to combat with untiring energy and signal success; and I cannot effectually expose the unfair and partisan spirit in which all questions relating to the Academy were dealt with by the conductors of the inquiry, without directing the attention of the reader to the trumpery nature of the special charges brought against the body, by its most conspicuous assailants, and for want of more substantial grounds of censure, eagerly welcomed by the committee, as affording a pretext for hostile animadversion in their most partial and disingenuous report.

Mr. Martin's evidence may be passed over with but

* Minutes of Evidence, 28th June, 1836, Q. 1066.

slight comment. Though characterized, in tone and substance, by that lasting feeling of resentment which had induced him, in revenge for the imagined slight encountered in his early career, pertinaciously to exclude himself from those academic honours which his maturer genius could not have failed to command, had he been willing to enter the lists as a candidate,—it was, perhaps, less spitefully depreciatory of the assailed institution, than the testimony of those whose exclusion from its ranks was not so clearly voluntary. As to the merits of his complaint, the whole case between the Academy and him is summed up in Sir Martin's answers to the questions numbered 2012, 2013, and 2016, in the printed Minutes of Evidence.

" 2012. Did not Mr. Martin complain that his pictures were exhibited in a bad situation; that he could not have a fair exhibition?—Mr. Martin is a gentleman for whom I have a very high respect; and I confess he is one of those artists whom I very seriously regret to find involved in the testimony which has been laid before you. Mr. Martin, at the age, I think, of twenty-two, twenty-four years ago, sent a picture to the Exhibition, of which he very naturally had a very high opinion, and which I have no doubt merited that opinion; and because this picture was not placed precisely in the position he thought it deserved, he considered himself injured; he considered his interests affected; and in fact I believe he either then, or shortly afterwards, withdrew from the exhibitions of the Academy. I am unwilling to say anything which may appear like passing judgment on the claims of my brother artists; and I should be sorry to be understood as impeaching the talent of any man, in or out of the Academy; but with reference to Mr. Martin, I have no hesitation in saying that I have a high respect for his talents, and that I believe his talents are respected by the members of the Royal Academy. If he had gone on as a young man of talent might reasonably be expected to do, and, instead of taking offence, had said to himself, 'I am young in the profession, and must undergo those trials and difficulties which all others have encountered, and to which juniors in all pursuits must necessarily submit,'—if he had continued to exhibit, I am convinced Mr. Martin would long since have become a full member of the Royal Academy.

"2013. I merely ask you whether he did not complain, as an artist sending his pictures to the Royal Academy, as not having been done justice to on more than one occasion?—He did, as many others have done. I have here an account of the pictures that have been excluded from the Exhibition, and received as doubtful during the last Exhibition, amounting to 590, and I will venture to say that there is not one artist engaged in the production of those pictures who, at the time he was smarting under the disagreeable sensations occasioned by finding his works returned, would not have said that the Royal Academy was a most pernicious institution, and that he had been very badly treated in having supplied works to an Academy the members of which were dull enough not to discover their merits.

"2016.' Can you disprove that Mr. Martin's picture which he names was ill placed, and that the other picture was injured?— The first statement is mere matter of opinion; I have no hesitation to assert that it was not ill placed. I assert that it was placed in a good situation, where it could be seen; it was not placed in one of the best situations. Mr. Martin also states that an Academician spilt varnish on his picture. I know nothing of this circumstance, and if any injury occurred to his picture it must have been accidental."—*Minutes of Evidence,* *15th July,* 1836.

As the evidence of Mr. Haydon supplies the most comprehensive illustration of the anti-academic feeling, and embodies the gravest of the charges brought against the Academy by those who were bent on its destruction, I cannot more effectually or more fairly state the case of the assailants, than by leaving that evidence to speak for itself. The reader will, therefore, find, *in extenso* in the Appendix, every question and answer recorded in the minutes of Mr. Haydon's examination, which bears

either on the public offences of the Academy, or the
private and personal injuries alleged by that gentleman
to have been inflicted by the body on himself.*

In perusing that evidence, the reader will naturally
make allowance for the evident and extraordinary excitement under which it was given, and of which it bears
the unmistakeable impress, wherever the Royal Academy
is concerned; exhibiting a state of feeling which could
not but lead in many instances to the substitution of
imperfect impressions of memory, or strongly biassed
conjecture, for well-ascertained fact. The most material
inaccuracies which it presents were noticed by the president, and the secretary, Mr. Howard, in their respective examinations, and the Appendix will supply the
reader with an opportunity of comparing, in many
instances, the unauthorized assertion with its authentic
and official denial.

At length, when the committee had fully exhausted
their inculpatory evidence against the Royal Academy,
they proceeded to summon before them the principal
officers of that institution,—the president, secretary,
and keeper. These functionaries, as representing the
parties supposed to be on their trial before this undis-
guisedly hostile tribunal, had been previously furnished
with a copy of the indictment on which they were
arraigned, in the shape of so much of the minutes of
evidence taken before the committee, as bore upon the
alleged defects and misdeeds of the Academy.

Sir Martin had watched, with feelings of just indignation, the partial character of the proceedings, and
the anti-academic spirit that marked the whole course
of the inquiry. It may, therefore, be easily imagined

* Appendix (A.)

ı 2

that, in obeying the summons of the committee, he was in no mood to conciliate their favour, or deprecate their hostility, by meekness of tone or deferential placidity of demeanour. He was little solicitous to disguise his strong sense of the injustice exhibited towards the Academy, in the eagerness with which the committee had invited the attacks of its assailants, and encouraged the vague and senseless vituperation which, in their evidence, supplied the place of authentic statement or specific charge. On some occasions, indeed, during his examination, when he expressed himself in terms of rather severe animadversion on the conduct and tactics of the anti-academic intrigue, the committee instructed the short-hand writer *not to take down his words;*—although it seemed but reasonable that, where the utmost license of attack had been encouraged, and all but solicited, on the part of the assailants, the right of public and indignant protest against public and malevolent misrepresentation, should be conceded to the parties thus put upon their defence.

It was, however, no part of the "mission" of the committee to exhibit anything approaching to "fair play" in their dealings with the Academic question. The reader of "Gil Blas" will recollect that, when the innkeeper at Xelva is called before the sham inquisitors, and interrogated as to the judaistic tendencies of his neighbour Samuel Simon, he is gravely admonished by the pretended commissioners of the Holy Office, that he is cautiously to abstain from giving any evidence that might tend to exculpate the accused : —

"'Mon ami,' reprit Laméla, 'vous oubliez qu'il ne faut point,' dans votre interrogatoire, excuser Samuel Simon. . . . . Vous ne devez dire que des choses qui soient contre lui, et pas un mot en sa faveur." *

* Gil Blas, vol. 2. Book 4. c. 1.

This was precisely the spirit that animated the committee throughout the investigation; and although they
could not go the length of excluding from the recorded
evidence the official statements of facts attesting the
public services of the Academy, *they carefully abstained
in their report from any recognition of those services,
or any mention of those facts.*

The official report of Sir Martin's evidence will be
found *in extenso* in the Appendix.*  It will there be
seen that, as regards him, the inquiry was conducted
on many points in the style and tone of a hostile cross-
examination.

The zeal of the committee, however, was not always
equalled by their discretion, and occasionally received a
check which afforded some amusement to the crowd of
eager listeners that filled the room during the president's protracted examination.  For example, the
attempt to bear down, by the weight of mere *doctrinaire*
authority, the expression of his opinions on subjects in
respect of which his official position,—indisputably the
highest in Europe connected with the art,—entitled him
to the outward semblance at least of deferential consideration, was in some instances strikingly unsuccessful, eliciting replies calculated to discourage the
exhibition of the complacent self-sufficiency which had
dictated the question.

"Are you aware," he is asked "that several celebrated
German writers have recently been strongly arguing against
academical institutions?—*A.* I am not.

"*Q.* Do you know that Monsieur Say, in a chapter devoted
to them in his Treatise on Political Economy, conceives they
are hostile to the fine arts?—*A.* I have seen it quoted, and

* Appendix (B.)

I 3

have no respect for the opinion of a political economist on the subject of the arts; for the principle of commerce and the principle of art are in direct opposition the one to the other.

"*Q.* Are they, or are they not sufficient judges of the effects of institutions, as proved by facts?— *A.* I do not conceive it is possible to speak decisively upon a general question like this. I say generally, as far as I am aquainted with the works of persons who apply the principles of political economy to the fine arts, that they are entirely mistaken in their views. They adapt to the arts a principle which belongs only to trade, and the moment you make art a trade you destroy it.

"*Q.* Does that observation apply to the evidence of such a man as Dr. Waagen, who is not a political economist?—*A.* It it is not my business to apply it; it is my opinion."

When it is borne in mind that the political-economical element preponderated greatly in the composition of the committee, it will be readily imagined that the application "*ad homines*" of Sir Martin's observations, was fully appreciated by the numerous auditory, and had a rather *piquant* effect to those among the by-standers who were friendly to the Academy, or impartial spectators of the contest between that body and its Parliamentary foes.

Further on in his examination, in answer to a member of the committee who, apparently with a view of suggesting an argument against the self-electing character of the Academy, asks, "Are not the same people in the situation of competitors and judges?" Sir Martin answers, with irresistible cogency of reasoning, and equally pointed significancy, *quoad* the competency of the judges whom he is addressing:—

"Most certainly: that is unavoidable, unless you select some other tribunal; unless you call the merit of the time before a tribunal not composed of artists. And, by-the-bye, that reminds me of a very curious statement in the evidence that has been given before this Committee, where a gentleman actually asserts that a knowledge of the art is not necessary in order to judge of the disposal of a diploma—that the public are the proper judges, and are perfectly competent to single out extraordinary talent the moment it appears. If that were the case, the establishment of an academy, would indeed be of no sort of consequence. If the public are competent to single out and discover talent themselves, it is in vain to talk of the distinction of R. A. But it is because the public are ignorant, to an extraordinary degree, upon the subject of the arts ;—it is because even those who are considered as the enlightened class of society, *who are even considered competent to legislate on all other points*, are incompetent judges of the arts, that it is necessary that it should be reserved for artists to decide, as to who are entitled to academic advantages."

Before I take leave of the subject, I must advert to one passage in Sir Martin's evidence, the effect of which has been most absurdly misrepresented, and which occasionally, even at the present day, affords an opportunity to the picture-dealing fraternity to attack his memory with the same malignity which they were wont to exhibit towards him in his lifetime. It occurs towards the close of his examination, in answer to one of a series of questions with which he was plied, with the view of extorting from him an admission that the Royal Academy were to hold the apartments about to be allotted to them in the new building in Trafalgar Square, merely on sufferance, subject to be ejected at any moment when the increasing number of pictures in the National Gallery might render additional accommodation desirable, for the purposes of the last-mentioned institution.

" *Q.* I will just put the case that one half of the building was not sufficient for the national pictures, do you think the nation have or have not a right to call for the National Gallery to give up the whole of the building for which the nation paid?—*A.* It is not for me to decide as to what are the rights of the nation, therefore I give no opinion upon that subject; but I beg leave to observe that I consider the Royal Academy a much more important institution to the nation than the National Gallery. I look upon it that a garden is of more consequence than a granary; and you may heap up a *hortus siccus* of art without producing any of the salutary effects which never fail to result from the operations of such a school as the Royal Academy. It would, therefore, I conceive, be an injury to the nation, as well as to the Royal Academy, if they were to be removed in order to make room for even the best works of the old masters."

The meaning of this passage is sufficiently obvious, and surely not open to cavil, as implying a want of due veneration for the works of those great artists with whose memory the brightest glories of the art are inseparably associated, and whose genius Sir Martin was ever indefatigable in holding up to the ambition of the aspiring student, as the proper object of his emulation. It has, however, afforded a pretext to more than one anonymous newspaper scribbler, in recent times, for the absurd and impudent statement that the late president had represented the exhibition of modern pictures at the Royal Academy as being of more importance than the national collection;—as if Sir Martin had gravely instituted a triumphant comparison between the result of one year's labour of contemporary British artists, presented in any given year on the walls of the Academy, and the most esteemed productions of departed genius, selected from the accumulated treasures of European art, and representing the intellectual toils of numerous successive generations—the fact being, that he had sought merely to mark the distinction between the claims of an establishment actively, perseveringly, and successfully engaged in the task of educating the artist, training and developing his powers through the whole course and range of necessary and systematic study,—and a *gallery*, which can do no more than silently exhibit the triumphs of the pencil,—affording, doubtless, valuable examples to the laborious and intelligent student, but which, without the aid of scientific precept and well-directed industry, would prove ineffectual to develop his latent genius, or imbue him with those pure principles of art, of which it in vain supplies the practical illustration to the uncultivated or ignorant observer.

With the avowedly high estimate formed by Sir Martin of the services of the Royal Academy, in promoting the cultivation and advancement of the arts, by the maintenance of its schools, and the incitement to exertion afforded by its honorary distinctions, he was clearly justified in looking upon the interests of that institution as of greater national importance than the mere formation of a gallery of the old masters;—much as he valued the effect of such an establishment, as an adjunct and aid to the operations of the Academy itself, in its mission of civilisation and public improvement. But it required all the malevolence of that picture-dealing quackery which it was his fortune in more than one instance to baffle and expose, to distort his well known convictions, on this point, into a feeling of disrespect for those great luminaries of art to whose fame he had rendered the most signal and enthusiastic homage, that the *combined* fervour of the poet and the painter could suggest.

Were the Vice-Chancellor of Oxford to be examined before a parliamentary committee, as to the expediency of appropriating the entire buildings of Christchurch and Balliol for the better accommodation of the over-flowings of the Bodleian Library, and dislodging for that purpose the whole academical staff of those venerable colleges, — unceremoniously sending dignitaries, professors, and students alike to the right about,—that learned and dignified functionary would not improbably intimate an opinion, that the maintenance of those time-honoured abodes of learning in their accustomed dignity and efficiency, was a matter of more importance to the country, than the convenient arrangement or accessibility of any large collection of books, however rich in the glories of ancient and modern literature.  But the expression of such a sentiment would, it appears, be considered by some candid critics as equivalent to an open avowal of contempt for Homer and Virgil, and a preference given to the Newdegate prize poem of the year, over Comus or Samson Agonistes !

Enough, and perhaps more than enough, has been said on the subject of the Fine Arts' Committee of 1836.  As far as it sought to carry into effect the views of the anti-academic intrigue, its result was wholly abortive.  In the Appendix will be found an extract from the Report*, containing all that relates to the position and claims of the Royal Academy.  The spirit which pervades it, is best characterized by Pope's well known line :

> " Willing to wound, and yet afraid to strike."

Studiously keeping out of view every fact and detail disclosed by the evidence, which could enlighten the House or the public as to the valuable and gratuitous

---

* Appendix (C.)

benefits conferred on the art and its professors by the
Royal Academy, the report abstains from all direct or
general censure of the institution; and while betraying
some slight aspirations for the advent of that mil-
lennium of taste and political economy, when all
academies and titular distinctions connected with the
art, shall be abolished, it throws out no hint of the
expediency of such salutary rigour as applicable to the
existing emergency.

# CHAPTER XV.

## 1837, 1838.

Opening of the New Building in Trafalgar Square. — Public Installation of the Royal Academy in their Apartments by the King. — Death of King William IV.—Accession of Her Majesty.—Official and Academic Details. — The Queen graciously confirms to the President and Officers of the Institution the Right of personal Access to the Sovereign, enjoyed during the preceding Reign. — Agitation for throwing open the Exhibition to the Public. — Interview between the President and Mr. Hume on the Subject. — Letter to Lord John Russell. — Renewed Attacks on the Academy. — Letter to J. Hume, Esq., M.P. — Official visit to Windsor Castle. — Diplomacy. — The Premier and the President. — Visit to Drayton Manor.

In the autumn of the year 1836, the Royal Academy vacated their rooms in Somerset House, and entered on the occupation of the apartments which had been assigned to them in exchange for their now time-honoured abode. Their formal installation in their new domicile did not, however, take place until the 28th April, 1837, when, previously to the opening of the annual exhibition, — then about to be presented for the first time on the walls of the new galleries in Trafalgar Square,—the King, attended by a numerous *cortége*, and accompanied by an unusual display of the pomp and circumstance of royalty, honoured the Academy by a visit, for the purpose of solemnly and publicly inaugurating their possession and tenure of that portion of the new building, from which such strenuous efforts had been made to exclude them.

There, standing under the portico of the newly-erected pile, surrounded by a brilliant circle of princes, ministers,

and great officers of state,—while the guard of honour,
drawn up in front of the building, presented arms, and
the band struck up the National Anthem amid the cheers
of the countless spectators who filled the vast area of
Trafalgar Square,—his Majesty publicly delivered to Sir
Martin, as president, the keys of the new academy, with
the gracious observation that they could not be entrusted
to better hands.

It was impossible for the King to mark more significantly his personal sympathy with the views, or
his recognition of the merits, of the Royal Academy.
By thus investing the proceeding of the day with
the attributes of a state visit, and communicating to
this delivery of possession, the character of a public
and emphatic ceremonial, his Majesty did everything
in his power to discredit the notion, so industriously
circulated and fostered by the anti-academic intriguers
and their parliamentary abettors, that the occupation
of the new apartments by the Academy was to be one
of mere sufferance, or even of uncertain tenure.  The
entire and exclusive dependence of the body on the
royal will and pleasure, was also practically asserted by
the observance of a form implying that they obtained
possession from his own hand; and, unquestionably, his
Majesty's intimate acquaintance with the circumstances
preceding and accompanying the removal of the Academy
from Somerset House, and his hearty concurrence in the
propriety of the course adopted by them, throughout the
protracted discussions connected with the new building,
were matters of so much notoriety, as to preclude all hope
in the minds of the adverse faction, that the Academy
could, in his Majesty's lifetime, be either bullied or
jockeyed out of a position, to which the personal favour
of the Sovereign afforded so important a guarantee.

The day was brilliantly fine ; and the scene was one of the most animated character, from the number of royal carriages, with their attendants in rich liveries, drawn up on either side of the entrance, — the bright uniform of the Guards forming the royal escort, and ranged in line in front of the building — and, " though last not least," the vast concourse of people collected in eager and excited curiosity, by the unusual display of the trappings of royal state, and joyfully hailing the appearance of their beloved Sovereign.

On returning to his carriage, after having inspected the apartments and made the usual tour of the Exhibition, the King paused for a few moments upon the terrace under the portico, to observe the striking *coup d'œil* which presented itself to the view, from that elevated position, and acknowledge the loyal acclamations which his presence elicited from the dense mass of spectators in the square below.  As these unmistakeable evidences of his well-merited popularity, and the unbought attachment of all classes of his subjects, rose in deafening shouts to the royal ear, from the upturned faces of the crowd, the President and those who were in immediate attendance could not fail to note the lively interest which his Majesty took in the scene, and his undisguised enjoyment of that frank and heartfelt homage, with which Britons alone can greet their Sovereign — a homage always spontaneous and impulsive; which, if sometimes capriciously withheld, in moments of political excitement, is ever the offspring of genuine feeling, unprompted by official zeal or municipal organization, — requiring no courtly *programme* for its direction, and obeying no *mot d'ordre* in its display.

The King was in excellent spirits, and, to all outward semblance, in perfect health; and amongst those who took part in or witnessed the proceedings of the day, no one could have anticipated the speedy termination of his Majesty's earthly career, which the lapse of a few short weeks was destined to bring about. His appearance and demeanour gave every external indication of bodily health and mental vigour; nor had he attained so advanced an age as to render a long continuance of his reign otherwise than reasonably probable. The ceremonial in question was, however, I believe, the last occasion, on which his Majesty appeared in the public exercise of any function or duty connected with his exalted station. His lamented death took place on the 20th June following.

In King William the Fourth the Royal Academy sustained an irreparable loss, the extent and importance of which could be fully appreciated only by those who, like Sir Martin, had enjoyed frequent opportunities of ascertaining the sentiments of his Majesty, on all matters connected with the claims and interests of that institution.

By the President himself, the death of a sovereign who had honoured him with every mark of official and professional confidence, and on all occasions evinced towards him the highest personal esteem and regard,— was felt not merely as a public, but as a private misfortune.

In common with all who had been admitted to frequent communication with the late King,—on occasions not restricted within the limits of official *routine*, or subject to the severest ceremonial rules of courtly *etiquette*, — Sir Martin retained through life a grateful remembrance of the frankness of spirit, the kindness of heart, and the cheerful affability which ever marked the social intercourse of his Majesty with those who had the honour of being received into the royal circle. The monarch who, endeared to all classes of his subjects, was universally lamented as a sovereign, experienced the still rarer fortune of being mourned by many as a friend.

At the earliest moment available for the purpose, after the accession of the Queen, the President conveyed to her Majesty, through the medium of the principal Secretary of State for the Home Department, Lord John Russell, the humble and dutiful request of the Royal Academy that the privilege of personal access to the Sovereign, on Academic affairs, enjoyed by the President and officers of the Institution during the reign of her Majesty's predecessors, might be continued to them during the present reign.

In the interview which Sir Martin had with Lord John Russell on the subject, his Lordship expressed some doubt as to the feasibility of the Queen's acceding to this request, on grounds referable to the official and ministerial arrangements connected with the new court. The President was, however, firm in declining to abide by the ministerial view of the case, and requesting that the point might be submitted to her Majesty's personal decision. This was accordingly done, and her Majesty was graciously pleased to signify her ready compliance with the wishes of the Academy, by recognising and confirming their enjoyment of the privilege in question.

The following extract from a letter to Miss Tunno (then on the Continent), written by Sir Martin a few weeks after the commencement of the new reign, contains some details on this and other points relating to her Majesty's accession, which will not, I think, be wholly without interest for the reader.

"London, 31st July, 1837.

. . . . . . . . . . . .

"We are here in all the agonies or ecstasies of a general election, the more exciting as it appears doubtful as to the result. I believe the king's death took place after your departure. Few sovereigns have been more generally lamented, or better deserved to be so; for he was kind-hearted, and honestly desirous of consulting the good of his people.

"The new reign, however, has begun prosperously; the queen has delighted everybody by her dignity, grace, and good sense. I had the honour of kissing her Majesty's hand at her first levee, the most crowded I ever witnessed, on presenting an address from the Royal Academy. The arts had an accession of dignity on the occasion. Three knights have been added to the lists of chivalry, in the persons of Sir Augustus Wall Callcott, Sir Richard Westmacott, and Sir William John Newton, miniature painter to the late king. These dignities, however, were proposed to be conferred by William IV., and were only confirmed by her present Majesty. On Tuesday last I had the honour of conducting her Majesty through the exhibition. She was accompanied by the Duchess of Kent; and I confess I was gratified and surprised to see how completely she appeared the same unaffected little girl, as when you saw her at the Private View,—easy, gracious, and graceful, without any studied assumption of majesty, or put-on air of importance. She has taken the Academy under her protection, and granted to us the same immediate access to her presence which we were allowed by her predecessor. This privilege is more than I expected; for, on urging the point to Lord John Russell, I was told there was to be no private secretary, and no access to the Queen but through the medium of her ministers. I requested, however, that the matter might be submitted to her Majesty; and the following day I had an official communication from Lord John, stating that she had been graciously pleased to continue to the Academy the same facilities of approach as usual."

In the year 1837, the anti-academic agitation assumed a new aspect, and called forth the energies of the President in its defence, on a point not previously imported into the controversy.

The expediency of throwing open the most interesting public monuments and repositories of art and science, in the metropolis, to the gratuitous inspection of the masses, had, for some time, been a favourite theme with the *dilettante-radical* party in the House of Commons; and their views on this subject, as far as the general principle was concerned, were shared, to a certain extent, by those genuine lovers and patrons of the art, whose more sincere and discriminating zeal in the cause of social improvement, was less ostentatiously paraded, but far more practically displayed. The free admission of the public to the British Museum and the National Gallery, if unproductive of any perceptible amelioration in the tastes or habits of the "great unwashed," had at least been unattended by the evils which had at one time been anticipated from this important concession. No wanton destruction of property, or vandal-like attempt to deface the precious objects of *virtù*, or the venerable relics of classical antiquity, thus disclosed to their admiring gaze, had marked the passage of the people, "*par eminence*," through the varied and accumulated treasures of taste and science to be found in those important public establishments.

The application of the principle, therefore, might, it was thought by many, be safely extended to all institutions of a national character, which contained numerous and permanent objects of general interest, or could boast of monuments appealing to the social and historical sympathies of the spectator. As far as this indulgence was sought, in reference to buildings, galleries, and museums devoted to public purposes, and sustained at the expense of the Government or the country, it was clear that the question was to be decided by considerations relating chiefly to the safe custody and careful preservation of the objects to be exhibited, and the comfort and convenience of those requiring access to them for useful and practical purposes, or visiting them from motives of a higher order than can be supplied by idle and unenlightened curiosity.

But it was obvious that whatever claim the nation at large might reasonably urge for gratuitous admission to institutions, the expenses of which were defrayed out of the national resources, no such right could exist as against an establishment dependent for its support on the pecuniary profits to be derived from the exhibition of works of art, — to which, consequently, free access could not be granted, without depriving the institution, — *pro tanto*, of its ordinary means of effecting the laudable public objects to which it was devoted.

The opponents of the Royal Academy, however, although fully apprised of all the circumstances which, in the case of that body, constituted a fair and unanswerable ground of exemption from the operation of the principle so strenuously invoked on behalf of the lower classes, eagerly hailed in its discussion a favourable opportunity for casting unmerited odium on the proceedings of the Academy, and a fresh outlet for the spirit of misrepresentation which was so perseveringly manifested throughout the anti-academic crusade. The conduct and guidance of the agitation appears to have been confided, about this time, to a gentleman, whose selection for that purpose, carried with it an air of absurdity bordering closely on the ludicrous; as it was hardly possible to point out in the House of Commons an individual whose temperament, habits, and career were more foreign to the pursuits of taste, or more at variance with the ideas and feelings on which they depend for their development, than the veteran reformer and redresser of fiscal abuses, Joseph Hume.

From this time forward, however, the initiation of every parliamentary attack on the Academy was entrusted to his intrepid though uninformed zeal; and the assailants of the institution were always sure of his ready co-operation in any plan that could be devised, with a view to its annoyance even before the period, when smarting under the infliction of Sir Martin's polished sarcasm — a sarcasm fairly provoked by deliberate discourtesy towards the President, and reckless mistatement of his opinions, on the part of Mr. Hume,—the latter had, to some extent, merged the simulated earnestness of the carefully-crammed advocate in the personal feelings of a somewhat roughly handled and thoroughly discomfited antagonist.

In the summer of 1837, however, Mr. Hume had not as yet adopted towards the Academy, or its President, so offensive a tone as to render the personal discussion of questions connected with its administration between himself and Sir Martin, a matter of difficulty or embarrassment; and in the ostensible pursuit of the objects involved in the movement for throwing open all public institutions of taste, art, and science to the people at large, he, in the month of May, in that year, sought and obtained an interview with the President at his house in Cavendish Square, for the purpose of impressing on the Academy the expediency of admitting the public *gratis* to the annual exhibition during a short portion, at least, of the period usually allotted to the annual display of works of art in that institution.

On this occasion a conversation of very considerable length took place between Mr. Hume and the President,

in which the former strenuously urged, with the utmost
of his ability, the views of which he was put forth as
the exponent and champion, while the latter fully
and calmly detailed the grounds on which he considered
it impracticable for the Academy to comply with the
suggestion. As might have been anticipated, neither
party succeeded in carrying conviction to the mind of
the other; but the interview passed off with every
appearance of good feeling on both sides, and every
manifestation of mutual courtesy and respect consistent
with the avowal of a conscientious difference of opinion
on the point in dispute. A detailed note of this protracted discussion was subsequently drawn up in
writing by Sir Martin, who was naturally desirous to
put on record the exact particulars of what passed on
an occasion to which reference was certain to be made,
with more or less accuracy, during the further progress
of the controversy. But in that spirit of truth and fair
dealing which ever characterised him, he submitted this
memorandum to Mr. Hume, in order that he might, by
the aid of that gentleman's memory, correct any error,
and supply any omission which might have found its
way into the statement, thus securing for his representation of the opinions and sentiments expressed on both
sides, the stamp and guarantee of unquestioned authenticity.

Mr. Hume, accordingly, after perusing the memorandum, returned it to the President with the suggestion
of a slight alteration on one or two points, in which a statement attributed to him seemed to require correction or
qualification, and the note was accordingly altered by
Sir Martin in conformity with the observation. I here
insert the document in its emendated and authentic
shape. By the indorsement in Sir Martin's handwriting,

the interview appears to have taken place on the 24th May, 1837.

> "*Minutes of a conversation with Joseph Hume, Esq., M.P., on the subject of Resolutions to be proposed at a meeting to be held at the Freemasons' Tavern, on Monday.*

"After a variety of observations as to the propriety and policy of opening all our public collections of curiosities and works of art to the public at large, and especially to the humbler classes, as a means of improving their taste and feelings, and giving them a relish for a better description of enjoyments than they are, in general, found to pursue, Mr. Hume stated, as a matter in contemplation to be proposed to the meeting, and advocated in Parliament, and in every other way, that the Royal Academy, as a return on their part for the occupation of so large a portion of a building erected at the public expense, should set apart one day, or more, during the week, as might be agreed upon, for the admission of the public *gratis* to the annual exhibition; that, on consulting with a variety of persons whom he considered competent judges in this case, he did not conceive that the funds of the Academy would be materially affected by this arrangement, as the privilege of free exhibition might be postponed during the two first weeks of admission, and in the mean time the Academy might have all the benefit of the public curiosity undisturbed; that if even some diminution of the income of the Academy did result from the proposed measure, they should regard it liberally, as a due and becoming tribute on their part to the benefit of the public, to whom they were so much indebted. Mr. Hume further observed that he thought it right to put me, as President of the Royal Academy, in possession of what was proposed, in order that I might take it into consideration, and see how far the Academy were disposed to promote measures which might tend to produce a general agreement, and put an end to contention and dispute; that he could have no view but the promotion of the fine arts, and the general improvement of the public taste, by introducing such regulations for that purpose, in our public establishments, as appeared best calculated to produce those effects, and might be consistent with all acknowledged rights and interests; that he considered the conversation confidential, and did not propose to make any public use of what might pass between us.

" After he had made his statement uninterruptedly, I observed that the Academy did not consider that, by their change of residence, they had incurred any new debt or obligation to the public; that we had simply made an exchange of apartments: that we had for the advantage of better accommodation to the arts, particularly to sculpture, given up a residence which had been provided for us by the king, of which we had been in undisturbed possession for nearly sixty years; a tenure which, although I supposed it could not be looked upon as a lease or covenant, to be enforced in a court of law, I thought I might say, considering the purposes to which that residence was applied, no reasonable, just, or prudent Government would be likely to interfere with or disturb; that, as to the return which, it was suggested, we should make to the public for the accommodation afforded to us in a building erected at the public expense, I must observe that Somerset House had also been erected at the public expense, and an express stipulation made by the royal founder of the Academy, that His institution should be accommodated there; and as the transfer of the Academy was a mere exchange for the convenience of the art, and we were assured by competent authority that we were to be in the new building on the same footing as in the old, there could, I conceived, be no new claim on us, or debt incurred to the public. I further stated, that with respect to a due return from the Academy for the advantage of having a portion of a public building devoted to its use, I conceived that if the Academy had no claim from the long-established occupation of their former residence, — if, in their present existence in Trafalgar Square, they had now for the first time received their local habitation as a generous gift from the Government,—they must be considered as making the fullest, the most ample, the most effective and legitimate return, in the support, for more than half a century, of the only effective school of art in the country, — in the establishment of professors in the different departments of the art, and the provision of every material and means of study necessary for its cultivation, and in the education of more than 1700 students; that I conceived these important services rendered to the public at the sacrifice of above 200,000*l.*, raised by the joint labours of artists and disinterestedly applied by them to public objects, formed a sufficient return for the house-room afforded to the Academy in a public edifice, without endangering and diminishing the necessary income of the institution by the measure proposed.

" To this Mr. Hume replied that the public did not consider the services of the Academy either so important or so disinterested as I represented them, and that I must be aware that great difference of opinion existed among the public, as well as in the House of Commons, as to the utility of that institution. He admitted that the maintenance of the school and the cultivation of the art must, to a certain extent, benefit every class of the community; but he considered that something should be conceded by the Academy in addition, for the gratification and improvement of the lower classes; and he did not allow that the members of the Academy made any sacrifice of their private interests, in devoting the funds created by the exhibition of their productions to public purposes, inasmuch as they had a favourable opportunity of showing their works to the public, and possessed an advantage over the other bodies of artists, by being selected for royal patronage, and placed in a building erected at the public expense.

" I directed Mr. Hume's attention to the grounds on which this preference had been accorded to them, viz., the support of the school of art, and the entire appropriation of their funds to the promotion of the arts, and the improvement of the public taste. I asked him if he could point out any other body of artists who could advance similar claims? The Society of British Artists, for example, maintained no school; the Water Colour Society did not profess to support any public object, and very reasonably and justifiably employed their funds for their own purposes, without any reference to public objects, and could therefore have no claim to similar consideration to that which was enjoyed by the Royal Academy. He observed that the societies I mentioned were comparatively in their infancy, and did not possess sufficient strength or means to effect the purposes to which I alluded. To this I replied that the Academy, from its first establishment, was effectively devoted to gratuitous instruction, and, as I conceived, gave ample compensation for whatever advantages it enjoyed. I stated that, with respect to the effect of the gratuitous admission proposed, I could not pretend to state what might be the opinions of the members of the Academy; but that, as far as I was able to judge, it would not only be injurious, but actually ruinous to the interests of the institution; that he must be aware that the British Museum, and the other public establishments which he proposed to include in the new arrangement, were all, more or less, supported by regular grants of public money, and were independent of any casual income from other sources; but that the Academy depended wholly for its support on the shilling receipts of the exhibition, which could not but be very materially affected by the periodical gratuitous admissions proposed, of which a large class of even that portion of the community which may be considered above the lower orders, would very gladly avail themselves.

"Mr. Hume observed that by opening all the establishments which might be said to minister to the gratification of public curiosity, simultaneously, the pressure on the Academy would be diminished, and the number of visitors diverted and dispersed in the pursuit of different objects of interest. As he appeared unimpressed by the objections which I had urged against his plan, I added that supposing the members of the Academy could be brought to acquiesce in the justice and propriety of his views, and even to be desirous of carrying them into effect, — a possibility which I could not for a moment admit — yet, as we were a royal institution, wholly dependent, as such, on the king, and responsible to his Majesty for our proceedings, the only mode we could adopt for such a purpose would be to solicit, by address, his Majesty's permission and sanction for so important a change in the nature and constitution of the establishment; — a change which we had no authority to make without his express approbation. I further remarked that as the National Gallery would be always open to the public, and as the works to be seen there were considered by those who were so anxious for the improvement of the public taste, as much better adapted to produce that result, than the productions of living artists, I could not but consider the proposed measure as originating in the same spirit of hostility against the Academy, as that which instigated the recent most partial proceedings of the Committee on the Fine Arts : that the Academy had always treated the aspersions of their calumniators with silent contempt, and would continue to do so, as we had the satisfaction to reflect that we were above the influence of their malignity.

" Mr. Hume said that he had not particularly attended to the proceedings to which I had alluded; but that from his knowledge of the chairman and several members of the committee, he should have expected the most perfect fairness and impartiality : that he was not himself mixed up in any of these matters ; that, with respect to the proposed meeting, he knew nothing of it until he was asked to take the chair, and that he was not aware of the existence of any such feeling towards the Academy, as I was led to suppose actuated some of those persons who were active in promoting the object which they desired to effect ; that he consented to preside at the meeting solely from a principle of duty and an anxious desire to assist in forwarding the great march of improvement, which promised, in its progress, to effect such beneficial results to the great mass of society.

" I said that, with reference to the Committee on the Fine Arts, Mr. Hume had but to look at the Report to ascertain the spirit which pervaded that document: he would there find that, although every feather and straw which misrepresentation could blow up in accusation of the Academy, was pompously brought forward, and the most frivolous and absurd imputations paraded, under an apparent impression of their importance, not a line of the direct and unanswerable evidence in favour of the Academy is quoted or referred to; while the Report pathetically laments that the works of those great artists, Messrs. Haydon and Martin (sent for exhibition about twenty years ago) were not hung to their satisfaction. I submitted to Mr.

Hume whether, well acquainted as he was with the various institutions in this country, and perhaps in many others, he knew an instance in which, after a course of seventy years, — with a hostility against it as rancorously vigilant to expose its errors, as mortified vanity and baffled presumption could make it, — any institution had come out of an investigation so rigid as that to which the Academy had been recently subjected, so perfectly untainted, so free from even a shade of rational crimination, as the Royal Academy? I asked him if he knew of any institution which made such sacrifices, or so disinterestedly devoted extensive funds of their own creation to public purposes or national objects?

"To my first query Mr. Hume made no reply; — to the second, he said he could at once name a society of which he was a member; — a society which sustained the arts long before the existence of the Royal Academy; — a society from which the Royal Academy might be considered an offshoot, and to which he had heard many eminent artists acknowledge they were indebted for the earliest stimulus which had been supplied to their exertions; — he meant the Society of Arts, Manufactures, and Commerce, in the Adelphi, which he considered to be a more disinterested institution than the Royal Academy, as the members had no personal interest in its proceedings, and subscribed for its support, which the members of the Royal Academy did not do for the maintenance of their establishment.

"I expressed my surprise at this observation, and asked him if the members of the Academy had not subscribed their works, and the proceeds of the exhibition of their works to the amount of above 250,000*l.*, which I considered a far more effectual subscription? I said that I did not look upon the Academy as an offshoot of the Society of Arts, but as having originated from the Royal Incorporated Society of Artists, the charter of which was now in our possession; that although I had a high respect for the society in the Adelphi, I considered their influence on the fine arts as of a very restricted character, and directed to very trifling objects, and that their services could not, as far as the fine arts were concerned, be for a moment put in competition with the claims of the Royal Academy.

" Mr. Hume appeared to dissent from this opinion, and again re-urged upon me the consideration that Parliament and the public would not be satisfied without some proceeding on the part of the Academy, similar to that which he had suggested, as a return for the position in which they were placed at the national expense.   To this I replied by repeating that the Academy had incurred no new debt by their location in Trafalgar Square; that I thought and I believed the members would agree with me that we made an ample return by the devotion of our money and our time to the promotion of important public objects;— that the interests of the country were more concerned in the preservation of the Academy than those of its members, who had no personal or selfish views to influence them in sustaining it. I asked what possible advantage could the eminent artists who composed the Academy derive from the existence of an institution whose direct object it was to raise up rivals to themselves? I observed that with respect to the interests of the existing members, it would be for their advantage if the exhibition were abolished; for there they sent their productions annually exposed to have their supremacy contested and their reputation en-dangered, if not entirely eclipsed, by the vigorous exertions of rising genius.   I further remarked that supposing the House of Commons could be induced (a contingency, however, which I thought rather unlikely, though I acknowledged there was no saying what might happen in a period of change and revolution like the present) to address his Majesty, humbly representing to him that his Academy was a most pernicious institution, and praying that his Majesty would be graciously pleased to with-draw from it his countenance and protection,—and supposing that his Majesty could be persuaded (a contingency which I conceived to be still more unlikely) in compliance with the prayer of his faithful Commons, to say to his Academy :—' You are no longer a royal institution; I dismiss you as unworthy of my patronage,'—and supposing further that the Academy was expelled from Trafalgar Square, in what way would the arts or the public benefit by its discomfiture?   Could it be imagined that the Academy would not still exist as an united body, and continue their exhibitions with equal attraction from the same

talent, and with every inducement, under a different denomina-
tion and in another place, to appropriate the profit of their
labours most prudently and justly, to their own purposes; and
would the Governmnet be much gratified in discovering that they
were to be called upon to advance a sum of 8000*l.* or 10,000*l.* a
year for the support of a school of art, which had been so long
more economically and judiciously maintained by the exertions
of a body of artists.

" Mr. Hume observed that the Academy would necessarily lose
much of its importance if deprived of royal patronage and the
advantage of a residence in a public edifice; and he had too
high an opinion of their liberality and patriotism, to suppose
that they would discontinue their support of those public objects
to which their attention is now directed.   To this I replied that
in the case which I had supposed, and which I considered to be
next to impossible, the expectation of such a sacrifice on the part
of the members of the Academy, would be rather unreasonable.

" Many other observations were made on both sides to the
same effect; but as it is impossible to detail in a small compass
all that was said in a conversation which lasted an hour and a
half, I close it here, believing that without pretending to adhere
to the actual words used, or the precise form and structure of
the sentences in which they were employed, I have accurately
and faithfully given the sum and substance of every material -
observation made by either party."

From what passed at the interview in question, Sir
Martin was induced to hope that the further discussion
of academic matters in the House of Commons, might
be distinguished by a little more courtesy, and a good
deal more candour and fairness, on the part of the
Radical opponents of the Academy.   In this, however,
he was disappointed.   The refusal to admit the public
gratuitously to the exhibition, even for a few days, was
too tempting a pretext for anti-academic declamation,
to be disregarded, or dealt with by rational argument.
The same system of one-sided statement and unreason-

ing censure was pursued with undiminished energy; and Mr. Hume was, as usual, foremost in the display of malevolence towards a body who had filled up the measure of their supposed delinquencies by declining to submit to his dictation in a matter where their interests were so deeply concerned. The Government, also, apathetic, if not actively hostile, took no pains to defend an institution, whose independence of ministerial authority was distasteful to the feelings, and perhaps rather offensive to the dignity of Downing Street and Whitehall; and it would appear, from the opening paragraph of the document which I am about to bring to the notice of the reader, that the views of Mr. Hume and his followers in the controversy in question, were to some extent favoured by one of the most distinguished members of the administration.

In the month of July 1837, Sir Martin put forth a formal and argumentative statement in vindication of the course pursued by the Academy on the subject of the gratuitous admission of the public to their exhibition, in a short pamphlet entitled " A Letter to Lord John Russell, her Majesty's principal Secretary of State for the Home Department, on the alleged claim of the public to be admitted *gratis* to the Exhibition of the Royal Academy." This *opuscule* contains incidentally a short but able exposition of the whole academic case, and many observations connected with those proceedings of the Committee on the Fine Arts, on which I have animadverted in the preceding chapter. It affords, therefore, some additional and valuable illustrations of a subject with which the memory of the late President is inseparably connected; it exhibits a manly and dignified assertion of the claims of the Academy; and as it is distinguished throughout by those graces of style and diction which ever characterised the productions of his correct and eloquent pen, I am induced to insert it here at length, in the conviction that no adequate idea could be given of its full force and argumentative effect, by means of extracts however judiciously selected.

"My Lord,

"In compliance with the wish expressed by your lordship, when I had the honour of an interview with you at the Home Office, I proceed to state some of the many reasons which render it not only inexpedient, but, as I conceive, unjust, to expect or require the Royal Academy to open its doors gratuitously to the public at any period during the exhibition.

"To the general principle of the measure advocated by Mr. Hume, no liberal or enlightened man can, I think, reasonably object. To improve the taste of the public, and to rescue the humbler class of society from the degrading influence of those gross and sensual habits in which they had been too long left to indulge undisturbed, must be considered as highly laudable objects; and every appropriate and reasonable means should be resorted to for their attainment.

"To throw open our cathedrals, our public museums, and other national establishments, under careful superintendence and judicious limitation, would appear to be considered by all parties as an obvious and strictly legitimate mode of effecting this desirable end. These structures and institutions are, in every just interpretation of the term, national property; they are sustained or assisted by what may fairly be looked upon as national funds, and they contain objects of interest or curiosity purchased at the public expense, and expressly stored up and displayed for the public use and enjoyment.

"How far the dignitaries of the church, who are charged with the care of Westminster Abbey and St. Paul's, may or may not be called upon to acquiesce in the proposed measure, is, however, a question with which I do not presume to interfere; I consider the matter only in reference to the Royal Academy, whose honour, character, and interests it is my duty to defend.

" If the Academy were circumstanced like the British Museum, or any of those institutions which derive their means of subsistence from the state, no good reason, I conceive, could beassigned why it should not be subjected to the application of Mr. Hume's principle.

" But the Royal Academy is not an establishment in any respect similar to those which I have described. Although instituted for the promotion of great national objects, and powerfully sustaining those objects, it is not a national establishment. Though rendering important public services, it is not, in any respect, supported or assisted, nor has it ever been supported or assisted, from any public fund. It contains no object of art or article of property which can, in any sense, be termed national, or over the use or disposal of which the public, or their representatives in Parliament, can have any legitimate claim to exercise influence or control.

" But it is said that the occupation by the Academy of a portion of the building in Trafalgar Square, erected at the public expense, gives the public a right to interfere in its concerns, and to expect some return, on the part of the Academy, for the accommodation thus afforded.

" To this it may be replied, that the Academy, by their removal from Somerset House, have incurred no new debt or obligation to the public. For the advantage of the arts, and the better accommodation of sculpture in particular, we have made an exchange of apartments; we have given up a residence which had been provided for us by our royal founder, King George III. — a residence which, when he disposed of his private property to the nation, he expressly stipulated should be constructed for, and secured to his Academy, in the newly-erected building of Somerset House, and which was so appropriated and surrendered to that institution accordingly.

" Of this residence the Academy have been in undisputed possession for nearly sixty years; and although their tenure, however binding in moral obligation, could not, I suppose, be regarded as having the force of a lease or covenant maintainable in a court of law, yet, considering the utility and integrity of the tenant, I think I may say that it was a tenure which no reasonable, just, or prudent government would be likely to interfere with or disturb.

" The habitation we have relinquished had been erected at the public expense, as well that to which we have removed; and as the transfer was made, not for the private advantage of the Academy, but for the convenience of the arts and the consequent benefit to the public, — and as we were assured, by competent authority, that we were to be placed in the new building precisely on the same footing as in the old, there cannot, I conceive, be any new claim on us, or debt incurred to the public, although we may be desirous, on the part of the arts, to acknowledge a due sense of the liberal conduct of the government, which so promptly facilitated an arrangement suggested for their advantage.

" With respect to the return which it is said the Academy should make for the favour conferred upon them, in having a portion of a public building devoted to their use, I beg leave to observe, that if the Academy could advance no claim of moral right from the long established occupation of their former residence, — if, in their present position in Trafalgar Square, they had now, for the first time, received their local habitation, as a generous gift from the state, — if even the heavy expenses of removal had been defrayed from the same source, — and they had found accommodation adequate to the great objects which the Academy has so long sustained, and worthy of the great nation which must benefit by their promotion *,—if even they were thus favoured, and furnished ' with all appliances and means to boot,' I could not hesitate to assert that the Academy must be considered as making the fullest, the most ample, and the most legitimate return for the house-room afforded them in a public edifice.

" The Royal Academy has supported for more than half a century the only National School of Art in the kingdom;—a species of institution considered of so much importance in most other civilised communities as to be supported by the state.

---

* " The eminent architect of the building has done everything for the accommodation of the Academy which skill could effect, under the restriction of space and means."

They have established professors and gratuitous lectures in the different departments of Art; they have instituted numerous prizes to excite emulation and stimulate industry: they have accumulated a valuable collection of casts, prints, and books, and provided every material and means of study necessary for cultivating the pursuits of taste; they have *gratuitously* educated more than seventeen hundred students, the most promising of whom have been enabled to pursue their studies in the schools of Italy, at the expense of the Academy, and the least successful of whom have been instructed in those acquirements which have qualified them to become useful agents of manufacturing improvement, when foiled in their ambition to fulfil a higher destination.

"These important services rendered to their country, at the sacrifice of nearly three hundred thousand pounds, raised by the joint labours of artists, and disinterestedly devoted by them to public objects, must, I conceive, under any just estimate of their value, effectually turn the balance in favour of the Academy, even though they decline to endanger their property and diminish their means, by opening their doors to a promiscuous multitude, or submitting a royal establishment to the tender mercies of Radical renovation!

"I might enlarge much farther on this topic, and trace the useful agency of the Academy through all its beneficial results. But your Lordship can need no such information from me. You are well aware that, in all enlightened ages, the importance of the Fine Arts has been acknowledged, and their promotion regarded as essential to the interests and the honour of a great nation. 'Kings and statesmen have thought the encouragement of their arts at home to be as much a part of their duty as the defence of their country in the field, or the maintenance of its interests in the cabinet. A taste for what is beautiful is one great step to a taste for what is good.'* If this taste has made any progress amongst our population, it is to the unassisted efforts of the Royal Academy that it must be mainly attributed.

"In vain shall we collect in National Galleries the productions of other times and other countries; — in vain shall we lodge in

---

* Mr. James, in his "Desultory Man."

gorgeous magnificence the mutilated gods of Greece, or the deified deformities of the Egyptian mythology, if we neglect to secure the co-operation of still more essential agents in the great cause of taste.   Considered with reference to their influence as a means of exciting genius to rival excellence, these splendid accumulations, however desirable and becoming the dignity of a great nation, can be regarded but as the ammunition of Art, which will be provided to little purpose, if we have not the ordnance necessary to its use, and the skill required to direct its application.   What effects have such stores produced in those countries where they have been amassed to an extent which we cannot hope to rival in the course of a century?   What triumphs of taste have been achieved through their means at Florence, or at Munich—at Dresden or at Dusseldorf?   Where are the *living* glories even of the Louvre or the Vatican, which shall be deemed to eclipse the lustre of the British School?

" A *hortus siccus* is highly useful in the study of botanical science.   It instructs the naturalist and gratifies the philosopher. But it is to the garden in which the ground is prepared,—where the seed is sown and the living plant is nurtured, that we must look for fruits or flowers.

" The schools of the Royal Academy, my Lord, are the well stocked and well cultivated garden in which the tender growth of native genius has been carefully attended to, and fostered to a vigour of vegetation, which may challenge competition with the horticulture of taste in every country of Europe.

" It is most important that no error should prevail on this subject ;—that we should not mistake the means for the end, or suppose that we have provided for the harvest, when we have spread the manure.

" Experience has proved that, compared to the quickening efficacy of a great practical school of Art like that which has been so long sustained by the Royal Academy, a national collection, however rich and extensive, exercises but a barren influence on the general mind ; for although it may facilitate or assist the vegetation of taste, it possesses in itself but little germinating or prolific power.

" It is somewhat mortifying, my Lord, that the merits and

services of the Royal Academy should be so little known or understood by the public, as to require to be thus explained and enumerated.   It may be said, indeed, to be rather extraordinary that an institution, unsurpassed, if not unexampled, for the disinterestedness and integrity of its proceedings, should be aspersed and misrepresented unceasingly as composed of selfish monopolists and mercenary traders in taste; — that it should be assailed with asperity even in the senate, without a voice being raised in its defence amongst those from whose better feeling and better knowledge we might reasonably have expected an indignant exposure of such calumnious imputations.

" The Royal Academy, my Lord, owe much to their Sovereign, but nothing to their country.   If a debt has been incurred, it cannot surely be on the part of those who, participating but little themselves in the honours and rewards which stimulate the efforts of ambition, in more favoured, though not more useful avocations, have yet generously devoted their exertions, for sixty-four years, to the promotion of objects of acknowledged public interest,— objects which, in other civilised countries, are anxiously provided for by national funds, and protected by national establishments.   But the Academy have so long, so quietly, and so unostentatiously pursued their useful career, that their services are received by the public as a matter of course,—as services to which they have a prescriptive right; and they seem disposed not only to undervalue and disregard them, but to exact still more from those who have shown themselves ready to sacrifice so much.

" To speak candidly, my Lord, the government may be said to be much more interested in the preservation of the Royal Academy, than the members of which that body is composed. What personal or selfish advantage can those eminent artists derive from the existence of an institution, whose direct object it is to raise up rivals to themselves?   What motive but zeal for the advancement of the arts and the honour of their country, can induce them to submit their works, already well known in the circles of taste, to the ordeal of an annual exhibition, subject to the animadversions of ignorance and malevolence, and exposed to have their supremacy contested, and their hardcarned laurels shaken, if not torn from their brow, by the vigorous grasp of rising genius?  But it may be reasonably alleged that the government have some interest in the preservation of an institution which has performed for them an important duty; a duty which, unquestionably, they would long since have been required to discharge, if the zeal and patriotism of the Academy had not furnished them with an excuse for neglecting it.

"This duty, my Lord, the Academy are still willing to perform without stipend or stipulation.  They are still willing to employ their time, their talents, and their funds, for the advantage of their art and their country.  But if their services are not considered of sufficient importance to insure them respect, and entitle them to protection; — if those whose office it is to watch over the great interests of the state disapprove of the manner in which the Academy perform their volunteered task; — if it be at length discovered that the affairs of art can be conducted more beneficially for the country under ministerial management, and that a fund of ten or twelve thousand pounds a-year can be appropriated for that purpose, the members of the Royal Academy will, I have no doubt, be among the first to hail the flattering prospect, and will readily surrender the privilege which they have been so long allowed to enjoy—that of supporting a National Institution at their own expense!

"It is always an ungracious task in bodies, as well as in individuals, to parade their merits, or expatiate on their services.  But there are times when the duty of self-defence must supersede all delicacy; — when we are called upon to assert ourselves, and vindicate the claims of truth and justice, against illiberal abuse and vulgar depreciation.  I have not in any respect exaggerated the services of the Royal Academy.  The returns laid before Parliament will sufficiently authenticate every statement I have made; and if I speak warmly, it is because I feel indignant that the slanderous assaults upon that Institution, should find countenance and support amongst those who ought to be the most prompt to repel them.

"I have had seven-and-thirty years' experience of the ability and integrity with which the interests of the arts have been attended to and promoted by artists, while disregarded by statesmen, politicians, and philosophers:—I have witnessed their honest zeal, while uncheered themselves by a single ray of patronage from wealth or power, and struggling through the difficulties of a pursuit in which failure is poverty and contempt, and success, compared with the rewards of coarser occupations, can scarcely be called prosperity;—I have seen their generous disregard of all private views or personal objects, in an ardent desire to promote the welfare of the arts, and the honour of their country; and I have felt proud of my profession. I feel, also, that at some sacrifice of health, time, and means, I have acquired the right to speak freely and without reserve, in defence of a body of men who are not allowed their just estimation in the scale of social utility, although they exercise functions important to the best interests of society, and, in every sense of the expression, may be said to deserve well of their country.

"I consider myself a disinterested witness in this cause; for I have nothing to hope for in its success, or to fear in its failure. All that can be done by my profession for an artist, my brethren have done for me. They have given me their confidence, and placed me at their head. The position is a proud one: no man can be more sensible than I am of the honour that belongs to it, or can more highly appreciate the kindness with which it has been conferred on me; yet I must confess that circumstances have rendered that position so onerous, in every way, that nothing but the grateful respect which I feel for those who have placed me in it, and the flattering assurance that, in the discharge of its duties, I have been fortunate enough to obtain their approbation, could justify me in retaining it even for a day.

"From what has been already stated, your Lordship will, I trust, see that Mr. Hume's *grand cheval de bataille,* his argument of compensation, has no just application to the Academy, and that no claim of interference on the part of the public or the House of Commons, can rest on that basis. But even if the demand for this concession were not brought forward as offensively* as unjustly,— were it unobjectionable alike in

---

* "I have been informed that, at the meeting at the Freemasons' Tavern, it was proposed by some patriotic advocate of popular rights that the Royal

motive and in manner,—it would still be as unreasonable as injurious to urge it on the Academy. The property thus required to be thrown open to indiscriminate access is neither the property of the public nor of the Academy. It belongs to individuals who have intrusted it to that Institution for an express purpose. It is composed of articles particularly liable to injury; and we have no right to use it in any manner likely to endanger its preservation, or which was not in the contemplation of those who committed it to our charge. If any damage were to take place, the injury would be without redress,—the public would not indemnify the sufferer, and the Academy could not be held responsible.

" Take, for instance, the Sculpture-room of the Royal Academy, filled, as it is at present, with most valuable works in marble, crowded in a space which allows scarcely more than two spectators to pass abreast between the different articles submitted to inspection. With what feelings would Sir Francis Chantrey, Sir Richard Westmacott, and Mr. Baily learn that productions on which they had been employed for years,—for which some thousands of pounds were to be paid, and for the perfect preservation of which they were responsible to the proprietors, had been thrown open to the promiscuous access of the mob; that a committee of coal-heavers—an assemblage of *connoisseurs* from Field-lane and St. Giles's—had been invited by the Academy to polish their manners, refine their feelings, and cultivate their taste at the expense of the unhappy artists, who must submit to whatever mischief or mutilation might be inflicted on their works, while exposed to so rough an ordeal of criticism?

" With difficulty, even at present, can the delicate projecting parts and limbs of figures and casts be protected from injury, in the press of that superior class of spectators, by whom the utmost care and caution are invariably exercised in their examination. Certainly, the eminent artists whom I have mentioned, if they were lucky enough to rescue their works in

Academy should not only be expelled from the building in Trafalgar Square, but that their funds should be seized upon, and distributed amongst the Art at large."

tolerable safety from one such exposure to an invasion of the populace, would take care how they incurred the hazard of a second inroad, and would prudently withhold their contributions altogether from an institution which had no longer the power to protect them.

"The rush of a crowd into the Miniature apartment would be still more likely to produce damage and depredation. The productions exhibited there are for the most part small and valuable; they are not very effectually secured on the walls to which they are attached, and are all in frames furnished with expensive glasses, liable to be broken on the slightest pressure. No vigilance of police or Academic superintendence could guard the property exposed to plunder in such circumstances, or baffle the furtive ingenuity with which such small objects would be wrenched from their places, pocketed, and carried off in the crowd. Even as it is, we find it impossible to prevent theft. Scarcely a year passes in which some miniature is not stolen; and the Academy has been so often called on to make good the loss, as to render necessary a public notice, that though the Institution would take all possible care of the works intrusted to their charge, they could not be responsible for damage or loss from accident, fire, or any other cause.

"But it is said that there is no danger; — that the French exhibition admits the public *gratis*, and the British Museum receives its thousands without any injurious result to the property of that institution. Neither of these instances, however, can, I conceive, be considered in point, as applied to the Royal Academy. The French Academy has an ample income from the state, and a gorgeous palace appropriated for the display of its productions; — its existence does not depend on such shilling-contributions as Mr. Hume's measure would not only materially diminish but effectually suppress. The public in Paris are admitted through the whole period of the exhibition; — they are not limited to a few prescribed days, and are not, by any such restriction, necessarily compelled, if they attend at all, to resort to it in inconvenient crowds. The French populace, also, I regret to be obliged to confess, are more sensible to the influence of works of art, — they are more qualified to enjoy the pleasures which such works afford, and less disposed to injure them, than the humbler classes of this country. Let those whose negligence of their feelings and interests has contributed to this comparative barbarism of our population, which they now appear to lament, — let those who have encouraged in them no taste but for intoxication, and have allowed them no pleasures but in the orgies of the ale-house or the brutalities of a boxing-match, — let these tardy advocates for popular refinement take the speediest means to remedy the evil they have caused. But they must not disturb the useful arrangements of a liberal and patriotic institution, or violate the rights of private property, for that purpose.

" The British Museum is open through the whole year. It affords ample space even for crowds to move about and disperse through its extensive apartments ; — its marbles are displayed in vast galleries, and not crammed into a semicircular nook like the Sculpture-room of the Royal Academy. The objects of curiosity in the Museum are principally enclosed in glass cases, and otherwise protected from injuries of accident or design. Those who cannot gratify their curiosity there to-day, know that they may do so to-morrow, or at some other convenient opportunity. The case is different with the Royal Academy : the exhibition there is open but for a short period; its days of free admission would necessarily be few and fixed. It is no disparagement to the other public shows of the metropolis to say, that from the nature and novelty of its display, it is in-finitely more attractive than any of its rivals. The annual receipts prove this : but Mr. Hume's " ingenious device " would soon degrade its character, and deprive it of its pre-eminence of profit. The higher classes would proudly absent themselves altogether ; a large portion of those who may be considered above the lower orders, would reserve themselves for an enjoy-ment at free quarters ; and the concourse of such company, thus narrowly confined, both as to time and space, would be pro-portionably impetuous in their movements, and irresistible by any force short of such a phalanx of police officers, as must aggravate the embarrassment of a crowd, without affording security from damage or depredation.

" But why does Mr. Hume, to whom those difficulties have been explained, continue to manifest an unfriendly feeling towards the Royal Academy? I can understand the motives which actuate some of his coadjutors or co-agitators. To the rabble of its opponents the *regal* designation of the Academy affords a sufficient provocation : but surely that institution might expect to find some favour in the eyes of a sound political economist ; for no Academic hand has yet been detected dipping into the national pocket. The Ways and Means have not been taxed for its support ; no item of charge on its account, in the annual estimates, has disturbed the equanimity or challenged the investigation of this vigilant guardian of the public purse. — I have heard Mr. Hume declare himself a friend to the Fine Arts. I cannot doubt that he is so, although he takes a rather singular way of showing it. Can he devise a cheaper means of promoting them than that which puts the nation to no expense? Has his experience furnished him with an example of any other institution, civil, military, or even religious, in which the labourers, though worthy of their hire, yet demand no pay, and perform valuable public services without fee or reward? Verily, the most niggardly spirit of parsimony might be well content to leave such a society unmolested. Can Mr. Hume complain that undue partiality for the votaries of taste has occasioned any offensive examples of ministerial profusion? Let him look at the Pension List ; does he find the name of an Academician there? — No! The arts are associated with science and literature, everywhere but in that state document. Passive and uncomplaining, artists are a class of men *qui ne savent pas trop se faire valoir ;* thoughtless visionaries in a world of dreams, — victims of an ambition that knows no taint of avarice, they are rarely found bustling in the crowd of Fortune's worshippers. They start no sly schemes of personal advantage, no cunning projects of patronage, to arouse, in our distinguished economist, his suspicions of peculation, or his jealousy of jobs.

" That the long course of slander to which the Academy has been exposed, may have produced an impression unfavourable to its influence and operations, on the mind of a gentleman whose studies may not have particularly qualified him to judge of such

matters, I can easily believe. Aware of the disreputable instruments employed to assail them, the members of that body
have always treated their libellers with contempt, and left them
to continue their avocation of calumny unnoticed. But imputations unrepelled are often taken as proved, by those who
have neither motive nor means to investigate their truth. After
the rigid scrutiny, however, to which the Academy has been
recently subjected, — after the publication of that farrago of
folly, vanity, and egotism, which, in the shape of evidence against
the Academy, has been paraded before the House of Commons
by the Committee on the Fine Arts, I cannot but express my
surprise that any candid or liberal mind should continue to be
influenced by misrepresentations so palpably absurd, — so
ludicrously malignant.

"I would ask Mr. Hume, in print, a question which I have
before put to him in private, and to which he appeared not to
have any ready reply. Can he point out an institution in this
or any other country, which, after an active career of seventy
years, and with an hostility against it as rancorously vigilant to
expose its errors as disappointment and malice could make it,
has stood more clear in its account, and come forth more perfectly untainted — more free from even a shade of rational
crimination—than the Royal Academy?

"Yet Mr. Hume and his friends are not satisfied: they demand
to open its doors, and summon Queen, Lords, and Commons to
their aid. But the Academy is safe in the enlightened protection of their Sovereign, and neither Lords nor Commons have
as yet responded to the call.

"Surely our new purveyors of *virtù* for the populace might
content themselves with the free admission of all classes to the
National Gallery. That collection, as well as the British
Museum, is open throughout the year; and the treasures it contains are considered by those who are so anxious to improve the
public taste, as far more effective for that purpose than the productions of living artists. That a few days' free access to the
latter should be thought of so much importance by the Committee of Taste at the Freemasons' Tavern, might appear as a
circumstance highly complimentary to our labours, if it did not

unfortunately excite a suspicion that the underworkers of the machinery considered the occasion as a favourable opportunity to strike a blow at the Academy, and compel that body to submit to an influence which they knew would degrade, and they hoped might destroy it.

" But these gentlemen will be disappointed: the time is not yet ripe for the triumph of their ultilitarian toils.   Academies and diplomas may still hope to survive the vigorous attacks of the Committee on the Fine Arts, reinforced even as it was by a heavy fire from the philosophic battery of a grave German Professor. The sagacious senator who conducted the process of assault with such politeness and impartiality willdoudt less recruit his discomfited powers during the recess, and study a more effective system of tactics for another campaign against Academic delinquency.   In the interim, however, we may be allowed to indulge in the reprieved dignity of *R.A.*; and *artificial* distinctions will probably be still employed to mark out merit for those rewards of respect and reverence, which quacks and pretenders would impudently grasp at and degrade.

" The Royal Academy has long been obnoxious to assailants of this character; but it has withstood too many storms to be shaken by a squall from such a quarter.   Its members have no paltry ends to answer—no personal objects to pursue.   Safe in their utility and their integrity, they may look with contempt on the crude, though crafty machinations of mortified vanity and baffled arrogance.   They are " armed so strong in honesty " as to be invulnerable in the squib-and-cracker warfare of vulgar scurrility; and there is no alternative that can be presented to them which they will not readily embrace, rather than submit to an interference inconsistent alike with the honour and the interest of an institution responsible only to their Sovereign; — an institution whose unassisted efforts have established the supremacy of British Art among the schools of Europe, and vindicated the genius of our country.

" Many other reasons might be adduced in support of the positions which I have advanced, were it allowable to occupy your Lordship's valuable time further on this subject.   If, encouraged by your kindness and your known attachment to the arts, I have already dwelt too long in illustration, and encumbered my argument with superfluous proof, you will, I trust, excuse an indiscretion which has resulted from an honest ardour in a good cause.

" The commencement of a new reign excites all the hopes and awakens all the energies of Art.   The character of the amiable and illustrious princess who has just ascended the throne of her ancestors, authorizes us to look forward confidently to a continuance of that protection which the Royal Academy has experienced from three successive sovereigns.   The gracious mark of favour which, with such amiable promptitude, Her Majesty has, on your Lordship's representation, accorded to the Royal Academy, encourages the expectation, that conversant as Her Majesty is with all those pursuits which form the objects of its care, the Queen will know how to appreciate their true value ; and her patriotism will combine with her taste, in securing for her country all those advantages which a liberal and judicious patronage cannot fail to derive from the grateful genius of the age.

" I have the honour to be, my Lord,<br>
" With great respect, your Lordship's very faithful Servant,

" MARTIN ARCHER SHEE."

Cavendish Square, 17th July, 1837.


If this masterly and dignified manifesto failed to set the Academy right with the public at large, to whom it was easier to echo a senseless clamour than to investigate its meaning or justice,—if it was ineffectual to check the hostility of the Radicals in the House, who cared as little for the facts as they did for the arguments involved in the subject,—it at any rate carried conviction to the minds of the few who, unbiased by prejudice, and approaching the question in a spirit of fair inquiry, could appreciate the significance of the statement and the cogency of the reasoning by which it was elucidated. By the real lovers and patrons of art it was hailed as a triumph of eloquent and convincing advocacy; and many were the evidences of its successful result, as an argumentative effort, which reached the author from quarters whence the voice of panegyric could not fail to be heard with just pride and satisfaction.  The venerable Bard of Memory writes to him as follows, in acknowledgment of a copy of the pamphlet:

" MY DEAR SIR MARTIN,

" A thousand, thousand thanks for your excellent and unanswerable letter.  You have overthrown the assailants—never, as I hope, to rise again. .

" Yours very truly,

" SAMUEL ROGERS."

" August 14th, 1837.

The subjoined letter from his valued friend Sir Robert Inglis, on so many subsequent occasions the able and zealous defender of the Academy in the House of Commons, will show that the president's arguments were fully appreciated by one at least of those to whose wisdom and candour, as legislators, the appeal was practically made in the form of a letter to the minister:

" 7, BEDFORD SQUARE,

" Saturday, 14th Oct., 1837.

" MY DEAR SIR MARTIN,

" I met you to day with shame, because I had not discharged the easy and grateful duty of thanking you, as I ought to have done, for your obliging attention in sending me a copy of your Letter to Lord John Russell.  I have read it with great interest.  I needed no conviction on the subject, having uniformly arrived at the same conclusion through the same arguments.

Your exposure and demolition of Mr. Hume are complete; and
I am much obliged to you for having furnished me with so
powerful and eloquent a statement of the rights and the wrongs
of the Academy which is so happy to have you for its chief, —
and which may indeed boast that it has you for its defender,
and *him* for its enemy. I do not, of course, agree with you in
one application of the phrase ' national property,'* in p. 2, and
I therefore think it more honest to say so at once.

" Believe me always, my dear SIR MARTIN,
" Very faithfully yours,
" ROBERT HARRY INGLIS."

" P.S. — I think you are mistaken in saying, p. 13, that not a
voice was raised, &c."


The late Lord Abinger, writing to him on the same
occasion, says :

" I cannot resist the desire of expressing my thanks for the
communication of your letter to Lord John Russell, and my
entire concurrence in all the arguments and sentiments so eloquently set forth in it. It is impossible for any man possessed
either of the power of reasoning accurately or of judging correctly, not to be convinced of the justness of all your principles,
and of the conclusion you derive from them; but I shall not be
surprised if you find it equally impossible to carry conviction
to the minds of those for whom principally you have published
your letter. There is a coarseness about the republicans of the
present day that is incapable of being softened by refinement or
good taste, and that marks but too plainly the stern despotism
which they would inflict upon their country, under the false
pretence of public rights. I doubt not, however, that you will
have the satisfaction of ranging on your side a majority of those
upon whose opinion at last the fate of the Academy must depend; and that though for the present you have cast your pearls

* This refers apparently to the cathedrals, which Sir Martin, in the second
paragraph of the letter, classes among the structures, &c., which he describes
as " in every just interpretation of the term national property."

before swine, the swine will not have the casting voice in disposing of them."

This prediction may be said to have been practically accomplished when, two years later, the contest between the Academy and its Radical opponents in the House of Commons was brought to a crisis, which ended in the signal discomfiture of Mr. Hume and his followers.   In the meantime, however, the letter to Lord John Russell, however conclusive in argument and incontrovertible in statement, had not precisely the effect of oil poured on troubled waters.   The tone of indignant and lofty defiance that characterised it when dealing with the assailants of the Academy, added fuel to the flames of their patriotic wrath, imparting fresh energy to their assaults, and additional venom to their abuse, on every subsequent occasion when the rights or interests of the Royal Academy were discussed or adverted to in the House of Commons.

As far as Mr. Hume was personally concerned, indeed, this gentleman had no just cause of complaint against the president, who had strictly observed all the forms of literary courtesy towards him, in those passages of the Letter, which alluded to his interference in the concerns of the Academy.   By no one of the *pseudo-dilettanti*, however, was the proceeding more deeply resented than by the great economist, who not content with redoubling his efforts to bring the rebellious body into due subjection to parliamentary omnipotence, exhibited his personal pique against the president in a manner so ludicrous, that it provoked the hilarity of the House, while by its ostentatious discourtesy it invited the infliction of that sharp retributive justice, so amply administered to him in the pamphlet which Sir Martin gave to the public at the end of the session of 1838; a production which filled the measure of his

offences against the dogmatism of pretentious incom-
petence, seeking to indoctrinate and mystify the public
mind on the subject of the arts. In the meantime, the
outspoken language of the letter to Lord John Russell
had not only increased the animosity of all to whom the
President was personally and officially obnoxious, by
reason of his strenuous defence of the body over which
he presided, but had also, absurdly enough, made him
a mark for political invective on the part of those whom
private interest, disappointed vanity, or utilitarian con-
ceit had arrayed in opposition to the Academy. Writing in the month of October, 1837, to Miss Tunno, who
had recently returned from a visit to St. Petersburg,—
where, in common with all other English travellers who
had been admitted within the range of the imperial
amenities, she was much impressed by the grave dignity
and apparent *bienveillance* with which the late Emperor
Nicholas I. exercised the courtly and ceremonious
functions of his exalted position,—Sir Martin says:—

" I suppose you can feel but little interest in the boisterous
contentions of the constitutional anarchy which we dignify in
this country by the name of political liberty,—after witnessing
the tranquil calm of paternal authority under the mild sway of
the magnificent Calmuck whose virtues and graces you have so
eloquently described. You have become a convert to the old
doctrine ' *sub rege pio*.' But what do you think of *my* being
attacked as a *rank conservative* and anti-radical in consequence
of the Letter to which you allude as having been mentioned to
you by Mr. A——. If you had been in England, you would
not have received your information on the subject at *second hand*.
At the earnest desire of some of my academic brethren, I was
induced to fire a shot among the rabble assailants of that institution, and have consequently made myself a target for all the
arrows of malignity, political and pictorial. But he who enjoys

the post of honour ought not to shrink from the post of danger. The Letter is a small affair, but you shall have a copy by the first opportunity."

The agitation connected with the question of gratuitous and indiscriminate admission to all public buildings and establishments, appears to have been vigorously prosecuted in the interval between the parliamentary sessions of 1837 and 1838. The promoters of this object had formed themselves into a committee, who met from time to time, and convened public meetings, at the Freemasons' Tavern, or some other favourite locality for popular demonstrations, in order to discuss the measures to be adopted for the purpose of enforcing on all whom it might concern a speedy submission to the authoritative edict of this self-constituted dictature. As might be expected, those public functionaries and officials, lay and clerical, who, exercising control over the question of access or non-access to their respective institutions, declined to obey the peremptory summons of Mr. Hume and his gallant band of popularity-hunting *dilettanti*, supplied the theme of much declamatory vituperation to the orators whose indignant eloquence adorned and enlivened these stirring debates; and it need hardly be said that the Royal Academy and their uncompromising President obtained their full share of the reprobation bestowed on such flagrant contumacy. In December 1837, a meeting was held at the Thatched House Tavern, St. James's Street, when Mr. Hume returned to the charge, and expressed himself concerning that body and its chief in terms of censure, and with certain inaccuracies of statement, that were not destined eventually to pass unnoticed or unrebuked; though it was not until after the system of sweeping abuse and disingenuous suppression of facts, had been again resorted to in the senate, in the course of the ensuing session, on the subject which had now become a kind of hobby with the eminent economist, that Sir Martin was at length induced to re-enter the field of controversy, with a direct exposure of that gentleman's proceedings and pretensions as an intruder in the domains of taste.

The " Letter to Joseph Hume, Esq., M.P., in reply to his aspersions on the character and proceedings of the Royal Academy," written and published in the month of July 1838, is unquestionably one of the most striking examples of contemptuous severity, and sarcastic vigour in argument, which the records of pamphleteering literature can supply. The very title-page gives rich promise of the slashing intrepidity, and felicitous *à-plomb* of satirical onslaught, that mark every page of the contents,—in a motto so happily chosen,—*ad rem* and *ad hominem*,—that in spite of the imposing plausibility of the reference to the noble author whose name is vouched on its behalf,* many a reader probably has indulged a natural, though in fact, ill-grounded doubt, as to its authenticity as a quotation. The passage is as follows :—" *Délivre nous, grand Dieu ! de ces amateurs sans amour, de ces connaisseurs sans connaissance !*

Notwithstanding the length of this remarkable *brochure*, I cannot bring myself to present it in a curtailed or imperfect form to the attention of the reader. Its publication under the then existing circumstances, is an incident demanding prominent notice in a biography of the late President; and there is hardly to be found in it a single paragraph which is not of obvious relevancy to the material facts of the contro-

* The Comte de Strogonoff, President of the Imperial Academy of St. Petersburg.

versy between the Academy and its assailants, or
strikingly illustrative of the talents, character, or
career of the writer. As a narrative, it sums up the
history of this particular episode of the anti-academic
intrigue, in a clear and rapid manner; and as regards
Sir Martin's personal connection with the events recorded
or alluded to, it has the claim of autobiography to urge
on the attention of the reader, and is legitimately entitled to supersede the statements, however authentic,
of any other chronicler of the President's actions or feelings. I accordingly insert it here, *in extenso*.

"SIR,

" In the report of a debate in the House of Commons,
on the subject of a small grant to the National Gallery, I perceive, by a speech attributed to you, that you have again
drawn your sword against the Royal Academy, and flourished
it with your usual vigour and *success*.

" There was reason to presume that you were somewhat sick
of the war which you had provoked, and that you would not
readily renew a contest in which you had acknowledged that
there was ' now no hope.' But ' *Ecce iterum Crispinus*,' appears to be your motto; and as you have on this, as well as on
a former occasion, made some animadversions on the Royal
Academy, which my duty to that institution impels me to
notice, I take the liberty by a direct address to solicit your
attention, and at the same time to refresh your memory as to
a name which, it appears, you found it rather difficult to
recollect.

" The ordinary detractors of the Academy are unworthy of
notice. The angry ebullitions of artists, disappointed in their
hopes, and suffering under the impression that their merits
have not been duly acknowledged, should be treated with some
indulgence, and passed over with a generous disregard. But
you, sir, are an important public character,—a distinguished
member of the senate; and statements from such a quarter

would undoubtedly be received with confidence, if their incorrectness were not pointed out and exposed.

"The task of this exposure, sir, I very reluctantly undertake to perform, having neither time nor taste for that species of public contention, in which your long-practised powers must give you an advantage so decided. But I am bound by position and principle to defend the interests of a valuable institution, which it would appear to be your favourite pastime to attack.

"It is plain, indeed, that in your scale of importance, the fine arts occupy but a very humble rank; otherwise you would have deemed it becoming and expedient to treat a body of artists honoured by the especial patronage of their sovereign, with somewhat more respect than the Royal Academy has found at your hands. If therefore, in dealing with your animadversions on that body, I should be betrayed into the practice of a similar freedom to that in which you have allowed yourself to indulge, I trust you will excuse the liberty, and attribute it to the influence of your own seductive example.

"You are, sir, evidently angry,—very angry, and like most people in a passion, your mental powers appear to be somewhat confused. Your memory, in particular, has been so impaired, as on a recent occasion to afford a very diverting instance of the failure of that faculty.*

"As your present assault offers nothing but a repetition of those complaints with which, in such a strain of querulous eloquence, you edified your audience at the Thatched House, in December last,—served up at second heat for the benefit of the Commons and the public,—I shall take leave to connect your tavern strictures with your senatorial effusions, and comment on each as the subject may require.

"You commence your parliamentary exposure by a declaration that ' you are quite indignant at the conduct of the Royal Academy.' Now, with the exception of the little *clique* of

---

* "Times" Newspaper, July 7th,—"In a letter written and published by the President of the Royal Academy, *he did not recollect his name* (laughter)."—*Mr. Hume's speech on the 6th inst.* This, sir, is " *the unkindest cut of all,*" and must be considered a very happy illustration of oblivious vengeance, and *non mi ricordo* wrath.

anti-academic malignants which may be properly designated as your 'tail,' and to whose wriggling and tortuous activity all your vermicular movements respecting the Academy may be traced, I believe that no other person in the community shares in the indignation which you express.   But rising still in your wrath, you assert that ' the Academy is the *meanest* and most *stingy* of all institutions.'

" These, sir, are harsh terms to be applied to a body of men whose individual utility, integrity and talent, rank as high in public estimation as your own ;  and as you are said to be peculiarly qualified to feel the full force of such aspersions, the offence they are intended to convey carries all the weight of peculiar personal aggravation.

" Your animosity, indeed, against the Academy, cannot be easily accounted for upon any principle which the experience of the most querulous public career supplies.   One would suppose that a number of artists might associate together for the purpose of raising the depressed arts of their country,—might disinterestedly devote their time, their talents, and their funds, to the support of an establishment which ought to be maintained by the state; one would suppose that they might be allowed to institute schools, lectures, and prizes, open for the gratuitous instruction and incitement of all who desire to devote themselves to the pursuits of taste,—that they might collect materials, models, and books for the purposes of study ; one would suppose that they might be permitted to carry on this not very censurable process for the greater part of a century, assiduously cultivating the genius of their country, and generously disbursing *their own money* for the public advantage, with an integrity untainted even by calumny itself, and an effect upon the taste of the time, which you alone, sir, amongst any respectable class of the community, will venture to deny ; one would suppose that they might establish an exhibition, open to all artists of merit, from whatever quarter they present themselves, and be even allowed to dine together *at their own expense,* with all that is illustrious, elevated, and distinguished in the land, as guests at their honoured board,— one would suppose that all this might be done not only with impunity, but with some little credit and consideration, without stirring the bile of a patriot, or disturbing the calculating machine which works in the cranium of a sound political economist. But your sagacity, sir, has discovered from such proceedings an extraordinary result; and you do not hesitate to attribute to the Royal Academy 'that the people of this country are in a state of ignorance with respect to the arts, that has no parallel in any other country in Europe.'

"I believe, sir, notwithstanding the *dilettante* drilling to which you have so patiently submitted, in order to fit yourself for the service in which you have engaged, you have not, as yet, obtained any particular distinction for your knowledge of the fine arts. Matters of taste do not appear to be in your department. Your sensibilities have never been excited to the manifestation of any interest in their behalf. Your invectives against the Academy, therefore, are as rash and intemperate as they are pointless and unprovoked. They betray a spirit of rancour and virulence more characteristic of private pique and personal enmity, than of that measured animadversion and regulated reproof, which a liberal reformer would employ even in the most ardent pursuit of public objects. But though your darts have been poisoned with the skill of a *Cherokee*, and your aim has been deadly, they have failed to inflict a wound; not from want of venom in the instruments, but of vigour in the arm by which they have been thrown.

"But to come to close quarters, and take your allegations in detail; the first count of that bill of indictment which you have thought proper to prefer against the Royal Academy is, that they have presumed to reject all the propositions which you have made to them, with respect to admitting the public *gratis* to their exhibitions. It is very true, sir, that the Royal Academy have rejected your ill-considered and unjust propositions, or, rather, I should say, demands: for, in that supercilious tone of authority which important personages know so well how to assume, they were told that 'neither the public nor the Parliament would be satisfied, unless the Academy made some return for the position which they enjoyed at the public expense.'

"The return,—the more than ample return made by the Academy for this accommodation, I have sufficiently shown in my letter to Lord John Russell. Your unreasonable demands, therefore, have been rejected by the Academy; and most unworthy would they have proved themselves of the trust reposed in them by their royal founder, as well as of the respect and confidence of their profession, if they had not rejected the modest demands, which required that they should disturb all their arrangements, alter their laws, and violate the interests of their art, in compliment to the new-born zeal for popular improvement which broke out at a meeting of a few gentlemen assembled as a committee at the Freemasons' Tavern.

"If, after the disinterested, the honourable course the Academy have pursued for so long a period,—if, conscious of the sacrifices they have made, and the valuable services they have rendered to their art and their country,—if, with every motive for manly firmness and just indignation, they should submit to the arrogant dictation to which you would subject them,—then, indeed, the Royal Academy would disgrace its title, and I should blush for my profession.

"Your next article of impeachment we find in a misstatement brought forward for the purpose of introducing an invidious contrast between the Society of British Artists and the Royal Academy. You tell the meeting at the 'Thatched House, that they should recollect 'that the Society of British Artists were obliged to provide not only exhibition rooms, but the whole of the expenses incidental to the establishment; while exhibition rooms, *and a portion of the expense of maintaining them,* were supplied to the Royal Academy *by the public.*'

"I must conclude, sir, that you are still marvellously misinformed as to the nature and objects of the two societies which you thus attempt to bring into opposition; for though some pains have been taken to enlighten you on the subject, I will not allow myself to suppose it possible that a gentleman and a legislator could intentionally suppress every particular which can be considered essential to a fair comparison,—and practise such a delusion on the meeting and the public, as must

result from the extraordinary statement that '*the two establishments were equally competing for public favour.*'

" With every respect for the society in question, and every
wish for their success,—I would ask, what possible claim of
competition with the Royal Academy your ingenuity can set
up for the Society of British Artists?  The former, the great
supporter of the arts for three-fourths of a century—the only
effective school for their cultivation in the kingdom—providing,
on a liberal scale, every material and means of study necessary
for such an establishment, and disinterestedly devoting large
funds of their own creation, to the noblest public purposes,—the *gratuitous* education of students without distinction
of class or degree, and the general promotion of the public
taste ; the latter society, a recent private speculation of a few
individual artists, for their own advantage,—without school,
scholar, or material of study ; pledged to no public duties, and
performing no public services ; with no other purpose than the
exhibition of their works, and employing their funds, as they
have an unquestionable right to do — solely for their own
benefit.

" Really, sir, the comparison which you have drawn between
these two institutions, does little credit to your discrimination,
and still less to your impartiality.

" But your zeal has carried you still farther ; and you do not
hesitate to assert that a portion of the expense incurred for the
support of the Academy, is supplied from the public purse.  You
are reported, sir, to be as peculiarly conversant in the lore that
relates to the outlay of the national funds, as you are vigilant in
preventing their misappropriation.  Can you adduce in support
of your assertion any grant of the public money to the Royal
Academy ?  Can you prove that a single shilling has been contributed by the Government towards the maintenance of that
institution, since its first establishment ?  If you cannot do
this, sir, you must allow me to express my wonder, by what
extraordinary process of misconception,—by what peculiar impulse of inaccuracy,—you have been led publicly to make an assertion, hazarded in the face of the explicit statement made to
you by me, in the conversation which took place between us on

the subject,—the minutes of which now lie before me,—an assertion, also, in the face of the still more explicit statement contained in my letter to Lord John Russell, of which you were furnished with a copy, and which I here quote :—

" ' The Royal Academy, although instituted for the promotion of great national objects, and powerfully sustaining those objects, is not a national establishment. Though rendering important public services, it is not, in any respect, supported or assisted, nor has it ever been supported or assisted, from any public fund.'—(*Letter to Lord John Russell.*)

" It is, perhaps, not to be expected that a gentleman engaged, as you are, in such numerous and important national affairs, should submit to be correct when dealing with the trifling concerns of the fine arts :  but, if you do condescend to include such matters within the wide sweep of your wing, we surely have some reason to complain that you allow yourself so lightly to hazard statements, the truth of which you do not take the trouble to investigate, and the injurious results of which you appear to disregard.

" Your next charge against the Royal Academy is advanced in the following observation :—(*Thatched House Speech, Times Newspaper.*)—' Mr. Hume would only say that it was his intention to call for returns to show what the Royal Academy, with all its privileges and advantages, had done for the cause of *science* and the arts.  He believed it had wholly failed in those respects, and that to this *failure* was to be attributed *the reluctance to give the papers which had been asked of the managers of that establishment.*'

" Your characteristic caution, sir, would appear to desert you in prosecuting your extraordinary hostility to the Royal Academy.  You are so anxious to strike, that you seize the first weapon of offence presented to your hand, and find that you have got hold of an edged tool, with which it is proverbially unsafe to meddle.  In the passage of your speech above quoted, you cast a very unworthy imputation on a body of artists who have long enjoyed the respect of enlightened and honourable men ; an imputation for which, if they could have given even the slightest cause, they would indeed deserve to be visited with the infliction of your interference in their concerns.　　Allow me to ask you, sir, on what authority you have been induced to offer them this public insult?　Upon what fact do you justify the offensive inference which you ingeniously draw from your own misstatement?

" The 'managers' of the Royal Academy have evinced *no* reluctance to supply the papers required of them.　They have no motive for concealment.　The more their proceedings are made known, the more their utility, their integrity, and their disinterestedness must become apparent.　The returns asked for by the House of Commons, at the instance of Mr. Ewart, were furnished as soon as they could be made out, after the king's permission (for which I immediately applied, and without which they could not have been granted) had been obtained for that purpose.

" That you, sir, were desirous of any information from the Academy, I learned on the 26th of September, by a communication from Lord John Russell, stating that you requested ' a return of the number of students sent abroad by the Academy, with the expense of maintaining them there, and other particulars concerning them ;'—Lord John politely inquiring if there was any objection on the part of the Academy to furnish you with the return in question.　To this I replied on the 27th of the same month, that the Academy could have no possible objection to supply the information asked for, or any other information that might be required of them : that the secretary, who had the books of the institution in charge, was then on the continent ;—that on his return, which might be expected in the course of a fortnight or three weeks, I would immediately lay his lordship's communication before the council, and I had no doubt the information sought for would be promptly furnished.

" The secretary returned about the time specified ; and on the 2nd of November, the earliest period at which, from the absence of members in the country, a sufficient number could be collected to form a council, the return was ordered to be made out and sent forthwith to Lord John Russell ; for, as you had thought proper to ask for it through him, it was presumed you wished to receive it through the same channel.

" Conscious that not a day had been suffered to elapse un-necessarily on the part of the Academy, it was with equal surprise and indignation we heard of your extraordinary out-break on the subject, at the meeting of the 16th December; and those emotions were not a little increased, when on the ap-plication of the secretary at the Home Office, he was informed that the return had been regularly received there; so that it ought to have been about six weeks in your possession, at the time when you thought fit to throw out an imputation so offensive to the feelings of gentlemen, who in their integrity defy your scrutiny, while they have the spirit to repel your aggression.

" But although the return in question has long been added to the vast and valuable mass of documents which your in-quiries, *de omnibus rebus*, must have accumulated in your state-paper office, and though you have been quite as long aware that the Academy were not answerable for the delay which called forth your illiberal remark, yet your candour has not prompted you to acknowledge your precipitation, or atone for your injustice.

" But although you have been a little unlucky in this instance, it must be confessed, sir, that you are a formidable foe, and appear to have all the resources of offence at your command. Your tactics provide for all contingencies; and when discom-fited on the ground of reason and argument, like a prudent general, you still have a reserve to fall back upon, and you anticipate victory from the operations of *fear* and *shame.*

" Thus, although ' the letter of the President of the Royal Academy proves that there is no hope at present from that quarter ;'—although the Dean of Westminster, ' Doctor Ireland, is immovable,' and the bishops, whom you flatteringly represent as *favourable to the employment of the golden key,* are, ' with one or two exceptions,' contumacious, and refuse to bow to your decree,—yet you do not despair.  You gird up your loins for a new encounter, and with the assistance of the overwhelming emotions to whose aid you turn in your distress, you are con-fident of ultimate triumph; for ' shame,' you declare, must compel the Academy to adopt the course you desire, ' when the

Society of British Artists have set them the example;' and the
' *threat* of inquiry which you have thrown out ' for the consideration of our ecclesiastical dignitaries, ' you have no doubt will
have a good effect.'

" It would appear, sir, that you have no objection to the use
of a *little intimidation* when it can be employed against deans
and chapters.

" But reinforced by the two powerful engines with which you
now take the field, Don Quixote's attack upon the windmill is
not to be compared to the vigour of your advance against
cathedrals and academies. You manœuvre your force, too,
with the judgment of a skilful engineer. You bring to bear
upon each of your opponents the battery most likely to be
effective; and you *terrify* the priests, while you *shame* the
painters.

" I do not presume, sir, to offer a conjecture as to the effect
which your fulminations may produce upon the right reverend
bench, or to judge whether enough of the church militant
spirit remains, to enable them to sustain with fortitude your
alarming menace. But for the Royal Academy,

" ' There are no terrors, Cassius, in thy looks.'

" Armed alike against fear or shame, in the proud panoply of
honour and truth, we disdain the recreant who would meanly
yield in such a cause; and when you attempt to batter in
breach, you will find the academic fortress more impregnable
even than the Tower;—you will be overset in the recoil of
your own guns, and catch, by rebound, the shame which you
would cast upon the Academy.

" I acknowledge, sir, I am not a little gratified to find that
the Society of British Artists have had the good sense and
spirit to reject your most unwarrantable propositions to that
body. In your application to them, you have not even the
flimsy pretext, which, though so fully exposed, you continue
to put forth as the justification of your attacks upon the
Royal Academy. Your orators cannot threaten *them* with ex-
pulsion, or demand the *seizure* and *distribution of their funds.*
But should your eloquence succeed in overcoming ' the great

difficulties' which you confess to have experienced 'not only from the Academy but also from the Society of British Artists,' you hold out to the latter a most seductive prospect of relief from the damage which you would inflict upon them, in these encouraging terms:

" 'You think it might, *perhaps*, be·necessary *as a matter of justice*, to supply the deficiency which the adoption of your plan would occasion in their funds *by means of a subscription.*'

" In plain English, sir, you would impoverish them first, for the benefit of those whom you are pleased to call the public, and subscribe to them afterwards (*perhaps*) for their own benefit.

" Really, sir, your process of patronage is peculiar and flattering. I do not see how the Society of British Artists can resist your eleemosynary munificence. They must yield at once to the promise of a compensation which is usually found to be so liberal, so *respectable*, and *so effective.*

" Unfortunately, sir, the fine arts have long been paupers in our *nation boutiquière*,—without home or settlement, beyond the sheltering roof of the academic workhouse. Yet I do not find in the extended course of your various public services, that you have ever suggested a poor-law for their protection, or brought forward any other measure for their benefit or advancement. Yet these are matters, sir, not unworthy the attention of a wise statesman.

" The candle-ends and cheese-parings of economical retrenchment may be rescued from the wasteful profusion of the public pantry—the *gold lace may be stripped from the state liveries*, and the length of the ladies' petticoats regulated again, as I believe it has been before, by legislative authority; and yet the national character may be defiled by sensuality, and brutified by intemperance.

" But although you profess to have found out at last that the arts are the only true and effective agents which can be depended on to refine and reform the manners and morals of your population, and although, in your tardy policy of improvement, you would anxiously make use of them for these purposes, yet what generous feeling do you manifest towards those to whom you now look for such important services?

"Instead of increasing their means, you would avowedly diminish them, and stamp on them the character of mendicancy as remuneration.

"You would invade their precincts like an enemy in quest of a contribution; you would tax them in proportion to the services they render you, and make them, without ceremony, the victims of their own utility.

"Verily, sir, I am afraid your name will not be recorded in the page of history as a patron of the fine arts.

"I now come, sir, to the last and least important topic upon which I shall presume to trouble you with a remark,—that which relates personally to myself.

"In one of the speeches to which my attention has been drawn, you are pleased to say that my letter to Lord John Russell was 'neither more nor less than a violent attack' upon the gentlemen who attended the meeting at the Freemasons' Tavern, when that assault upon the Royal Academy took place, which appears so conspicuous in its proceedings, and so offensive in its debates.

"I think, sir, if you had adverted to this assault (which the members of the Academy considered as demanding especial notice), and if you had condescended to read with due attention the letter in question, you would have perceived that you had improperly characterised it. You would have seen that it is not an attack, but a defence,—a remonstrance against unprovoked insult and meditated injury,—a tardy exposure of long continued calumny,—and a calm and correct statement of claims unjustly disputed, and services unacknowledged and ill-requited.

"The members of the Academy, sir, were quietly pursuing their occupations, congratulating each other on their escape from the formidable denunciations of the parliamentary committee on the fine arts—philosophically contemplating the dawn of that bright day which is to arise for them, in the newly-awakened zeal with which their interests are advocated, as — aids to mechanics and manufacturers. We were, in short, sir, disinterestedly, diligently, and without helping hand from patriot or politician, working the only machine by the operation of which you now find you can hope to effect the social improvement you desire — the promotion of the fine arts; when, lo! rumours of wars again reached our ears, — new modes of annoyance, new measures of molestation were concerted against us. Though we could not be conveniently dislodged from our position, we might at least be harassed in our quarters. New levies were accordingly brought into the field; and you, sir, the most experienced leader of your time, were judiciously selected for the command.

"You will recollect, sir, that I did not seek the encounter in which my defensive movement is represented by you as a violent attack. I had not sufficient confidence in my powers to volunteer in such a fray.

"*You* first called to arms, and struck the first blow!

"I did not, sir, obtrude myself on your attention. You did me the honour to demand a parley, in which you detailed your intended operations. I did not hesitate to acknowledge the justice of your principle when applied, under proper regulations, to establishments supported by national funds, and containing objects of national property. But I explained to you, sir, in nearly the words of my letter to Lord John Russell, ' that the Royal Academy was not, in any respect, an establishment which answered to this description; that it had never derived support from any public fund, and that it contained no object of art, or article of property which could in any sense be termed national, or over the use and disposal of which, the public or the Parliament could have any just claim to exercise influence or control.'

"I further explained to you, sir, that for the better accommodation of the arts, and for the advantage of sculpture in particular, we had made an exchange of apartments, and given up a residence provided for us by our royal founder, George III., which, after sixty years' undisputed possession, we had every reason to consider our own.

"In my simplicity, sir, I had flattered myself that by these representations I had made some impression on your mind in favour of an institution, whose integrity malice itself had not dared to asperse, and whose members had devoted nearly three hundred thousand pounds to the promotion of public objects, without making a single inroad on the national purse.

"But I was not aware, sir, how fully the *tenacem propositi virum* of Horace was exemplified in your character. You were inflexible in resolution, and inexorable in hostility; the war-whoop sounded from every quarter; and all the powers of the state were invoked to disturb, at least, if they could not destroy us.

"It cannot be considered surprising, if 'the din of all this smithery' should have aroused in us the slumbering spirit of resistance, and made expostulation take the air of defiance. We feel, sir, that the Royal Academy has some merits to plead, which should secure it from the awkward interference of busy and incompetent meddlers, whose professed good intentions can make no atonement for the disturbance they excite, and the mischief they occasion.

"We object, sir, to be cast in the new mould which your plastic patriotism would prepare for us—we decline to be cut and carved according to the peculiar fashion which your new-born zeal for popular refinement may choose to inflict upon us.

"In expressing these sentiments, sir, I have given way to no violence, and made no attack on gentlemen, to many of whom I have the honour to be known, of whose good intentions I cannot doubt, and in whose views, as far as they relate to institutions maintained at the public expense, I have expressly stated my concurrence. But, I must beg leave to dispute the justice of extending those views to the Royal Academy; and I cannot acquiesce in the propriety of their attempt to invade the interests, and violate the independence of that establishment.

"I regret that those gentlemen should inconsiderately lend their aid to the designs of persons who avow their desire to overthrow the Academy; and I conceive that the tone and spirit which betrayed the true character of its assailants, ought to have prevented all co-operation with them for such a purpose.

"You will excuse me also, sir, if I observe, that your

eloquence would have been more to the point, if, instead of describing my letter as violent or intemperate, you had tried your hand at disproving the facts, and refuting the arguments which it contained.

"You have essayed however to give a political turn to my remarks, which they cannot justly be said to bear, and which it is unnecessary for me to disclaim.    Politics, sir, are high matters in which I have never presumed to interfere.

> 'In moderation placing all my glory,
>   While Tories call me Whig, and Whigs a Tory.'—*Pope.*

"With your politics, sir, whatever they may be, I conceive I have nothing to do; but I must take leave to dispute your taste, and I cannot submit to your authority as a Dictator in the regions of *virtù.*

"I deny your statement that 'I have spoken of *radicalism* as hostile to the arts;' although I have protested against 'the renovation of a royal establishment' by some of those who are said to preach that doctrine.   I do not know, sir, what precise meaning you may attach to the word *radicalism,* or whether you are ambitious of being considered an apostle of its creed. I trouble not myself with what may be its political interpretation; but as to its influence on social life—on all that softens the manners and purifies the enjoyments of man—I do not scruple to avow, that if, as the proverb teacheth, 'The tree is to be known by its fruits,'—from some 'sour specimens produced in your 'unweeded garden,' I should not expect the flowers of taste to flourish under its shade.

"In alluding to the little awkward squad of restless and fretful malcontents, to whom I have taken the liberty of assigning a peculiar position in your *rear,* I never once thought of their principles, moral, political, or religious.   I am quite aware that their desire is not to revolutionise the state, but the arts.   It is not the cabinet they would confound, but the Academy.   They do not want to expel the ministers from Downing Street, but the *monopolists* from Trafalgar Square;— the object of all their hopes, labours, and lucubrations being, to establish a *dilettanti* democracy—an interesting anarchy of Art—

a general topsy-turvy of taste, in which effrontery may flourish, and quackery reign triumphant.

"But you, sir, not only accuse me of traducing *radicalism* as 'hostile to the arts,' but you state that in doing so, I forget that many years ago 'I published an opinion, that the arts flourished more under the *cap* of liberty, than under any *other form* of government.'

"Considering, sir, how difficult you have found it to recollect my *name*, I cannot but feel surprised that you should profess such a lively recollection of my *opinions*,—that you should have burthened your intellectual storehouse, charged as it is with matters of such deep moment to courts and cabinets,

'Where all wise saws and maxims may be found,'

with the remembrance of a trifling production so little congenial with your cast of mind, and so little worthy the attention of a political philosopher of your calibre.

"But to do you justice, sir, I am not so vain as to suppose that the work in question ever gained admission to your library, or that you ever read a line of it; otherwise your respect for yourself, and the place in which you spoke, however regardless you may be of what is due to me, would not have permitted you to hazard so evident a misstatement of the opinions it contained, as that which you have thought proper to advance. Luckily, sir, my powers of recollection are not quite so defective as yours, as you will perceive by the following quotation, from the persual of which it will be found, that availing yourself of one of those resources of argument, to which I understand, you profess to think it, in some cases, allowable to resort, you have maintained that 'black is white,' and ascribed to me opinions the direct reverse of those which I have either published or professed.

"' That the arts flourish only under a free government, is an opinion *not so easy to establish as agreeable to maintain.* The author, as a friend to freedom, would be pleased to find the position confirmed by experience, and would see with pride the cap of liberty exclusively decorated with those attractive ornaments. Unfortunately however, *it does not appear that the*

*brightest eras of taste have been coincident with the purest periods
of freedom, and the splendid days of Pericles and Alexander, of
Augustus, of Leo, and of Louis le Grand, would seem to countenance an opposite doctrine.* The Muses, like most other
ladies, are fond of homage and attention,—they are attracted
by splendour, and conciliated by politeness; and notwithstanding
the warm assurances to the contrary, of some very respectable
poetical and philosophical authorities, it is *not quite* certain, that
in a contest for their favour, they would not *prefer the prince
to the republican.*"[*]

"But lest it should be supposed that the sentiments expressed in a previous publication ('Rhymes on Art,') might
countenance your statement, I beg leave to introduce a passage
from that work:—

> 'What, though in Greece when Ammon's glory swayed,
>   When prostrate Rome Augustus' power obeyed,
>   In latter days, when Leo's lustre shone,
>   And gorgeous Louis graced the Gallic throne ;
>   What, though like rockets from the hand of Time,
>   Through Life's long gloom shot sparkling and sublime,
>   These Meteor Ages of Mankind were given
>   To mark with cluster'd stars the mental heaven,
>   And pour their blaze on earth's astonished view
>   *When Freedom's cloud-encompassed orb withdrew.*
>   Britain, for thee a brighter age expands,
>   Bless'd Rock on which the Church of freedom stands,
>   From whose pure Shrine expelled with Idol power,
>   Anarch's grim Gods a Pagan world devour;
>   Britain, for thee when calmer hours arrive,
>   And our cold year the unsheltered Arts survive,—
>   For thee *remains to prove* what radiant fires
>   Gild the clear Heaven where Liberty inspires.'
>
> *Rhymes on Art, p.* 30.

"I trust, sir, that should you condescend again to notice
the opinions of so humble an individual as I am, you will try
to recollect them more accurately; for misrepresentation,
whether it be the result of negligence or design, must always

---

[*] "Elements of Art."   Canto 2, p. 140.

be considered discreditable to a controversialist, and unworthy of a gentleman.

" In throwing myself thus in the gap to repel your ungenerous assault upon an institution which merits your respect as a patriot, your admiration as an economist, and your gratitude as a man of taste, I am perfectly aware that I become a mark for the arrows of low and vulgar malignity. You have yourself received many shafts from the same quiver; and though I do not for a moment presume to compare my small-ware proceedings with your wholesale and important operations, I may observe, that you, as well as I, have experienced ' that to be busy is some danger,' even when the most disinterested intentions are directed to the most laudable objects.

" At an early period of my progress, with a rashness which is said to be characteristic of my country, I ventured to raise a feeble voice in the cause of the arts, neglected and disregarded as they were,—and in defence of a profession then little favoured by the public or the state. The attempt was surely pardonable, though perhaps presumptuous. But as the follies, the vanities, and the prejudices which chilled the heart of genius, had not been spared—as I ventured to remonstrate against the frivolous pursuits of the wealthy, and the unpatriotic apathy of the great,—as the ignorant critic—the trading connoisseur, and the timid truckling artist met their deserts, —the vain and the venal were aroused to an enmity which has followed me more or less, unappeased even to the present hour.

" Yet age has not brought with it prudence; and after a lapse of seven-and-thirty years since I first broke a lance with the vandalism of the day,—behold! I am again in the field in the same cause.

" I shrink not, sir, from the encounter, even though you come forward as the great Goliah of the fray. As to your allies of the pencil and the pen, I shall only say, *sans façon;*

> ' *Let baffled quacks in rabid rage* "abuse
> My father, mother, body, soul, and muse!"'

" Let them swear 'by all the gods!' that I am a bad

painter, a worse poet, and, to crown all, an academic monopolist! Whatever my claims may be, the censure of such assailants I defy. Their praise indeed, might be fatal; for,—

> 'Of all mad creatures,—if the learn'd are right,—
>  It is the *slaver* kills, and not the bite.'—*Pope.*

"I advocate, sir, no private or personal object. Selfish interests have never prompted my pen; my pencil has never courted the dispensers of patronage or fame, nor have I ever sought to gain by intrigue, what talent could not procure for me. On personal grounds I do not believe I have an enemy; —on such grounds I should grieve to deserve one. But if an unflinching zeal in the cause of the arts,—if an honest ardour in defence of an institution, whose services entitle it to the respect and gratitude of the country, should expose me to the shafts of professional malevolence, the rancour of party, or even the frown of authority, I am ready to abide the consequences and to pay the penalty.

"I have the honour to be, Sir,

"Your obedient Servant,

"MARTIN ARCHER SHEE."

"Cavendish Square, 10th July, 1838."

If, as we have seen, the letter to Lord John Russell created some sensation in the circles of taste, the epistle to Mr. Hume afforded a still more piquant treat, not only to the friends of the Academy and the true patrons of art, but to all who, without bias or prejudice, had watched the progress of the anti-academic agitation, and were capable of appreciating the subject and the persons involved in the controversy.

I must here record the humorous comment passed on it by one who united the clearest head and the soundest judgment, with the most original wit that has graced and enlivened the social annals of this century.

The Rev. Sydney Smith*, in a note to the author, acknowledging the receipt of a copy of the pamphlet in question, says: "I have written on my copy

"Spernit *Humum* fugiente pennâ."

But however the world of art and literature might enjoy the signal triumph of wit and reasoning over humbug and pretension, the publication in question was not calculated to find much favour in the eyes of a ministry to whom it was of vital importance to humour the susceptibilities of so doubtful an adherent, and formidable parliamentary *condottiere* as Mr. Hume; while they were little concerned to rescue the Royal Academy from unjust aspersion, or maintain it in the possession of its existing rights.

It was not without a full appreciation of probabilities, and something of a prophetic spirit that Sir Martin, in the concluding paragraph of the letter, had adverted to "the frowns of authority," as amongst the contingencies to which his fearless advocacy of the academic cause

---

* While recalling the memory of the great "laughing philosopher" of the age, I cannot refrain from placing before the reader another characteristic example of that quaint and peculiar wit for which the immortal Canon of St. Paul's was so distinguished; although the letter in which it occurs has no reference to the subject discussed in the text. It is however, a pleasant and amusing memorial of his intimacy with the late President, and conveys a happy illustration of Mr. Smith's epistolary style. The document will speak for itself. It was no doubt written during the prevalence of some *anti-Puseyite* epidemic.

June 5th, 1843.

"Dear Sir Martin,—In case the rumour should prove true that the Protestant religion is to be abolished, I wish to make interest with you for something in your church—and that we may converse upon these matters, I beg the favour of you to dine with me on Saturday 24th, at a quarter after seven.

"Ever yours,<br>"SYDNEY SMITH."

"Sir M. A. Shee."

might expose him; and it is certain that, from this period, whenever the whig element predominated in the direction of public affairs, he neither . expected nor experienced from the " powers that be," any amount of observance or personal courtesy, which the narrowest estimate of official conventionality could have withheld from the combined claims of his position and his character.

During the summer months of 1838, Sir Martin occupied with his family a small house on Richmond Hill—a locality for the beauties of which he felt all the enthusiasm of a genuine Londoner.  The description of this rural retreat and its advantages, in the subjoined extract from one of his letters to Miss Tunno, is connected with some characteristic traits of thought and feeling which may not, perhaps, be without interest for the reader.

*To Miss Tunno.*

"Richmond, 2nd September, 1838.

.        .        .        .        .        .        .

" You have been *advised* (according to the mercantile phrase) of our removal to Richmond.  We have got a little tenement, under the name of Stanley Cottage, on the hill, just opposite the Star and Garter, the largest room of which is about eight feet square, but with the most beautiful and extensive prospect which this celebrated scene of cockney conviviality affords. Our *domicile* is on so small a scale that the family can barely cram into it.  The exercise of hospitality is quite out of the question, for, as the *residents* sit at dinner, the servant can hardly pass round the table to perform the duties of attendance; and a single guest would embarrass the establishment beyond the power of arrangement, or the hope of elbow-room.  The house, however, is not without an air of respectability; and we have a *lawn* before the door as large as a moderate-sized Turkey carpet, so that our pride is saved while our pleasure is consulted.

We are within a stone's throw of Richmond Park, when we are inclined for a woodland walk, and the Thames may be said to flow at our feet — for we have only to descend for a few yards the slope, in front to reach the river, when our recreations are disposed to take an aquatic direction. You see in what an amiable spirit I am inclined to estimate the blessings I possess. Will you tell me that I am *querulous* and discontented after this manifestation of philosophic enjoyment? In truth, I should be dissatisfaction personified, if I did not partake, in some degree, of the disposition to be pleased which influences on all occasions the little circle in which 'I live and move and have my being.' I do what I can now and then to gloom the domestic horizon. I look out for a black spot in the distance, and spy an approaching storm. But it won't do. I am sure to discover, in some quarter of the heavens, a kindly glow — a gleam of sunshine — to dissipate my clouds and brighten the darkest atmosphere of my moody imagination. The weather has been most favourable to us. I trust you have been equally fortunate, and that you and your fair companions have been able to enjoy it without interruption or drawback. It must be a tempestuous season, indeed, that would interfere with the pleasures of the boys under your roof. I know myself how independent one feels, there, of all atmospheric influences, and can no more doubt of their enjoyment than of my own, in the same situation.

.     .     .     .     .     .     .     .

"I find you have been cultivating *vital* Christianity in the puritanical pages of . . . . . I read a *little* of the book at Taplow Lodge, and quite enough to sicken me of its folly and fanaticism. One might be amused by the weakness of such self-satisfied bigots, if the mirth arising from their absurdities were not checked by the indignant feelings excited by their presumption, and the arrogant tone in which they at once condemn and commiserate the. *small* portion of their fellow-creatures, who refuse to wrap themselves up in the same cloak of sanctimonious security."

Another letter, written from the same locality, in the course of the same month, contains some rather amusing details of an official visit to Windsor. The reader will see that, on some occasions, it required the exercise of a little diplomacy, and the exhibition of a little firmness, on the part of the President, to retain and assert the academic privilege so graciously conceded by the Queen; the enjoyment of which was somewhat grudged to that body by high ministerial susceptibilities.

*To Miss Tunno,*

"Richmond Hill, 20th Sept. 1838.

"MY DEAR MISS TUNNO,— What do you think of our *rencontre* on Tuesday? Like a lightning flash the (to me) most agreeable of all aspects, appeared and vanished. I have not yet recovered the vexation, mortification, and even *shame* of suffering such an opportunity of exchanging a few words with you to be lost. But we passed each other with such a railroad rapidity, that before I could get down one of the glasses (for, as you will readily believe, they were *all up*), and make a deaf post-boy hear, your carriage was out of sight; and as I took it for granted you were on the wing for the review, I thought it hardly fair, for my gratification, to detain you, as the proceedings were about to commence when I left the Castle, and the delay might prevent your obtaining a favourable position for observation, as crowds were collecting from all quarters. After all, this is making out but a bad case; and I feel that I ought not to have suffered you to escape me, but should have tried *a race with Cole* [Miss Tunno's coachman], even though I might be indicted for endangering the lives of her Majesty's lieges on the highway. You will conclude that I was at Windsor *on business*, and will naturally wonder that I should have chosen so bustling a day for my visit, when it was so little likely the Queen would be at leisure to receive me. The fact is, that being out of town, and not attending to the Windsor news, I had made my arrangements before I was aware of the proceedings that were about to take place. The position in which I found myself on the occasion was rather curious, and somewhat embarrassing; as I shall explain, knowing, as I do, that *state affairs* are always *safe* with you. I believe you are aware that the Queen, notwithstanding *much reluctance* evident on the part of the ministers, agreed to allow the President of the Academy the same direct access to her which her predecessors had always granted to the Academy; and in accordance with this privilege I had, through the medium of Sir Henry Wheatley (privy purse) an audience of her Majesty on academic affairs. As it was necessary to obtain the royal sanction and signature to the diplomas of the four lately elected members, to enable them to vote at the election, in November, of associates,—and as I was anxious to effect this object before the Queen went to Brighton, I wrote to the Baroness Lehzen (Sir Henry Wheatley being absent in Yorkshire); with whom I had some acquaintance, and whom I knew to be in high favour at court, to procure me the interview with the Queen which I desired. I adopted this course, though I feared the baroness would probably wish to avoid the responsibility of allowing herself to be made a medium of communication on the occasion; but I was anxious to keep clear of the minister, who, I knew, would immediately offer, *most kindly*, to get my papers signed without any *trouble on my part*. On Tuesday, accordingly, I took my letter and the documents to Windsor, and sent it with my card to the baroness. After waiting for a short time, I was told the baroness was engaged with the Queen; but my letter should be delivered to her the moment she was at liberty to receive it. In the meantime we were offered refreshments, and informed that luncheon would be ready for me at one o'clock. In a few minutes, however, a page came to inform me that Lord Melbourne would be glad to see me in his room. I found his lordship with a paper in his hand, which I immediately recognised as *my letter open*. He asked me if I wished to get her Majesty's signature to any of my papers, and said that he was then immediately going to the Queen, and would get them signed without occasioning me any further delay. He seemed somewhat *dry* in his manner, as if not quite pleased. I told him that I had written to the baroness, of which he said he was aware, as she had sent him the letter, of which I was also aware, as I saw it in his hand; but I wished him to understand that I had no desire to conceal that I

had done so.   I expressed myself much obliged by his kindness, but as the privilege accorded to the Academy, of immediate access to the sovereign, was a great honour, and highly valued by that body, it would be a breach of duty on my part, to waive it on any occasion, or on any authority short of her Majesty's command.   He inquired if I had yet seen the Queen on any academic business.   On being answered in the affirmative, and [informed] that the privilege in question had been granted, by express command of her Majesty, in an official communication from Lord John Russell, he agreed to inform her Majesty that I was in attendance, and let me know the result.   In about half an hour, he came forth from the royal presence, and gratified me by a communication which I certainly did not *then* expect, that the Queen would receive me almost immediately.   The baroness, who also appeared, apologised for not having sent me an answer, and said she sent the letter to Lord Melbourne, as the person who could best obtain for me the interview I required. In a few moments a page came to usher us into the presence of the Queen, whom we found attended by a tall lady in waiting (I believe Lady Portman).   I never saw her Majesty look so well.   She was very gracious, signed the diplomas, and withdrew to prepare for the review.   Delighted to get my business so well over, I declined taking luncheon, turned my back upon the gay scene, though the military were all assembled in the Little Park, and set off for Richmond without delay.   Among documents which I had to submit to the Queen, was an address from the Academy, soliciting her Majesty to sit to *their President* for a whole length, to be placed in the Academy with the portraits of her predecessors, to which she has assented.   .        .
.      .      .      .      I hope that both you and your fair companions have derived health and pleasure from your excursion ; and though I myself could live between the wainscot and the wall through the year, like a house rat, I am convinced that change of air and scene is as salubrious as agreeable.   In accordance with this doctrine, I am about to make a visit of a few days to Sir Robert Peel, at Drayton Manor."

Sir Martin's contemplated visit to the illustrious

statesman mentioned in the concluding paragraph of
the preceding extract, took place accordingly in the
course of the ensuing week.   The circle whom he found
assembled at Drayton Manor included some of the most
conspicuous politicians of the conservative party, to
whom his recent passage of arms with the formidable
champion of economic radicalism and utilitarian *virtù*
did not, to say the least of it, render his appearance
less welcome, among the guests of the great opposition
leader.   A question addressed to him at dinner, on the
day of his arrival, with laudable gravity, by his distinguished host, to the following effect: "Sir Martin,
did you bring Mr. Hume down with you in the train
to Birmingham?" was no doubt productive of much
hilarity among the listeners, who had but recently
chuckled with intense enjoyment over the lesson administered to that gentleman, in his newly-assumed
character of a *dilettante*, by the caustic pen of the
President.   But what renders this visit of Sir Martin
to Drayton chiefly memorable is the fact that he there
and then first became acquainted with an eminent contemporary, whose public career he had long watched
with admiring interest, and whose social character
and intellectual attainments he ever after held in the
highest estimation:—one whose short but brilliant
career exhibited the most signal triumphs of forensic
and parliamentary talent; and who, had he not been
prematurely cut off in the zenith of his fame, and the full
development of his rare mental powers, would have,
doubtless, adorned and dignified the bench, as he had
graced the bar and charmed the senate; while, according
to all human probability, his acute judgment, clear and
comprehensive views, and persuasive eloquence, would
have ultimately placed him in the foremost category of

political success, and commanded the most coveted distinctions of ministerial or diplomatic ambition.

With the world at large, the memory of the brightest genius, displayed and chiefly restricted within the bounds of an active professional career, is sadly, and, if I may be allowed the term, impressively transient. But to many who witnessed his success in the House, and to all who had the opportunity of observing, and the means of appreciating his varied forensic abilities, it will be superfluous to add to the above description, the honoured and lamented name of Sir William Follett.

# CHAPTER XVI.

## 1839.

Formidable Parliamentary Attack on the Royal Academy. — Motion of Mr. Hume, and Order of the House of Commons, for Returns of the Receipts and Expenditure of the Academy. — The Academy resolve to refuse obedience to the Order. — Petition of the Royal Academy to the House of Commons. — Embarrassment of the Ministry. — Their ineffectual Attempts to alter the Purpose of the Academy. — The "Count-out." — The Debate on the Motion. — Victory of the Academy.

THE year 1839 was a memorable one in the annals of the Royal Academy. In that year they were destined to encounter and repel a parliamentary attack, which, if successful would have been fraught with consequences fatal to their independence, and destructive of their most valued privileges. For the courage which prompted, and the skill which conducted to a triumphant issue, their fearless resistance to the formidable power of the House of Commons, they were mainly indebted to the firmness, energy, and talent of their President. Cordially and frankly, indeed, was he supported throughout every stage of the crisis, by the approving confidence of his academic brethren. But ready as they were to adopt, at his suggestion, the intrepid course dictated by a wise and courageous foresight, such vigorous counsels could never have prevailed, or been attended with so gratifying a result, had one less determined in spirit, or less energetic and judicious in action presided, over their deliberations.

The time seemed well chosen for an assault on the academic fortress.  The feeling of envious discontent, so natural to those who, conceiving themselves entitled by transcendent merit to the highest honours of the Academy, saw no immediate prospect of attaining their wishes, was still industriously fostered by the small band of ultra-Liberal politicians who espoused their cause in the House; while the aspect of the court and the position of the ministry afforded encouragement to the malcontents, and led to the most sanguine expectations of success, in their meditated onslaught on what they loved to describe as the stronghold of an injurious monopoly.

" The King's name," according to the words of inspired wisdom, " is a tower of strength;" and during the reign of William IV., the Royal Academy and those who were most actively engaged in directing its councils had practical experience of the truth of that venerable axiom.  Viewing the institution itself with a kind of affectionate partiality, as the creation of his royal father, and entertaining towards its existing head a feeling of strong personal regard and esteem, the King could be fully relied on for effective countenance and unhesitating support against the assailants of the Academy, on all occasions when the rights and privileges guaranteed to the body by their august founder, were the objects of attack.  While insisting emphatically on their peculiar character as emanating from the royal will, and absolutely dependent for their collective existence and powers of action, on the personal pleasure of the Sovereign, the Academy well knew that his Majesty fully acquiesced in the practical results of this honourable though somewhat anomalous position, and for his own satisfaction, as well as in their interest, would protect them in the enjoyment of every advantage and immunity involved in this state of privileged dependence.

So long as the affairs of the Academy remained on this satisfactory footing with regard to the Sovereign, and the personal favour of his Majesty afforded the President frequent opportunities of unreserved communication with their royal patron on all questions affecting the interests of the institution, the absence of ministerial support against their parliamentary assailants, and the perfect readiness of individual members of the Government to sacrifice the Academy on the altar of radical popularity, were matters of little account in the estimation of those who were most zealous for the maintenance of its existing position.

But the death of King William IV. had materially altered the aspect of affairs, and deprived the Academy of a vantage-ground in the contest, which they had little prospect of regaining. Not, indeed, that their theoretic relations with the Crown were ostensibly disturbed; for, as we have already seen, his Majesty's august successor had, at the earliest period when her royal pleasure could be taken on the subject, honoured the President by the gracious assurance that the peculiar privilege of personal access to the Sovereign enjoyed by the official representatives of the Academy, in conformity with the original laws of the institution, should be continued to them during the present reign. But it could not be expected that, under existing circumstances, the communications of the Academy with the Crown should exceed the limits prescribed by the strict letter of courtly *étiquette* and official routine. The personal interest taken by King William IV. in the concerns of the Academy, and his gracious condescension in allow-

ing to the President those extra-official opportunities
for the free expression of opinion in relation to its affairs,
which Sir Martin so frequently enjoyed, were advantages
extraneous to the theory of academic privilege, and inconsistent with the altered circumstances of the Court,
in its social, if not in its constitutional character.

The change of reign had necessarily been attended
with a corresponding change of persons in the royal
*entourage.* The Court of King William, consisting as
it did of the united households of his Majesty and Queen
Adelaide, though like all courts, reflecting with tolerable
fidelity the tendencies of the royal mind and will, was,
during the latter years of his Majesty's reign, but little
influenced by the prevalent tone of ministerial society.
The majority of the courtly functionaries in permanent
attendance on the King were indebted for their appointments to the personal friendship or esteem of the Sovereign; while, in the case of those whose advancement
could be traced to ministerial favour, their official
gratitude was due not to the existing, but to a long
defunct ministry. On the other hand, all the high
personages composing the household of the Queen Con-
sort, from the Lord Chamberlain and the Master of the
House downwards, held their places at the will and
pleasure of her Majesty; whose royal discretion in these
matters was not, either upon constitutional principles
or by prescriptive custom, necessarily controlled by
ministerial predilections, or affected in its exercise by
the fluctuations of party.

The result was that the ordinary social and political
atmosphere of Windsor Castle and the Pavilion, during
the greater part of King William's reign, exhibited anything but a sympathetic acquiescence in the views of
the Cabinet for the time being; and as far as the in-

fluence of prevalent feelings could affect the tone of the royal mind, that influence was probably obstructive of the personal wishes of the minister, on many points of minor importance which, although not of the essence of his ministerial supremacy, he would gladly have presented to the royal judgment as affected by considerations of political expediency and parliamentary success.

In the court circle of those days, Sir Martin could reckon many warm friends and admirers; while to all he was an object of personal esteem and good will; ever experiencing, on his visits to Windsor and Brighton, an attentive courtesy and cordial welcome from those in attendance on their Majesties, that effectually softened the restraints and annoyances of *étiquette*, and practically neutralised all that was theoretically irksome in courtly duties.

The favourable dispositions evinced by his Majesty towards the Royal Academy and its head, were therefore not likely to be injuriously affected by the opinions of those who formed the ordinary society of the palace; and as far as the interests of the body were supposed to be identified with the personal and official claims of the President to a large measure of respect and consideration, it is probable that no attempt of the party of " progress " or " movement " to curtail the power or diminish the *prestige* of the Royal Academy, could have recommended itself to the approval of the Court.

These times had, however, now gone by.  A new set of actors filled the scene; and, as a necessary consequence of the youth and sex of the Sovereign, the ministerial element was triumphantly predominant in all the stately and courtly arrangements of the new reign.

The opponents of the Academy had now, therefore,

every reasonable assurance, that if their plans could be so shaped and matured as to secure the active co-operation, or even the passive acquiescence of the Government, they would encounter no formidable obstacle in the views and feelings of the Court; nor could they anticipate the existence, at any future period, of a state of affairs more propitious to their designs of academic subversion, as far as the *personnel* of the ministry and the intellectual characteristics of their chief were concerned.

Great as were the mental powers of Lord Melbourne, and high as he deservedly ranked as an able parliamentary debater, a skilful political leader, and an accomplished man of the world, — his *insouciance* with regard to all matters of public concern not directly affecting the higher interests of the state, or tending to modify the relative position of the contending parties in the daily strife for power, was all but a proverbial peculiarity. This *poco-curante* spirit, — co-existing as it did with a cultivated intellect and social qualifications that disarmed political hostility, and conciliated the regard of all who came within the range of his personal influence,—was naturally viewed in the most indulgent light by his numerous friends and admirers; and if sometimes a theme of jocular sarcasm, was seldom the object of grave censorious comment. It mattered little, however, to the class of interests which he thus dis‑regarded, that his neglect was ascribable to other causes than general want of enlightenment, or defective perceptions in matters of taste. The result was practically the same. He would probably not have professed, with King George II., to "hate *boetry* and *bainting;*" nor would he, like the great Lord Kenyon, have taken the superficial dimensions of a picture as the criterion of its comparative value. But of practical sympathy with the interests of art, science, or literature, he was as guiltless as the august monarch and the learned judge whose eccentricities of view, in such matters, are so happily illustrated by the well-known traditional anecdotes to which I have alluded.

That Lord Melbourne, or any other leading statesman, should formally originate, or actively promote, any plan for the parliamentary suppression of the Royal Academy, was, perhaps, more than the most sanguine among the assailants of the body ventured to anticipate. But there seemed good grounds for hoping that the fate of any hostile motion to be made in the House of Commons, at the suggestion of the anti-academic party, would, at all events, be left to the uncontrolled discretion or caprice of the House, without any real attempt on the part of the minister to influence their votes on the occasion; even though the proceeding, as one avowedly directed against an institution under the especial protection of the Crown, might be thought to require some faint show of opposition from the Treasury Bench.

At the period in question, the two great parties, Liberal and Conservative, were so nicely balanced in the House, that it was of the highest importance to the minister to keep in good humour the extreme radical section of that assembly, by playing into their hands on all occasions where no broad party principle was at stake. The most determined enemies of the Academy were, as we have seen, among the leaders of this section; and it may be fairly presumed that the sarcastic severity and open defiance with which the pretensions and efforts of their Coryphæus had been treated in the " Letter to Joseph Hume, Esq., M.P.," had not much tended to mitigate the unreasoning hostility of these " *Connoisseurs sans connaissance.*"

The Academy had, under the circumstances already detailed, afforded to the Committee on the State of the Fine Arts, and to the House at large, all the information respecting the laws, internal arrangements, and practical working of the institution, which the most active spirit of parliamentary inquiry could reasonably desire.  In doing so, however, they had, as the reader will recollect, carefully and successfully guarded themselves from any recognition of the right of interference in their concerns, which a section of the House, at the instigation of the " high art " fraternity, were solicitous to assert;—supplying the returns sought for by Mr. Ewart's motion,— not in compliance with any order of the House,—but in obedience to the will, or rather by virtue of the personal sanction of their royal patron.   The returns in question were not, as the reader will bear in mind, furnished until the pleasure of his Majesty had been formally taken on the subject; and they were then transmitted, not directly to the authorities of the House of Commons, but to the Principal Secretary of State for the Home Department, to be by him communicated, if he should see fit, to that august assembly.

It appears, from the letter to Mr. Hume, that some further information, in answer to an application from that gentleman, made to the Academy through Lord John Russell, had been furnished through the same high official channel, in the autumn of 1837.   These returns were, no doubt, also applied for with a view to parliamentary discussion on academic matters; but in this, as in the former instances, the Academy had kept clear of all direct communication with the House, and acted ostensibly in the exercise of a discretion, controlled and controllable by the royal will alone.   It was, therefore, not without laying himself open, in some degree, to the charge of disingenuousness, which Sir Robert Peel, in the course of the subsequent debate, — when the Academy successfully tried their strength against their parliamentary assailants,— more than insinuated against the honourable member, that Mr. Hume, in the month of March 1839, in giving notice of a motion for certain returns from the Royal Academy, appended to that notice some words intimating that the information sought for was *in continuation of former returns.*

This notice of motion must, I presume, have appeared among the Orders of the Day, in the columns of the daily papers; but it had, no doubt, escaped the observation of the academic authorities; for it appears that when the motion was made by Mr. Hume, in pursuance of his notice, at half-past one in the morning of the 15th of March, 1839, the parliamentary friends of the Academy were not on the alert to resist or question it;— and the House, probably reduced to a very small and very drowsy remnant of its members, at that late hour of the sitting, treated the proceeding as a matter of course, and made the order without discussion.   According to the statement of Sir Robert Peel, as found in the report of the debate above referred to: " The order was moved for and procured at half-past one in the morning, when the attention of honourable members was not much called upon—and when, if it had been, their jealousy would have been entirely lulled by the words which the honourable member for Kilkenny appended to his notice."   Sir Robert goes on to say that, " the honourable member for Kilkenny,— not, perhaps, with any disingenuous intention, although a more apparently disingenuous appendix to a motion he (Sir R. Peel) had never seen—had led honourable members and the House astray."

The returns called for by the order were as follows, viz. : —

" A return of the amount of money received for admission, and of the number of persons who visited the exhibition of the Royal Academy of Arts in each of the years 1836, 1837, and 1838 ; distinguishing the entrance money from the proceeds of the sale of catalogues, together with the amount paid in salaries and perquisites to each person employed in that establishment in each of those years ; also the miscellaneous expenses under separate heads in each of those years; and the average number of students who have attended the Life School, and that of the Antique, in each of those years."

This, it will be perceived, was the first direct practical assertion, on the part of the House, of its authority to investigate the concerns, and inspect the accounts of the Royal Academy.   To have yielded obedience to the order in question, would, in the eyes of the President, have been to concede the whole principle on which they had so strenuously insisted, and acquiesce in that responsibility to the House of Commons, which they had never ceased to deny and repudiate.   The object of the proceeding was manifestly the enforcement of this responsibility, and the establishment of a precedent which should authorise and inaugurate a course of vexatious and frivolous interference with the affairs of the institution, on the part of the House, at the instigation of the few members of that assembly who were bent on promoting the hostile views of the anti-academic coterie.

The order having been formally notified to the Academy, that body did not hesitate long as to the course to be pursued on the occasion.   The manly and spirited view which the President took of their position and duty, in reference to this embarrassing crisis of their affairs, had only to be developed with his usual clearness, and urged with his accustomed force of argument, to command the ready and cordial assent of his colleagues, who had the most unbounded reliance on his judgment and discretion, and a well-grounded confidence in his power of defeating this fresh *manœuvre* of their enraged and hitherto baffled opponents.

The Academy resolved that, — COME WHAT MIGHT, THEY WOULD DISREGARD THE ORDER, AND WITHHOLD THE RETURNS.   It was decided that they should take no step implying any recognition on their part of the proceeding of the House, until after the lapse of the usual period within which, in the ordinary course of parliamentary matters, returns so ordered are expected to be forthcoming; when, according to the precedents by which they were guided on the occasion, they had reason to believe that the order would be reiterated in a more peremptory form.

The result was in accordance with their expectations. In due course of time they received a fresh notification of the order, which, under the circumstances, could not be deliberately disobeyed, without risk of calling down the formidable vengeance of the House on the body at large, or at any rate, on those who, in public estimation, represented its collective existence, and were responsible for the management of its affairs.

To the President, however, who was the strenuous adviser, and would probably be the victim of this unusual contumacy, the prospect of the worst consequences which the wrath of exasperated radicalism,—reinforced by the Speaker's mace and the small-sword of the Serjeant-at-Arms,—could inflict on him personally, had but few terrors.   The session was now so far advanced that the most flagrant breach of privilege, or contempt of the House, could not be visited, even in the case of obdurate impenitence, with more than a few weeks compulsory residence in Newgate. But though perfectly willing to encounter, if necessary, the dread ordeal of a summons to the bar of the House, and the subsequent committal which might probably ensue, on his avowing his personal responsibility for the act complained of, — Sir Martin was careful to shape the academic course so as to afford the House an opportunity of gracefully retreating from a step, which they could hardly follow up without exposing themselves to the ridicule of the country, in an unseemly and perhaps, after all, an unsuccessful contest.

The course suggested by the President, and willingly adopted by the Academy, was admirably calculated to effect this object; while it raised the anger of Mr. Hume and his friends to the highest pitch of exasperation, and caused some embarrassment to the Government, whose conduct throughout the affair, if not prompted to some extent by an unavowed sympathy in the views of the assailing party, would be fairly open to the charge of pusillanimity.

The Academy determined on addressing the House, by a petition of the whole body, which should explain in the fullest manner the peculiar nature of their constitution and functions, assert their exclusive dependence on the personal pleasure of the Sovereign,—appeal confidently to the history of their unintermitting exertions and acknowledged services in the cause of the arts, as affording a sufficient reason for their being allowed to continue in the management of their own concerns unmolested by parliamentary interference,—and conclude with a respectful request that the House would be pleased to rescind the order for the returns in question.

The preparation of so important a document was, as the reader will readily surmise, mainly entrusted to the President; and those who are familiar with the peculiar characteristics of his style, cannot fail to recognise his clear, vigorous, and eloquent pen in the most important and effective portions of this able defence of the institution over which he presided. Although it contains some statements and arguments, couched in language nearly identical with that which Sir Martin had employed on other occasions,—when coming forward as the champion of the Academy, under circumstances already brought to the notice of the reader,—I do not feel myself at liberty to omit any portion of this remarkable and dignified remonstrance, the effect of which would be materially injured by curtailment; nor without the aid of its perusal *in extenso* is it easy to appreciate, in all its bearings, the position and proceedings of the Academy at this momentous crisis of their affairs.

*The humble Petition of the President, Council, and Academicians of the Royal Academy.*

" Your petitioners beg leave to approach your Honourable House with the profound respect and reverence which are due to so important a branch of the Imperial Legislature.

" Actuated by those feelings which it is alike their duty and their desire to cherish, your petitioners have with regret to acknowledge the receipt of an order of your Honourable House requiring ' a return of the amount of money received for admission, and of the number of persons who visited the Royal Academy of Arts in each of the years 1836, 1837, and 1838, distinguishing the entrance money from the proceeds by the sale of catalogues; together with the amount paid in salaries and perquisites to each person employed in that establishment in each of those years; also, the miscellaneous expenses, under separate heads, in each of those years; and the average number of students who have attended the Life School, and that of the Antique, in each of those years.'

"Although the integrity and disinterestedness with which the affairs of the Royal Academy have been invariably conducted preclude all motive or desire for concealment, yet your petitioners humbly conceive, that the position of the Royal Academy, with respect to its funds and the sources from which they are derived, is such as should exempt its pecuniary arrangements from compulsory inspection, or the interference of an authority which might possibly, by artful means, be unduly obtained and vexatiously exercised; and the employment of which, unless absolutely necessary for some great public object, could not fail to be annoying to the Academy.

" Under this impression, and as the existing guardians of an institution which they are anxious to transmit, unimpaired in honour and independence, to those who may succeed them in its direction, your petitioners feel imperatively called on to submit most respectfully to your Honourable House the following considerations ; confident, that if the circumstances to which they refer had been previously brought under the notice of your Honourable House, they would have had sufficient influence on your liberality to prevent the issue of the order in question.

" If, in the performance of this duty, your petitioners should be betrayed, either in matter or expression, into any irregularity inconsistent with the forms proper to be observed in addressing your Honourable House, they trust it may be regarded with that liberal indulgence which you have always manifested towards unintentional error and involuntary offence.

" The plan of the Royal Academy was conceived and matured by artists, not more for their own advantage, than to promote the interests and honour of their country.  It was submitted by Sir William Chambers, and other eminent artists his contemporaries, to the judgment of George III.  That monarch, to whose zealous patronage of the arts justice has never yet been rendered, immediately perceived the importance of the object they had in view, and at once constituted the society they proposed to form, a Royal Institution, under his own immediate protection.  He assigned to it apartments in his own palace, was graciously pleased to allow to its President and principal officers the privilege of direct access to the royal presence on all matters relating to its interests; and, for the first seven years of its existence, generously supplied its deficient means, to the extent of five thousand pounds, from his privy purse. The growing attraction, however, of their labours in the exhibition, soon enabled the members of the Royal Academy to relieve their royal benefactor from this burthen, and to sustain the establishment by their own exertions.

"When the hereditary property of the crown was, by a new arrangement, transferred to the nation, the sovereign, with a liberal solicitude for the interest of his Academy, expressly stipulated that an appropriate residence should be provided for it, in the newly-erected building of Somerset House. Apartments were accordingly so appropriated there, and formally surrendered to the Academy, whose members retained undisturbed and undisputed possession of them, for nearly sixty years. Circumstances, however, having occurred which afforded a favourable opportunity of procuring a more convenient habitation for the arts, by the transfer of the establishment to Trafalgar Square, an arrangement for that purpose was agreed to, under the sanction of the late King, William IV., and with the liberal assistance of Earl Grey, then prime minister. In consequence of this arrangement, your petitioners were induced to relinquish the apartments in Somerset House, to which long occupancy and long service had given them a moral, if not a legal right, in exchange for those which form the present abode of the Royal Academy. It is proper to observe here to your Honourable House, that this exchange, though anxiously desired for the advantage of the arts, was not carried into effect by the Academy, without the fullest and most unequivocal assurances that they were to be placed in the new building precisely on the same footing as in the old, and that their liabilities, local or personal, were not to be in any respect altered or affected by the change.

"If your petitioners had conceived that by their removal they should incur any new obligation — if they had supposed that they should be rendered amenable to any new authority, or subjected to any other responsibility, save that which they owed to their sovereign,— from whose gracious hand the President of the Academy received the keys of the building they now occupy, — they could not have hesitated a moment to decline any advantage or accommodation that was to be purchased at such a price.

" But whatever may be their pretensions, legal, moral, or equitable, to the undisturbed occupancy of their present habitation, your petitioners readily admit that their best title is the use they make of it — the purpose to which it is applied.  If your petitioners cannot hold it by this tenure, they desire not to advance any other claim.  How far the Royal Academy has fulfilled the covenants implied under a lease of this kind, they now respectfully submit to the decision of your Honourable House.

" The members of the Royal Academy have zealously supported, for two-thirds of a century, the only regular, effective, or national school of art in this kingdom, comprising separate accommodations for the study of the antique, the living model, and the works of the old masters in the school of painting; all under the superintendence of the ablest professors.

" They have instituted professorships for gratuitous lectures in painting, sculpture, architecture, perspective and anatomy.

" They have established an annual exhibition, to which all artists, without distinction, are allowed to send their works.

" They have instituted prizes in the different schools, to stimulate the industry and excite the emulation of the students.

" They have accumulated a valuable collection of casts, prints, and books, and provided every material and means of study necessary or expedient for the cultivation of the pursuits of taste.

" They have gratuitously educated according to the best principles of the art, nearly two thousand students, the most promising of whom have been enabled to pursue their studies in the schools of Italy, at the expense of the Royal Academy, and the least successful of whom have been instructed in those acquirements which might qualify them to become useful agents of manufacturing and mechanical improvement.

" Your petitioners might enlarge much further on this topic, and trace the useful agency of the Academy through all its beneficial results; but they would humbly represent to your Honourable House, that they have already stated such public services as may be reasonably considered of some account in sustaining the character of a people for civilisation and refinement.

" Your petitioners would respectfully observe, that public services of this nature have been deemed so important in the estimation of all other enlightened communities, as to have been anxiously provided for at the expense of the state.

" These services have been rendered to their country by the members of the Royal Academy, at the sacrifice of nearly three hundred thousand pounds, derived from the joint labours of artists, and disinterestedly devoted by them to the promotion of national objects, while they were themselves uncheered by national encouragement, or any stimulating hope of national reward.

" In thus sustaining the interests of the fine arts, and upholding, at their own expense, for the greater part of a century, an institution which they had just grounds to expect would have been maintained *for* them rather than *by* them, your petitioners humbly conceive that British artists have established some claim to public consideration, and that the career of the Royal Academy presents a case unexampled in the history of the arts, in any other age or country.

" The reflection will not fail to occur here to your Honourable House, that if the time and talents thus employed by the members of the Academy in support of important national objects, had been devoted to the promotion of their own personal and private interests, according to the practice of other societies of art established in the metropolis, they would have produced no inconsiderable addition to the emoluments of the least lucrative, the least mercenary, and the least favoured profession to which ambition or industry can be directed in modern times.

" In the mode in which the large sums thus expended by the Academy have been appropriated to the different agents employed in its management, a congenial spirit of disinterestedness has prevailed. The art, not the artist, has been considered. The establishment has not been allowed to swallow up the means which were intended for the promotion of its object. The most ordinary duties of the institution could not be adequately executed for the remuneration attached to them, if zeal in the cause did not prompt those exertions, which a calculating self-interest would certainly refuse, unless tempted by a more liberal reward.

" The office of President is without emolument — a post of honour, and, as such, a source of expense to the holder, both in time and means, which no ordinary professional income can sustain without serious inconvenience.

"The Keeper and Secretary, the principal officers on whom the working of the institution depends, and who are obliged to devote almost their whole time to the duties of their different stations, could not, on their respective salaries, maintain the humblest rank of respectable artists, without resorting to the aid of their professional exertions.

" Even in the ministrations of humanity towards their distressed brethren, and the less fortunate members of their own body, the Academy, anxious not to cripple the means of promoting their primary object, — the interests of their art, — have apportioned their benevolence with a sparing hand ; and the unhappy victims of taste who in their hour of need resort for assistance to those funds which they have contributed to create, find in their academic resources, not an asylum of repose after a life of toil, not a security for comfort in declining age, but merely a refuge from actual destitution.

" The portion, however, of their means thus employed, scanty as is the provision which it affords, has been hallowed by its application.

" From a fund thus restricted, the necessities of many claimants have been relieved, whose talents entitled them to expect a more prosperous fortune.

" To the Royal Academy was Wilson indebted for support in his declining years ; and the widows of Hogarth and Woollett have found succour from the same source, under difficulties from which, if genius have any claim to public consideration or reward, the merits of these eminent men should have enabled them to secure such dear connections.

" What may be the just claims of a body of artists who have thus acted it is not, perhaps, for your petitioners to say ; but they trust your honourable House will not consider that they have formed a very presumptuous estimate of the deserts of the Royal Academy when they assume, that if they are not entitled to praise, they might at least expect to escape reprobation.

"Yet has the Royal Academy been the object of incessant attacks, not only from those who may be supposed to be influenced by feelings of personal or professional disappointment, but also from quarters to which they might have reasonably looked for the exercise of a calm and dispassionate judgment on their proceedings. Even your honourable House has witnessed a severity of animadversion upon the character and conduct of the Royal Academy, which only the most unequivocal and well-ascertained evidence of delinquency can be supposed to excite or justify.

"But it was on the transfer of the Academy to its present abode, that the hostility against it appeared to assume a systematic character.

"The most strenuous exertions had been used to obstruct the projected removal of the Academy; and when the hope of effecting that object failed, the measure, which could not be prevented, was itself converted into a new and more effectual engine of molestation.

"Although, as has been already stated to your honourable House, the Royal Academy had for a period of sixty years possessed a residence, erected, like that in which they are now placed, at the public expense, and although, during that long period, no guardian of the public interests had considered himself entitled to disturb their arrangements, or to investigate their affairs, yet were your petitioners now told, in a tone of authority, that they must not hope to be longer indulged with similar forbearance; that, as they were allowed to occupy a portion of a public edifice, they must submit their concerns to public scrutiny, and conduct all their proceedings according to the good pleasure, and under the *surveillance* of persons who would represent themselves to your honourable House as assertors of the public rights.

"To follow up these denunciations, mis-statements the most

gross and absurd were industriously circulated, as to the institution and its members.

" Public meetings resounded with angry declamations against academic monopoly and corporate exclusion. If your petitioners had been defaulters, convicted of applying the public money to private purposes, instead of spending their own for the public benefit, they could not have been followed by a louder hue and cry of condemnation. It was even proposed, that the funds of the Academy should be seized and distributed in a general scramble among the other societies of art, and the doors of our exhibition rooms were to be forced open for the promiscuous admission of the populace. Committees were formed, petitions to the sovereign and the Legislature presented, and various returns demanded from the Academy in the name of your honourable House.

" On the first application of this kind, although somewhat surprised at such a requisition, in the case of an institution which depends upon its own resources, and which has never either sought for or received assistance from any public fund, yet your petitioners did not hesitate to solicit the permission of their late royal patron and protector, King William the Fourth, to supply all the information then required.

" In this proceeding your petitioners were actuated by a desire to mark their respect for your honourable House, and at the same time, to take the opportunity of laying before the Parliament and the public, such an authentic statement respecting the constitution and laws of the Royal Academy as would enable them fully to understand the nature, the objects, and the operation of that institution.

" This information, in the most ample details, has been supplied by the Academy in various returns, furnished to the Secretary of State for the Home Department, for the purpose of being laid before your honourable House, and also, in the copious evidence given by the president and officers of the Academy before the Parliamentary Committee on the Fine Arts. By these means, the institution, through all its functions, educational and financial, has been unreservedly laid open to general inspection, and submitted to an investigation as rigorous as the most active spirit of scrutiny could devise or direct.

" Having thus afforded every elucidation which can be considered necessary for any useful purpose, or which ought to be required to satisfy the most searching curiosity, your petitioners respectfully submit to your honourable House, whether they can be justly called upon, by farther acquiescence, to allow of an interference in the concerns of the Royal Academy, inconsistent with the character of an institution which rests upon its own resources, and is responsible only to the gracious sovereign from whom it derives its honours and its name,—whether your petitioners can be justly required to submit to an interference which claims to examine into the minutest details of an expenditure, which they who do not contribute to supply, cannot reasonably desire to control,— an interference also which, in its operation, could not fail to be injurious to the arts, by disturbing the tranquil exercise of those duties which the Royal Academy was constituted to perform.

" In humbly submitting to your honourable House these statements, your petitioners beg leave to observe, that they have not voluntarily obtruded themselves or their concerns on your attention. Your petitioners have been called forth from the studious retirement of their pursuits and habits, to remove unjust aspersions, and repel unprovoked aggression. Actuated by no selfish motives, having no personal interest to promote, your petitioners approach your honourable House with the just confidence of men who conceive that in their humble sphere they have done some service to their country. On their own account, your petitioners have nothing to desire; they solicit no favour, no indulgence, no advantage, which a due consideration of the public interest may not determine to be just and expedient.

" The Royal Academy depends for its security on the strength of its own means. Whether it shall or shall not be allowed, in its present position, to continue in the unmolested exercise of its useful functions, as a great school of art, can be matter of little moment personally to its existing members; but your petitioners humbly conceive it must be of some importance to the public,

and to the rising race of students, who are indebted for their
professional education to its liberality.

" That the Academy has been actuated, from its first establishment, by a disinterested zeal for the promotion of the arts, has
been sufficiently proved by the undisputed statements submitted
to your honourable House respecting that institution.

" Your petitioners, who are now the guardians of its honour
and the administrators of its means, are willing to persevere
with the same zeal in the same cause.  They are willing to
devote their time, their talents, and their funds, to the support
of the same national objects.

" But it surely cannot be considered unreasonable, if they claim,
as a condition of this obligation, the unmolested management of
an institution which owes its existence to their predecessors,
and which is still maintained by the exertions of those who have
succeeded to their duties and their rights.  They feel that they
have done their best to uphold the character of the British
School of Art in honour and credit.  If others can do better,
your petitioners do not wish to stand in their way; and they
would ·be the last to obstruct the adoption of any measures
which national liberality may suggest, or national means accomplish, for the more effectual attainment of those objects to
which all the efforts of your petitioners have been directed,—
the prosperity of the arts and the honour of their country.

" Fully confiding in the wisdom and justice of your honourable
House, your petitioners most respectfully express their hope
and trust, that in consideration of the statements herein set
forth, your honourable House will be pleased to rescind the
order of the 14th of March last.

" And your petitioners will ever pray."


The petition, so drawn up, was entrusted, for presentation, to the amiable and accomplished member for the
University of Oxford, Sir Robert Harry Inglis, who had,
on more than one previous occasion, made some ineffectual attempts to stem the torrent of vituperative injustice

by which the claims of the Royal Academy were over-
borne, in every incidental discussion that took place in
the House on matters connected with the arts. The
petition, as laid on the table, had appended to it the
following signatures :—

MARTIN ARCHER SHEE,
  President.
RICHARD WESTMACOTT.
EDWARD HODGES BAILY.
ABRAHAM COOPER.
THOMAS UWINS.
CHARLES LOCK EASTLAKE.
WILLIAM WYON.
DAVID WILKIE.
FREDERICK RICHARD LEE.
HENRY PERRONET BRIGGS.
AUGUSTUS WALL CALLCOTT.
ALFRED EDWARD CHALON.
FRANCIS CHANTREY.
WILLIAM COLLINS.
RICHARD COOK.
THOMAS DANIELL.
JOHN PETER DEERING.

WILLIAM ETTY.
HENRY HOWARD, Secre-
  tary.
WILLIAM HILTON.
GEORGE JONES.
CHARLES ROBERT LESLIE.
EDWIN LANDSEER.
WILLIAM MULREADY.
THOMAS PHILLIPS.
HENRY WILLIAM PICKERS-
  GILL.
RAMSAY RICHARD REIN-
  AGLE.
ROBERT SMIRKE.
ROBERT SMIRKE, Jun.
CLARKSON STANFIELD.
JEFFRY WYATVILLE.
WILLIAM WILKINS.

An able article in the " Art Union " for August, 1839,
probably from the pen of the accomplished writer who
then held the post of editor of that deservedly popular
periodical*, bears the following striking testimony to the
merits of this memorable petition :—

" It is quite impossible to peruse this document with indifference. The bitterest and most prejudiced opponents of the
Academy cannot but admit that for purity of style and clearness
of argument,—for a tone at once firm and respectful, energetic,
yet by no means arrogant,—it may be classed with the best

* Mr. S. C. Hall.

models of composition in the English language. It meets every
point at issue, it combats every assertion of wrong-doing, it is
calm and temperate throughout, and yet justly indignant against
calumny ; — it urges claims to the consideration, praise, and
gratitude of the country, strongly, yet without a shadow of
boasting ; it appeals to the justice of the Legislature for protection, not as an entreaty, but as a right ; it is, beyond
question, the most eloquent prayer and protest that . for many
years has been laid upon the table of the House of Commons,
and might do honour to the most accomplished writer of the
age."

The petition was presented and laid upon the table on
the 8th July; and shortly afterwards Mr. Hume gave
notice of his intention to move " that the return to the
order of the 14th March last be made forthwith."

In the meantime the Government had been fully
apprised of the course which the Royal Academy intended to pursue, by means of personal communications
between the President and one or two of the principal
members of the administration; and as the time approached when the contest was to be brought to a decided issue by a division on Mr. Hume's motion, the
debate on which would necessarily involve the consideration of the matters put forth in the petition, the ministerial authorities in the House could not but be alive to
the awkwardness of their position, in a struggle where
an open espousal of the cause of one or the other of
the contending parties, might be productive of results
which, as dangerous either to the stability or to the
character of the administration, they were in either
case desirous to avert.

Circumstanced as the Academy was, in relation to
the Crown,—and resting their case as they did on statements admitting neither of contradiction nor cavil,
which, in the estimation of all candid and dispassionate

observers, fully entitled them to the active support of
the Government in the impending trial of strength,—it
was clearly impossible for Her Majesty's ministers in the
House of Commons to take an avowedly hostile part
against them.   Nor, under the circumstances, could the
Treasury Bench decently resort to the cowardly policy
of remaining wholly silent and passive on the occasion.
On the other hand, the manly and straightforward
course which the Academy had a right to require at the
hands of the representatives of the Crown, was little
likely to recommend itself to the adoption of a ministry,
whose fear of alienating a few ultra-radical supporters
was not counterpoised by any personal sympathy with
the interests they assailed, or any desire to do justice to
the Academy, by a public and practical recognition of
services which could not be denied, but which, from
some incomprehensible cause, the leading members of
the administration were most reluctant to acknowledge.

To come forward boldly, and cast the shield of official protection over a body that could advance such legitimate claims on the respect and gratitude of the House
and the country,—to throw the weight of ministerial influence into the scale, for the purpose of repelling a parliamentary attack on the Academy, instigated, as they well
knew, by motives of private malevolence,—this was
undoubtedly the line of conduct which justice and common sense combined to dictate to the ministry.   Such a
course could not possibly have been attended with any
immediate risk to their parliamentary ascendancy; for in
the event of their joining issue with their radical allies
on this point, they would have infallibly secured the
ready co-operation of the great Opposition leader and a
numerous body of his political adherents.   Neither was
there any technical difficulty in the way of such a pro-

ceeding; there was nothing in the circumstances of the case, up to that point, which could so far excite the constitutional susceptibilities of the most rigorous stickler for the omnipotence of the House, as to suggest the danger of any loss of dignity in the rescinding of the order. The Academy had indeed, in their own councils, resolved *not to obey*, and to *brave the consequences of disobedience;* but the judicious wording of their petition carefully avoided all open manifestation of this intended contumacy, and maintained throughout a tone of suitable deference for the august assembly to which it was addressed.　The Government, however, could not have acted towards the Academy in this fair and frank spirit, without giving mortal offence to Mr. Hume, and thereby seriously endangering the amount of parliamentary support which that gentleman and his adherents vouchsafed to the Melbourne administration.

The course eventually pursued by the Government was fraught with the usual inconveniences affecting a trimming or vacillating policy.　They did their utmost to avert the crisis, by urging the Academy to waive their objections to the order ; and these efforts having proved ineffectual, they were at length induced to give the academic cause a partial and hesitating support, which, while it must have been highly unpalatable to the originators and promoters of the motion,—whose defeat it contributed to secure,—left the credit and the grace of victory to the frank, generous, and energetic advocacy of Sir Robert Peel, and his able coadjutors on the Opposition side of the House.

Within a few days of that on which Mr. Hume was expected to bring forward his motion, Sir Martin, at the request of Lord John Russell, waited upon that nobleman at the Home Office ; when his lordship, expressing his regret at the course of action contemplated by the Royal Academy,—strongly urged the expediency of their conceding the point on which they had taken their stand, and supplying the returns called for by the order, without bringing the matter to the test of a hostile debate and division. But great as was the President's respect for the judgment of that eminent statesman, there was little likelihood that he should be deterred from a line of conduct resolved upon, after the most mature deliberation on his own part and that of the Academy, by the fear of displeasing or embarrassing a ministry in whose goodwill towards the body and the interests they represented, he had so little reason to confide. Sincerely impressed by the value of the services rendered by the Academy to the arts, and the strong claim they had thereby established on the esteem and support of the Government, he could not but feel that the conduct pursued in their regard by the existing ministry, was not less ungrateful than ungracious. Devoted as he had been to the academic cause, and bearing for so many years the brunt of the illiberal warfare waged against the institution, he was little inclined to acquiesce in a view of their position, which would practically belie the principles he had ever asserted on their behalf, and render futile the efforts which, at a vast expense of time and mental exertion, he had made,—and hitherto successfully made,—to sustain them in the enjoyment of their original rights. Justly valuing the social pre-eminence conceded to him as the head of a body occupying a dignified place among the intellectual institutions of the country, and honourably connected with the person of the sovereign,—he was fully resolved that the Royal Academy should never, as such, be reduced, under *his* presidency, to the humiliating necessity of courting the favour of the minister, or subserving the intrigues of any party, or section of party in the House of Commons. If the Academy,—as they were content to do,—should continue to perform, with gratuitous liberality, at their own expense, those didactic and administrative duties towards the art, and the rising generation of artists, which in all other countries recognizing the importance of the interests involved, are undertaken at the charge of the state,—they were fully determined that it should be on the condition of retaining unimpaired their complete independence of all parliamentary or ministerial interference, and their exclusive responsibility to the sovereign.

During the discussions which, under the Pontificate of Clement XIV., preceded the issuing of the Bull for the suppression of the Jesuits, the general of that formidable order was sounded as to the possibility of their abandoning some of their privileges, and submitting to some additional control, in order to avert the danger of the threatened suppression. His answer, it will be recollected, was in these words:—"*Sint ut sunt,—aut non sint!*"

In a similar spirit, the Academy repudiated all notion of a compromise with an enemy bent on their destruction with an ardour of vindictive malevolence, not inferior to that by which the intrepid disciples of Loyola were justly or unjustly assailed. "If," said the President, "Her Majesty's Government are of opinion that the services of the Royal Academy are not such as to entitle them to official countenance and support, against the assaults of their parliamentary foes, at this crisis of their affairs, we are sorry for it; but we are content to abide the consequences, whatever they may be, of this low estimate of our claims. The Government will of course act according to their discretion in the matter; but *our minds are made up.* We are *unanimous* in our determination of resistance to what we consider an improper and inadmissible interference in our affairs; AND WHATEVER MAY BE THE RESULT, WE WILL NOT SUBMIT TO THE DICTATION OF MR. HUME AND HIS FRIENDS."

The Home Secretary, however, did not disguise his strong disapproval of the academic proceeding. "I think it an ill-advised measure," said his lordship, "and I wish my opinion to be communicated to the Royal Academy."

"I shall certainly not fail to communicate your lordship's opinion to my colleagues of the Academy," rejoined the President; "but notwithstanding the high respect entertained for your lordship by the members, I cannot hold out the slightest prospect of their being induced to depart from the resolution they have formed;" and with this observation, the President took his leave.

A day or two later, he received a private and friendly note from the First Lord of the Treasury, requesting a few minutes' conversation with him in Downing Street. On his arrival at the Treasury in obedience to this summons, Lord Melbourne greeted him with that easy and seemingly frank cordiality, which gave such a charm to his official, as well as to his social intercourse. His lordship expressed much good-humoured surprise at the unwillingness of the Academy to grant the returns, and avowed his inability to understand what inconvenience or injury could possibly result to them, from compliance with the wishes of the House of Commons on the occasion. In answer to this, the President entered fully into the academic question; explaining the nature and origin of the institution,—recapitulating the history of their long and perfectly gratuitous services,—pointing out the benefits which had accrued, and were still likely to accrue to the interests of taste in this country, from the disinterested exertions of the body,—and insisting on their right of exemption from all liability to the inquisitorial annoyances sought to be inflicted upon them, for the gratification of professional spite and private malignity, in the persons of a few disappointed and envious individuals.

The witty and sarcastic pen of the Rev. Sydney Smith has immortalized that remarkable peculiarity of Lord Melbourne's character, which induced him to avow or affect a careless ignorance of matters brought under his official notice, which, in reality, had claimed and obtained their full share of his acute and ready attention. In apparent accordance with the habit of mind thus ascribed to him, and perhaps in pursuance of this singular system, the Prime Minister listened to the details relating to the object, functions, and services of the Royal Academy, as one but little acquainted with the peculiar character and attributes of that body. " Well, Sir Martin," said he, " from what you tell me, I must say, that if an institution of this nature is necessary for the country, I do not see how we could well have it on cheaper terms."

" *If* such an institution is necessary, my Lord !" rejoined the President, repeating his words with astonished and somewhat indignant emphasis. " All I can say is, that if your lordship considers it unnecessary, you are the first great minister of a great country who has ever held such an opinion."

This remark elicited of course a disavowal of any intention to depreciate the importance of the fine arts as objects of public attention, and the interview passed off without any apparent diminution of cordiality on the part of the minister. His interposition, however, was not more effectual than that of his distinguished colleague, in recommending to the President of the Academy a modification of the policy which that body had made up their minds to pursue. It was plain that the parliamentary difficulty, such as it was, could not be evaded, and that the Government would, practically, have to elect between Mr. Hume and the Academy, in the approaching struggle.

In the meantime, two counter petitions had been drawn up and presented to the House, deprecating all concession to the claims and remonstrances of the Academy. One of these was the petition of a single artist; and the reader will easily and correctly anticipate the statement, that it emanated from the arch-assailant of the Academy—Benjamin Robert Haydon; the other purported to be " the Petition of the London Artists."

That it was but ill entitled to so comprehensive a designation, may be collected from the fact that it exhibited but *seven signatures*, among which figured of course the names of the principal anti-academic witnesses, whose hostile evidence was so eagerly recorded by the Fine Arts Committee of 1836.

On the other hand, while this select *junta* were modestly assuming to represent the wishes and opinions of the profession at large, a petition in support of the academic cause, signed by seventy artists, not members of the Academy, and in no way connected with it, except as contributors to the annual exhibition,—was presented by Sir Robert Inglis; and another, similar in its object and purport, bearing the signatures of 120 students of the Royal Academy, was entrusted for presentation to Mr. Emerson Tennent, and laid on the table accordingly.

In reference to the exertions made by the attacking party to enlist their professional brethren in the cause of anti-academic agitation,—exertions which exhibited so pitiful a result,—the number of the " Art Union " from which I have already quoted, contains the following pertinent observations. " It is to the honour of the Academy, and of the artists generally, that all possible efforts—that labour, stimulated by the bitterest hostility, and warranted by the almost certainty of success, should have drawn into one focus the combined exertions of only seven artists, and one artist, out of about 800 who live by the profession in London alone."

On the 23d July, the day fixed by the notice of motion, Mr. Hume rose to open his case against the Academy, in a thin house; from which, as he proceeded in his address, the members gradually dropped off one by one, either from want of interest in the subject, or (possibly) through some preconcerted arrangement among those who were desirous of getting rid of the motion without a trial of strength between its abettors and opponents.

The process of *depletion*, as applied to the House, went on so rapidly and satisfactorily, under the influence of the honourable member's oratory, that before he had elaborated more than a few energetic sentences,—full of significant import as to the fate that awaited academic delinquency,—the member for Carlisle, Mr. Howard of Corby, having noted the gradual reduction of the mem-bers, below the constitutional standard of deliberative competency, suddenly interrupted the flow of Mr. Hume's incriminatory eloquence, by the fatal words, " I move that this House be counted." In vain did the honourable member for Kilkenny,—throwing up his clenched hands above his head, with a gesture of half frantic indignation,—loudly denounce the unfairness of the proceeding. The result was inevitable; the numerical deficiency was incontestable, and the House was "up" in two minutes.

This "count out" having disposed of the motion, together with all other orders of the day, it was necessary to begin *de novo*, by giving fresh notice of motion for a future day. This Mr. Hume did at the earliest possible moment. But this state of things necessarily involved the delay of a week, in bringing on the renewed motion; and at that advanced period of the session, there seemed every probability of its being displaced, and again postponed, through the press of other and more important public business, of which there is generally a considerable arrear to be rapidly disposed of on the eve of the prorogation. There was thus a chance of the question being thrown over altogether, until the next session; a contingency that would have been highly satisfactory to the Government, and the cause of much disappointment to the anti-academic cabal. The Academy, however, were by no means desirous to evade the contest, merely for the sake of postponing indefinitely a crisis which was certain to recur sooner or later, and for which they could not expect to be better prepared at any future period. Fortunately for them, and to the great exultation of their assailants, no adjourned debate or other parliamentary casualty disturbed the order of the day on the 30th July, so as to interfere with Mr. Hume's intention of bringing on the motion.

The debate, which commenced at seven o'clock, was protracted until past one; and although the attendance of members was thin throughout, and the numbers who divided fell far short of what might have been expected on an occasion when the leaders of the two great parties in the state, both contributed their eloquent and forcible advocacy to the cause of one of the contending parties, the discussion was of a very animated character, and being almost entirely engrossed by speakers of high parliamentary reputation, and much political weight, was full of interest even for those who were present in the character of unconcerned and impartial observers of the contest.

Mr. Hume's speech was of course condemnatory of the Royal Academy, whom he accused of "contumacious conduct," and personally calumnious of the President, whom he represented as having written and published opinions unfavourable to the academic principle, at a time when he was not a member of the body,—insinuating that he had adopted or expressed different views, in consequence of his election as a royal academician. It could not but be perfectly well known to those who, in prompting Mr. Hume for the performance of a part so unsuited to his peculiar qualifications, had suggested to him this exhibition of reckless and bungling malevolence, that it involved two mis-statements; and that as regarded the change of views alleged to have been produced by the attainment of academical honours, the charge was an unqualified falsehood.

The first publication which Sir Martin gave to the world was, as we have seen, the "*Letter to Noel Desenfans*," which made its appearance in 1802, more than a year after his admission to the full honours of the Academy,—his election as R.A. having taken place in February 1800. It was therefore wholly untrue that he had published opinions hostile to academics, or indeed discussed the subject at all in print, before his election into the body. The assertion that he had, at any time, advocated views unfavourable to the existence of such institutions, was equally incorrect, although less obviously the suggestion of deliberate mendacity. The chief pretext for this absurd and often-repeated misrepresentation, was to be found in a note to " Elements of Art," a work published in 1809, where the question of the utility of annual or periodical *exhibitions* of the works of contemporary and living artists, is slightly touched upon, and some doubt expressed upon the subject—a subject wholly distinct from any consideration of the benefits to be derived from an academy, considered as a school of art, and an institution conferring honorary distinctions on the successful votary of art, whose legitimate ambition they are designed to stimulate and sustain, by the hope and prospect of their attainment.

With the public at large, however, " *the Academy* " was " the Exhibition," and nothing more; so that in the minds of many who were unacquainted with the real nature and functions of the former, its individuality might well be confounded with, and its fate involved in the condemnation, of the latter. But in point of fact, the language in question amounts to no more than the statement of a point as open to debate, and in no sense pledges the author to the affirmative of any proposition affecting the abstract expediency of the system of annual exhibitions; the object of the passage in the text, and the note appended to it, being simply a caution to the student to avoid a class of error into which he might possibly be betrayed, by an undue anxiety to arrest at once the eye of the spectator, among a crowd of works of varied character, submitted contemporaneously to public observation,—instead of devoting himself to the due elaboration of his work, in a strenuous endeavour to achieve the kind of sterling merit most appropriate to the subject, apart from all consideration of mere exhibition effect.

No one can have perused "Rhymes on Art,"—of which "Elements of Art" is in fact the continuation or supplement,—without being fully alive to the fact that the author's best energies were applied to the further and full development of the principles involved in the establishment of the Royal Academy, and the successful promotion of the objects which that institution was so well calculated, as it was designed, to advance and sustain.

Mr. Hume was followed in the debate by Sir Robert Harry Inglis, who, in an argumentative and forcible speech, moved that the order be rescinded. This counter-motion having been seconded and effectively supported in a short speech by Mr. Philip Howard, Mr. (now Sir Benjamin) Hawes, the member for Lambeth, spoke with great force and effect in favour of the exemption of the Academy from the system of vexatious interference with which they were threatened; expressing a strong opinion that no case had been made out against them which would justify the house in demanding these returns; and dwelling emphatically on the fact that the occupation by the body of their former apartments in Somerset House, had been founded on a direct personal grant from the favour of the crown, and that they were then in possession of their apartments in the new building, as an equivalent on being removed from their original premises.

After some observations from Mr. Warburton, — of course condemnatory of the Academy, and infavour of enforcing the returns, — the motion, no doubt to the great relief and temporary elation of the assailing party, was supported at some length by a leading member of the cabinet, viz., the Chancellor of the Exchequer, Mr. Spring Rice (now Lord Monteagle):— although it is to be remembered that the speech of the right honourable gentleman was so complimentary the Royal Academy, and so candid in its express or implied admission of the inutility of the motion, that his subsequent vote in its favour must be ascribed rather to a punctilious desire of vindicating the principle of the omnipotence of the House of Commons, than to the supposed existence of any necessity for the assertion of that principle, for the purpose of obtaining the information involved in the returns which the Academy sought to withhold.

The Chancellor of the Exchequer was followed by Sir Robert Peel, on whom the attention of both parties had been for some time anxiously fixed, each being convinced that the result of the debate could not but be materially affected by the course which the great leader of the opposition might deem it expedient to take on the occasion.   Not indeed that, on the one side, much hope, or on the other, much fear existed, that the cause of the assailants would be actively supported by the skilful and eloquent advocacy of the right honourable baronet; but his silence during the argument would have been felt by the friends of the Academy as more certainly disastrous to the interests at stake, than his absence from the division; as they felt that his open and frank espousal of those interests might decide more than one wavering vote, or, at any rate, delay the departure of some few political supporters who,—perfectly indifferent themselves as to the subject of the debate,—would, as a matter of course, remain to strengthen that side which appeared to enlist the sympathies, and merit the support of their accustomed leader.

The sanguine anticipations of the academic party on seeing Sir Robert rise, were not destined to be disappointed. Nothing could be more judicious, more earnest, or more ably argumentative than his advocacy of the academic cause. He discussed in great detail the conduct and proceedings of the Academy, exhibiting an accurate knowledge of their constitution and functions, and bearing a willing and emphatic testimony to the efficiency and disinterested nature of their public services. He spoke, as from his personal observation, of the great sacrifice of time, trouble, and private convenience, at which the engrossing duties of the presidency had been gratuitously discharged by the two eminent individuals who had successively filled the chair,—the late and the existing President;—and he appealed forcibly to the justice and good feeling of the House, to show their sense of the merits and integrity of the body, by rescinding the unnecessary and vexatious order into which he intimated that the House had been inadvertently betrayed, partly through the means of the words appended to the notice of motion, concerning which he remarked, as above mentioned, that "*a more apparently disingenuous appendix to a motion he had never seen.*" The right honourable baronet concluded by expressing his conviction that the institution had not been forgetful of the great trust which was committed to it, had fulfilled the object for which it was established, and had exercised its power in a manner which every true friend of the arts must approve.

To Sir Robert Peel succeeded Mr. Ewart, who of course supported the motion, and who, in his turn, was answered by the President of the Board of Trade, Mr.

Poulett Thomson (afterwards Lord Sydenham), who declared his belief that there was no public body or institution so pure in principle, or which had more effectually answered its end; and after a speech in favour of the motion from Mr. Wyse, Lord John Russell closed the debate by a forcible appeal in which he strongly urged on the House the expediency of rescinding the order, ably seconding the views and arguments of Sir Robert Peel, by a line of reasoning which should have been conclusive against the motion in the minds of all true economists ; as he pointed out that the Academy, as at present constituted and conducted, was the means of a pecuniary saving to the country.

" The returns " he urged, " could not be demanded on the ground that honourable members did really require any additional information, for the evidence of the President and Secretary before the committee furnished all the information which any such returns as were then moved for could possible supply. If the House thought proper, they might come to a resolution declaring that the slight advantage which the Academy derived from the state, ought no longer to be continued. It would then be for the Academy to determine what course they might think proper to pursue. If the House intended to interfere for the purpose of putting an end to the income which the Academy derived from the exhibition of pictures, then it would be their duty to make provision for defraying those expenses, and for giving that encouragement and assistance to young artists, which now devolved upon the Royal Academy. The academicians dispensed instruction, they promoted art, and they exercised charity. If Parliament deprived them of their income, Parliament should attend to those objects to which that income had heretofore been applied. He readily admitted that it might be quite right to take measures for improving the public taste in architecture, painting, and sculpture; but undue interference with the Academy was clearly not calculated to promote those ends: to harass and vex the Academy by this species of inquisition was at once inexpedient and unjust."[*]

After a short reply from Mr. Hume, the House divided, when the numbers were:—

For enforcing the returns . . . 33
For rescinding the order . . . . 38
———
Majority . . . . . 5

The names of those who voted in the division were as follows:—

*Minority.*

ATTWOOD, T.
BARING, F. T.
BRIDGEMAN, H.
BROTHERTON, J.
BROWNE, R. D.
EWART, W.
FIELDEN, J.
FINCH, F.
GORDON, H.
HOPE, H. T.
HUME, J.
JOHNSTON, GENL.
LEADER, J. T.
LUSHINGTON, C.
MUSKETT, G. A.
NORREYS, SIR. D. G.
O'BRIEN, W. S.
O'CONNELL, D.
O'CONNELL, J.
PARKER, J.
RICE, RIGHT HON. T. S.
SCHOLEFIELD, J.
STANLEY, HON. E. J.
STOCK, DR.
THORNELEY, T.
TURNER, W. A.
VIGORS, N. A.
VILLIERS, HON. P.
WAKLEY, T.
WALLACE, R.
WARBURTON, H.
WILLIAMS, W.
WOOD, SIR M.
WORSLEY, LORD.
WYSE, T.

*Majority.*

ACLAND, SIR T. D.
ACLAND, T. D.
BROCKLEHURST, J.
BURRELL, SIR C.
CAMPBELL, SIR J.
COLE, LORD.

* The author was present under the gallery during the debate in question. The above quotation from the speech of Lord John Russell is given on the authority of the report in the "Art Union" for August, 1859.

| | |
|---|---|
| Divett, E. | Palmer, G. |
| Douglas, Sir C. E. | Palmerston, Viscount. |
| Fremantle, Sir T. | Peel, Right Hon. Sir |
| Gaskell, J. M. | Perceval, Colonel. |
| Gordon, Hon. Capt. | Philips, M. |
| Graham, Rt. Hon. Sir J. | Pigot, D. H. |
| Grimsditch, T. | Richards, R. |
| Hastie, A. | Russell, Lord John. |
| Hawes, B. | Rutherford, Rt. Hon. A. |
| Holmes, W. | Sibthorpe, Colonel. |
| Howard, P. H. | Steuart, R. |
| Inglis, Sir R. H. | Thomson, Rt. Hon. C. P. |
| Maule, Hon. F. | Thompson, Alderman. |
| Mildmay, P. St. John. | Waddington, H. S. |
| Morpeth, Viscount. | Wilbraham, G. |
| Morris, D. | Wilmot, Sir J. E. |
| Oswald, J. | Wood, G. W. |

The contest, it will be seen, was a close one; and the numbers who took part in it were, it might be thought, too few to justify a confident prediction as to the fate of any similar motion in the ensuing session, if brought forward at an earlier period of the parliamentary campaign, when a fuller House might be secured by the exertions of the leading members who, on either side, took an interest in the question. In point of fact, however, the result of this debate was not only a victory, but a most decisive victory, for the academic cause. Neither in the next nor in any subsequent session, during Sir Martin's presidency, was there any effectual attempt made to revive the discussion of that claim of parliamentary interference with the internal arrangements of the Academy, which had in this instance encountered so determined a resistance, and met with so signal a check. The redoubtable "seven" were completely baffled and discouraged; nor was it till a few years later, that they ventured on another and

equally unsuccessful attempt to destroy the Royal
Academy, through the instrumentality of the House of
Commons; when Mr. Hume, their faithful and persevering agent in Parliament, brought forward, but did
did not venture to press to a division, a motion for an
address to the crown, humbly entreating that the
Royal Academy might be ejected from their apartments in Trafalgar Square.

# CHAPTER XVII.

## 1839—1846.

Change of Ministry.—Sir Robert Peel Premier.—His Relations with the
Royal Academy and the President.—Social Popularity of Sir Martin.—
Royal Strangers.—The King of Prussia.—The late King of Saxony.—
Mr. Hume's last parliamentary Assault on the Academy.—Its Failure.—
Decline of the President's Health.—Peculiar Nature of his Complaint.—
Death of his Brother.—He resigns the Presidency.—Touching and gra-
tifying Address from the Academy.—He recals his Resignation in com-
pliance with their Wishes.—Considerate Kindness of Sir R. Peel.—Grant
of a Pension on the Civil List to Lady Archer Shee, in acknowledgment
of Sir Martin's Merits and Services.—Similar and gratifying Recognition
of his Services by the Royal Academy, with the Sanction of the Queen.
—Partial Restoration of his Health.—His last Appearance at the Private
View of the Exhibition.—He presides for the last time at the Grand
Dinner.—Death of Lady Archer Shee.—Her pension re-granted to Sir
Martin's three Daughters.—Sir Robert Peel.—The last Act of his official
Life.

THE preceding chapter virtually closes the history of
the protracted contest in which Sir Martin was engaged,
on behalf of the Academy, during the earlier period of
his occupancy of the academic chair. With the single
exception (already noticed) of an abortive attempt to
address the Crown, to which I shall presently more
particularly advert, the remaining years of his presidency were undisturbed by any hostile proceeding of
the anti-academic *coterie* of sufficient importance to
claim the interest of the reader.

Before the disheartened assailants had sufficiently
rallied from the despondency consequent on their parliamentary failure, to attempt any efficient re-orga-

nisation of their plans, the aspect of political affairs underwent a change which they could not but feel to be highly unfavourable to their views. From the moment when Sir Robert Peel was once more in power, as the head of a strong conservative government, their chances of success in any attack on the Academy, through the medium of the House of Commons, were reduced to the lowest degree of probability. Thenceforth, until the final retirement from office of that able, intrepid, and patriotic minister, the highest interests of the arts were comparatively safe under a Government which, if powerless to control or direct in their favour the caprices of public opinion, or the uncertain flow of parliamentary liberality, were, at any rate, ever ready to afford them a friendly and effective countenance.

It is seldom, indeed, that a British minister has at his command those abundant sources of public patronage, which, under the despotic rule of a Richelieu or a Colbert, are available for the development of genius, and the liberal remuneration of its most ambitious labours. But the exhibition of a generous sympathy with the pursuits of the artist, and a graceful recognition of the social claims of those who sustain the character and illustrate the triumphs of art, will sometimes afford an effective substitute for the more substantial reward that ministerial prudence is bound, however reluctantly, to withhold. To the ardent and imaginative temperament of youthful genius, the hope of social distinction supplies an active stimulus, to which the prospect of wealth, as an incident of success, is usually very subordinate; and even at a more advanced period, in spite of the disenchanting experience of life, the consciousness of high public estimation, and the flattering homage of society, in its highest and most intellectual development may in some degree compensate the deficiency of that worldly prosperity, the extent of which is to be appreciated by reference to a financial standard alone.

Assuredly, if the enjoyment of—

" Honour, place, observance, troops of friends,"

may be taken as the test, few of Sir Martin's contemporaries could be said to surpass him in the outward evidences of a successful career. The feeling entertained towards him by the body over which he presided, was not less affectionate in its estimate of his moral and social worth, than eager in its recognition of his public and official services: and the triumphant result of the recent parliamentary contest had raised this feeling to a pitch of enthusiasm, which it seldom falls to the lot of any man to excite among the competitors whom he has distanced in the pursuit of a common object of ambition.

The struggle itself, which, in its commencement and early stages, had attracted but little notice from the press, and consequently excited but a moderate amount of interest beyond the immediate circles of art, was too striking in its character, as ultimately developed, and especially in its termination, not to enhance, in a conspicuous degree, the public importance of the body, and shed an additional lustre on the social position of their chief.

The victory, to which the judicious eloquence of Sir Robert Peel had so greatly contributed, was probably a source of some vexation to the ministry, who had sought to avert the discussion of claims they found it equally inconvenient to recognise or dispute; nor did the firm tone and attitude adopted by the President throughout the contest, or the success which ultimately attended that timely exhibition of firmness on his part, much tend to diminish the personal disfavour, of which he appeared to be the object, in some high official quarters during the ministerial sway of the Whigs.

With their illustrious successor, however, no feeling of this nature, could operate to the prejudice of one who, in asserting the rights and vindicating the services of the Academy, had acted in accordance with Sir Robert's own estimate of their duties and their claims. The more frequent personal communications between the President and the great leader of the conservative party, consequent on the resumption of office by the latter, had the effect of greatly developing the feelings of esteem and regard, which that eminent statesman was, on many remarkable occasions, prompt to exhibit towards the President ; and during the remaining period of Sir Robert's administration, the relations of the Academy and their chief with her Majesty's Government were on a most satisfactory footing, and such as to afford to those most interested in the permanency and efficiency of the institution, a guarantee against the intrigues of its enemies, almost as effectual as that which, in the previous reign, the personal favour and sympathy of the sovereign had so abundantly supplied, as a counterpoise to ministerial disfavour or indifference.

In the summer and autumn of the year 1842, Sir Martin was honoured by the sittings necessary for the purpose of enabling him to execute the state wholelength portrait of the Queen, to be placed in the apartments of the Royal Academy, for which her Majesty had, at their request, graciously consented to sit. This picture formed the President's principal contribution to the annual academic display in the following year. It represents the Queen in the robes of state and the royal diadem of brilliants usually worn by her Majesty on opening or proroguing the session of Parliament, and in the act of ascending the steps of the throne in the House of Lords, on one of these august occasions. This work, from which no engraving has been executed, was, at the close of the exhibition, and, according to its original destination, placed in the council room of the Royal Academy, in Trafalgar Square, a position which it still retains.

In the spring of the year 1842, the visit of the King of Prussia to London, — an incident which attracted an unusual degree of attention among all classes of London society, — afforded Sir Martin an opportunity of being made personally known to an illustrious prince, whom at that time the united voice of literary and scientific Europe hailed as the ardent admirer and enlightened patron of every species of intellectual merit; while his easy unaffected demeanour, and simple unceremonious habits, obtained for him among the most sanguine votaries of continental freedom in England and elsewhere, the fullest credit for those liberal tendencies in his political creed, which, whether sincere or not, at that period of comparative tranquillity, were destined to be rudely tested at the disastrous epoch of 1848.

While in England, his Majesty exhibited much interest in all matters pertaining to art, science, and literature, and a flattering wish to become personally acquainted with the most eminent individuals connected with these various departments of mental exertion. With a view of more effectually gratifying this laudable curiosity, Sir Robert Peel solicited and obtained his Majesty's attendance at a *déjeûner* in

Whitehall Gardens, to which the prime minister invited a brilliant and distinguished circle, composed of all that was most distinguished in public and official life, with the most conspicuous celebrities of the literary and scientific world, expressly summoned for the purpose of being made personally known to the *Roi philosophe*, who was so well qualified to appreciate their social and intellectual claims.  Sir Martin, alike officially and personally entitled to the distinction, was included in the list of those who were brought together for this interesting ceremonial, and had the honour of being presented in due form to his Prussian Majesty, whose affable and engaging manners, — of which he had on this as well as on subsequent occasions, ample opportunity of judging, — made a most favourable impression on the mind and memory of the President; while he was equally struck by the unaffected good sense and total absence of constraint and pretension, which marked the demeanour and conversation of his Majesty.

There was also at that time in London, another continental sovereign, with whom Sir Martin was brought into social contact, by the chances of official life and private hospitality.  This was the late King of Saxony, the *éclat* of whose position as a crowned head visiting the English capital, was so greatly eclipsed by the political and dynastic interest connected with the name and *antécédens* of his more important brother potentate, that his presence in London attracted comparatively but little notice among the public at large; although from the Court and the ministry he did not fail to meet with every respectful attention to which his exalted rank so justly entitled him.  However severe may be the rules of *étiquette*, as observed in the different courts of Germany on state occasions, there is perhaps, in the ordinary routine of daily life, less practical *gêne* connected with the movements of the august personages for whose benefit these stern canons of ceremonial discipline are retained and enforced, than the peculiarities of our national character contribute to impose, as the inevitable penalty attached to the splendours of royalty among ourselves. It may well be, therefore, that the illustrious individual in question found his advantage in not being so completely "*the observed of all observers*," as he probably would have been but for the accidental coincidence of his visit with that of his royal brother of Prussia, and that he enjoyed, as an unusual luxury, the privilege of visiting the different objects of public interest with which London abounds in the eyes of every intelligent foreigner, without that superabundant publicity, and those eager demonstrations of cockney curiosity, which to some extent trammelled the proceedings, while they no doubt gratified the self-love of the more conspicuous "lion" of the day.

To those, however, who, like the President, were socially or officially brought within the range of his notice, and honoured by a personal introduction to him, his Majesty's demeanour was not less strikingly indicative of good sense and kind feeling, than that of the Prussian monarch, whom he appeared somewhat to resemble in simplicity of manners and amiability of character; while, among his own subjects, he enjoyed an amount of popularity, less ostentatiously manifested perhaps, but destined, as the event has proved, to be of a far more solid and durable nature.

We have seen that on his election as President, Sir Martin had been chosen to replace his predecessor, Sir Thomas Lawrence, in the two most distinguished societies, of a combined convivial and intellectual character, which are to be found within the range of this peculiar branch of our national statistics,—*the Club*, and the Society of Dilettanti. Without being a regular attendant at the respective meetings of these celebrated confraternities, he had a high appreciation of the charms of that refined and often brilliant social intercourse, of which, in their periodical *réunions*, they supplied the most striking examples ; and his presence at both was sufficiently frequent to render his brother members fully alive to his conversational merits, and occasion his appearance among them to be hailed as a valuable addition to the *programme* of the evening. Among the survivors,—now alas ! comparatively few,— of those who in his time adorned the lists of these two eminent associations, there are not wanting those who recur with pleasure to the period when their meetings were enlivened and graced by the eloquent converse, and unaffected courtesy of demeanour, which were the never-failing characteristics of the late President, and dwell with emphatic eulogium on the memory of his varied acquirements, his attractive society, and high moral worth.

In the month of July 1844, occurred the last parliamentary attack upon the constitution and privileges of the Royal Academy, which Sir Martin's presidency was destined to witness. On this occasion Mr. Hume was again entrusted with the conduct of the assault, and doomed again to encounter a signal defeat, in his character of anti-academic champion. In some respects, indeed, the result was more mortifying, and more fatal to the hopes of those who enlisted him in the cause, and supplied him, although scantily enough, with the ammunition of argument, in a contest for which he was personally so ill-provided, than the debate and division of July 1839. For if, in the last-mentioned conflict, the victory was achieved by a small majority in a thin house, the forces arrayed against him in the House in July 1844, proved sufficiently formidable to dispose of the question without the formality of a division.

The course determined by Mr. Hume and his friends was that of moving an humble address to the Crown, entreating her Majesty to withdraw her royal favour and countenance from an institution so prejudicial to the interests of " high art" as the Royal Academy.

From the known sentiments of Sir Robert Peel, then prime minister, with regard to the claims and merits of the Academy, no reasonable doubt could be entertained that a motion so framed would be met by an open, decided, and strenuous ministerial opposition ; nor could the result, under the circumstances, afford a more legitimate subject of speculative conjecture.

The subjoined letters from Sir Robert to the President will effectually serve to acquaint the reader with the course pursued by the minister on the occasion, and the success which attended the adoption of this resolute policy.

(Private.)

"Whitehall, 20th July, 1844.

" My dear Sir,—Mr. Hume is again meditating an assault on the Royal Academy.

" He commenced it a few nights since, and failed from the House being counted out in the middle of his speech.

" He proposes an address to the Crown, of which I enclose a copy, one portion of which implies that there has been a departure from the original intentions of George III. in founding the Academy.

" Perhaps you can inform me on what this implication is founded.

" It may be convenient that I should have a general account of the funds of the Academy, including the sums received from admissions to the exhibition and other sources.

" A general account, also, of the purposes to which the annual revenue has been applied.

" Your own intimate knowledge of the subject will suggest to you any other information which may enable me with effect to do that which I am well inclined to do, — defend the Academy, and resist the attack upon it, made ostensibly by Mr. Hume, but prompted probably by professional enemies of the institution.

" I think Sir Robert Inglis (who has left London, I believe) was furnished with materials which enabled him to state with advantage the claims of the Academy to public confidence and support.

" Is there any publication to which I could refer, and the reference to which might save you the trouble of sending me the details which I ask for ?

" Believe me, my dear Sir,

" Very faithfully yours,

" ROBERT PEEL."

" Sir Martin Archer Shee, &c."


It is almost superfluous to state that in compliance with the request contained in this letter, the President supplied Sir Robert with abundant and satisfactory materials for vindicating the character and conduct of the Royal Academy.

On the 23rd July Sir Robert Peel writes as follows :

" Whitehall, 23rd July, 1844.

" MY DEAR SIR, — I return to you, with many thanks, the accompanying papers.

" Mr. Hume and his motion were at a great discount in the

House of Commons last night.  He met with no support, and did not venture to divide.

" The feeling of the House was strongly and decidedly in favour of the Royal Academy.  I doubt whether five members would have voted with Mr. Hume had he taken a division.  I hope we have effectually discouraged future attacks; but I cannot answer for a gentleman who boasted that he had ' the impudence of the devil.'

" Believe me, my dear Sir,

" Very faithfully yours,

" ROBERT  PEEL."

" Sir Martin Archer Shee, &c."

With the notice of this abortive attempt, the history of the anti-academic agitation, in and out of Parliament, as far as that agitation is connected with the record of Sir Martin's official career, is brought to a close.

Long before the date of Mr. Hume's motion for an address to the crown, the health of the President had given serious indications of approaching failure, although no perceptible diminution of his mental or bodily energies had been exhibited either in the contributions of his pencil to the annual exhibition, or in his manner of discharging those public functions of his office which most severely taxed his intellectual powers and physical strength.  As early as the spring of 1842, some slight symptoms of the distressing malady that afterwards took permanent hold on his constitution, had manifested themselves in a form which was easily confounded with the ordinary results of dyspeptic derangement; and the hopeful anticipations of his family and friends long failed to appreciate the gravity of ailments apparently admitting of so intelligible and re-assuring an explanation.  He complained of a constant feeling of giddiness ; and although no unsteadiness of gait, or languor in his movements when in public, in society, or indeed in his domestic circle, appeared to add weight to the statement, — often made in a half-jocular manner in answer to the ordinary inquiries concerning his health, — he frequently declared that he found it difficult to avoid reeling like a drunken man.   It was not, however, until the summer of 1843, that the complaint exhibited itself suddenly in the shape of decided *vertigo*, the nature and violence of which could not reasonably be referred to any cause connected simply with the organs of digestion.   Nevertheless, the earlier attacks having apparently yielded to the ordinary treatment applicable to aggravated forms of dyspepsia, his medical advisers were still not unwilling to persude themselves, or to acquiesce in the hopes of his family, that the usual remedies of change of air, temporary relaxation from all kinds of business, and strict attention to diet, might produce a favourable change, and gradually effect his perfect restoration to health.

Accordingly, having to a certain extent rallied, he found himself sufficiently well, at the beginning of the month of August, to accompany Lady Archer Shee and other members of his family on a visit to his friend, the late Mr. Robert Vernon, at whose hospitable mansion in Berkshire, he had, in several preceding years, passed a portion of the autumn vacation.   While at Ardington, he was again violently attacked by his vertiginous complaint, which, partially disappearing, returned with undiminished severity at intervals, accompanied by violent retchings that were evidently the result, and not otherwise connected with the cause, of the fearful giddiness under which he laboured.   Obliged to shorten his stay at Ardington, and return to London for advice, he was ordered to the sea; and on complying with the medical mandate, he seemed to derive considerable benefit from a residence of a few weeks at Brighton, at the end of which, he returned to Cavendish Square in apparently improved health. He was again, however, suddenly and violently attacked by the complaint, in its most distressing form, on the 10th December in that year, the day on which the distribution of gold medals to the successful competitors in the schools of the Academy was to take place; and the attack was so severe as not only to incapacitate him from the performance of his official duties on the occasion in question, but to confine him for several days to his bed room, in a state of great discomfort and prostration of strength. At the end of a week or ten days, he rallied so far as to be apparently restored to his average state; and during that winter and the ensuing spring, although occasionally threatened with a return of the more violent symptoms of his complaint, and never altogether free from the sensation of giddiness, which had, as may be supposed, a very depressing effect on his spirits, he was able to continue the practice of his profession, and to resume his official labours, with but little diminution of that zealous assiduity in their performance, which had throughout distinguished his career as President.

Fortunately, the parliamentary assault on the Academy which was, as we have seen, unsuccessfully made during the session of 1844, was far from entailing on him such an amount of mental exertion as had been involved in his conduct of the academic defence during the more formidable campaign of 1839. But to one who took so conscientious a view of the obligations imposed on him by his occupancy of the academic chair, and the responsible position which he consequently filled in reference to a vast class of public and private interests connected with the prospects and statistics of art in this country, — what may be termed the ordinary routine of his duties and occupations as President, was attended with an almost daily sacrifice of time, thought, and personal convenience, that constituted a very serious and perplexing addition to the cares of a laborious profession, and the many claims, domestic and social, which assert their importance in the every-day life of most men engaged in the active pursuits of the world.

His cordial sympathy with the struggles of unfriended talent, and his feeling of paternal kindness for the youthful votaries of the art, were so universally known, that utter strangers applied to him, without hesitation, for advice and guidance, in reference to their own hopes and prospects, or those of their children and relatives, on occasions where a doubt existed as to the most judicious course of elementary study, or when the question of following the art, as the main pursuit of life, was the subject of personal deliberation or family debate.

Easily and cheerfully accessible to all who could urge on his attention the most slender claim of connection with those interests of taste, of which he considered himself, as far as his means and ability would permit, the natural guardian and protector, he never grudged the time employed, at whatever inconvenience to himself, in listening to their statements, resolving their doubts, correcting their views, and, — where he conscientiously could do so, — stimulating their enthusiasm, or cheering them under temporary discouragement. Few days passed without his more important avocations experiencing some interruption from these unauthorised inroads on his time, and appeals to his considerate kindness.   Nor were they indeed restricted to matters assumed to be peculiarly within the range of his official or professional sympathies; as his connection with literature was often appealed to as a claim for similar good offices towards the humbler and less fortunate votaries of the muse.

When the various circumstances which, during many anxious and active years of his presidency, had thus combined to challenge and divide his attention, are fairly taken into account, it will be no matter of surprise that the strain on his mental energies, at the age of seventy-four, began to exhibit results of a serious character, in reference to his bodily health; and although the peculiar nature of his complaint appeared somewhat to perplex the minds, as it certainly baffled the sanative skill of the eminent medical men whom he, from time to time, consulted on his symptoms, there can be little doubt that his ailments were referable to some irregular or irritating action on the brain, resulting from a too continuous action of that mysterious organ.

The summer of 1844 came and passed away, without any material increase of his illness; and in the month of August he was able to enjoy the cordial hospitality of his valued friend, Sir George Staunton, during a fortnight's visit which, with Lady Archer Shee and his family, he paid to that amiable and accomplished man, and eminent *savant*, at his beautiful residence of Leigh Park.   There, amid the most enchanting scenery which the genius of the landscape gardener can produce or develop in a region not remarkable for any striking features of natural beauty,—and in the enjoyment of society so congenial to his taste and feelings as that of his worthy host, whose engaging vivacity, varied knowledge, and genuine kindness of heart, communicated to the social atmosphere of Leigh a peculiar charm, that can never be effaced from the memory of those who were so fortunate as to experience its exhilarating influence—the President seemed, in great degree, to recover the natural buoyancy of his spirits, and to gain ground in the daily and hourly struggle with his depressing complaint.

On leaving Leigh, he again sought the benefit of sea air, in a residence of a few weeks at Brighton, in the fresh and bracing climate of the East Cliff, with, apparently, the same satisfactory result as in the previous year.

The ensuing winter, however, was marked by a gradual diminution of physical strength, and a very perceptible increase in the ordinary or normal symptoms of his complaint; and as the spring approached, the growing conviction of his mind that the progress of time and disease would speedily disqualify him for the active duties connected with the academic chair, became sadly and painfully strengthened. Conceiving himself hardly justified in retaining a position which, in his case, had required the exercise of so much bodily and mental energy, of which he now felt or feared himself to be no longer capable,—and unwilling to monopolise the highest honour and greatest worldly prize of his profession, after he had ceased to be competent to the performance of the chief functions attached to its enjoyment,—he resolved on resigning the trust which he had for so many years discharged with untiring and conscientious assiduity.

With great exertion, and at the expense of much bodily suffering, he had contrived to complete a couple of pictures as his contribution to the approaching exhibition; works which, in this biography, at least, deserve a passing notice, as being not only the last which he exhibited, but the very last productions of his pencil. One was a half-length portrait of Madame Ralli, the wife of one of the partners in the eminent Greek mercantile firm of that name; the other was the portrait of a valued and attached friend, then as now, well known and highly esteemed in the circles of taste, literature, and science, — Mr. Benjamin Austen. The first-mentioned picture was, I believe, considered as no unfavourable representation of the very lovely subject whose likeness it seeks to perpetuate. It was certainly not deficient in vigour or pleasing effect as an attractive female portrait. The last, still conspicuous on the walls of that dining-room, the graceful and brilliant hospitality of which is, fortunately, not yet traditional among those of our generation who appreciate the rare union of the " feast of reason and the flow of soul" with the brightest triumphs of gastronomic science, was pronounced by competent critics, to be a production which would have done honour to the most vigorous period of Sir Martin's professional career.

The death of his elder and only brother, which took place rather suddenly, in the month of May of that year, naturally contributed to increase the depression produced by the state of his own health, and to aggravate the symptoms of a complaint exercising an injurious action on his nervous system. This near relative, between whom and Sir Martin the warmest fraternal affection ever subsisted, had been for many years resident in his brother's family; and although his health had recently exhibited signs of decay, such as might be reasonably looked for at his advanced age, (he had completed his 80th year) these indications of

the progress of time had not led Sir Martin to anticipate for him so rapid a termination of his life.

On the 27th May, 1845, Sir Martin, in the following
letter, formally communicated to the council and
members of the Royal Academy, his intention of retiring
from the office of President.

*To the Council and Members of the Royal Academy.*

"Cavendish Square, 27th May, 1845. ·

" GENTLEMEN,— With sincere regret I address you for the
purpose of announcing my respectful resignation of the honourable office of President of the Royal Academy, which, through
your favour, has been conferred upon me for fifteen successive
years.

" I will not, gentlemen, attempt to express the feelings under
which I thus relinquish a position which I have always regarded
as the proud distinction of my life, and the highest honour to
which an artist can attain. But advanced age, severe and long-
protracted illness, with other causes, have conspired to unfit me
for active exertion, and admonish me that to make way for
more vigorous powers is as much a measure of justice to the
Academy, as of release to me from a responsibility which I am
no longer competent to undertake. As I can truly say that I
have never shrunk from the performance of any duty, which the
interests of our art or the Academy appeared to require of me,
I trust I may confidently hope that, in now withdrawing from
the field, in my 76th year, I shall not be considered as deserting
my post, or quitting it prematurely.

" According to the ordinary course of nature,—even if disease
should not anticipate the result of time,—my lease of life must
soon terminate ; but while I exist, gentlemen, I shall remember
with pride and gratitude the undeviating kindness, the (I may
almost say) affectionate consideration which you have always
shown to me.  ·

" Through a long period of personal, professional, and social
intercourse, you have amply proved to me how much a spirit of
generous confidence and cordial co-operation, may contribute to

animate the zeal, to lighten the duties, and lessen the anxieties of those who are called to act for others in any official or responsible character.

"You may readily, gentlemen, supply your chair with a President more competent than I am to support the dignity and perform the functions which belong to it. But, perhaps, without presumption, I may say that you will not easily find a President more honestly desirous to promote the cause of the arts than I have been, or more anxious to sustain, in due estimation, the honour and character of our profession.

"That you may long continue to merit, as you have well merited, the support of the public, the respect of your country, and the approbation of your Sovereign, is the sincere wish of,

"Gentlemen,
"Your most faithful and grateful humble servant,

"MARTIN ARCHER SHEE."

On the same day, he addressed the subjoined letter to Sir Robert Peel, as the channel through which he could most appropriately convey to the Queen, the respectful intimation of his intended resignation of an office which he had the honour to hold by virtue of Her Majesty's royal saction.

"Cavendish Square, 28th May, 1845.

"MY DEAR SIR,—When you so kindly favoured me with a visit some weeks since, in Cavendish Square, I took the liberty of mentioning my intention of vacating the chair of the Royal Academy.

"The advanced period of my life (in my 76th year) a severe illness of nearly three years' continuance, under which I still suffer, and other considerations, have unfitted me for active exertion, and render my retirement as expedient for the interest of the Academy, as necessary for my release from the pressure of duties which I am no longer competent to discharge.

"Although most reluctant to obtrude any personal concern

of my own on the notice of the Queen, I cannot but consider it my duty humbly to notify to her Majesty, as the august head and protectress of the Royal Academy, my respectful resignation of the distinguished office of President, which, by her Majesty's gracious sanction and signature, as well as the unanimous choice of my brother academicians, I have been permitted to occupy down to the present time.

"Many considerations connected with the Royal Academy, as well as strong feelings of personal respect towards yourself, would, my dear sir, render it most gratifying to me, if I might hope to effect this announcement to her Majesty through your good offices. I fear to encroach on the liberal indulgence to which I have been so often indebted; but your kindly acceding to my wish on this occasion, would relieve me from the awkwardness of an official communication, which, as I have no precedent to follow, I sometimes doubt if I am authorised to make.

"Excuse, my dear sir, this last, as well as the many other troubles which I have given you; and believe me to be, with the greatest respect, most faithfully and gratefully yours,

"MARTIN ARCHER SHEE."

"The Right Hon. Sir Robert Peel, Bart."

Sir Robert having kindly complied with this request, he in due time communicated to Sir Martin the gracious expression of her Majesty's regret that the state of his health should have rendered it expedient for him to vacate the President's chair.

The effect of the announcement on his brethren of the Academy was, however, far beyond what mere sympathy for his sufferings, and friendly regard for his person, would naturally produce. Impressed with the strongest faith in the value of his services, and the warmest feelings of gratitude for his energetic, skilful, and wholly disinterested conduct, in the judicious management of the affairs of the institution, they could not readily acquiesce in the results of a step which deprived their councils of the chief elements of wisdom and weight, on which they depended for the maintenance of their position and rights. Such was their confidence in his judgment, — such their reliance on his administrative ability, and legitimate influence in those official and political circles whose favour and good will it was of material importance to conciliate, — that his secession from the office of President was looked upon by the members as an event fraught with embarrassment and danger to the best interests of the Academy.

It is certainly no disparagement of the many eminent and able men who at that time adorned the ranks of the royal academicians, to say that, however high was their mutual estimation of each other, there was no one who, in the general view, combined in himself so many requisites, moral, intellectual, and social, for the effective performance of the duties attached to the chair, as their existing President. Even assuming that the state of his health might for the present, or indeed permanently, disqualify him for an active participation in the ordinary routine of their affairs, they felt that his name was a tower of strength, and his spirit a bond of union amongst them, which they could not, without absolute necessity, bring themselves to relinquish. The memorable result of their deliberations, in this state of mind, will be presently stated. It is indeed recorded in a shape which must effectually exonerate Sir Martin's biographer from the charge of partial exaggeration, which the foregoing estimate of the temper and feelings of the Academy, at this particular period, if wholly unsupported by proof, might possibly suggest.

The fifteen years during which Sir Martin had filled

the academic chair, had been, as we have seen, a period
not only of active and unceasing exertion, on his part,
in the affairs of the Academy, but of great social and
official *éclat*, which gave to his occupancy of that distinguished position, a prominence in the eyes of the
world, that the presidency,—originally connected in the
minds of men with the intellectual as well as the professional triumphs of Sir Joshua,—had scarcely retained
when held by the two immediate successors of that
great artist.   Not indeed that the social estimation of
Sir Thomas Lawrence could be considered inferior to
that of his most eminent contemporaries ; but when
called by the unanimous assent of his brethren to
occupy the vacant chair, he already stood so high in
the favour of the world, that his official pre-eminence
seemed to add but little to the *prestige* of a popularity
which in his personal, as well as his professional character, he so extensively enjoyed.   His discharge of the
duties connected with his office, though marked by good
sense and gentlemanly demeanour, was not, moreover,
of a character to attract public attention, or create
any particular interest, beyond the immediate *entourage* accompanying their performance ; and although
always representing the Academy with grace and propriety, on the rare occasions when his official character
was conspicuously *en évidence* beyond the walls of
Somerset House, his position in the eyes of the public
was far less completely identified with that character
than with his individual merits and success as the most
eminent portrait painter of his day ; and he evidently
did not conceive that his tenure of the office involved
any duties of hospitality or representation, calculated
to disturb the tranquillity and comparative seclusion of
his bachelor establishment.

But the circumstances that attended Sir Martin's presidency, were of a nature to concentrate on the office itself, a large amount of attention which had not been previously, or at any rate, recently bestowed on it by the public : and his personal discharge of its functions was of a character greatly to enhance the degree of interest which extraneous causes had tended to create on the subject.

The public discussions in Parliament and in the press, on the destination of the new building in Trafalgar Square,—the distinguished favour and countenance exhibited, on all occasions, towards the Academy and its official representative, by King William IV., and the great impulse given to popular curiosity on the subject of the institution, by the transfer of their abode from Somerset House,—all contributed to this result ; — and probably at no time since the establishment of the Royal Academy, had its affairs and administration occupied a larger space in the public eye, than during the period over which Sir Martin's active discharge of the presidential duties extended.

Thus, if in the case of Sir Thomas Lawrence, *the President* was often lost sight of in the popular and admired artist, Sir Martin may said to have experienced, or exemplified, a directly contrary process ; — his professional *status* being, with the public at large, to a great extent merged in the *éclat* of his official rank, and the *prestige* of his personal and social qualifications for its sustainment.

The fact of his being, so to speak, more officially conspicuous than his more recent predecessors, was not without its influence in imposing upon him a variety of social duties, or obligations of expediency,—beyond the strict limits of his academical functions, — involving not only a serious sacrifice of time and trouble, but great additional expense; — while, on the other hand, his professional practice (except as regards the royal commissions with which he was honoured during the three or four last years of King William's reign) received no perceptible impulse from his official character ; and as years wore on, he was, in common with the few survivors of his most eminent contemporaries, and by the operation of laws to which every long protracted professional career is more or less subject,— gradually superseded in the practical favour of the public, by more youthful, if not more vigorous, candidates for fame, in that branch of the art to which he had devoted his chief attention.

When, in addition to this, it is remembered that of the three Presidents who had successively occupied that distinguished post since the death of Sir Joshua, Sir Martin was the only one who had not held, together with the presidency, a lucrative appointment, the emoluments of which far more than counterbalanced the additional annual expenditure inseparable from the occupancy of the academic chair, — it will be no matter of surprise that the substantial results of his honourable and laborious career should have proved very disproportionate to the amount of social and worldly distinction with which it had been attended,— and that his necessary abandonment of all professional exertion involved a diminution of income, which was far from being unimportant,— even with reference to the limited scale within which he contemplated reducing his expenditure, upon his retirement from official and active life, —and afforded, in itself, a strong additional motive for resigning an office entailing on its possessor a heavy annual expense.

Early in the month of June, Sir Martin went down with his family to Brighton, from the air of which place he had on many occasions derived so much benefit, that he had it in contemplation to make it his residence during the short period which, in the failing state of his health, he anticipated as the limit of his earthly career. Beyond a respectful and regretful acknowledgment, from the council, of the receipt of the letter announcing his resignation of the presidency, no intimation of the course intended to be adopted by the Academy, on the occasion, had been given or hinted to him, in any way, previously to the communication which I am about to lay before the reader. The delay had not occasioned any surprise, or suggested any conjecture on his part; as he was well aware that a certain time must elapse before the subject of his letter could be formally and officially brought under the notice of the general assembly, and that the body would be anxious to address him in reply, in terms which would most effectively give expression to their kind and cordial feelings towards him. He was, however, wholly unprepared for the contents of the following address which was forwarded to him at Brighton, towards the end of the month of July.

*" To Sir Martin Archer Shee, President of the Royal Academy.*

" We, the members of the Royal Academy, expressly convened in general assembly, on the 23rd ult., having listened with painful interest to the correspondence between you, sir, and the council, on your proposed resignation of the presidency of the Royal Academy, beg most respectfully and, at the same time, most earnestly to reiterate the sentiments of the council, namely, the deepest concern at the step you have contemplated, and entire sympathy in the afflictions which have led to it,—the anxious hope that you may be speedily restored to health, and our unanimous wish that you may be persuaded to withdraw a resolution alike adverse to the interests of the Academy, and to our own feelings.

"Our long experience of your delicate and conscientious sense of duty assures us that your temporary and unavoidable absence from the business of your office, from these sad causes, has been your paramount motive in this proposition; but while we bear in mind your efficient occupation of the chair till within a few months, we cannot but entertain the confident expectation that this pressure of indisposition will be relieved, under Providence, in such a manner as to restore to us, ere long, your valued superintendence.

"The less onerous duties of the presidency will readily be performed by deputy; and with the liberty of occasional reference to you, sir, we shall each and all of us redouble our vigilance in our several departments, so as to secure the order and efficiency of our institution, and to relieve you from all unnecessary anxiety and burthen. And while we are assured that you will excuse the extreme reluctance with which we contemplate your relinquishment of a position demanding such rare qualifications, and which we should find so much difficulty in adequately supplying, we rely on your wonted generosity to acquit us of disregard of your private wishes, with respect to the cares and labours of office, and your relief from those large personal sacrifices which you have so long made in our favour.

"Ever mindful of the debt of gratitude we owe to you, not only for the admirable manner in which you have presided over us during fifteen years, but for the signal acts and services which you have rendered this institution during nearly half a century —as the unwearying contributor to its means, the accomplished and eloquent advocate of its nobler interests, as the firm and uncompromising upholder of its laws and independence, and as our triumphant champion in the hour of need—to these honourable claims to our veneration and respect, permit us to add the assurance of our affection to you personally, inspired by the parental and conciliatory conduct of your presidency; and we seize the opportunity afforded us by this occasion, of acknowledging these sentiments in the fullest and most cordial manner, as equally due to ourselves, and to you, sir, as our beloved President.

"Hoping that you may be induced to delay your retirement from the chair, on the present occasion, and that our request may be consistent with your health and feelings,

"We have the honour to remain, Sir,

"Your affectionate friends and colleagues."

This address bore the signatures of the whole body of royal academicians and associates.

Such an appeal was irresistible. While a hope remained that the severity of his complaint might yield to the beneficial influence of rest and sea air, and that the pressure of disease might not be so great as wholly to disqualify him for occasional mental exertion, he could not but feel that acquiescence in the wishes of his admiring and affectionate colleagues,—so earnestly and considerately expressed,—was an imperative, and under the circumstances, a pleasing duty. Without hesitation, therefore, he hastened to assure them of his readiness to resume, at their request, the distinguished position of which their grateful partiality still considered him the fittest occupant, in spite of the physical infirmities which in great measure incapacitated him from its duties.

On the 8th August he received the following letter from the prime minister, Sir Robert Peel, for the contents of which he was as little prepared, as for the communication from his colleagues of the Royal Academy, which I have just recorded.

(Private.)

"Whitehall, 7th August, 1845.

"My dear Sir,— You probably are aware that, some years since, a new arrangement was made by Parliament respecting the grant of pensions on the civil list by the Crown.

s 2

"A sum totally inadequate to the purpose for which it is granted, for it is limited to 120*l*., is annually placed at the disposal of the Crown, with a power to apply it to the reward of personal services to the Sovereign, of public service, or of distinguished literary or scientific merit.

"Several distinguished men (such being the principle of the grant) have had no difficulty in receiving a pension on the civil list, as an acknowledgment of merit. Among the number are Professors Owen, Faraday, Airey, among men of science; the names of Southey and Moore were also included.

"The acceptance of the pension involves no personal obligation to the minister, and imposes no fetter on the perfect independence of the recipient.

"I fear that your career in art has been more honourable than profitable, and that the office of President of the Royal Academy, while conferring the highest distinction, subjected you to many demands upon your valuable time, and indeed to many pecuniary charges.

"From these considerations, and also from the consideration that you entirely fulfil the conditions which Parliament has attached to the grant of a civil list pension, by eminence in literature and art, I shall have the greatest satisfaction in proposing to the Queen that a pension for life, to the amount which has been usually granted of late years,—namely, 200*l*. per annum— shall be assigned to you as a mark of the royal favour, and acknowledgment of public service.

"It may be agreeable to you that this pension, instead of being granted to yourself, should be granted for her life to Lady Shee; and, if this be the case, I shall have equal pleasure in submitting the name of Lady Shee to her Majesty.

"Believe me, my dear Sir,<br>
"With sincere esteem,<br>
"Most faithfully yours,<br>
"ROBERT PEEL."

"Sir Martin Archer Shee, &c., &c."

It will be collected from what I have stated above, that Sir Martin's pecuniary means on his retirement

from active life, were not such as to render this proposed addition to his income either unacceptable or
unimportant; and the considerate delicacy with which
the proposal was communicated to him, was of a nature
to remove every scruple of pride that might have interfered with its acceptance, and impart to a substantial
benefit, the character of a graceful and complimentary
tribute to the value of services, in the recognition of
which he could not but find a legitimate source of
gratification. The suggestion of substituting the name
of Lady Archer Shee in the grant of the proposed
pension, was peculiarly satisfactory, and was, as may
well be supposed, gratefully acquiesced in by Sir Martin.
While conveying to the thoughtful and friendly minister
the expression of his acknowledgments on the occasion, he found himself called upon, by the unexpected
turn of the academic deliberations on his proposed
retirement, to request the exercise of Sir Robert's good
offices in explaining to the Queen that notwithstanding
the recent announcement of his intended resignation,
the unanimous wishes of his academic brethren had
imposed upon him the duty of remaining at his post,
should such a course be honoured with her Majesty's
approbation. As the best means of acquainting Sir
Robert with the exact position of affairs upon the point,
Sir Martin enclosed to him a copy of the address which
had produced this change of intention on his part.

The following letter will show how fully Sir Robert
appreciated and entered into the feeling which had
dictated the proceedings of the Academy on the occasion.

"Drayton Manor, 14th August.

"MY DEAR SIR,—I have written to the Queen on the subject
of my last letter, and have not a doubt, from my knowledge of

her Majesty's sentiments and feelings with regard to you, that her Majesty will cordially approve of my recommendation.

"I have read with the utmost satisfaction the excellent, the touching address of the Royal Academy, as honourable to those who have conceived it, as to him to whom it has been presented.

"No one has done so much as you have done to encourage that high and honourable feeling which has prevailed among the members of the Royal Academy, and which dictates their appeal to their honoured President.

"You have a right to be doubly proud of this address, as evincing the success of your exertions to maintain the elevated character of British artists, and also conveying to you the tribute of their grateful and affectionate esteem.

"Believe me, my dear Sir,

"Very sincerely yours,

"ROBERT PEEL."

"Sir Martin Archer Shee, &c. &c."

The Queen having signified her Majesty's gracious approval of the arrangement suggested by the minister, the grant of the pension was accordingly made to Lady Archer Shee; and the royal warrant, made out and drawn up on the occasion, commemorated in emphatic terms the distinguished public services of Sir Martin, during his fifteen years tenure of the office of President of the Royal Academy.

The members of that institution, not content with having given so striking a proof of their esteem and admiration for their President, as was implied in their unanimous entreaty that he would retain his position as their head, were anxious to mark in a more substantial, if not a more significant form, the high sense they entertained of his personal and official merits, and their grateful appreciation of the sacrifices which he had made in the cause of the arts. They found in the circumstances connected with the munificent bequest of one of their most eminent and lamented members, an additional motive for a proceeding suggested to them by exceptional services on the part of Sir Martin, and for which they had no precedent in the previous history of the Academy.

The reader is probably aware that under the will of the late Sir Francis Chantrey, the Royal Academy will eventually come into the possession of a very large sum of money,—being, in fact, the great bulk of that distinguished artist's property, — which, in their hands, will be available for the general purposes of the institution, and the effective promotion of those objects for which it was established. The will, in conferring this gift on the Academy, contained a direction that out of the income of the property, an annual sum of 300*l*. should be paid to the President for the time being; but the period when this contribution towards the hitherto gratuitous expenses incidental to the occupation of the academic chair was to take practical effect, was of course postponed until after the termination of the life-interest in the property reserved by the will in favour of the testator's widow; and as this amiable lady was greatly Sir Martin's junior, it was in the highest degree improbable (and no one would have more devoutly deprecated the chance than himself) that by surviving her, he should be placed in a position to benefit by the clause in question.

His colleagues of the Academy, however, could not but feel some regret that while a pecuniary advantage, of a very moderate character indeed, but still of importance in lightening the burthens of the office, was reserved for his immediate or remoter successors in the President's chair, he, and perhaps he alone, should be excluded from its enjoyment, whose devotion to the interests of the institution had combined with other causes to entail on him an amount of mental labour and active exertion, far beyond what the ordinary duties of the presidency had imposed on any of his predecessors. Actuated to some extent by this feeling, in addition to their earnest wish to bestow on him some signal and emphatic mark of their grateful affection, they resolved, subject to the approval of their august patron and protectress, to anticipate, in Sir Martin's case, the effect of the Chantrey bequest, by assigning to him during the remainder of his life an annual sum of 300*l.* out of the academic funds.

They were too well aware of the sensitive and scrupulous independence of his character, to allow of the matter being broached or hinted at to himself, during the course of the deliberations which took place in the council and in the general assembly, on the subject of this unusual proceeding; and so well were their measures concerted, and their precautions taken to secure his total exclusion from their councils on the occasion, that the first intimation of the project received by him, announced at the same time its perfect completion and ratification by the gracious approval of the Queen, under her Majesty's own hand, and testified by the royal sign-manual appended to the address from the Royal Academy, submitting the measure for her Majesty's sanction.

His feelings on receiving this new and unexpected proof of the affection of his colleagues, and the gracious favour of his sovereign, will be best understood on perusal of the subjoined letter, addressed by him to the members, academicians of the Royal Academy, on the 24th October, 1845 :—

"Brighton, 24th October, 1845.

"GENTLEMEN, — To say that I have been as greatly surprised as deeply affected by the communication which has been personally made to me by our worthy secretary, would very inadequately express the feelings which that communication has excited.

"You had already, gentlemen, turned the balance of obligation greatly against me, and far exceeded in acknowledgment all that the most partial appreciation of my pretensions could have imagined or contemplated. The flattering proof of affectionate consideration with which you had honoured me, would repay a life devoted to such services as I have had the pride and pleasure of performing for the Royal Academy. The distinguished honour derived from the position of President has always been considered as its appropriate reward; and your cordial approbation of my conduct in the chair has enhanced that honour to the utmost limit of which it is capable.

"Believe me, gentlemen, I neither expected nor desired, nor conceived that I deserved any other remuneration ; and if I had been aware of your resolution of the 28th of August, before it passed through the regular forms of the Academy, I should have deemed it my duty respectfully and gratefully, but firmly, to oppose it. But with that delicacy towards me which has characterised the whole proceeding, you have allowed me no opportunity of objection or remonstrance; and the first intimation I received of the measure in question, was the official announcement of its completion by her Majesty's sanction and signature.

"You have thus, gentlemen, ingeniously enforced your intentions by royal authority, and kindly endeavoured to lighten the weight of the favour you have conferred, by giving its acceptance the air of a duty. The generous spirit, gentlemen, in which this further testimony of your regard has been voted by the Academy, and graciously confirmed by the Queen, makes me feel that hesitation on my part would be ungracious to both.

"But let me not, gentlemen, be suspected of an affectation

which would seem to ascribe more than its due proportion of influence to this consideration. In profiting by your liberality, it would be a very unworthy feeling which could induce me to withhold from you the satisfaction which I am sure you will derive from the acknowledgment, that you will have afforded an effective addition to an income which long continued illness, and the consequent interruption of professional occupation, had rather inconveniently diminished.

" At my advanced period of life, gentlemen, it were vain to hope that the future may render me more worthy of your favour than the past. You have, however, proved that you are willing to value my deserts according to that liberal calculation which takes the will for the deed. With a full security, therefore, that any effort which I may hereafter be able to make in your service will be regarded under this indulgent estimate, I remain, with equal respect, regard, and gratitude,

" Most faithfully and affectionately yours,

" MARTIN ARCHER SHEE."

The excitement consequent on a succession of occurrences which, however gratifying in themselves, were calculated to agitate an already weakened nervous system, produced some temporary aggravation of his distressing complaint. From this, however, he gradually rallied; and although the symptoms of old age began to exhibit themselves unmistakeably in the change of his outward appearance, and the absence of that bodily activity and firmness of step, which had marked his demeanour and movements until within a comparatively short period, his spirits recovered their tone, and his intellectual vigour remained wholly unimpaired. The state of his health still imposing upon him the necessity of avoiding all bodily fatigue and continuous mental exertion, he passed the winter and early spring at Brighton; and while, as regards the ordinary and routine duties of his office, his place was efficiently supplied by Mr. George Jones, the amiable and accomplished Keeper of the Academy, he was able to communicate his views from time to time, on all subjects of exceptional importance or interest, to his academic brethren, with his usual clearness, and undiminished vigour, through the medium of epistolary correspondence.

On the 10th December, the anniversary of the establishment of the Royal Academy, and the period when the annual election of officers for the ensuing year takes place, he was as usual, unanimously re-elected President; and the biennial ceremony of the distribution of gold medals having again come round, the discourse which he had prepared for delivery on that interesting occasion, two years previously, when he was suddenly prevented by severe illness from discharging the duty in question, was, at his request, read to the students on his behalf, by the worthy Keeper.

The President had at one time indulged a hope that the state of his health might admit of his officiating in person on this important anniversary; but he was reluctantly induced by the remonstrances of his family and his medical advisers, to refrain from an attempt which it was feared might retard his apparent progress towards a qualified convalescence. ' He determined, therefore, to husband his strength through the winter, by carefully avoiding every unnecessary mental exertion and unusual demand on his physical energies, during the period that would intervene before the opening of the exhibition in 1846, in the hope that he might be sufficiently recovered to undertake the duty of presiding at the Academy dinner.

In this hope, on the accomplishment of which his mind was most earnestly bent, he was not doomed to disappointment.   Ere the important period arrived, the most incapacitating symptoms of his complaint had so far yielded to the influence of medical treatment, and the beneficial operation of rest, and freedom from engrossing occupation, that he could contemplate, without much apprehension, the bodily fatigue and the far more serious mental exhaustion inseparable from the effective performance of the duties connected with the ceremonial of the day.   He therefore determined on going up to London a few days before the opening of the exhibition, in time to be present at the private view, and superintend the arrangements of the council, in reference to the approaching dinner.   It was arranged that Lady Shee should accompany him to town; and although it was considered of importance that he should not long absent himself from Brighton,—to the pure and bracing air of which the gradual improvement in his health seemed in great measure attributable,—they proposed to prolong their stay in London for a few days beyond the period of the academic ceremonial, in order to be present at the christening of their first and only grandson, the recently-born child of their youngest son, at that time occupying with his family Sir Martin's house in Cavendish Square; — an occasion of some domestic interest in itself, and which, from the state of the male representation of the family,—not only among Sir Martin's own descendants, but throughout that branch of his ancient house with which he was more immediately connected,—appealed very forcibly to those ancestral sympathies, which, be it weakness or not, retained, to the last, a strong hold on the mind and heart of one whose career had added fresh distinction to an honourable name.

A day or two, however, before the time fixed for the

President's journey to London, a slight, or what appeared to be a slight cold, with which Lady Archer Shee was attacked, induced her to abandon her intention of accompanying Sir Martin in his visit to the metropolis, her medical attendant being of opinion that at her advanced period of life, and in reference to the general condition of her health, which had been for many years extremely delicate, the journey in question would not be unattended with risk. There seemed to be nothing in the circumstance itself, to justify any apprehension as to the result of what appeared a trifling indisposition; Lady Shee having been long subject to attacks of a similar character, which, frequently recurring, yielded without difficulty to medical treatment of a simple and chiefly precautionary nature. Sir Martin, therefore, left Brighton without any particular anxiety on her account, and with no more serious mental disquietude on the occasion, than was involved in his disappointment at being deprived of her society during his intended short stay in town.

His brethren of the Academy had of course had due notice of his intention to preside at the dinner, and were prepared to greet his re-appearance among them with affectionate cordiality. But although the failure of his health, and the circumstances attending the resignation and resumption of his office, were generally known in the circles of art, nothing had occurred in connection with the public discharge of his official functions, to prepare them for the evidence of his partial recovery, which his presence at the opening of the exhibition so satisfactorily afforded. His appearance at the private view, therefore, was, to the far greater proportion of the distinguished visitors who filled the exhibition rooms on that occasion, an unexpected event; and no one who, like the writer of these pages, witnessed the effect it produced on the brilliant assemblage that were there congregated, will easily forget the flattering and spontaneous testimony thereby offered to the President's great and well-merited social popularity.

At that period, the royal visit to the exhibition was, according to established custom, arranged to take place on the same day as the private view to which the *élite* of the *connoisseur* and fashionable world were admitted by tickets: the Queen, and such members of the royal family, officers of state &c., as were privileged to form part of her Majesty's *cortége* on the occasion, being attended and conducted through the exhibition rooms by the President and officers of the establishment, in the first instance; the holders of tickets (with the exception of those whose presence was commanded by the Queen), not being admitted into the rooms until after the departure of the royal party.

The gratifying duty of attending her Majesty and the Prince on their visit to the Academy was discharged for the last time by Sir Martin on this occasion; and in the course of its performance, he was honoured by the gracious exhibition of a cordial interest in the state of his health, on the part of his royal and august visitors. I may be pardoned for mentioning, in particular, that the late Duke of Cambridge, with characteristic amiability and genuine kindness of heart, expressed much apprehension lest the President should suffer from the fatigue of the day, and urgently pressed him to avail himself of the support of his Royal Highness's arm, in making the tour of the rooms with the royal party. Although much reduced in strength, and aged in appearance, within the preceding year, Sir Martin was, however, fully adequate to the performance of his courtly duties on this occasion; and having allowed himself a short interval of rest after the departure of the Queen, he re-entered the exhibition room, at the fullest moment of the private view, and when no one but his brother members anticipated his appearance among them. His arrival was greeted with the most unmistakeable demonstrations of surprise and gratification, from all quarters of the room. Peers, prelates, statesmen and *savans*,—courtiers and *literati* thronged round him in a kind of chorus of congratulation, with an enthusiastic cordiality, too evidently unpremeditated to be suspected of insincerity or exaggeration; while the highest, the noblest, and the most courted of the fair visitors who graced the Academy by their presence on that occasion, vied with each other in the eager exhibition of friendly and respectful interest in his improved health, and cordial satisfaction at his unexpected return to the scene of his official and social triumphs.

These striking evidences of the estimation in which he was held, personally, as well as officially, by all that was most distinguished among his contemporaries, were a source of legitimate satisfaction to all most nearly connected with him, and to those,—and they were not a few,—both in and out of the academic circle, on whose sympathies he had the strong claim of long and intimate friendship. It was, indeed, to the few members of his own family who were present, a moment of exultation, to be appreciated by those alone who knew how he was estimated in his domestic circle, and how fully his rare and noble qualities of mind and heart justified their feelings of devoted attachment and veneration.

The following day (Saturday 2nd May), he once

more, and for the last time, presided at the annual dinner, which was, as usual, brilliantly attended, and where his last public accents were listened to with an interest greatly enhanced by the circumstance which rendered his presence on the occasion an event wholly unlooked for, until within eight-and-forty hours of its occurrence.  He had the gratification of being supported by the prime minister, Sir Robert Peel, who, in the absence of the Lord Chancellor, occupied the seat next to the President on the right hand of the chair; and whose warm sympathy with the objects and interests which Sir Martin had most at heart in his official capacity, to say nothing of the proofs of personal regard for which he was indebted to that able and patriotic statesman, rendered his proximity during the discharge of the duties of the day, peculiarly agreeable to the President.

Some touching verses, inserted a few years back in a number of "Household Words," and which purport to have been suggested by Sir Martin's last appearance in the academic chair, on the interesting occasion in question,—verses conceived and written in a spirit of the most kindly sympathy with his declining health, and with a just appreciation of his rare intellectual and oratorical powers,—appear to indicate on the part of the writer, whom strong circumstantial evidence would seem to identify with the most popular author of the day, an impression that the effects of Sir Martin's long and distressing illness were perceptible, in the diminished energy with which he went through the arduous task imposed on him by the programme.  This may possibly have been the case, as far as regards the mere physical power required to make his voice distinctly and emphatically audible, in every part of the large room where the academic banquet takes place. But if the testimony of some of the most distinguished among his brilliant auditory can be relied on, it would seem that neither in matter nor in manner,—neither in justness of idea nor appropriateness of language,— neither in soundness of view nor in grace of delivery, did his various addresses from the chair, on that day, fall short of the high standard of excellence which his previous efforts, on similar occasions, had established in the minds of his friends, as connected with his usual performance of the duty in question. Certain it is that his brethren of the Academy were loud and earnest in the expression of their gratitude for his exertions on the occasion; while the impression that remained on his own mind, as to the degree of success by which these exertions had been attended, in the estimation of those around him, appeared as satisfactory as his character- istic diffidence of his own powers would ever allow him to entertain.

Although much fatigued at the close of a day which had taxed his physical and mental powers to the utmost, he returned to Cavendish Square in high spirits, and deeply gratified by the occurrences of the evening. But alas! a sad reverse of feeling awaited him. During his absence at the Academy, a letter from Brighton, from one of his daughters, had arrived by the evening post, containing a very unsatisfactory report of Lady Shee's health, and, without in words betraying the extent of the apprehensions under which the writer laboured, suggesting the expediency of Sir Martin's return to Pavilion Colonnade on the ensuing day.

Though this unlooked-for summons spoke not of im- mediate or even probable danger, its real significance was but too justly appreciated by the foreboding fears of those to whom it was addressed, as well as by Sir Martin himself, when, early on the following morning, the sad intelligence, studiously and judiciously withheld at the late hour of his return from Trafalgar Square on the previous night, was necessarily communicated to him.

The matter admitted of no delay. Accompanied by his eldest daughter and one of his sons, he started for Brighton by the earliest available train, and arrived in Pavilion Colonnade about one o'clock in the afternoon; when, to his unspeakable grief and dismay, he found the beloved sufferer rapidly sinking, and by the acknowledgment of the eminent medical men in attendance, apparently beyond the reach of all human skill. The complaint, which, during the first few days, had exhibited merely the symptoms of a slight cold, had suddenly assumed the alarming character of inflammatory *bronchitis;* and so rapid was the progress of the fearful malady, that, at the time of Sir Martin's arrival, she appeared to retain but a partial and intermitting consciousness; and the awful change in her countenance proclaimed at once, but too significantly, the near approach of death. Lady Archer Shee expired at four o'clock on the following morning, Monday, the 4th of May, 1846. Had it pleased God to prolong her life until the 19th of December, in the same year, she would have seen the fiftieth anniversary of her marriage with Sir Martin.

The sudden disruption of the most cherished and holiest of earthly ties, after so long a lapse of years, during which its influence had been fully and gratefully appreciated by one whose ideas of happiness and enjoyment were wholly centred in *home*, was a calamity, on the severity of which, under the circumstances, it would

be superfluous to enlarge.   Those to whom the amiable
and endearing qualities of Lady Shee's character were
best known,—and there are few whose memory is more
affectionately cherished by numerous surviving friends,—
can alone estimate the loss which Sir Martin sustained
in the death of the most devoted of wives, and one of
the brightest spirits that ever chased the shadows of
care and despondency from the domestic hearth.

Happily it is no part of the duty of the biographer
to dwell minutely on the details of an overwhelming
and lasting grief.   It will suffice to say, that the blow
was one, from the effects of which Sir Martin cannot
be said to have ever completely rallied; nor could any
other result be anticipated in the case of one who, at
the advanced age of seventy-six, with shattered health
and an enfeebled nervous system, retained all the
warmth of heart and ardour of domestic affection, which
had characterised him in early youth, and throughout
every subsequent period of his life.

The unexpected announcement of Lady Shee's death
produced a most painful sensation among the numerous
attached friends and admirers who, but two days previously, had joyfully hailed Sir Martin's reappearance at
the Academy, in the discharge of his arduous duties
as President, with heartfelt congratulations and every
gratifying evidence of personal regard.

Among those who most truly appreciated the sadness
of his bereavement, no one was more prompt or more
considerate in the exhibition of a friendly sympathy,
than Sir Robert Peel; and in the midst of the many
engrossing and harassing cares of his high position,—at
the moment threatened by that combination of opposite
political elements which so soon after resulted in his
final removal from power,—he hastened with the most

thoughtful kindness, to provide, in his ministerial capacity, against the consequences, to Sir Martin and his family, of an event which had necessarily the effect of rendering nugatory the gracious act by which the Crown had emphatically recognised the President's eminent merits and services, but a few months previously. The pension granted, according to the minister's kind suggestion, to Lady Archer Shee, had of course ceased on her lamented death. But a very few days had elapsed after the occurrence of the mournful event, ere Sir Robert Peel, with every expression of kindly feeling appropriate to the circumstances, conveyed to Sir Martin the assurance that when the proper period arrived for bringing under her Majesty's notice the question of the apportionment of the sum to which the Crown is restricted, in its annual appropriation of pensions on the civil list, he was desirous and prepared to propose to her Majesty the gracious renewal of the royal bounty to the President, in the shape of a pension of the like amount as that which had been awarded to Lady Shee, to be granted for life to Sir Martin's three daughters, and the survivors and survivor of them.

It is due to the memory of one of Sir Martin's most attached and most valued friends — the late Lord Denman — to state, that on receiving the intelligence of Lady Archer Shee's death, his lordship, without any previous communication on the subject with Sir Martin or his family, and in apparent ignorance of the strong personal regard entertained towards the President by the Prime Minister, which rendered the suggestion superfluous, immediately wrote to Sir Robert Peel, calling his attention to the fact that the lapse of Lady Shee's pension had, under the circumstances, frustrated the gracious intention of the Crown in its creation.

Although it is certain that, with his feelings towards the President, Sir Robert had not overlooked, and was incapable of disregarding, the expediency of bringing the matter afresh under the gracious notice of the Queen, with a view to its satisfactory arrangement,—yet the genuine kindness of heart and frankness of spirit which dictated the proceeding of the illustrious Chief Justice, in addressing, for such a purpose, a minister with whom he had but slight social relations, and whose views were generally considered antagonistic to the great political party with whose brightest glories the name of Denman is inseparably associated, cannot but command the grateful acknowledgment of Sir Martin's biographer.

It need hardly be said, that Sir Robert's kind and thoughtful consideration for the future interests of those surviving relatives in whom Sir Martin's affectionate anxiety was now chiefly centred, afforded the latter as much satisfaction as, in the deep affliction which over-whelmed him at the moment, he was capable of receiving from any event connected with his worldly affairs.   Nor, however painful the effort, did he fail to express to Sir Robert, by a few lines under his own hand, the grateful sense he entertained of the kindness of the minister, and the favour of the Crown.   Her Majesty having graciously acquiesced in the recommendation of the First Lord of the Treasury, the affair was carried through in due course; and on the 28th June, in the same year, Sir Robert again wrote to the President, to acquaint him with its final completion and ratification by the Royal Sign Manual.

In the interval which had elapsed since the first communication addressed by him to Sir Martin on the subject, the suicidal policy of that portion of the Conservative party which felt itself called upon to revenge the wrongs of " Protection " on the sagacious and far-sighted minister — who had not hesitated, at all risks, to avow and act upon his conscientious, though tardy conversion to sounder theories of commercial and economical science, — had, by throwing their weight into the scale of the Whig-Radical party, on a division involving parliamentary interests of secondary importance, succeeded in placing the administration in a minority, under circumstances which involved the necessity of their resignation; and at the period when the warrant for the pension to Sir Martin's daughters was submitted to the Queen, for her Majesty's signature, the seals of office were retained by Sir Robert Peel and his colleagues, merely until the completion of the new ministerial arrangements should have definitively pointed out the hands into which they were to be transferred.

In the friendly letter which, as I have stated, announced to Sir Martin that the proposed arrangement had been fully carried into effect, by the gracious sanction of the Queen, Sir Robert emphatically, and alas! too prophetically, stated that the transaction was *the last act of his official life,* — a phrase which, in the estimation of him to whom it was addressed, and indeed by its own obvious significance, implied a resolution on the part of that distinguished statesman, to pass the remainder of his life free from the trammels of office, and in the enjoyment of that political independence, for the want of which the patriotic labours and ill-requited sacrifices of his ministerial career, had afforded him such questionable compensation.

In reply to this communication, Sir Martin wrote as follows :—

"Brighton, June 30, 1846.

"MY DEAR SIR,

" An occasional aggravation of the persevering malady under which I still severely suffer, rendered me quite unable yesterday to acknowledge your gratifying letter, communicating to me that the Queen had been graciously pleased to comply with the arrangement respecting the pension to my daughters, which your considerate kindness recommended to her Majesty. The manner and spirit in which this favour has been conferred upon me, so much enhance its value, that I should prove myself most unworthy of it, if, reluctant as I am to trespass on your attention at a moment when your mind must be occupied by matters of the highest national as well as personal interest, I could hesitate, even at the risk of indiscretion, to repeat the assurance of my heartfelt gratitude. The indulgence which I have always experienced from you, and the generous sympathy you have shown for my incurable domestic calamity, convince me that you will justly appreciate feelings which, however strongly excited, cannot always be adequately expressed.

" You allude, my dear sir, to your retirement from office. During a long life, I have never allowed myself to be influenced by any political or party feeling; — a conduct which I conceived to be most befitting my position as an artist. The rancorous hostility, however, with which you have been recently so unjustly assailed

'by those
Whose sons will blush their fathers were thy foes,'

has extorted from me one instance of a departure from a policy so long observed, and compels me to declare my conviction, that the important services which you have rendered to your country, the generous sacrifices which you have made to her interests, and the extraordinary powers you have displayed in effecting your patriotic objects, have secured for you a proud station amongst the most eminent statesmen that the annals of history have ever presented to the admiration and gratitude of an enlightened people.

" Pardon, my dear sir, this political outbreak of a man, who, though not wise enough to be silent, is too old and too honest to be insincere.

"That you may enjoy all the blessings that health, fame, and fortune can bestow, is the ardent prayer of,

"My dear sir,

"Most faithfully and gratefully yours,

"MARTIN ARCHER SHEE.

"To the Right Honourable Sir Robert Peel, Bart."

# CHAPTER XVIII.

## 1846—1850.

Gradual Decay of Sir Martin's physical Powers.—Distressing Characteristic of his Complaint.—Unimpaired Vigour of Mind.—His Thoughts on the revolutionary Movements of 1848 and 1849.—Death of the Bishop of Llandaff.—Sir Martin recommends Mr. Macaulay to the Queen as his Successor in the Academic Professorship of Ancient Literature.—The Great Exhibition.—Death of Sir Robert Peel.—Last Moments of the President.—His Death.—His Funeral.—His Character.—Conclusion.

THE few remaining years of Sir Martin's life which his biographer has to record, were not such as to admit of any extended notice. Passed in retirement and comparative seclusion, amid the constant suffering attendant on a chronic complaint, and the gradual decay of his physical powers, they present nothing in the way of incident, to arrest the attention of the reader, or to retard the close of a narrative already, perhaps, too circumstantial in details of little general interest.

During Sir Martin's residence at Brighton, and even before the death of Lady Archer Shee, the character of his singular complaint appeared to undergo a material change, exhibiting itself no longer in the form of sudden and violent giddiness,—resulting in the most distressing phenomena of sea-sickness,— but presenting the normal condition of a permanent vertiginous affection, from the depressing influence of which he never for a moment felt himself entirely free.

One of the most painful circumstances connected with this state of the brain or the circulation, was its invariable and immediate aggravation by the act of reading or writing. How greatly the discomfort of the feeling itself, was enhanced by the privation involved in the necessity of refraining from the use of his eyes in reading, can be fully understood by those alone who, like himself, have been accustomed to look upon books as amongst the strictest necessaries of life, and who have ever found, in their aid and companionship, the most effective safeguard against *ennui*, and the surest refuge from the ordinary cares and anxieties of existence.

The total exemption of his mental faculties from the gradual process of decay observable in his outward frame, although highly consolatory to those around him,—whose pride in his intellectual superiority was a cherished feeling, the disturbance of which, by the manifestation of any failure of mind or memory on his part, would have been felt by them as a severe trial,— only served to render more acute the annoyance he himself experienced from a state of things which seemed to condemn his still bright and vigorous intellect to a dreary inactivity. Fortunately, however, the evil admitted of material alleviation. With three unmarried daughters, resident under his roof, and wholly devoted to the task of promoting his happiness and comfort, he was at no loss for effective means to obviate the worst results of the merely physical incapacity under which he laboured. That he drew largely on the resources thus supplied by filial affection and solicitude, may be easily inferred from the fact, that, during the last two or three years of his life, he usually required the services of a reader at every moment of the day, not passed out of doors, or devoted either to his meals or to the necessary cares of his invalid condition. The somewhat severe duty in question was cheerfully undertaken, and performed with unflinching assiduity by those on whom it naturally devolved; but even *their* persevering zeal could hardly suffice to maintain the untiring activity necessary to supply the wants of his all but insatiable appetite for intellectual food.

The annoyance which he acknowledged himself to experience from the suspension of their task, during even a short interval,—under circumstances when he had only the resource of that silent musing which, in the case of many who have entered on the declining period of life, seems to afford a not unpleasing occupation,—was explained by him as connected with a peculiar characteristic of his mind, that, on such occasions, had a tendency to aggravate the ordinary symptoms of his complaint.

It was, he said, impossible for his brain or his imagination to remain quiescent for any lengthened period, during which neither books nor conversation enforced an outward claim on his attention. The memories of the past, the uncertainties of the present, the contingencies of the future,—not only in reference to himself and his *entourage*, but often in relation to matters of public interest, philosophical, literary, or political,—would, by turns, and with an obtrusive pertinacity against which he in vain essayed to struggle, excite the activity of his brain, in every variety of imaginative speculation, anxious reflection, laborious reasoning, and sometimes hypothetical argument.

This was probably the result of a long-established habit of mind, originating at a period of life when this speculative and gratuitous exercise of the intellectual faculties was attended with highly beneficial results to his powers of reasoning and his rare gift of eloquent expression. But this species of mental fermentation, innocuous as it might have been in a system unweakened by time, and unassailed by disease, could not co-exist with so much physical debility and functional derangement, except at the risk of increasing the ordinary evils attendant upon both.

It might be truly said of him,

*" I suoi pensier' in lui dormir non ponno ;"*

and he felt that his only resource was to direct this too ready wakefulness of thought into a calm and peaceful channel, by occupying it with subjects of sufficient interest to fix and repay his attention, without calling into permanent activity those higher functions of mind of which, while fully possessing the use, he could not with impunity allow himself the continuous exercise.

It need hardly be said, that, while his mental faculties remained thus unimpaired, every subject of importance connected with the interests and management of the Royal Academy, that was brought under his official notice, was sure not only to command his ready and anxious attention, but to receive the benefit of a judgment as sound, and arguments as convincing, as had formed and maintained his opinions in the brightest days of his academic career.

The manual operation of writing was, as I have said, a cause of greatly increased discomfort, and was therefore seldom resorted to by him on occasions of this description. But the process of dictation was equally effective for the purpose of conveying his sentiments, with distinctness and accuracy, to the friendly colleagues who sought his guidance or advice in the administration of those affairs which could no longer enjoy the advantage of his active participation.　His written communications, addressed from time to time to his brethren of the council, on matters which appeared to call for the expression of his opinion, or the development of his views, exhibited, to the very last, those characteristics of clearness of thought and vigour of diction, which had ever distinguished the productions of his pen.

Time did not fail to produce its usual effect in gradually lightening the burthen of his affliction, and restoring to his mind and spirits a calm and even tone. Thus, although his bodily health experienced no permanent improvement, his interest in passing events, and the great questions which were agitating the world, and convulsing continental society, in the years 1848 and 1849, was sufficiently strong to exhibit itself to those around him with that vigour of thought and energy of expression which had marked the enunciation of his opinions in by-gone days.

The subjoined letter, addressed by him to his attached friend Miss Tunno will afford some evidence in support of this assertion, while it is curiously illustrative of the peculiar nature of his physical ailment.　Begun with his own hand, it seems to have been interrupted by that disheartening aggravation of the ordinary symptoms of his complaint, which, as I have said, invariably attended any continuous exercise of his eyes, in reading or writing.　But although its merely manual completion required the employment of another hand, the style and substance of the letter leave no doubt as to the clearness of the head, or the activity of the mind, from which it emanated.

" *To Miss Tunno.*
" Brighton, Feb. 14, 1849.

" Often during many months past have I most eagerly desired

to write to you, my ever dear and excellent friend; often have I attempted to do so, and as often have I been obliged to desist, from the utter inability to carry my intention into effect. I will not say how much this has grieved me; for notwithstanding my long experience of the considerate kindness of your disposition, I have never been able to get rid of the impression that I must appear to you as ungrateful as neglectful, in suffering from any cause (short of the absolute suspension of all my rational faculties) an interruption, on my part, of the correspondence with which you have so long indulged me, and from which I have derived such sincere gratification. Though not having quite so decided an excuse to plead for my silence, I think I may reasonably say that he may be considered as nearly approaching to that imbecile state, who finds himself unable to *write*, or *read, talk*, or even *think* on any subject, without bringing on himself an aggravation of all the inflictions of a complaint which admits of only partial alleviation, and yields to no remedy within the range of medical science. You may be well assured, my amiable friend, that not all the infirmities of age and disease, combined to test the endurance of man, could suffice to deter me from attempting, at least, to prove to you, by my own hand, that however the head may fail in its functions, the homage of the heart is still yours, in as warm a glow of affection and admiration, as your many excellent and attractive qualities ever excited in the earliest period of our acquaintance,— if other difficulties did not co-operate with my vertiginous enemy to counteract my intentions. You are aware, I believe, that I have been long under the *surveillance* of a domestic board of health, consisting of three fair guardians and divers assistant functionaries, generally considered as *relieving* officers; but, as far as I am concerned, as little effective in that capacity as the most callous official commemorated in the far-famed Andover Union. Now, my fair guardians,—though, as you well know, mild, gentle, and amiable in all the ordinary concerns of life,— where my health or comfort appears to be at all in question, are so energetic in expostulation, so absolute in exacting submission to prescribed rule, that, for peace as well as policy, I find it necessary to yield to their sway. Indeed they are so utterly unhappy, so alarmingly apprehensive of consequences, if they see a pen in my hand, or suspect any meditated infraction of dietary or other sanative regulations, that it would not only be ungracious but ungrateful to persist in any proceeding which must appear to them like a perverse opposition to just and rational remonstrance.

"Thus, my dear friend, though a warm friend of liberty, am I reduced to passive obedience, under petticoat coercion and the resistless sway of female virtue. Even the wretched scribble which I with such difficulty write, and you I fear cannot read, has been perpetrated by stealth,—two or three lines at a time,—in those few snatches of opportunity and short relaxations of attention, which unavoidable circumstances will occasionally extort from the most anxious and untiring vigilance. But you have little reason to regret those obstructions which so effectually impede my epistolary efforts. I am no very amusing correspondent;—what can a letter from me now contain but details of dulness and disease,—records of suffering and sadness? Shut up as I am in my cave for three fourths of the year, visiting nobody, and admitting no visitors except the members of my own family; half blind from an affection of the optic nerve, hearing little at one ear, and nothing at the other; helpless in motion, and lethargic at rest;—my position may be considered as a kind of living death: I am defunct before my time, as to all the purposes and pleasures of social intercourse. I exist in a dreamy state of semi-conscious nonentity; without the energy to repress the excitement of active thought, or power to resort without injury to the slumbering resource of meditation. Pardon, my ever dear friend, this long trespass on your patience and your feelings, which only your indulgent kindness can excuse, and nothing but the ardent desire to rescue from the imputation of neglect or decay, the lasting attachment which your admirable qualities have inspired, could have induced me to inflict upon you.

"I have suffered, my ever dear friend, the penalty of disobedience, by being rendered unable to continue, by my own pen, a letter which I fear you will find illegible; for you will have perceived that my hand fails me even more than my head.

This unlucky check, you may suppose, unavoidably disclosed my secret operations; and my sensitively apprehensive guardians are loud in eloquent reproof of my evasion of their authority. They even threaten a strait waistcoat, if I should make a second attempt to elude their vigilance. Thus circumstanced, I am compelled to entrust the remainder of my epistolary indiscretion to the agency of the fair and kind amanuensis, whose assistance has so often called forth my grateful acknowledgment; but, as I have adopted a more intelligible interpreter, I will also, for your sake, change my theme, and ask you what must be the preoccupation of mind of him who could scribble a long epistle to man, woman, or child, at a time like the present, without even an allusion to politics? What do you think of the frightful "antics played before high Heaven" by the Sovereign People, in what is called, *par éminence*, the *civilised* part of the world? There cannot surely be a dry eye amongst the angels if, as we are assured by poetical authority, they weep for the folly and frenzy of mankind. If I were *at large* again, and competent to any active prudential proceeding, I think I would rush to the Zoological Gardens, and request admission to the assemblage of wild beasts collected there, to avoid all community of intercourse with the wilder and more savage animals called men. A menagerie of monkeys is an asylum of sages, compared to the lunatic gatherings of patriots and politicians. If any sceptic should enquire for the locality of the infernal regions, he may be sure to find it in that hell upon earth, — that political Pandemonium, — a convention for the regeneration of man. What a pity that Providence, in its wisdom and mercy, did not constitute a world of women; to show that the virtues and charities of life are not inconsistent attributes of humanity; and to prove that faith, truth, justice, generosity, and common sense are yet to be found, at least in the *better half* of the human race.

Unwilling, my kind friend, that the close of my letter should continue the depressing tone which too much characterises its commencement, I have anxiously avoided a topic ever present to my mind, and which must darkly cloud the short remainder of my existence; but in a desire to relieve the painful feeling, which, I well know, has always prompted you to share in the afflictions of your friends, I am bound to tell you that Time has worked its usual effect, and that I can now speak and think of the lost companion of my life, without those convulsive bursts of emotion, on the first interview with any friend who was acquainted with her virtues. But though the stunning influence of sorrow has been somewhat assuaged, I still suffer under a solitude of the heart, which cannot be removed even by the constant attentions, and soothing endearments of the most affectionate family that ever shed a ray of comfort on the gloom of declining years and decaying faculties. But no more on this subject."

The gradual progress of bodily decay is as sad a theme to dwell on in narration, as it is a melancholy spectacle to contemplate from day to day. It is, however, nearly all that remains to be told by the biographer, in closing his record of Sir Martin's long and honourable career. Fortunately, his evil of declining strength, while productive of much discomfort, was not aggravated by acute suffering; and the unimpaired vigour of his mind enabled him, almost to the last, to sustain his interest in passing events, as well as in the incidents and feelings which make up the sum of domestic and family life. On the occasion of the marriage of his second son, in the month of August, 1849, with the daughter of the late John Richard Barrett, Esq. of Milton House, Berks, he presented to the bride an admirable production of his pencil, in a portrait of her husband, painted in the early youth of the latter,—a work which the President always looked upon as one of his most successful efforts. Being desirous either of making some slight alteration in a portion of the *accessoire*, or of repairing an almost imperceptible injury to the colouring of the face, which he fancied he discovered in the picture after it had been subjected to the process of cleaning, he one day, for a few minutes, and for the last time, resumed his palette and pencils, which had remained untouched by him since the spring of 1845. But, alas! the uncertainty of sight, incident to his complaint, rather than any ordinary failure of the organs of vision, soon warned him that his operations were very hazardous; and he desisted from the attempt with a sigh. The picture in question claims an additional interest in the eyes of the owner, from the fact that it was the last work on which the once vigorous pencil of the President, traced its now expiring line.

The death of his friend Dr. Coplestone, the Bishop of Llandaff, caused a vacancy in the office of Professor of Ancient Literature in the Royal Academy. This honorary professorship,—a merely nominal chair,—is one of four or five similar appointments connected with that institution, which were originally created, and have been retained in its organization, for the purpose of associating with the body a few eminent men in the literary and scientific world. There are no duties attached to the office, except that which may, in the words of the civilian or scientific jurist, be described as a " duty of imperfect obligation," viz. that of being present at the annual dinner; while free admission to the exhibition, including the private view, and the disposal of two other tickets for that interesting occasion, constitute, with the right of attendance at the dinner, the measure of the privileges attached to the appointment. It is, however, a distinction involving a graceful and complimentary recognition of high intellectual claims, on the part of the Crown and the Academy, and has been proportionably valued by the eminent men on whom it has been conferred.

Unlike the rank of R.A. or A.R.A., and most of

the other official appointments in the body, the office of Professor of Ancient Literature, and the other honorary professorships in the Royal Academy, are not the subject of election by the Royal Academicians. The nomination is made by the Queen, on the recommendation of the President. The vacancy in question, therefore, afforded Sir Martin an opportunity, of which he gladly availed himself, of testifying his admiration for one of the greatest writers and most distinguished men of his time, by humbly submitting to her Majesty the name of the Right Hon. Thomas Babington Macaulay, as a fit successor to the deceased prelate. Mr. Macaulay was accorddingly dulyappointed Professor of Ancient Literature in the Royal Academy, in the room of the Bishop of Llandaff.

The project of the great industrial exhibition, when publicly ventilated in the early part of the year 1850, forcibly arrested Sir Martin's attention, and from the first enlisted his ardent sympathy in favour of the objects sought to be attained by the promoters of that magnificent work. He felt and spoke on the subject with a degree of enthusiasm, such as is seldom manifested by those whose lives are visibly hastening to a close, and who are consequently liable to that engrossing pre-occupation of thought, which leaves but little space for ideas and reflections having exclusive reference to the material interests and prospects of that busy world, the " fashion " of which is, for them, rapidly passing away.

Earnestly desirous that the Royal Academy,—as the representatives of an important section of that social fabric which the gigantic undertaking was intended to consolidate, expand, and develop,—should cordially co-operate in forwarding the enlightened and philanthropic views of the illustrious Prince to whose happy suggestion the memorable and gloriously executed idea may, I apprehend, in its origin, be unhesitatingly ascribed, Sir Martin addressed to his colleagues of the Council an earnest and animated appeal on the subject, strongly urging upon them the expediency of marking their approval and appreciation of the design, by a liberal pecuniary subscription towards its expenses. It is almost superfluous to add that the Academy, animated by feelings of congenial liberality, and fully sharing the views of their venerable President, were prompt in acting on his recommendation. A sum of £500 was duly voted and contributed by the Royal Academy to the funds of the undertaking.

As the year 1850 proceeded, the rapid decay of Sir Martin's physical powers gave unmistakeable warning of the speedy termination of his earthly career. But though reduced to a state of great bodily weakness, and exhibiting in his frame and countenance the usual characteristics of approaching death, his mental faculties betrayed no symptom of decay, nor did his interest in books or public affairs appear to flag.

The melancholy death of Sir Robert Peel, which occurred but a few weeks previous to his own decease, was to him a source of the most painful regret; he was indeed sensibly and deeply affected by it  On the morning after the day when the news of the sad accident had reached Brighton,—in answer to an anxious inquiry after his own health from one of his family, he exclaimed, with melancholy emphasis, " What does it matter how *I* am? —when the ablest and most virtuous statesman in the country lies at the point of death? What is the value of *my* life in comparison with *his* ? "

It was the last occurrence which was destined to call forth any manifestation of excited feeling on his part.

Within a few weeks, he was reduced to a state of extreme debility and exhaustion, which, in most cases, would have suggested to the sufferer, especially to one so far advanced in years, the expediency of remaining in bed. But although the act of getting up, and the operation of dressing, could not be achieved without much laborious exertion on his own part, as well as on the part of those in attendance on him, he continued to make his daily appearance in the drawing-room, and occupy his accustomed arm-chair for the greater part of the day, and the whole of the evening, until within less than three days of his death; and, down to the same period, the services of a reader were still in daily requisition, with the same unintermitting continuance, during the entire portion of the twenty-four hours which he passed out of his bed-room.

At length, on the night of Friday the 16th of August, the total prostration of his system, and the utter incapacity for spontaneous movement which he exhibited when about to seek his bed-room for the night, made it evident that the struggle could not be further prolonged. He was, however, perfectly collected; courteously exhibiting, as he ever did, a considerate and regretful consciousness of the trouble which his helpless condition necessarily entailed on those around him, while removing his clothes and placing him in bed.

" Do not," said he, addressing his sons, who were in close attendance upon him during this process, " do not wish for long life; you see the state to which I am reduced." This was the last connected sentence that he uttered. He lingered during the Saturday and Sunday, in a state of continued, or but partially interrupted unconsciousness. On Monday the 19th, about six in the afternoon, he breathed his last. He had completed his eightieth year, on the 20th of the preceding month of December (1849).

All his children—three sons and three daughters—and two out of three daughters-in-law, to whom he was scarcely less endeared by his unvarying kindness and affectionate demeanour, had the melancholy satisfaction of being present at his last moments.

On being apprised of his decease, the Council of the Royal Academy made a communication to his family, pointing out the expediency of following, in his case, the precedent established in that of his distinguished predecessors in the chair, by making arrangements for his interment in St. Paul's Cathedral, with the usual solemnities of a public funeral; and offering, on the part of the Academy, to take upon themselves the arrangement and responsibility of so much of the ceremonial as related to the attendance of the members, and the proceedings to be observed within the walls of the institution on the occasion.

Many reasons, however, irrespective of the earnest desire which Sir Martin had been frequently heard to express, that no such display should take place in the event of his death, and that he might be conveyed to the grave in as quiet and unostentatious a manner as possible, combined to render acquiescence in the kind and respectful suggestion of his academic brethren unadvisable, in the judgment of those members of his family with whom the decision of the question rested.

It has been seen that on his retirement from active life, his circumstances were far from wealthy; and although any public honours, spontaneously paid to his memory, would have been productive of the highest gratification to his children, and in their view well worth the pecuniary sacrifice which might be involved, it was by no means certain that the amount of public interest created by his death would, in its outward demonstration, be sufficient to outweigh those prudential considerations which, in reference to the state of his property, rendered it, *primâ facie*, inexpedient to incur the formidable expense inseparable from the proposed public funeral.*

The four last years of Sir Martin's life had been passed in such complete seclusion from the busy world, that the ever-advancing tide of time might be said to have long since rolled its oblivious waves over his name, as far as any impression (among the general public) of his existence as a *living* celebrity was concerned. How completely this was the case, may be gathered from the fact that on the announcement of his death, through the usual channel, in the obituary of the daily press, his name, character, and career remained wholly unnoticed by the principal organs of public opinion. His decease, too, occurred at a period of the year when his many surviving friends and admirers in the front rank of social, political, and intellectual life were absent from London, and would therefore have been unable without great inconvenience to pay him the tribute of respect involved in a personal attendance at his public obsequies.

Under these circumstances, the proposal of the Council was respectfully and gratefully declined; and it was determined that the funeral should take place at Brighton with the strictest privacy; the attendance being, with two exceptions, confined to members of his own family.

On the evening of Monday, the 26th August, the funeral office of the Roman Catholic Church was performed over his coffin, at his residence in Pavilion

---

* I have been assured that the cost of Sir Thomas Lawrence's funeral and interment in St. Paul's amounted to about 700*l*.

Colonnade, in the presence of his family, by the Rev. Mr. Rymer; and on the following morning his revered remains were removed to their last earthly resting place, in the Brighton Cemetery; the burial service of the Church of England having been previously read over them in the adjoining parish church.

Six mourners alone followed him to the grave, viz: his three sons, his step-grandson, Lieutenant William George Cubitt*, of the 13th Bengal Native Infantry (then a youth of fourteen years of age), the son, by her first husband, of Sir Martin's fondly beloved and warmly attached daughter-in-law, Mrs. William Archer Shee,— his friend, the Rev. Richard Cook, the respected clergyman of St. Peter's, Brighton, who accompanied the funeral *cortége* from Pavilion Colonnade, and, at the request of Sir Martin's family, officiated in the performance of the ecclesiastical rite in the church and at the grave; and Mr. Scott, Sir Martin's able and highly esteemed medical attendant.

A plain stone slab, surrounded and protected by an iron railing, marks the place of his interment. The inscription simply records his name and office, &c., with the respective dates of his birth and death.

---

* While recording the name of this gallant young soldier, in connection with the last offices paid to one who stood to him in the relation, and felt for him all the affection of a grandfather, I cannot deny myself the pleasure of noticing the incidents of his subsequent career, which have conferred the most honourable distinction on that name. Lieut. Cubitt was one of the little band of heroes who for five months successfully defended the Residency at Lucknow against the numerous and ferocious enemies by whom they were so closely and perseveringly besieged. In the disastrous affair of Chinhut, while serving with the volunteer cavalry, he performed an act of chivalrous and truly Christian valour, by rescuing three disabled men of H.M.'s 32nd Regiment, whose lives he saved at the imminent risk of his own; a service which has been appropriately requited by the glorious decoration of the Victoria Cross. Lieut. Cubitt was dangerously wounded at a subsequent period of the siege.

By a somewhat rare instance of good fortune in the case of an octogenarian, whose marriage had taken place more than fifty-four years previously, and who was the father of a large family, he was survived by *all the issue* of that marriage, viz: six children, and three grandchildren.

His descendants are as follows:

Three sons.

1. George Archer Shee, m. 16th Oct., 1842, to Jane Seymour, third daughter of Sir Thomas de Trafford, Bart., of Trafford and Croston, Lancashire.

2. Martin Archer Shee, m. 9th August, 1849, to Louisa Catharine, youngest daughter of John Richard Barrett, Esq. of Milton House, Berks.

3. William Archer Shee, m. Feb., 1843, to Harriett, daughter of George Harcourt, Esq., and widow of Major Wm. Cubitt, of Catton, Norfolk, Assistant Military Secretary to the Governor-General of India.

Three daughters.

Anna,<br>
Mary,       } Archer Shee, unmarried.<br>
Eliza Jane,

Three grandchildren, the issue of the marriage of his youngest son, William, viz. :—

Mary,<br>
Martin,<br>
Harriett.

---

Before closing this imperfect record of Sir Martin's social, professional, and official career, I must endeavour by a few details illustrative of his personal and moral individuality, to supply something of that which is necessarily wanting to the accuracy of a biographical portraiture, so far as it deals merely with the narrative of facts and actions; however distinctive may be the characteristic evidences which they inferentially afford.

In one important, not to say essential, particular, I have to regret a more than usual deficiency in the materials necessary to effect this object; for I am not in a position to supply the reader with any pictorial representation of the "outward man," which would convey even the faintest idea of his personal appearance, as it dwells on the memory of those who knew him most intimately. There is not in existence any good, or indeed moderately satisfactory, likeness of him, either from his own hand or that of any other artist.

In or about the year 1813, at the request of Messrs. Cadell and Davies, the publishers, he sat to an artist of great subsequent celebrity, the late John Jackson, R. A., for a chalk drawing, to be engraved for an expensive and interesting work then in course of periodical publication, entitled "The British Gallery of Portraits," each number of which contained biographical notices and engraved portraits of several eminent men of the day. Whatever may have been the merit of the drawing, it is certain that the portrait, as reproduced in the engraving affixed to the biographical sketch of the late President, presents a singularly unfavourable version of his countenance and air. It conveys, indeed, a most erroneous impression of the habitual aspect of a face at all times conspicuous for intellect and acuteness, and usually characterised by a peculiar and winning animation.

A slight sketch,—little more indeed than an outline,—made some dozen years later by a near relative, was also engraved, as the frontispiece of one of the monthly numbers of the "European Magazine," with a result still more wide of the mark; for the likeness, faint and unsatisfactory as it was in the original sketch, wholly evaporated in the process of engraving.

At the earnest entreaty of his friend Mr. Ellis, whose portrait he was painting on a large half-length canvas, about the year 1816 or 1817, he introduced into the picture what was intended as a likeness of himself, but was certainly anything but a favourable illustration of his proficiency in that valuable branch of science, termed *self-knowledge*.

With these exceptions, nothing that can be described, even by courtesy, as a likeness of the late President, is now extant. The last-mentioned work, were it otherwise satisfactory as a portrait, could not be made available in the way of a frontispiece to this biography: and certainly the reader would be merely misled by the reproduction opposite to the title-page, of either of the engravings to which I have referred, as a likeness of Sir Martin.

In stature he was under the middle size,—not measuring, I believe, even in his youth, more than five feet five inches. His figure was compact and muscular, rather stout in proportion to his height, and at one period suggesting some anticipations of corpulency, which, however, owing probably to his active and abstemious habits, were never realised.

His features were far from regular; but there never was perhaps a countenance of greater or more varied capability of expression; nor one that more distinctly bespoke the man of wit, feeling, and intellectual energy. His smile had a peculiar and winning brightness,—his frown, when he *did* frown, and frown *in earnest*, was scarcely less remarkable in its expressive sternness. The singular formation of his brow, which presented an unusual prominence of the frontal processes, contributed, in moments of excitement or deep mental preoccupation, to give to his aspect a character of *intensity* and resolution, such as I have never observed to the same extent in any other human countenance. It might be said, without much exaggeration, that he had

"An eye like Mars, to threaten and command;"

and whoever once witnessed the flash of that eye, in certain rare moments of sudden and serious displeasure, could not easily forget it.

There is a curious anecdote connected with the peculiar frontal development to which I have adverted, that may perhaps assist the impression conveyed by the above very imperfect description.

In the summer of 1813 he met with a very severe accident, while occupying with his attached and highly valued friend, the late Mr. Tooke *, the driving seat of that gentleman's barouche, on their return from Hampton Court, where, with the principal members of both their families, they had passed the morning in a *lionising* visit to the palace and gardens.

In driving through the town of Richmond, the hind wheel of the carriage, driven by Mr. Tooke, came in contact with a post; and the occupants of the box seat were precipitated with great violence to the ground; Mr. Tooke sustaining a severe injury to one of his legs, which placed him on crutches for some weeks, while Sir Martin (then Mr. Shee), who fell on his head and face, fractured his nose, but was not otherwise seriously hurt.

The accident occurred within a very short distance of the residence of Mr. Julius, the well known surgeon,

---

* Thomas Tooke, Esq., F.R.S., the eminent statist, whose name is so intimately and honourably associated with the development of economic science in this century. Mr. Tooke died in the early part of the year 1858, at a very advanced age. The Tooke Professorship of political economy in the University of London, a chair recently inaugurated, has been established as a just and graceful tribute to his memory, and a standing record of his distinguished attainments in that branch of knowledge. He was one of the late President's warmest and most intimate friends.

whither the sufferers were immediately removed; and they were fortunate enough to obtain his prompt and valuable aid.

On examining Mr. Shee, whose face was disfigured with blood, and exhibited in other respects unmistakeable traces of its recent collision with the *pavé*, Mr. Julius assumed an aspect of portentous gravity; and instead of applying himself at once to the re-adjustment of the injured organ, he began hastily to press with his thumbs those salient points of his patient's brow, which, in their singular prominence, suggested to him the idea of serious mischief to the *os frontis*. "Oh! my dear Sir," said Mr. Shee, laughing in spite of his *nasal affliction* and general soreness, "don't be alarmed. *That* is only *the nature of the beast!*" "Ha!" eagerly exclaimed the surgeon, "I am greatly relieved to hear you say so."

It is no easy matter to convey to the reader a distinct idea of Sir Martin's conversational powers, or of that peculiar charm of manner by which their effect was so greatly enhanced. His colloquial style was marked by an appropriate elegance of diction, not often met with, at least in the same degree, even in the most distinguished *causeurs* of his own time, and still more rarely found in the present generation, which rather affects an idiomatic simplicity; while *Slang*, in a more or less mitigated form, seems gradually encroaching on the domain of familiar conversation, even among the highly educated classes of society.

Facility and general correctness of expression may be fairly expected, from all in whom a vigorous natural intellect has been carefully developed by regular and assiduous cultivation. But the habitual flow of Sir Martin's language was strikingly exceptional, in its ease, grace, and precision.   It is related of Charles Fox, that on one occasion, when expatiating on the eloquence of his great rival Pitt, he thus noted a distinction between his own oratory and that of his illustrious antagonist, to the advantage of the latter. " It is true," said he, " that *I* never want a word; but Pitt never wants *the right word*."   I might almost venture to assert that this emphatic and significant eulogy was, in a subordinate and colloquial sense, fairly applicable to Sir Martin.   It mattered not what was the subject of discussion, whether serious, jocular, or trifling;—whatever fell from his lips in argument or conversation, was habitually expressed in language the accurate propriety of which could hardly admit of a cavil, and in the style or turn of which it would have been difficult to suggest an improvement.   The ordinary level of every-day discourse, even among the *élite* of intellectual life, will often require from the most profound thinker and brilliant talker, the contribution of a triviality or a truism to the onward flow of unpretending chat.   But Sir Martin had, in most cases, the art of clothing the familiar idea in a garb that rescued it from insignificance.

If he had not the piquant causticity of Rogers, the sparkling and epigrammatic pleasantry of Luttrell, or the matchless and impulsive union of satire and hilarity that distinguished the unrivalled Sydney Smith, he exhibited a clear and brilliant lucidity in thought and phrase, that permanently sustained the admiration of the attentive listener.   Perhaps the chief characteristic of his conversation was the absence, at all times, of the *commonplace* element, in the expression of his thoughts, opinions, and feelings.   Even when the sentiment or maxim he uttered affected no claim to the merit of originality, and appeared to do little more than embody the result of ordinary experience or reasonable reflection, it was impossible not to be struck with the peculiar felicity of the terms in which it was enunciated.    In this respect he might be said to illustrate, in no small degree, Pope's well known definition of " wit : "

> " True wit is nature to advantage dressed ;
>   What oft was *thought,* but ne'er so well *expressed.*"

On no occasion was this happy command of language more conspicuously displayed, than when he was tempted to indulge in the light and graceful *badinage* so appropriate, according to the ideas prevalent in the more chivalrous traditions of his country and his youth, in addressing the fair sex.   A strain of complimentary *persiflage,* the substance of which would have seemed hyperbolical, and almost preposterous, from one less eloquent and refined, flowed from his lips in such animated and choice phraseology, that in the ears to which it was addressed,—however generally averse to the accents of flattery,—its charm was never impaired by the sense of its exaggeration, nor its effect marred by a doubt of its earnestness.   This result was no doubt greatly facilitated by the peculiar advantages of his *abord* and demeanour. It is not too much to say, that, judged by the polished and elaborately courteous standard of the old school, his manner towards women was *perfection*; delicate in its tact, chivalrous in its respectful deference, flattering in its watchful and devoted attention.

It was, however, as I have intimated, an *old school manner*—a graceful relic of bygone days—a style characteristic of the best specimens of a class now socially extinct—a style better suited to powder, embroidery, and court-ruffles, than to the high-lows, *Knickerbockers,*

and *wide-awakes*,—the voluminous beard and head reck-
ing with tobacco-smoke, of the modern English gentleman;—a manner more consonant to the imposing
gravities of the minuet, or the decorous graces of the
original quadrille, than to the frantic whirl of the *deux-
temps* waltz, the hot-haste of the galop, or the *confiding
affection* of the polka.

It will be collected from what I have said above,
that the late President's conversational superiority was
not habitually that of the epigrammatist or utterer of
*facetiæ*, however he might occasionally indulge in light
pleasantry or shine in repartee.  I cannot therefore support my statement of his colloquial merits, by the species
of conclusive evidence which a string of successful *bons-
mots* would supply; and in recording a trifling anecdote
or two in connection. with the memory of his social
successes, I am merely attempting to convey some
faint idea of the graceful tact, and acute readiness of
thought and expression, which distinguished his conversation.

My first illustration exhibits him in the character of
a courtier, under circumstances of some embarrassment,
from which his skilful extrication,—without the slightest
compromise of truth or sincerity,—by means of a judiciously arranged phrase, was a source of great hilarity,
and a theme of jocular panegyric, to the brilliant but
friendly and partial circle by whom it was witnessed.

He was at Windsor Castle, just about to commence
the portrait of Queen Adelaide, in the presence of
several of the distinguished functionaries of the court
and visitors at the Castle, grouped around his easel,
and watching the proceedings with interest.  Her Majesty, whose kindness of heart and unaffected affability
of manner were proverbial, had just taken her seat in

the chair; and as the President was intently studying the most judicious point of view for the representation of the royal countenance, that illustrious lady, with an amiable smile, and in the unmistakeable accent of sincerity, said to him: "Oh! Sir Martin, I pity you, indeed, for having such a subject!"

What answer could be made to such an observation, under the circumstances? The truth of the implied criticism on her Majesty's personal appearance, as deficient in picturesque attraction, was unfortunately too obvious, and too evidently in accordance with her own profound conviction, to render an express disclaimer or denial of the difficulty, morally or decorously possible. Silent acquiescence, on the other hand, would have been *gauche*, not to say disrespectful. What was to be done? The courtly painter was not for a moment at fault.

"Madam," answered the President without hesitation, "I shall hope to have the honour ere long of showing your Majesty on the canvas, *my impression of your Majesty's claims* as a *subject! !*"

It was a case where, practically; *nothing was to be said;* and I think it will be admitted that he could have scarcely said *that nothing*, more gracefully or judiciously.

The subjoined *trait* is still more slight; but it can also boast a certain degree of characteristic individuality, in connection with the social *manière d'être* of the late President. It was related with great enjoyment of its *finesse*, by the late Bishop of Llandaff, to a clergyman of that diocese, on whose authority I record it.

While in conversation with Sir Martin in Cavendish Square, during the progress of the fine portrait of the Bishop painted by the late President, his lordship happened to relate some interesting details of the

career of an humble philanthropist well known in
Monmouthshire and the neighbouring counties — a
poor schoolmaster of the name of James Davis, who
during a long life of poverty, patient toil, and self-
denial, had devoted himself with extraordinary energy,
perseverance, and success, to the task of improving the
moral, religious, and material condition of the still
poorer classes among the peasantry of that region; —
combining the fervid zeal of the missionary, with the
charitable and earnest benevolence of the good Sama-
ritan.   The Bishop described in glowing colours the
humble faith, the untiring activity, and truly Christian
virtues of this good man, winding up his panegyric
by the following comprehensive summary of his merits.
" In short, my dear Sir Martin," said his lordship,
" such was his character, and such his career, that had
he belonged to *your* Church, I have little doubt that he
would have been *canonized*."   The President turned
from his easel, and made a low bow to his Right Reverend
sitter.    " I am delighted to find," said he, " that your
lordship entertains *so high an opinion of our Church !* "
Until the failure of his health, and the peculiarly distressing nature of his complaint, had produced their
natural result on his habitual state of mind and feeling,
he generally exhibited, when not under the pressure of
any immediate or serious anxiety, an elasticity and
buoyancy of spirits, in the society of his family and
intimate friends, rarely to be found in those who have
numbered " threescore years and ten."   He was, indeed, subject to occasional fits of depression, and had
a constitutional tendency to view the contingencies of
the future *en noir*.   But his gloom, if sometimes deeper
than was fairly justified by the circumstances in which
it originated, was never traceable to moroseness of temper,

or any habit of mind akin to *ennui*. Impetuous, rather than irritable, in his disposition,—and when roused, sufficiently energetic and outspoken in expressing his feelings of displeasure,—he was wholly free from the slightest tinge of vindictiveness, and was incapable of harbouring any permanent feeling of resentment, even against those of whose conduct he had most reason to complain. On the other hand, if he were ever accidentally betrayed into an unjust censure or hasty condemnation of any one under his authority, even in a matter of trifling importance, or in the case of the lowest servant in his establishment, the unhesitating and generous frankness with which he acknowledged and apologised for his error of judgment, amply atoned for any mortification that might have been occasioned by his unintentional injustice. No man had more completely the art of conciliating the regard, while he commanded the promptest obedience, of those under his control.

Of the high moral tone of his mind and feelings, the reader can, I think, himself form a judgment from the contents of the foregoing pages. Truth, honour, and duty were the mainsprings of his career, and the principles that regulated every act of his life, of which the venerable precept, "*Fay ce que doy, advienne que pourra,*" would be the appropriate motto.

I cannot perhaps better illustrate the peculiar attributes of his mind and character, than by recording two maxims or rules of moral duty, which he strenuously urged on the adoption and observance of his children; and of which, as to the first I *know*, — and as regards the second, I *religiously believe*, — that he enforced the inculcation by his own example.

"Never," said he, "put from under your hand in writing, a line or a word which you would be ashamed or afraid to hear proclaimed at Charing Cross: and never harbour, for a moment, in your mind or heart, a thought or a feeling which you would blush to acknowledge before the assembled world."

His insatiable love of reading, and the varied range of his studies, have been already noticed. It need hardly be said, that like most men of superior intellect and ardent imagination, he was fully alive to the charms of literary fiction. No one certainly enjoyed a good novel more thoroughly than he did, or felt more grateful to those whose creative fancy can for a time supersede the dull realities of life, in the mind or attention of the reader, by the vivid impressions and engrossing interest conveyed and excited by a well constructed tale, — beguiling him from the remembrance of his own cares, by the fictitious joys or griefs of the airy phantoms which are evoked and paraded in life-like semblance before him.

Somewhat sceptical in the earlier periods of the development of the *Pickwickian faith*, he was suddenly and permanently converted to more *orthodox views* on the subject, by the perusal of " Oliver Twist; " since which time he did full justice to the merits of the prolific and original pen which has achieved such extended popularity, in what may be almost described as a new department of romantic literature.

Nor was he less fully alive to the claims of the great rival *romancier*. One of the last works of fiction which elicited his enthusiastic praise, and beguiled the tedium and discomfort of his rapidly declining health, was " Vanity Fair; " and I have a double pleasure in recording his high appreciation, not only of the literary talent, but of the great artistic proficiency, exhibited by the author, who, in his twofold command of the pen and

the pencil, as the felicitous and striking interpreter of
thought and fancy, may be well apostrophised in the
words of Horace—

*" Docte sermones utriusque linguæ."*

In tracing this imperfect record of the mind, the character, and the career of the late President, I have not
thought it expedient to attempt any critical analysis of
his merits, or any systematic description of his labours
or peculiar attributes, as a painter.  Apart from any
question of my personal qualifications for discussing
such matters, I am conscious that my judgment, while
dealing with claims in the recognition of which I feel
so deep an interest, would be not only open to the suspicion, but subject, in fact, to the bias of a partiality
that would impair its authority, and, in the mind of the
reader, nullify its results.

The permanent rank which Sir Martin Archer Shee
is destined to occupy in the history of the art, is a
question which no observations of mine can affect.  Those
of his social and professional contemporaries who survive, are well acquainted with the productions of his
pencil; but the most elaborate description, however
accurate in itself, would convey no distinct idea of his
merits or his style to the reader who may be unfamiliar
with his works.

If I have been less guarded in the assertion of his
poetic and general literary claims, it is because I have
at the same time, laid before the reader such evidence
in support of my statement as will enable him to test
its accuracy, by the standard of his own judgment, taste,
and feelings.  The result will, I feel confident, serve to
acquit me of the charge of exaggeration in my estimate
of Sir Martin as a poet, a prose writer, and a satirist.

His powers as a speaker are, to the present generation,

and must necessarily remain, matter of traditional report. But I can appeal with confidence to some valuable corroborative evidence on the subject. One of the most gifted and accomplished writers of the day, Earl Stanhope, in a late volume of his valuable History, has recorded his personal testimony in favour of the rare grace and ability with which Sir Martin discharged the arduous duty of presiding at the great annual dinner of the Royal Academy; and I may add that, at an early period of my own forensic life, the example of the President, as a correct and graceful speaker, was earnestly and emphatically urged upon my attention by one who may almost be said to be himself the highest living authority in matters of oratory;—one who, while in the senate he successfully contests the palm of eloquence with the first parliamentary speakers of the day, is, in his own profession, recognised without controversy or question, as the most accomplished speaker and the most consummate advocate at the Bar.

In adverting to the moral and social merits of Sir Martin, I am aware that I have occasionally expressed myself with a warmth of eulogy which to some may appear excessive or misplaced. But I cannot affect to solicit the indulgence or deprecate the satire of the reader, for the emphatic manifestation of feelings amply justified by the qualities of mind and heart which have called them forth. On these points, it is obvious that no more competent witness can be found than one whom long personal and daily experience has qualified to speak, with earnest conviction and grateful remembrance, of those virtues which, as a biographer, he is called on to record; and I feel that I should exhibit a species of pusillanimity if, while bearing, as I am bound to do, my testimony to the existence and striking development of rare moral excellence in the subject of this biography, I could be influenced by the fear of encountering the sneer of the cynic, or the open ridicule of the scoffer, to withhold or qualify the full tribute of earnest admiration and affectionate respect which I owe to his revered memory and his honoured name.

# APPENDICES.

---

## (A.)

*Benjamin Robert Haydon,* Esquire, called in ; and Examined.

1050. Mr. *Ewart.*] MR. HAYDON, you are well known as a celebrated painter ; have you devoted much of your attention to the general system-of academies ?—I have.

. . . . . .

. . . . . . .

. . . . . .

1053. Have the artists themselves, since the establishment of academies, been inferior or greater than those who flourished before?—Inferior.   Giotto, Massaccio, Lionardo da Vinci, Bartolomeo, Michael Angelo, Raphael, Giorgione, Titian, Correggio, were all produced from schools, and *before* academies.   And there have been no men equal to these great men since in any way, —that must be acknowledged.   The inference must be obvious.   I consider academies all over Europe were signals of distress thrown out to stop the decay of art, but which have failed most egregiously, and rather hastened it.

1054. They were instituted for the purpose of elevating art ?—Yes; for kings thought all over Europe, by dignifying members with titles, they would produce genius; it has not succeeded; the result of that is proved.

1055. Does this result, in your opinion, apply equally to England?—Decidedly. When the Royal Academy was founded, we had great men; we have never had such men since. Previous to the Royal Academy, there were Wren, the architect, Hogarth, the satiric painter, Reynolds, Barry, Wilson, Gainsborough, Banks, Gibbons, Roubilliac, &c.* and certainly there have been no such men since; though it has been the fashion of the academy to run down Barry, because he could not colour, and was deficient in light and shade, Dr. Johnson says, " There is a grasp of mind in his works, that no other English work possesses." The Adelphi pictures are a set of pictures to illustrate a principle, like the great works of Greece and Italy; they are the finest things done in England by an English artist (though Fuseli's Milton Gallery is more poetical); Barry's work is at the Society of Arts. Dr. Johnson was right, though of art, technically, he knew nothing.

1056. What was the origin of the Royal Academy? —It originated in the very basest intrigue: there was a chartered body of artists, out of which twenty-four directors were annually elected by the constituency; then these directors, having got the sweets of power once, naturally, as all men do, wished to keep it, and they wanted to be elected again; but the feelings of the constituency, who knew right from wrong, refused to consent to it, and sixteen of these directors were voted out; these men had the ear of Dalton, the King's librarian, and they persuaded Dalton to persuade George the Third to found a Royal Academy, which George the Third consented to do, and thus the other eight directors that were left seceded and joined the sixteen, giving themselves a majority of four, because they limited the number to forty in the new academy. All the exclusive laws were thus carried, which the artists complain of, and have been the cause of the whole of the bad passions, intrigue, injustice, cabal, heat and turmoil in English art ever since.

* Flaxman, though a student, was refused the gold medal.

1057. The academy has no act or charter like other public bodies ?—No; they only exist by the royal pleasure; they cunningly refused George the Fourth's offer of a charter, fearing it would make them responsible; they are a private society, which they always put forward when you wish to examine them, and they always proclaim themselves a public society when they want to benefit by any public vote.

1058. Do you approve of the Royal Academy as a school of instruction ?—I do in a great measure, but not altogether. I approve of there being one keeper in the antique, and the young men being instructed by one man in that school, but I totally disapprove of the system in the life academy, which succeeds it; where there is a succession of visitors among the academicians; the whole forty take it in turns to instruct the young men; the consequence is, that an academician who is an historical painter, instructs them this month, then comes a landscape painter to instruct them the next month; and if it is the historical painter, he tells them to draw correctly, and not to mind colour or effect, but the outline; he goes, and then comes the landscape painter, and he tells them to think of colour and effect only, not to attend to outline. I appeal to the Committee if that is a reasonable mode of instruction, after coming from the upper schools of the antique. I should say not. An extraordinary illustration of that I can give you: a very celebrated landscape painter at the academy brought down a large quantity of plants in pots, orange and great lemon-trees, and put them all round a naked figure on which he wanted to set off the flesh of the model and make an Eve of it; the absurdity was so great, the young men were more inclined to laugh than anything else.

On this principle I say there should be two keepers, one for the life, and one for the antique, or an assistant to the keeper for the life, and the instruction would go on more soundly, or both schools should be under one instructor.

1059. What is the process of admission ?—First of

all, you have a letter to the keeper of the antique, to show that you are a competent drawer.

1060. Who gives him the letter ?— Any gentleman who knows him and his morals can give him the letter.

1061. Dr. *Bowring.*] Is that letter a testimony to his artistical talent or his character ?— Only to his moral character; he makes a drawing to prove that the one he has brought is his own; that is very sensible; he draws, and it is compared with his first drawing, and if approved, he is admitted as a student by a specific council, and afterwards he goes into the life academy.

1062. Mr. *Ewart.*] What is the process of instruction ?— The keeper comes in every night, or in the course of the day, and corrects the drawings of the young men. We had Fuseli; he was a very eminent keeper, though he might not be in a style of art so pure, yet he had the habit of elevating ambition and exciting the ideas of young men in a high degree.

1063. What do you disapprove of principally in the Royal Academy ?— Its exclusiveness, its total injustice. The body is benefited by some of the works of the most eminent men in the world, and they deny them the right of preparing pictures for the public, on which their existence depends, after they are hung up. Mr. Martin gave an extraordinary instance of their hanging a picture of his; some of the academicians dropped a quantity of varnish, and ruined the picture, and he was unable to get admission to mount up and get it off, and he suffered a whole season by this unreasonable oppression. May and June are the very existence of an artist who is working for bread, and who depends on the effect his works have in these months, for the existence of a whole year afterwards. It was infamous to injure an eminent man's work, and deny him a just remedy. In fact, the academy is a House of Lords without King or Commons for appeal. The artists are at the mercy of a despotism whose unlimited power tends to destroy all feeling for right or justice; forty men do as they please, it is the fact; the people have an appeal constitutionally, but the artists have no appeal; the academy is a House of Lords without appeal. It is an anomaly in the history of any constitutional people, the constitution of this academy; I cannot conceive how it could have been framed, upon investigating it. It is extraordinary how men, brought up as Englishmen, could set up such a system of government. The holy Inquisition was controlled by the Pope, but these men are an inquisition without a Pope.

1064. Do you think that it is a system which involves undue patronage on the part of some, and induces self-abasement and dependence on the part of others?— Certainly, I think the moral character of English artists is dreadfully affected: not so much as twenty years ago; twenty years ago they were in such a state of abject degradation, that the mention of an objection against the Royal Academy would have ruined immediately any artist, as it ruined me. For though the artists all agreed with me in my assault, they were so frightened, they set upon me to prove they had no connexion. Wilkie was so frightened, he refused to be seen with me in the streets. They were the most abject slaves in Europe at that time.

1065. Has that affected the arts themselves as well as the moral character of the men?—I think it must have done so.

1066. Have you suffered in your reputation and emoluments by the injustice of the academy?—I was ruined entirely by their injustice. There is a great mistake abroad; I should like to have the power of saying that it is a supposition that I began by attacking the Royal Academy; I lost at first many friends and patrons in consequence of that belief. There never was a greater mistake; I believe a great number of academicians, my fellow-students, know I was industrious and indefatigable; I gave offence to no one. My first picture was painted in 1806, and exhibited in 1807, and was well hung, and purchased by Thomas Hope. Then I began a much greater picture, " Dentatus," well known in the art, and in Germany, and which was for Lord Mulgrave, my employer.  He begged me to keep it for the British Institution.  I told him I was a student of the academy, and wished to support the Royal Academy, as I derived the greater part of my knowledge studying there.  I then sent " Dentatus" to the Royal Academy, and that picture contained principles which I am now lecturing on at this period of my life, and which are received with the greatest enthusiasm by scientific audiences.  I have never been able to add a single principle of the construction of the form of man as a species, since that period, when I was twenty-two years old, because I got them from the Elgin Marbles.  This picture was hung in the great room, in the same place as the other ; and after two days it was taken down and put in *the dark*, on the assertion that I occupied the place of an academician, when, instead of an academician's picture, a little girl in a pink sash was put there to fill the place.

1067. Not the picture of an academician ?—Certainly ; and in the ante-room there was no window at that time, therefore it was destruction to an artist of any reputation to have a picture of that class put in that position, which cost him two years painting.  I will show the Committee the consequence : my employer, Lord Mulgrave, began to believe I had no talent ; yet while I was painting the latter part of that picture, my room was crowded with people of fashion five and six deep.  Directly the academy put it into the dark, I never saw a patron or a person of fashion, rank or fortune for a year and a half near my room, and I am perfectly convinced these academicians have such experience of people of fashion, because they are in perpetual contact with them at dinners, on private days and in society, that they knew the effect of putting a picture of that class in such a situation on my particular friends, who were all people of the highest rank, would be destruction to me, as it was ; they have been very much ashamed of this conduct since.  I perpetually inquired who were on the committee ; I wrote to Sir Martin

Shee; I asked him if he was on the committee; he said he *adopted* the conduct of the committee, but he evaded the answer; this was in 1809, but I found he was on the committee of 1809, by their own official statement. The consequences were so dreadful, that I lost all employment, and a handsome commission was taken from me, and I never had another commission for sixteen years. That is one of the consequences of the present system, and I myself have been the victim. Through all my great works I was supported by opulent men, T. Hope, Jeremiah Harman, Lord Ashburnham, Sir George Beaumont, &c., as a matter of charity and sympathy; they were disgusted at my treatment. Afterwards I put my name down for an associate in 1810; I had not a single vote. I sent the same picture to the British Gallery the year after, and it beat one of the committee in contesting for the premium, and won the great prize. The academy refused me admission in 1810, and in 1812 I attacked it, so that the honourable Committee will see I did not begin, as is generally supposed, by a turbulent and violent attack on the authorities in art. I then tried to found a school, and produced Eastlake, the Landseers, Harvey, Lance, Chatfield; but here the academy opposed me, and destroyed my school by calumny. One of my pupils sent a drawing to the Academy for admission, and put "Pupil of B. R. Haydon;" I told him he would be refused; he was so. Three months after he sent a new drawing; left out my name; he was *admitted:* he then tried for student, and was *refused* because he could not draw; and when Lawrence selected the best draughtsman among the young men to go to Italy to copy Michael Angelo, he selected this very young man, because he drew so beautifully.

1068. Mr. *Brotherton.*] You made one application? —Yes, as Wilkie did. I was perfectly justified in so doing; I thought, and the public think, I was deserving to be elected, in consequence of the certainty of the principles on which "Dentatus" was painted; I might have painted twenty academic pictures in the time I painted this one.

1068.* The academy had no reason to complain of you in the first instance ?—No, not in the least; I had done nothing to offend them.

1069. What was the period when your first public controversy began with them ?—In 1812 I attacked them in "The Examiner," under the signature of the "English Student," which was well known as being myself; I never denied it, I acknowledged it; I considered myself as a portion of a class of artists which had suffered by the foundation of the academy; I knew nothing about them personally and individually, till I came in contact with them on an election for professor of anatomy. The first suspicion in my mind was excited by coming in contact with them on this question; Sir Anthony Carlisle had written in "The Artist," that anatomy was perfectly *useless*, and he was perfectly convinced it was without avail in the art; Sir Charles Bell had published a most beautiful work on the anatomy of expression. There was a contest for the professorship, and I myself canvassed several academicians; I found them determined to elect Sir Anthony in opposition to Sir Charles Bell, except Mr. Hoppner, and though he was a private friend of Sir Anthony Carlisle, he told him in his conscience he could not vote for him. Then arose my suspicions of the sincerity of the academicians for the benefit of high art, or the advance of the taste of the people; for this was a palpable instance of a most extraordinary nature; because they rejected the most competent man who had written in favour of a science, and preferred the one who had written against it, for the interest of the artist.

1070. Mr. *Ewart.*] Why is it England has never established an historical school as in other nations ?—Because the progress of the art was stopped at the reformation in religion.

. . . . . . .

. . . . . . .

I think that obstructed the arts entirely in this country,
and I think portrait painting got a-head from the neglect of Government; and painting being no longer a
matter of state protection, it has never recovered itself.
It went on in that condition till George the Second's
time; then appeared the native artist, Hogarth; and
then the King (George the Third), under the supposition of advancing the art, founded the Royal Academy,
which, from the state of the country, and the patronage
of portrait painting, being the only part of the art which
obtained a market, has done nothing but embody portrait painters in power, to the destruction of high art
altogether. And though, from the character of the
English, the native vigour of the English character and
its constitutional habits, it has contrived to obtain a
high character in every other species of art except historical painting, because there is always a market among
individuals, historical painting alone suffers from the
want of state patronage, as in the reign of Edward the
Third. That is my view of the question.

1071. Why do you think the academy as a body has
not wished to advance the interests of the nation in historical painting?—Because the portrait painters will
lose their importance the instant the state votes money
for high art.

1072. Do you think the taste for the higher kinds of
art has increased or diminished since its establishment?
—Among the nobility (though the nobility are our
only patrons) it has diminished immensely, since the
death of Sir George Beaumont, and from academical
influence; for at the great dinner where all the nobility
assemble, portrait is mostly before their eyes by the
tricks of the portrait painters. In Thornhill's time there
was a greater feeling for what was grand in art than
now, for the moment the dome of St. Paul's was built,
it was painted. In Charles the Second's time, Verrio
adorned Hampton Court and the British Museum.

That feeling went out gradually, in proportion to the absence of state employment and the influence of the academy. Now the academy is founded, all the world desires to see the exhibition, as it is a spring show of little pictures, portraits, and little pieces of furniture; such works become the object of every person to purchase and artists to produce. And at the same time we owe an everlasting obligation to portrait painting, for had there been none after the Reformation, the art would have gone out entirely; and the desire to be painted, from the domestic feelings of the English, which are very strong, has kept the art continually afloat, from the destruction of the Catholic religion to the foundation of the Royal Academy, which embodied the *esprit de corps* of portrait painters, in despotic power, when it was too powerful before, for it had killed Hussey, a man of genius, patronised by the Duke of Northumberland, and embarrassed Hogarth.

1079. Do you think the British Gallery of service?— Of immense good.

1080. Do the Royal Academy approve of it?—They tried to obstruct it and destroy it in every possible way. When it was first founded, in the reign of George the Third, in consequence of the influence behind the curtain (the academy is always behind a curtain), they objected to it on the principle that it was unfair to the Royal Academy, though it is now a second academy in corruption. The exhibition of old pictures has done great good to the public. It is too much controlled by a Mr. Seguier, who curries favour with the academy, and gives their pictures the best places, though seen before in the academy. Had the directors persevered, they would have carried public encouragement; but a publication called " Catalogue Raisonné," proceeding from the academy, wherein they were all scurrilously attacked for the best thing they had done, in exhibiting old pictures, disgusted the best patrons of the art. The academy feared the improvement of the people's taste.

. . . . . .

1082. Do you think the taste of people can be improved or injured by the exhibition of pictures ?— Very much injured.

1083. How ?—By the glare of colouring, a competition to outshine each other without reference to art. I have known some academicians send their canvas only with a head on it, and wait to finish it till they saw what would be hung by the side of it, and dress up the thing in a week for the public, like an automaton. Think of that, and Titian taking eight years about " Peter Martyr !"

. . . . . . . . .

. . . . . . . .

. . . . . .

. . . . . .

1106. You have adverted to the Royal Academy, do you think they would aid in the accomplishment of such a plan ?—I do not think they would now; they made an attempt in 1792 to get 5,000*l.* for a gallery of honour; Opie, Flaxman, West, all made public proposals about a species of gallery of honour; then the British Gallery applied to Mr. Percival for 5,000*l.* annually, to encourage the art, and was refused. After the battle of Waterloo a sum of money was devoted to a monument for Waterloo; a committee was formed, and they were directed by Lord Castlereagh to apply to the Royal Academy as to the best mode of disposing of the money for the arts, and they returned no answer; and Lord Castlereagh then said the thing had better be given up.

. . . . . .

. . . . . . .

. . . . . .

. . . . . .

1114. Have you ever known any appeals of the kind

you have alluded to having been made to Government for a parliamentary vote ?—Yes, continually ; the British Gallery applied for 5,000*l.* a year ; I have had three petitions presented in the House by Lord Brougham, by Lord Durham, and Mr. Ridley Colborne, and I have corresponded with all the ministers for twenty-five years, up to Lord Melbourne ; I think it singular that the excuse always was, " Now is not the time." Mr. Percival said, " Now is not the time, because it is war ;" then came peace, and then was not the time, for we were so much embarrassed in consequence of the war. I think, in a great measure, the Royal Academy has kept up that feeling ; I know that at a large dinner at Sir George Beaumont's, who was one of the best patrons of art, and which consisted of the greatest portion of royal academicians, the whole thing was discussed, and Sir George said they threw cold water on it, and said it was not wanted in the state of the art, though they might have competed for it ; he was decidedly favourable, and did all he could to advance it with all his might. I have a notion, that in consequence of my attack and their hatred against me, because they used me unjustly, I being the most prominent person in advising those things, if I were to die, they would come forward and promote the thing ; and if they came forward as a body it would be done.

.    .    .    .    .    .

.    .    .    .    .    .    .

.    .    .    .    .    .

1118. You have made some reference to the mode in which you would apportion the National Gallery for works of British artists ; what do you think of the plan which is now in fact carrying into execution, of appropriating a part of the National Gallery for the exhibition of the annual pictures, not a selection, but an annual contribution of artists ?—I think it will ruin the art and the academy too. I am perfectly convinced, on every principle of common sense and justice, after a whole body of artists have been suffering for years, to let the Royal Academy get into that national building, and take the advantage of a national vote, and not having a single law altered, or a single injustice corrected, is the most extraordinary thing I ever heard of in my life. I would not let them into the gallery, but devote that portion of the gallery to a native collection, leaving such spaces as there would be in the other part for the cartoons. In the first place, that plan is most desirable, for persons may look in and go away with an improved notion, and I would gradually fill it with the best works of native genius, as they successively appeared, and the Royal Academy should not be admitted.

1119. You seem to think a national collection should be, as nearly as possible, for the eternal works of art, not for the ephemeral productions of the year?—Yes, a species of mausoleum for all that is great and grand in the nation. If we had a thing of that sort, when the foreigners come, we should have something to show them: while some of the best known works of art are rotting for want of space (my own "Judgment of Solomon" and "Lazarus"). Von Raumer would not speak of English art with the compassionate forbearance he now thinks it deserves, as to historical painting. Why is that? He comes to the Royal Academy, and sees a series of whole-length portraits standing on tiptoe, and he goes away and says they cannot put men on their legs ; but if the fine works were gradually purchased and put in a gallery, year after year, in the course of twenty years there would be a fine collection. The "Edinburgh Review" said, the great error in this country was the hurry to get things completed, everything is to be done in a year or two, whereas the Louvre took a hundred years.

1120. Did you ever, in any foreign exhibition, see a portion of the gallery devoted to an English school?—No; there were some works of Reynolds in the palace of the Grand Trianon.

1121. You find, of course, the national galleries of foreign countries distributed into the Italian school, the Flemish school, and the German school, but did you ever see an English school?—No; we have not got character enough for it yet: that is one of the consequences of the formation of a Royal Academy, giving power to men whose object it is to keep it up at the expense of the art, and the greatest men in it. An academician said to me, " The art was a thing the academy had a right to keep to themselves;"—a pretty principle for the instruction of the people.

1122.           .           .           .           .           .

.           .           .           .           .           .           .

.           .           .           .           .           .

Since the reign of Louis Fourteenth, the principle of putting power into forty men's hands and elevating them by making them royal, and allowing them to elect each other, has become ruinous; because the people do not value the greatest genius if he be deprived of such distinctions, however God Almighty may have distinguished him. Hogarth opposed the formation of our academy, and foretold it would be governed by the worst artists. Exactly as he predicted, a bad artist, called Farrington, who had leisure for intrigue from want of employment, got to rule the academy; he it was who caused Reynolds to resign, and expelled Barry. Reynolds wanted to elect an architect academician, to teach perspective ; by law no man could do this who was not an R.A. Nothing could be so proper. Farrington, merely to thwart Reynolds, opposed it, and beat him. Reynolds, to whom the academy owed its consequence, resigned, having been infamously treated : the public took Reynolds's part. Barry was expelled for proposing reforms, and the moment he died they adopted them.

1125. *Chairman.*] You approve of academies as a means of conveying instruction in that which is positive in art, but you object to them as obnoxious, so far as they attempt to control taste and genius ?—Yes, in so far as they exceed schools I disapprove them. I mean that all academies should be reduced to schools; these are the principles of my opposition to all academies, and I hope this Committee will have a good effect in Europe as well as in England. The artists in France and Germany desire it as much as we do.

(B.)

Sir *Martin Archer Shee*, President of the Royal
Academy, called in; and Examined.

1916. *Chairman.*] HAVE you any observations to
make upon the evidence which has been sent to you by
the Committee ? — I believe, in the evidence which has
been given before the Committee, as to the origin of the
academy, it has been stated to have arisen in the *basest
intrigue.* In answer to that, I beg leave to read to you
an account of the origin of the academy, derived from
sources which I believe to be rather more authentic and
correct : " The dissolution of the incorporated body of
artists was owing to the indiscriminate admission of
members. At the period of the separation, the number
amounted to 141, of whom a large proportion were of a
very inferior order. When the society was first instituted, due respect was shown to the eminent artists, who,
by the propriety of their conduct, and the esteem in
which they were held, gave dignity to it, and by their
excellent performances, contributed most to the popularity of the exhibitions. They were, therefore, for a
while, considered to be the persons most proper to have
a large share in the government of the society. While
that sentiment prevailed, it proceeded with success.
But it was not long before ambitious desires began to
operate, and the votes at elections being equal, many of
the members who had little title to confidence and distinction, aspired to the direction of the institution, and
by combining together, they were, by their numbers,
enabled to effect their purpose. They ejected two-thirds

of the respectable members who filled the offices of trust, and placed themselves in their room; and forming a majority out-voted those whom they had permitted to remain. The principal artists, seeing the impossibility of restoring order and proper subordination, after some vain attempts, soon withdrew from this society; and without delay formed another plan, in which they avoided the errors which caused the destruction of the incorporated body they had quitted. It was now seen that no society of this kind could be lasting, unless it were more limited in its members; and that it could have no national dignity, without the avowed and immediate patronage of the Sovereign." This is a quotation from the "History and Life of Sir Joshua Reynolds," by Mr. Farrington, and not written with a view to be brought forward on any occasion like the present. I beg leave to refer to another authority on the same subject — the origin of the academy: " The artists who formed the exhibition at the Spring Garden Room having obtained a charter, it might naturally be supposed that the society would be placed in a situation, and furnished with the means, of cultivating their mutual interests to the best advantage; but unfortunately they were scarcely collected, when dissensions arose, which in the course of three years caused an irreparable breach, and in the end, a total dissolution of the incorporated society. This event was in a great degree occasioned by the loose and unguarded manner in which the charter was composed; for it did not provide against the admission of those who were distinguished neither by their talents as artists, nor by their good conduct as men. In consequence of this indiscriminate admission of persons, many of the inferior practitioners were no sooner seated, than they began to cavil at the conduct of the directors, though they were the original founders and chief supporters of the society; and a party was soon formed, by whom it was resolved to exclude several of the principal directors from their official situations, although they had no complaint to allege against them." This is a quotation from an account of the establishment of the Royal Academy, in the introduction to Mr. Edwards' "Anecdotes of the Arts;" and was not written with any view to the present inquiry. Now it may be proper that I should point out to you the individuals who have been represented to this Committee as guilty of "the basest intrigue." I think it will be admitted that no language can be found stronger in reprobation, stronger in contempt and vilification of individuals, than the expression which I have quoted. The artists who have been thus represented as guilty of "the basest intrigue" in forming the Royal Academy, were, Sir Joshua Reynolds, the greatest portrait painter that ever lived in any country, and one of the most respectable men that ever graced the annals of society; Benjamin West, the greatest historical painter, I have no hesitation in saying, since the days of the Carracci, a man as respected in private life, as he was admired for his talents. In addition to these two gentleman, I would mention the greatest architect of his day, Sir W. Chambers, the architect of Somerset House, a man celebrated in his profession, and respected by all who knew him. I would also add to these, the name of Paul Sandby, the greatest landscape painter in water colours of his day; and several others whom I might mention, if it were not occupying too much of the time of the Committee. This is the account of the origin of the Royal Academy, drawn from the sources which I have mentioned; and the Committee will of course give it whatever weight they may consider is attached to it.

1917. The observations of the witnesses who have been examined were not directed against individuals composing the Royal Academy at the time of its formation, but against the system and against the formation of the system ?—I believe that is as it may be understood by those who read the evidence.

1918. Refer to any part of the evidence where allusions have been made to the individuals who composed the academy at the time?—Of course no evidence brought forward would be so indiscreet as to mention names.

1919. How many individuals formed the academy at its first formation?—Forty.

1920. Proceed to any other observations which occur to you proper to be answered in the evidence?—There is another observation which I would beg leave to remark upon. It has been, I believe, generally asserted in the evidence, that the Royal Academy has been exceedingly hostile to the interests of the great body of artists; that they have on all occasions interfered to the prejudice of the higher departments of the art. I think that is pretty clearly stated in the evidence.

1921. You will find by the evidence that it referred to the system and not to the individuals?—I speak of the Royal Academy, and the Royal Academy is a body composed of individuals. They have been accused of having a direct interest in depreciating the arts; they have been accused of invariably acting with a hostile spirit to the higher department of the arts; they have been represented as a "clique of portrait-painters," actuated by a mean and selfish desire to promote their own views at the expense of their profession.

1922. You consider these charges to be unfounded?—Most certainly; the grossest and most unfounded charges that ever were made.

1923. Be so good as to state the reasons on which you consider those charges do not justly lie against the Royal Academy?—The contradictory testimony of the witnesses themselves sufficiently refutes them. It has been stated in evidence that the arts have retrograded since the establishment of the Royal Academy. It has been stated by another evidence that the Royal Academy has impeded the progress of the arts, and that their state is now much lower than it was before it was established. Another evidence thinks the arts are in a much *higher* state now in this country than those of France and Germany, particularly in historical painting.

Another evidence states that the arts are making such progress, that "Let the Royal Academy do what they will," it is impossible for them to stop the progress of improvement.    What does the Committee think of that ? Another evidence thinks the academy has done a great deal; that it had nursed and brought the arts into repute.    Another important evidence states, that the Royal Academy, by embodying the *esprit de corps* of portrait-painters, "killed Hussey the painter and embarrassed Hogarth."    Now I beg leave to observe, that Hogarth died some years before the Royal Academy was formed.    His death took place in 1764; the academy was established in 1768.    I have said that Hussey also died before the establishment of the academy.    This, I find, is incorrect.    He died in the year 1788, at the age of 78 ; having long before retired from his profession, and settled in Devonshire, in easy circumstances, and cannot, therefore, be well considered the *victim of academic assassination.*    It appears to me, that after the statement which I have thus made of the inconsistencies appearing in the evidence which has been brought forward, it is not necessary to enter into a further explanation of the effect which the Royal Academy has had upon the higher branches of the arts in this country.    I find the utility of academies has been very much questioned.    One gentleman, who seems to have taken a more philosophic view of the case than those who have co-operated with him, describes academies as universally injurious to the arts.    An academy, I believe, means a school, a place where something is taught, where information is communicated, where the means of knowledge are given to those who are disposed to obtain it.    If I understand what an academy is, it means that; and how such an institution can be injurious to the interests of society, I cannot well conceive. I can well imagine that a particular academy, by its injudicious construction and by its mal-administration, may be so mismanaged as to convert a great good into a great evil.    That result has been asserted of the

Royal Academy; but it remains to be proved, and I hope will be required to be proved upon different evidence than that which has been brought forward on the present occasion. The power which the academy possesses of conferring distinctions, is another grave imputation cast upon them by these gentlemen; they do not see the propriety of an artist being allowed to put " R. A." after his name, or why he should be graced by any particular honour or distinction; whatever merits he may have attained, whatever skill he may have acquired, or whatever services he may have performed in art, they do not conceive that he should be singled out and distinguished from the general mass of his profession, or that the Sovereign of the country should confer upon him any mark of his favour. I am now referring to the testimony of a witness who disapproves of all distinctions whatsoever; but, indeed, I may say, that the whole current of the evidence runs in that channel; aristocratic distinctions are represented as promoting inequality in the arts, as raising one man above another, without his having any just claim to superior talent. It is not for me to enter into an abstract discussion of the merits of artists, or the effect of these distinctions in society. That social system might perhaps be the best, wherein wisdom and virtue alone should be the objects which call for the respect and homage of mankind. I should be the last to oppose such a system were it practicable; but, unfortunately, every man does not show his wisdom in his face, nor are his virtues blazoned on his breast; a mark of honour or distinction, therefore, is a stamp set upon merit, for the purpose of pointing it out to those who have no other means of ascertaining it. Whether that is a proper politic or patriotic institution in society, it is not for me to determine. But I apprehend it is not necessary to go further into that subject.

1924. Is there any other charge brought against the academy upon which you wish to make a remark?—The funds of the academy and their management have furnished a large chapter in the evidence which has been laid before this Committee. The academy have been accused of mismanaging their funds, and perverting them to private objects and private purposes.

1925. State the evidence in support of that assertion? —The following statement appears in evidence : — " According to the printed returns to Parliament, there are more than 600 individuals, not members, who exhibit annually therein, on the one hand ; and 45 on the other, either members or associates. Those 600, although the money is in a great measure raised from the exhibition of their works, have not the slightest control over the charity fund ; and the 45, or rather 40, academicians, have an absolute control over it ; and I should add that these 45 have positive claims. There are salaries and superannuations to themselves, and pensions to their widows, according to the laws ; and the 600 have no claim whatever. They may, possibly, on the recommendation of an academician, obtain assistance, but it is precarious ; and that it has been insufficient is proved by the necessity artists have been under, of establishing two benevolent institutions." I think that makes out the observation. Upon an average of the ten last years of the academy, the disposition of its funds for the relief of distress among its members amounts to 490*l.* per year ; that is, to the members of the academy. The sum allotted by the academy in donation to persons wholly unconnected with the academy, persons having no claim as members or relatives of members, but artists, many of whose names are hardly known to the academy, but by their recommendation and their distress, — the sum devoted to this purpose amounts to 460*l.* a year ; as large a sum, I believe, as any other society established in this country expends for similar purposes.

1926. Are those two sums of 490*l.* a year and 460*l.* a year, averages?—Averages for the last ten years. Previous to the last ten years a much larger proportion was given out of the academy than to those in it. The gross amount of sums expended in pensions to decayed members of the academy, since its establishment, is 11,106*l.* 5*s.* 9*d.*; ditto of sums expended in donations, during the same period, to distressed artists, not members of the academy, is 19,249*l.* 13*s.* 3*d.*; but the times have become worse, and the members in the academy have been more distressed, and consequently have had a much larger claim upon the funds which they have created.

1927. Would not the times be also worse for those who are out of the academy?—Yes, no doubt. Those two sums together amount to 950*l.*, appropriated by the Royal Academy to the distress of their brother artists, in and out of the academy. With respect to the formation of two other societies for benevolent purposes, the Committee will be surprised to learn that those two societies have been in a. great measure established by members of the Royal Academy. Conscious that the Royal Academy was not a mere charity fund, that it was appropriated to a higher purpose than the mere maintenance of the distressed, that it had for its objects the promotion of the arts, the cultivation of the public taste, and the improvement of our manufactures, — conscious that these were its legitimate objects, and that any money applied to other purposes was in some degree a departure from the original contract of the institution, the members of the academy did not conceive themselves warranted in devoting a larger portion of their funds, to merely benevolent purposes. They have therefore assisted and promoted the establishment of the two societies alluded to. One of those societies I will say, not only was originated by the members of the Royal Academy, but supported by them; and were it not for the zealous and liberal exertions of a member of the academy now present, it would have long since fallen to the ground, and the unfortunate objects relieved by it, would have lost the succour they have since obtained through its means. The gross sum subscribed by different members of the academy in aid of the two benevolent funds amounts to 2,202*l.* 18*s.*

1928. What sum is annually received from individuals at the exhibitions?—Sometimes 5,000*l.*; but the average is between 4,000*l.* and 5,000*l.* The Committee are desirous of knowing how the funds of the academy are employed. The funds of the academy are employed first, in maintaining the establishment, in remunerating the officers, the professors, visitors and servants, and for all the purposes which such an institution is found to require for the maintenance of the schools, and the expenses of the exhibition. To these objects, together with the pensions and donations to which I have already alluded, the funds of the academy are appropriated; but upon this subject the secretary or treasurer will be more competent to inform the Committee than I am, I only mean generally to state that there is no other application of the funds. It has been stated that the academy are pensioned, and that they are paid for what they do. The institution of the academy is perhaps one of the most disinterested that ever was known or established in any country. I will venture to say that there is no instance of an institution in which the funds are managed with more pure integrity, and where so little is appropriated even to the wants of those who are employed in the performance of its duties; the remuneration of the officers is upon the narrowest possible scale. The keeper of the academy, whose whole time is devoted to the duties of his office, and who has hardly leisure to pursue his profession, receives only 160*l.* a year.

1929. Mr. *Brotherton.*] Has he any apartment?—He has an apartment also in addition. The keeper of the academy is always selected from those artists who are conspicuous for the highest qualifications in the art.

1930. Who is the present keeper?—Mr. Hilton.

1931. Is he an historical painter?—Yes. The next officer in the academy is the secretary; his salary is 140*l.* a year, with an allowance for house, coals and candles. The next is librarian of the academy, whose salary is 100*l.* a year; the librarian has no other privileges. There is a treasurer also, who is not appointed by the academy, but by the King. It was originally considered that as his Majesty was the founder of the academy, and supported it in the first instance, it was proper that the officer who had the management of the funds should be under his Majesty's control and sanction. That arrangement has been continued by the academy ever since to the present day. The treasurer is Sir Robert Smirke, and his salary is 100*l*.

1932. *Chairman.*] Is the time of Sir Robert Smirke totally absorbed in his duties of treasurer, the same as the other officers?—No.

1933. Does he act by deputy?—No, he acts personally, and takes great interest, great care, pays great attention, and keeps the books in an order which would be creditable to any establishment.

1934. Has he no assistance?—None from the academy that I am aware of. The other expenses of the academy consist in the general meetings. The members attending are, I think, allowed 5*s*. each. That, I fancy, was originally intended as a means of discharging whatever expenses might be incurred in going or returning. I do not know that it can be considered as a very profitable remuneration to the members of the academy generally.

1935. Was it intended originally to insure their attendance?—So far as the bonus of 5*s*. can be expected to operate upon them. The council of the academy is a body which has the conduct of its business, consisting of eight members, chosen by rotation in the academy. At every meeting of the council there is 2*l*. 10*s*. distributed among the members who attend, which upon an average amounts to 5*s*. or 6*s*. also. The visitors of the academy are allowed a guinea a night for their attendance. They attend between two and three hours; they must attend two hours, but their attendance generally extends to more. There are the professors also of painting, architecture, perspective and sculpture. The professor of sculpture has been established recently. The academy were under the impression that it would be useful to sculpture in general if the principles of the art were more clearly developed by an able sculptor, than they are upon the general principles of the art, as applied to other branches. I therefore took the liberty, on a former occasion, of suggesting to the academy the propriety of establishing a professorship of sculpture. The academy, always zealous in the cause of the profession, and anxious to promote the welfare of the art, adopted that suggestion; and Mr. Flaxman, one of the ablest sculptors of the day, was appointed to that duty. Mr. Westmacott succeeded him, and now regularly delivers his lectures on sculpture. There is a lecturer on anatomy, who was appointed from the most eminent men of the profession of surgeons. Those lecturers have each 60*l.* for six lectures; that is, if they deliver six lectures; if they deliver no lecture, they have no remuneration.

1936. Mr. *Brotherton.*] Has the academy a dinner?— They have an annual dinner, and by the laws of the academy they are allowed to invite 140 persons. It has been stated in the evidence that the members of the academy have the power of issuing tickets, and the president particularly has been stated to have the power of distributing tickets for that dinner. I beg leave to say, that is totally unfounded. The members of the academy individually have no power whatever.

1937. *Chairman.*] Who has the power?—The dinner is regulated by the council of the academy for the time being.

1938. Are not the council themselves members of the academy?—They are, but I speak of them as individuals. There is not perhaps in Europe an example of an annual dinner so peculiarly constituted. The Committee will be surprised when they hear that the invitations are regulated by election. It is found upon an average that if 140 guests are invited, a sufficient number will attend to fill the room; and the proportion is generally so well preserved, that there is hardly an instance of any inconvenience being felt, either by a lesser or a greater number attending. I believe I have known one occasion on which the council of the academy were obliged to have a table spread in an adjoining apartment. The process of the invitation is this : there are a great many invitations which are called official; that is, invitations which the academy deem it proper to issue as a matter of course; first, to the Princes of the Royal Family, and any foreign princes or other foreigners of high rank to whom the academy desire to pay attention, such as the *corps diplomatique;* the principal ministers of state, and the heads of certain public bodies are also invited, and any celebrated characters, such as those distinguished in war, as the Duke of Wellington, Lords Nelson, St. Vincent, Hill, Anglesey, &c.; persons of that description are always invited.

1939. And of course any distinguished artists or literary men?—Yes; distinguished foreign artists have frequently been invited; and men of literary and scientific eminence, such as Byron, Walter Scott, Davy, Rogers, Moore, Babbage, and many others.

1940. You place them of course before the persons who are distinguished in war ?— We may place them so perhaps in our own estimation, but we pay some attention to the institutions of society, and are willing to assign them such stations as those institutions prescribe. As artists, perhaps, we should be more disposed to approve of celebrity in the pursuits of peace, than in those of war; but I leave that point to be settled by the State. The secretary reads the lists of guests invited the previous year; any vacancies are filled up, which may have occurred, from the death of celebrated individuals, or some other cause. The process of invitation is this : if the president (who has not the power incorrectly ascribed to him in the evidence) wishes to propose a guest, he writes the name of the individual on a slip of paper, to which he attaches his own signature; being warned that the individual proposed must be a person distinguished for exalted rank, conspicuous station or great talent, or an acknowledged patron of the arts.

1941. Does not the suggestion place talent and merit before rank and station ?— I am not aware of the exact collocation of the words; but I believe the Royal Academy, being a royal institution, conceive that it is their duty to act according to the acknowledged scale and gradation of precedence which is generally adopted in society.

1942. If a dinner is given for the arts, would it not seem more proper to invite the guests according to their eminence, as artists or persons connected with the arts, than simply according to their station ?— The dinner is given in order to interest the nobility of the country,— those persons who must necessarily be the promoters and employers of artists,— in the productions of the year. The president states the person, his name is read out by the secretary, the balloting-box is brought forward, and he is immediately either admitted or rejected, according as he is thought to answer the description which the laws of the academy point out; and so it proceeds : the next member in seniority is called upon to name his friend; and thus they go through the number of vacancies which by accident, or any other cause, remain on the list. This is the regular course of proceeding; and I do not believe there is an instance of any person being invited because he happened to be the private friend or relative of an academician.

1943. The persons who nominate the guests on these occasions invariably act on public motives ?— Yes; they scrupulously confine their invitations to those persons whom they think likely to reflect credit on the academy, and most likely to patronise and protect the arts. The academy are further charged in the evidence with electing good artists merely for their own purposes as members of a private institution, and not from any public motive. One gentleman is asked, " Are there not many eminent artists in the academy ?" He answers, " *Yes;* " but immediately correcting that unfortunate admission, he says, " a *few.*"

1944. Are there not many eminent artists out of it ? — I hope no member of the academy would say, " Yes ; a few."

1945. Would you say, " Yes, many ?"— I have no hesitation, for one, to say that there are many eminent artists out of the academy. I think the evidence will bear me out in stating, that one of the principal objections that have been made to the existence of the Royal Academy is its constant exertion to depress the arts, particularly in the higher department, and to discourage historical painting, and everything which tends to its promotion. Now, it is extraordinary that the very same evidence, or at least a portion of it, which contains this imputation, acknowledges that an attempt was made some years ago, by West, Flaxman and Opie, to bring forward a plan for a gallery of honour. (Flaxman was not a member of the academy at the period alluded to ; but this sort of mis-statement runs through the whole evidence.) Now it must be admitted that it was an extraordinary mode of discouraging the higher branches of art, for one of the ablest members of the academy, a portrait painter, Mr. Opie, to project a plan so well calculated for their promotion.

1946. Did they do this under the sanction of the academy, or under its express orders ?— Expressly under the sanction of the academy, who approved of every proposition that was made.

1947. Did the academy appoint them for the purpose ?— No, they appointed themselves ; but the academy approved of and promoted their views to the utmost of their power. Their zeal so far outstepped their discretion (for I am sorry to say it is not always discreet to make public exertions even for public objects), that they endeavoured to promote that object which it is said to be the interest of the academy, from the corrupt nature of the system, to obstruct and depreciate.

1948. How long is that since ?— About the end of

the last century.  I beg leave to state, that there has been
no subject more constantly before the members of the
Royal Academy, or that has more constantly influenced
their exertions than the consideration of the best means
of promoting the higher department of the arts.  There
has been nothing within the power of the academy —
nothing within their influence, either in-doors or out of
doors — nothing they could say — no remonstrance they
could offer — no representation which would reach the
ears of the great, that they have not zealously employed
for the purpose of raising the arts in this country, and
inducing the Government to step forward in their behalf.
In corroboration of this, I am sorry to be under the
necessity of introducing the name of so humble an
individual as he who addresses you; but what I conceive to be a duty to the academy obliges me to mention
it.  Subsequently to the plan of Mr. Opie, a plan was
brought forward by Mr. Flaxman and myself for the
purpose of procuring encouragement in the higher departments of the arts, strongly stating that although the
academy had used every exertion for the cultivation and
education of artists, they had not the means of patron-
ising them when educated; and that, therefore, something was required to be done by the state.  This plan
was so far advanced that an address was prepared,
which I had myself the honour of drawing up, to be
presented to the administration of that day.  It was
found, however, that as the academy was a Royal Institution under the immediate patronage and protection
of his Majesty, it would be disrespectful to him to present an address to his ministers; particularly, as before
the measure could be completed, it must have received
the royal sanction.  The academy, therefore, changed
their purpose, and an address to his Majesty was drawn
up by Mr. Flaxman.  Every artist who knows any
thing of the name or the talent of Flaxman, will be
aware of the extraordinary zeal which influences him on
all occasions in the cause of the arts.  In his address he
pointed out the absolute state of depression of the higher

department. The address was presented; I do not know what influence or what means were employed to counteract it, but it was productive of no result. This was in the time of George III. I mention the circumstance as affording another *extraordinary instance* of *the disposition of the academy* and *the tendency of the system* to obstruct the progress of elevated art. In addition to this, I would mention (and here again I am sorry to say I am under the necessity of introducing myself), that an exertion was made some years ago in the same cause; and it is curious, that a portrait painter should be the first person during a considerable number of years, and at a time when the patronage of the great was essential to him, to come forward and issue a rather strong remonstrance on the subject of the arts. I refer to a publication called " The Remonstrance of a Painter." I am sorry to appear egotistical in introducing this work on the present occasion, but the duty I owe to the academy requires it. I believe that no exertion on the part of those gentlemen who pique themselves so much on their love of the arts has been pointed out previous to that period. · Many gentlemen will bear me out in the assertion that an institution which has been acknowledged to produce considerable benefit to the arts, originated from that publication; I have the authority of some members of the institution to say, that in consequence of the effect which that little publication produced, they were led to exert themselves, and the British Institution was formed in consequence. I beg leave also to say, in illustration of the disposition and tendency of the Royal Academy to *depress* the arts and to *discourage* the higher department, that the only exertion which was at that time made on the subject, was made by a member of the Royal Academy, and by a portrait painter too, notwithstanding that *the evil spirit of portraiture* is represented as so unfavourable to the higher department of the arts. I allude to a letter which I had the honour of writing to the directors of the British Institution, and which originated in this way : I had the honour of being intimate with Sir Thomas Bernard, who was the founder of the British Institution, a man of the most respectable character, full of zeal for the arts, but who acknowledged that he had not much knowledge on the subject.   I was in the habit of communicating with him when that institution was founded.   I have in my possession documents to prove that a good many of the regulations concerning it had passed under my review.   In a conversation with him, the late Sir George Beaumont, and, I think, the present General Phipps, I took the liberty of pointing out what persons of their rank and consequence could effect for the arts, if they thought proper to follow up the proposed objects of that institution with the support which they deserved.   Sir Thomas Bernard and Sir George Beaumont said, " Why cannot you let us have some plan or project ?   Let us have your ideas on the subject ? "   I observed that it was not for me to dictate to men of their consequence and station.   They, however, urged it so strongly, that I sat down and wrote what I conceived might be a short letter, contained, perhaps, in a sheet of paper; but according to the old observation, which says, " let no man say he will write a *little* book," I found my letter, instead of being included in a sheet of paper, amounted to about 90 pages. I found that it was in vain to remonstrate, or to represent to those gentlemen that they could effect a great deal for the arts, if some practical plan was not brought forward, which they might be disposed to carry into execution.   I accordingly drew up a plan.   I am far from saying it was a wise plan ; I am far from insinuaing that many members of the profession, and gentlemen out of the profession, were not capable of drawing up a better plan than mine, but, such as it was, it was laid before the committee of directors of the British Institution, and in furtherance of the objects recommmended in it, they applied to the Government for 5000*l*. a year, which was the limit of the sum which I had proposed as necessary for its execution.   The application for this sum has been stated in evidence; but it would not answer the purpose of that evidence to mention who was the author of that plan; that it was produced by an academician and a portrait painter : that has not been mentioned in the evidence, and therefore it is that I supply it. As an additional illustration of the desire of the Royal Academy to promote the cultivation of the higher department of the arts, I would state that the late president of the Royal Academy, Sir Thomas Lawrence, a *portrait painter*, actually involved himself in great pecuniary embarrassment by the purchase of a large collection of drawings by the most celebrated masters. At the death of Sir Thomas Lawrence, so anxious were the members of the Royal Academy that this valuable collection should be preserved entire, and retained in this country, that, on the motion of a member, at that time professor of painting, and who is also a *portrait painter* (Mr. Phillips), the academy voted 1,000*l*. towards a subscription for the purchase of the collection in question, on the express condition that it should be placed in the British Museum, and rendered available for the general study of artists, and the improvement of the public taste. I think I have proved, by a series of circumstances, that the Royal Academy have omitted no opportunity of promoting the arts in the higher department.

1949. Mr. *Hope*.] Is not this a proof rather of the exertions of an individual than of the body?—Of course the latter circumstance respecting the British Institution is, but it shows the disposition of the members of the academy to promote the interests of the arts.

1950. Does it show more than the exertions of a single member of the academy?—No; but the exertions of that single member included with others, may be taken as inferring the disposition of the academy.

1951. Mr. *Pusey*.] Do you not consider that the Royal Academy, in electing you as their president, showed they did not disapprove of those exertions of yours on behalf of historical painting? — I should suppose so.  There are such a variety of imputations and aspersions thrown on the academy throughout the whole of the evidence, that it would detain the Committee much longer than they would be disposed to hear me, if it were possible to go through them all.  If there is anything of which the Committee think proper to call for an explanation, I shall be most happy to give them all the information in my power.

1952. *Chairman.*] Have you considered the effect of academies generally on the fine arts? — I have.

1953. What is the result of your investigation on that subject? — The result of my investigation is, that academies, on the whole, do good to the arts; though, as I said before, it is necessary to know the particular academy to which the Committee allude, its construction and its principles, before we can say whether that good result will be produced.  An academy, in the abstract, means only a school; and I think schools are good things.

1954. If I understand you right, you approve of academies when they are simply schools; you disapprove of them when they tend (as has often been attributed to academies) to introduce mannerism and other similar faults, in fact when they fetter the genius of the artist instead of confining themselves to giving instruction? — Academies, I conceive, are like all other institutions producing a mixed effect.  I know of no institution that has not its defects, and so have academies; but it is on the whole that you are to consider whether an academy is a good thing or a bad thing.

1955. Upon the whole, do you consider them bad or good? — Upon the whole I consider them good.  They operate in a variety of ways.  An academy is not to be considered solely with reference to the existing artists of the time; it is to be considered with reference to the whole institution of the arts of the country.  An academy exerts great influence on the public as well as on the artist; it is not confined to the mere office of education; it promotes the public taste by its exhibitions.

1956. You think it should be something more than a mere school, if I understand you right?—I do. I think an academy should be an institution which gives every opportunity to rising talent, which should be open to all ranks for admission; which should furnish every means of instruction that the nature of such an institution admits of; and I think it should be the means of conferring honour and dignity on the profession of the arts; for one of the effects of an academy is that it enables an ignorant and uncivilized population to acquire some respect for the arts; it gives them an idea that they are objects of some consequence, and not merely confined in their results to the display of a picture on a wall, or a statue in a square, but that they produce a serious influence on the whole scheme and structure of society. By the honours and distinctions which have been connected with the institution of academies, the public are taught to respect the arts and to know their value; for one of the evils of the arts is that their merits do not lie upon the surface.

1957. Mr. *Brotherton*.] Does the Royal Academy in your opinion answer the description you have given?—In my opinion, the Royal Academy, in every respect, answers the description I have given.

1958. *Chairman*.] Does it familiarize the mind of the population of the country with the arts?—So far as the academy has the power, it does.

1959. How does it do so?—The Royal Academy exists by the contributions of the public to their exhibitions.

1960. I understood you to state that it brought the arts home to the population of the country?—Of course.

1961. How is that performed?—The Royal Academy since its establishment has educated nearly 1,800 students. Those students have not all become Raphaels and Michael Angelos; they do not even all become artists. They receive the education which the academy affords them gratis; and if they have not talents for the higher class, they drop into humbler occupations; they spread through the country, and they are employed in the manufactures in various ways.

1962. Can you give us many instances of persons educated in the Royal Academy now employed in manufacturing districts in the country?—I am not sufficiently conversant with those districts to be able to do that. I have, however, no doubt of the fact. I conceive that it is a very reasonable conclusion.

1963. Are you aware that evidence has been given by manufacturers themselves of the extreme want of artists educated as you have described; and I believe that only one case has been mentioned of persons educated in the academy applying themselves to manufactures?—I have not seen that evidence. I speak merely with reference to what must be, I think, the conclusion of every reasoning mind upon the subject. For instance, there have been 1,800 students educated in the Royal Academy; what has become of those men? They have not all become artists.

1964. Is not the effect of some of these fostering bodies frequently to make persons artists who really have not that strong bias for art which would be desirable; and those persons having once become artists, will not condescend to pursue the lower branches of the art connected with manufactures, and that therefore they are neither useful in one way or the other? — That is an evil which must always attach to every scholastic institution; because if you give the means of instruction to an individual who is not calculated to avail himself of that instruction, who has neither talent nor sense to conduct himself under the opportunities of that instruction, the institution which gives it to him is not answerable for the consequences.

1965. Should not the institution see first whether the person is really capable of pursuing the calling which he is about to follow? — Allow me to state that that is utterly impracticable. There is nothing more constantly within the experience of the artist, than the fact that young men who appear to come forward with a flash of talent that dazzles their friends and those who know them,— who appear great geniuses, and who sometimes think themselves great geniuses,— are found, after a few years' application, so completely to retrograde, as to exhibit no merit whatever. The only test we can have in the academy with respect to the estimation of a student who applies for admission, is his industry. The student whom we find to apply himself diligently, however dull he may appear, however slow he may be in his operations, may brighten into a man of genius; but there have been so many instances of flashes of talent coming out at an early period, which have been extinguished in smoke, that there is nothing which the academy is so suspicious of, as that precocious exhibition of talent.

1966. Are you aware of the opinions of the celebrated director of the gallery of Berlin, Dr. Waagen, being unfavourable to academies generally, and only favourable to them in the light of being simply schools of instruction ?—I have the pleasure of being acquainted with Dr. Waagen, but I had not the slightest conception that that was his opinion.

1967. It has been stated by Dr. Waagen, " That the natural result of the academic institutions consequently was, that on comparing a number of specimens of the different schools, such as those in Paris, Petersburgh and other places, all exhibited a striking similarity of manner ; while in the earlier times, and the earlier method of teaching, the character of the schools of different nations, and that of each individual artist was entirely original and distinct. By this academic method which deadened the natural talent, it is sufficiently explained, why, out of so great a number of academic pupils, so few distinguished painters have arisen. The three most distinguished artists, which, for instance, Germany produced in the eighteenth century, namely,

Mengs, Denner, and Dietricy, owed their education, not to academies, but were educated after the old manner; so in our own days, the two most distinguished of the living artists of the German school, Cornelius and Overbeck, have risen to eminence in the most decided opposition to the academies; and the most eminent English artists, namely, Sir Joshua Reynolds, Barry, Wilson, and Flaxman did not receive their artistical education in an academy. That these men, when they were already celebrated artists, became members of academies, has nothing to do with the question, which is simply this, whether the academies have attained their objects as institutions of instruction. With this, another injurious effect of the academies has been connected, by means of the official distinctions which the academies enjoy through the influence of the State. They have attained a pre-eminence over all the artists that do not belong to the academies, which the academies watch over very jealously, and have thus introduced into the freedom of art an unsalutary degree of authority and interference. It occurs often that a very mediocre artist, of which every academy counts some few among its many members, stands much higher in the State as an academician than the most talented artist who does not belong to an academy. As the majority of mankind look more on authority than on genuine merit, it has occurred often that a moderate artist, being an academician, has found plenty of employment, while artists of considerable talent who do not belong to such an institution remain unemployed and unnoticed;" do you or do you not agree in that opinion?—I cannot agree generally with Dr. Waagen. He has stated some points on which academies may produce an injurious effect; but my opinion is that, upon the whole, an academy, like a university, being a place where education is to be received and communicated, is a useful institution. I think gentlemen do not sufficiently distinguish between *concomitants* and cause and effect. It does not at all follow that because

Homer and Hesiod were great poets and never went to school, that therefore schools are bad.

1968. I asked you if you were of opinion academies were only good in so far as they were schools, but that academies generally were productive of bad effects; do you agree with that opinion?—I say I agree in some points with Dr. Waagen, but not on the whole.

1969. Then you do not agree with him in the opinion, which pervades his evidence, that academies are only good if they are places of instruction, and not good in the usual sense in which the term "academy" is applied?— No, I do not. I think academies are good in the same way that universities are good, conferring honours and distinctions, furnishing the means of education, and stimulating the rising race to obtain those honours and distinctions.

1970. Are you aware of the opinion of Horace Vernet, a celebrated painter, upon academies?—No further than I find it quoted in the evidence.

1971. Are you aware that he suggested the suppression of the French Academy at Rome?—I am not.

1972. Are you aware that several celebrated German writers have recently been strongly arguing against academical institutions?—I am not.

1973. Do you know that Mons. Say, in a chapter devoted to them in his treatise on political economy, conceives they are hostile to the fine arts?—I have seen it quoted, and have no respect for the opinion of a political economist on the subject of the arts; for the principle of commerce and the principle of art are in direct opposition the one to the other.

1974. Are they or are they not sufficient judges of the effects of institutions as proved by facts?—I do not conceive it is possible to speak decisively upon a general question like this. I say generally, as far as I am acquainted with the works of persons who apply the principles of political economy to the fine arts, that they are entirely mistaken in their views. They adapt to

the arts a principle which belongs only to trade; and
the moment you make art a trade you destroy it.

1975. Does that observation apply to the evidence of
such a man as Dr. Waagen, who is not a political economist?—It is not my business to apply it; it is my
opinion.

1976. Is the Royal Academy self-elected?—They
elect their own members, subject to the sanction of the
King.

1977. Are those proceedings public or private?—
Private.

1978. To whom is the Royal Academy responsible?
—To the King.

1979. Do you consider that, in the important branch
of architecture, the Royal Academy has afforded all the
instruction necessary to advance the art of architecture
in this country?—I do not; but I consider that the
academy have exerted themselves very much to afford
that instruction; and as far as their means and the inconvenience of their locality would allow, they have
done everything in their power for the architecture of
the country.

1980. Have the students in the academy had the
opportunity of studying from the architectural casts belonging to the academy?—Not to the extent that could
be wished, because the rooms of the academy would
not admit of it. Some years ago the Royal Academy
purchased a celebrated collection of architectural casts
belonging to the late Sir Thomas Lawrence, for which
they gave 250*l.*; and feeling that their own apartments
allowed them no means of disposing of those casts
which would enable them to become available to the
students, it was agreed and determined by the academy
to present them to the British Museum, upon the express condition that the museum should so display
them as to render them available for the study of
artists.

1981. In the course of rotation does it ever happen
that landscape-painters are placed in the situation of

instructors to students in historical painting?—If the question means to refer to the appointment of the visitors, whose office it is to attend the school of the living model, then, I say, landscape painters have been sometimes appointed ; and many of those landscape painters are perfectly competent to the duty.

1982. Mr. *Hope.*] Are they appointed in rotation, or are they elected?—That is a mis-statement in the evidence, like many others. They are not appointed by rotation ; they are annually elected, and their appointment is laid before the King, and sanctioned by His Majesty, who reads the list with great attention before he affixes the royal signature.

1983. By the majority of the academicians?—Yes, at a regular assembly of the academy called for the purpose, on the 10th of December.

1984. *Chairman.*] Do you consider that the half of the National Gallery, which is now to be given up to the Royal Academy, is to be understood as belonging exclusively to the Royal Academy, or as held in trust for the benefit generally of the fine arts?—I consider the Royal Academy itself is a trust for the benefit of the fine arts, since they were appointed by the King for the purpose of cultivating and improving the arts of painting, sculpture, and architecture.

1985. The academy consists of 40 members?—Sixty; 40 academicians, and 20 associates; with six associate engravers.

1986. Do you conceive a body of that small number, and which is self-elected, is sufficiently comprehensive to watch over and represent the general interests of the arts in this country?—I do.

1987. You consider them quite sufficient?— Quite sufficient.

1988. Do you consider a self-elected body better suited to the character of a national institution than a body more comprehensive than the Royal Academy, and elected more on the representative system ?—I conceive that all the evils which resulted from the dissensions alluded to in the extracts which I have read to the Committee, would arise from the very nature of the constitution which you have just described; inasmuch as persons necessarily of little skill and less knowledge, not having the same means or the same opportunity of acquiring a perfect acquaintance with the claims or talents of artists, would be created their judges.

1989. Then you approve altogether, both of the present limited number of academicians, and the principle of self-election which exists in it?—I do. My reasons are these: when the academy was first formed, I apprehend it was not constituted solely with a view to the actual state of the arts at the time; and as a proof of that, it was with considerable difficulty that the number of the academy could be filled up; and it has been even stated in the evidence, that in consequence of the difficulty of finding artists competent to the situation, many persons were admitted members who could have no chance of being elected in the present day. When an institution like the academy is established, it is not founded merely with a view to the present state of the interests which it superintends, but with a prospective view to the state to which those interests may advance; and it has been ascertained by the practice of other nations, that 40 is a liberal allowance of distinguished persons in existence at one period, in any art or science. In France 40 members were considered sufficient to represent the literature of 30 millions of men; and I should be proud indeed of my profession if there could be found, at any one time, 40 artists of such eminence as to be secure of transmitting their names to posterity. I am anxious to explain my sentiments on this subject; because it may appear to some persons an invidious or unpopular opinion, that 40 members are fully sufficient to represent the interests of the art, and to furnish a stimulus to the rising race to obtain possession of the honours it confers. In addition to this, I would refer to the history of the arts from the establishment of the Royal Academy up to the present time, and it will be found that there is scarcely a single instance of any very eminent artist who was not a member of the Royal Academy, or who might not have become so if he had taken the proper means of obtaining that distinction. I consider this fact as affording a full proof of the competency of the number of 40 to include, *in due succession*, all the eminence of the profession.

1990. Is there not a law of the Royal Academy prohibiting any of its members belonging to any other institution or society of artists in London ?—Yes.

1991. Do you or not think that partakes of an exclusive character?—I think that the law is no longer necessary in the academy; and the academy have long ceased to act upon its spirit. The academy, as it was originally formed, and as it is now established, depends on the contributions of the public. It was therefore necessary to guard the institution sufficiently to prevent a decline of the funds, from a deficiency of the talent that was requisite to attract the public. It became essential, therefore, that the members of the academy should be restricted from contributing their exertions to any other establishment.

1992. Mr. *Hutt*.] You say that the spirit of the regulation has ceased to be acted upon ; has it not been acted upon in a very recent case ?—Only in this way, in the case of Mr. Cockerell. If Mr. Cockerell had become a member of the Society of British Architects, and had made no reference to the academy, I am convinced the academy would never have taken notice of the circumstance. But Mr. Cockerell, feeling a delicacy on the subject, applied to the council of the academy for advice on the occasion. The reply to Mr. Cockerell was simply this, that the council are an executive body ; they have nothing to do but to execute the laws of the institution, and conduct its affairs according to those laws. They could therefore only refer him to the laws of the academy, which they conceived to be conclusive on the subject, until they were removed.

1993. *Chairman*.] Do you think it quite fair that the

academy should have the arrangement of the pictures of artists who themselves do not belong to the academy ? —Most certainly ; it would be impossible it should be otherwise.

1994. Do you not think it would be fairer that those artists, an immense number of whose pictures are annually sent to the academy every year, should have persons more or less appointed by themselves, or in whose appointment they had some part, rather than by persons belonging to a separate society ?—The Royal Academy is formed with certain regulations, and all artists are invited to exhibit with the Royal Academy according to those regulations.

1995. I am only asking you as a fact, whether they do not arrange the pictures, and whether you think it perfectly fair that the Royal Academy should arrange the pictures of persons who have no authority in the appointment of the persons who arrange them ?—I think it perfectly fair. No person· is called upon to exhibit there who does not like to do so, and does not think it his interest to do so.

1996. Have they not the power, if they so chose, of putting their own pictures in the best places ?—Most certainly.

1997. Mr. *Hope*.] How do you reconcile that with your former statement, that the Royal Academy is a trust ? — A trust to be executed under the laws of the Royal Academy, as prescribed by their sovereign. This trust they execute according to those laws, and if they did not execute them according to those laws, they would betray the cause for which they were appointed, and would justly call down upon themselves the indignation of the King. Every institution must have regulations.

1998. I will just put these two propositions: the persons who arrange the pictures are members of the Royal Academy, and the persons whose pictures are sent to be arranged are most of them not members of the Royal Academy ; therefore the persons who are members of the Royal Academy have in this instance an advantage over the artists who are not members of the Royal Academy ?—Most certainly. It would be a most extraordinary institution if there were no advantages to be derived from it.

1999. Then there are not those advantages derived to the great body of artists which are derived to the academicians themselves from the institution of the academy? —Those advantages are extended to the whole art in succession.

2000. There are no peculiar advantages derived to the academy ?—No, there are no peculiar advantages that are not open to the whole profession to attain in succession.

2001. Have not the academicians the arrangement of the pictures ?—They have.

2002. Is not that an advantage ? — I say it is.

2003. Is not that an advantage which the other artist exhibitors have not ?—Most undoubtedly; and cannot have, under any institution; they neither have it at the academy, the British Institution, nor at the Suffolk-street Gallery.

2004. Mr. *Hope.*] Is not the possession of any peculiar advantage, by members of the academy, in some degree incompatible with the exercise of a trust for the benefit of art in general ?—No, quite the contrary; because if the members of the academy had no advantage from their station to reward them for the exertion which they make to obtain it, I cannot conceive who would go through the toil that such a process requires. The academy furnishes not only a school of instruction, but it is a means of reward; it is a means of distinction; it is a means of stimulating the rising talent of the time. The man who is made a royal academician, is pointed out, and justly so, for his talent to the public as a distinguished artist. The diploma tells him he is selected for particular pre-eminence and skill in his profession. There is no man who may not obtain that distinction, if he has talent enough, and disposition to go through the preliminary probation, which all professions require from the junior race, of competition.  It is a great mistake, which appears to run through the questions which have been asked me, to consider the academy as if they were an exclusive body of 40 or 60 individuals, distinct from what is called the great mass of the profession.  The academy, in all fair estimation, includes the whole of the profession; because it invites the whole profession to come forward and show they are capable and deserving of being raised to that rank, which other artists have obtained.

2005. Are not the same people in the situation of competitors and judges ?—Most certainly; that is unavoidable, unless you select some other tribunal; unless you call the merit of the time before a tribunal that is not composed of artists.  And, by-the-bye, that reminds me of a very curious statement in the evidence that has been given before this Committee, where a gentleman actually asserts that "a knowledge of the art is not necessary in order to judge of the disposal of a diploma," that the public are the proper judges and are perfectly competent to single out extraordinary talent the moment it appears.  If that were the case, the establishment of an academy would indeed be of no sort of consequence. If the public are competent to single out and discover talent themselves, it is in vain to talk of the distinction of R. A.; but it is because the public are ignorant, to an extraordinary degree, upon the subject of the arts; it is because even those who are considered as the enlightened class of society, who are even considered competent to legislate on all other points, are incompetent judges of the arts, that it is necessary that it should be reserved for artists to decide as to who are entitled to academic advantages.

2006. Mr. *Pusey.*] Are you of opinion, in the same way, that it is not considered advisable for the under-graduates in our universities to elect the professors, that in the same mode the exhibitors in general should not choose judges of art and directors of artistical education ?— Precisely; the principle would be ruinous and destructive to the interests of the art were it ever established; it would be calling in ignorance to decide upon ability.

2007. Mr. *Hope.*] When they become judges, do they cease to be competitors ?— No; but allow me to say that it is impossible you can call in one artist to decide on the work of another, without considering him in some sense as a competitor for public favour. That is a case arising from the nature of things, unless you adopt some other tribunal. If the general mass of artists, out of the academy, were called upon and allowed a voice in the distribution of their works, that office must be executed by some appointed individuals; those appointed individuals must be directors; they must be judges; they must be called upon to say whether this picture or that is fit for exhibition, or whether this deserves a prime place or not.

2008. Is that not a serious objection to an academy at all ?— I think not.

2009. I wish to know whether the academy might not be more extended so as to comprehend a greater number of the artists of this country, and who might be elected upon a more representative system than the one that exists at present. In putting that question, I do not mean that all students should be admitted to elect those who are to decide upon questions with reference to the arts, but I mean that the present system should be considerably enlarged; do you object to such an enlargement of the present system ?— I do; for this reason, that in proportion as you extend any distinction conferred, you destroy its value, and you prevent the same ambition from operating upon those who wish to obtain it.

2010. Do not the academicians consider it a year particularly favourable to them when they are members of the hanging committee ?— That depends on circumstances. In my experience, which I am sorry to say now extends to 36 years, I never knew a more disagreeable duty; I have known several persons refuse it; and nothing but the strongest representations could induce them to submit to the drudgery of hanging the pictures. Upon a very recent occasion, one of the persons appointed to hang the pictures remonstrated in the strongest manner, and actually declined to perform the office; and nothing but the representation of the council, that it was his duty, could induce him to undertake it. So far is it from being considered by members an office which they are proud or pleased to assume, that they look upon it as a charge of great delicacy, great difficulty, and as exposing them to many invidious reflections. The fact is, that any gentleman who is not acquainted with the nature of an exhibition of works of art, can hardly form an idea of the difficulty of arranging it. With respect to the exhibition of the academy, it is arranged in this way: those members who are not of the council, for the time being, are not admitted to the rooms during the process. It might be supposed that the members of the academy generally would have the power of dictating where their own pictures should be placed, and of coming in and disapproving of the situations allotted to them. This is not the case; they are, as I have said, excluded; and no member of the council is allowed to utter a word to any artist out of the academy, as to the situation in which his pictures are placed.

2011. Is it not usual for the members of the hanging committee to place their own pictures in the best situations? — By no means; there is an artist here present who is far from placing his own pictures in the best situation; he had the liberality to withdraw from the last exhibition two or three of his pictures, when he was arranger, in order to accommodate artists not members of the academy. Other members of the committee acted in the same liberal way, on the same occasion. Gentlemen who are appointed to this disagreeable office, so far from seizing the opportunity of thrusting themselves forward in all the conspicuous places, generally have the delicacy to send a smaller contribution than usual. Mr. Leslie has exhibited only one small picture this year, although he was an arranger. Many do not exhibit at all. Upon one occasion when I was an arranger, I would not exhibit, because I would not expose myself to the possible imputation of having placed my own pictures in a favourable situation.

2012. Did not Mr. Martin complain that his pictures were exhibited in a bad situation; that he could not have a fair exhibition ?—Mr. Martin is a gentleman for whom I have a very high respect, and I confess he is one of those artists whom I very seriously regret to find involved in the testimony which has been laid before you. Mr. Martin, at the age, I think, of twenty-two, 24 years ago, sent a picture to the exhibition, of which he very naturally had a very high opinion, and which I have no doubt merited that opinion; and because this picture was not placed precisely in the position he thought it deserved, he considered himself injured; he considered his interests materially affected; and, in fact, I believe he either then, or shortly afterwards, withdrew from the exhibitions of the academy. I am unwilling to say anything which may appear like passing judgment on the claims of my brother artists, and I should be sorry to be understood as impeaching the talent of any man, in or out of the academy; but with reference to Mr. Martin, I have no hesitation in saying that I have a high respect for his talents, and that I believe his talents are respected by the members of the Royal Academy. If he had gone on as a young man of talent might reasonably be expected to do, and, instead of taking offence, had said to himself: " I am young in the profession, and must undergo those trials and difficulties which all others have encountered, and to which the juniors in all pursuits must necessarily submit,"—if he had continued to exhibit, I am convinced Mr. Martin would long since have become a full member of the Royal Academy.

2013. I merely ask you whether he did not complain, as an artist sending his pictures to the Royal Academy, as not having been done justice to on more than one occasion?—He did, as many others have done. I have here an account of the pictures that have been excluded from the exhibition, and received as doubtful, during the last exhibition, amounting to 590; and I will venture to say that there is not one artist engaged in the production of those pictures who, at the time he was smarting under the disagreeable sensations occasioned by finding his works returned, would not have said that the Royal Academy was a most pernicious institution, and that he had been very badly treated in having supplied works to an academy the members of which were dull enough not to discover their merits.

2014. Are you aware that Mr. Martin exhibited his pictures in foreign countries?—I understand he did.

2015. And are you aware that he found, as he stated, that much greater fairness and equity were exhibited to him there, than in the Royal Academy in this country?—I am aware of it from the evidence; but I do not see what bearing that has on the conduct of the Royal Academy.

2016. Can you disprove that Mr. Martin's picture which he names was ill-placed, and that the other picture was injured?—The first statement is mere matter of opinion; I have no hesitation to assert that it was not ill-placed. I assert that it was placed in a good situation, where it could be seen; it was not placed in one of the best situations. Mr. Martin also states that an academician spilt varnish on his picture; I know nothing of this circumstance, and if any injury occurred to his picture, it must have been accidental.

2017. Have not the academicians who exhibit their pictures at the annual exhibition the privilege of previously varnishing and cleaning those pictures, which other artists who exhibit at the same time have not?—Yes.

2018. And re-touching?—Yes; that is one of the advantages possessed by the members.

2019. Do you consider that a fair advantage, and one of those privileges which, according to your previous evidence, you consider beneficial for the interests which the academy hold in trust for the public? — I consider it perfectly fair; it is one of the privileges, one of those advantages which the institution grants, and which are alluded to in the diploma of his Majesty; for if the Royal Academy did not confer upon its members any advantages which were not possessed by the whole art at large, I do not see what effect it would have as offering a stimulus to ambition, or a reward to ability.

2020. You think it a proper advantage? — I do. When I say so, however, I must add, that it is one of those advantages of which I myself have made very little use, and I should have no kind of objection to see it abolished. But the members of the academy are naturally interested in the appearance of the exhibition, because the prosperity of the institution depends on the impression which that exhibition makes on the public. If by allowing the members to varnish or re-touch their pictures, the academy can render the whole exhibition more worthy of attention, and more likely to be attractive, they are justified in so doing. They could have no objection to allow the same privilege to the artists at large if it were possible; but the number of exhibitors renders such an extension of it impracticable. Even now, it is with great difficulty that the members of the academy who exhibit can be accommodated. I have sometimes waited for days before I could get even to see whether a picture of mine wanted to be varnished, because there were scaffolds and ladders over and above it, and members at work upon them.

2021. Mr. *Hutt.*] Is it not done at all other exhibitions? — I do not know what may be the practice elsewhere; but other exhibitions have no reference to the academy.

2022. Have they not also this advantage, the right of hanging their own pictures first, consequently taking the best places? — No; a committee of three are appointed by the council to arrange the pictures; those three gentlemen place the pictures to the best of their judgment. If any member of the council, or if the president comes down to the academy, and thinks hatt he sees anything unfair, improper, or ill-suited to the situation, he expostulates with those who have the arrangement; and if he finds that he does not succeed in effecting an alteration, he brings the matter before the council, and the whole council decide whether the committee have arranged the works in question properly or not.

2023. *Chairman.*] But the persons who hang the pictures, and the persons who criticise the hanging of the pictures, and the persons who judge finally of the correct decision of the hanging committee, are all academicians?—To be sure, it is impossible it should be otherwise.

2024. Mr. *Hutt.*] In speaking of the Royal Academy and its advantages, is it your opinion that since the foundation of the Royal Academy the arts have made any marked improvement in this country?—A very decided improvement; it is admitted, even in the evidence, which I have commented upon this day, and by the best authority (for certainly Mr. Martin's talents entitle me to say that he is the best authority among those who have been examined), that such is the progress of the arts in this country, that even the malpractices, or perhaps I should say (for he does not make use of that precise term), the exertions of the academy cannot succeed in effectually opposing it.

2025. Hogarth, Reynolds and Gainsborough were all previous to the formation of the Royal Academy?—Yes; and if by that observation it is meant to infer that I think there are as great artists now as Reynolds, Hogarth, Gainsborough, &c., I have no hesitation in saying that, in my opinion, there are greater artists than Gainsborough now living. With respect to Reynolds, I am willing to admit that he has no equal in the present day. I ought, perhaps, to apologise for expressing an opinion which appears in some measure to limit the talents of my profession; but I believe even the vainest of my brother artists (and painters and poets are acknowledged to have a little dash of vanity in their composition) will confess that Reynolds was not only the greatest artist produced by this country, but the greatest artist that was ever produced by any country in his line ; that, however, does not alter my position that the arts have made great progress. Were I at liberty to mention the names of some eminent individuals, what a display could I make of the talents that exist around us, which do honour to the academy and their country!

2026. Where there was one good artist in the time of Reynolds, there are fifty at present ?—Yes.

2027. You think that is materially owing to the academy ?—Yes; I do not mean to say that in the natural progress of things a certain amount of encouragement would not have a tendency to advance the arts to a considerable extent ; but I am quite convinced that the influence of the Royal Academy, and the desire existing in artists to become members of such an institution, have stimulated them to greater exertions, and that the manner in which the academy brings about an intercourse between artists and those persons of exalted station, who must be looked upon as their natural patrons, operates materially to promote the best interests of the profession.  It has been asserted throughout the whole course of the evidence which has been given before this Committee respecting the academy, that it is a mere private institution, conducted for its own private purposes.  In fact, its members have been represented by some of the witnesses as so many selfish traders, sacrificing the best interests of the art to their own personal views.  Now I would just beg leave to ask what possible interest the members of the academy can have in effecting the discreditable objects imputed to them?  What personal interest has Sir David Wilkie, Sir Francis Chantrey, or any other eminent member of the academy, in sustaining an institution which is represented as so pernicious in its influence ?—If he were low-minded enough to be actuated by the sordid spirit ascribed to the members, he would say, "Let the academy be abolished ! It only tends to create and multiply artists. I am already in full possession of the public favour, and as well known as I desire to be ; I do not want to exhibit my works; the public are well acquainted with my *studio;* if they require anything from my talents, they will seek me there. The exhibition is a grievance ; the academy raises up rivals who may take the bread out of my mouth." That is what would be said by such men, if they were under the influence of the low, mean, and unworthy feelings ascribed to them. As an academician, I feel that I speak the sentiments of the whole body, when I assert, with pride, that no such vulgar, discreditable motives can be discovered in any part of their proceedings. As far as relates to the more distinguished members of the institution, it would be to their individual advantage that there should be no academy. They derive little benefit from an establishment which occupies, so unprofitably, their time and attention, and obliges them to enter into an annual competition with all the rising talent of their country.

2028. *Chairman.*] Do they contend upon an equality ? —Perfectly ; under any rational application of that term.

2029. Are not the preferences which have already been mentioned inconsistent with equality?—I have already admitted that some advantages belong to the members of the Royal Academy; but I will explain what I mean. I allude to an equality, not of *rights,* but of opportunities. It would be absurd indeed to suppose that all works, good, bad and indifferent, could be *equally* well placed or seen in an exhibition ; but, in illustration, I will give an instance. In the present exhibition there is a work of great ability, by an artist whose name I will mention, Mr. Knight; it occupies a considerable space. To make room for that picture, in, I may say, one of the best situations in the exhibition, several pictures of the members of the Royal Academy were obliged to be removed. That gentleman does not complain that he has not the opportunity of showing his talents. I could go through numerous other instances in which the best works of non-members have been brought forward in most conspicuous places, as in the case of Mrs. Carpenter, Messrs. Simpson, Charles Landseer, Roberts, Partridge, Morton and others,—all artists of great talent, for whom the academy have felt proud in showing their respect, by placing them in a favourable position before the public. They do not complain, because, perhaps, at an earlier period of their career, some work of theirs, which they conceived to be of considerable consequence, may not have been placed to their satisfaction in the exhibition. They do not on that account fall foul of the academy, and with a kind of parricidal spirit, assail and slander the institution to which they are indebted for the best part of their education.

2030. Has not the Royal Academy got one half of the National Gallery?—Not at present.

2031. It is to be devoted to it?—Yes.

2032. And to that one half of the National Gallery the public cannot go, unless they pay 1s.?—I consider that half that building is to be the National Gallery, and the other half the Royal Academy.

2033. That half of the National Gallery is not open to the nation?—Certainly not; the Royal Academy being dependent on the receipts from the exhibition must necessarily charge the same sum for admission as where they now are.

2034. Do you consider the new National Gallery is commensurate with the greatness of this nation?—Certainly not.

2035. Do you think it proper, then, if it is not itself large enough, half should be given away to another institution?—I did not say it was not large enough; I say, as a structure erected for the purpose of a national gallery and a royal academy, it is not so extensive as a great nation like this would be expected to produce;

but I say that that part of the structure which is to be devoted to the National Gallery, is fully ample for any pictures which the National Gallery have now to place in it; and not only fully ample to receive those pictures now, but will be fully ample for many years to come; and I trust, should the period arrive when it will be necessary for the convenience of the collection of the nation to extend its locality, that room and space sufficient will be found to accommodate it.

2036. Do you consider, if the national pictures were to be too numerous to be contained in the half of the National Gallery, which is now to be devoted to the purposes of the National Gallery, that the Royal Academy would then have to give up the half which they possess in consequence of the increased number of the national pictures to be exhibited?—I conceive that the Royal Academy is to be placed in the apartments connected with the National Gallery, precisely on the same footing as they are now in Somerset House. That is the foundation on which the academy has thought it prudent to remove; and that is the position in which I conceive them to stand.

2037. Do you consider that if the half of the building was not sufficient for a national gallery, the nation who paid for the whole of the building have a right to demand the other half now occupied by the Royal Academy or not?—I cannot pretend to say what right the nation possesses; all I can say is, that the Royal Academy has been placed in the apartments which they now occupy by the express donation and command of his Majesty; that when his Majesty was pleased to transfer the property of the King to the nation, a stipulation was made that the Royal Academy, as well as the Royal Society and the Society of Antiquaries, should have accommodation in the new building. The plans and the arrangement of the different apartments were all submitted to the Royal Academy for their approbation, and sanctioned by the president and council. The academy have enjoyed these apartments ever since, precisely on the same footing, by the favour of their Sovereign, and the honourable tenure of their integrity and utility; they are to be placed in their new position, on the same terms upon which they held the old; and I conceive that it would not be to the credit of any government to disturb or remove them.

2038. You do not mean to deny that the public have paid for the whole of the building of the National Gallery; may they not, therefore, when they think it right, place the Royal Academy in some other position, and if it is deemed for the national welfare, take the whole of the building? — The public paid for the erection of Somerset House; at the period of its erection, there was an express condition that a portion of it was to be devoted to the Royal Academy. The academy, understanding that it would be a convenience to the Government to obtain their apartments in Somerset House, and feeling that it would be an advantage to the arts of the country to have a more enlarged space for the display of their powers, proposed this change or rather exchange of residence. The academy give up that which they have a right to consider their own, and of which they have been in possession for upwards of half a century; and they receive in return the apartments in which they are to be now placed.

2039. If you consider it for the convenience of the Government and the academy that the Royal Academy might be shifted from Somerset House elsewhere, would it not be right that they should be moved from the projected situation in the National Gallery, if it were for the good of the nation? — I must observe, that that seems to be begging the question. I do not conceive that such a measure could be for the good of the nation.

2040. Might it or might it not be? — I do not think it possible that it could be.

2041. I will just put the case, that one half of the building was not sufficient for the national pictures, do you think the nation have or have not a right to call for the Royal Academy to give up the whole of the building for which the nation paid ?—It is not for me to decide as to what are the rights of the nation; therefore I give no opinion upon that subject; but I beg leave to observe, that I consider the Royal Academy a much more important institution to the nation than the National Gallery; I look upon it that a garden is of more consequence than a granary; and you may heap up a *hortus-siccus* of art without producing any of the salutary effects which never fail to result from the operations of such a school as the Royal Academy. It would, therefore, I conceive, be an injury to the nation, as well as to the Royal Academy, if they were to be removed, in order to make room for even the best works of the old masters.

2042. Has the school of perspective been conducted in an entirely unexceptionable manner by the Royal Academy?—The professor of perspective has not recently delivered his lectures; and as far as relates to the non-performance of his duty, the course of instruction in the schools must be confessed to be incomplete. The academy have forborne to press on the professor of perspective the execution of his duties, as strongly as they might perhaps be expected to do,—partly because many of the members consider the process of lecturing as ill-calculated to explain the science of perspective;—and partly from a delicacy which cannot perhaps be perfectly justified, but which arises from the respect they feel for one of the greatest artists of the age in which we live. He of course receives no emolument during the cessation of his lectures.

2117. *Chairman.*] Have you any observations, Mr.
Howard, to make on the evidence that has been given
before this Committee on the subject of the Royal
Academy?—I wish to lay before you a few mis-statements which I think I observed there. First, the Royal
Academy did not refuse a charter from George IV.,
for fear that it would make them responsible. A charter
was neither offered nor desired. Neither Banks nor
Flaxman was known to the public before the establishment of the Royal Academy, as asserted. They were
both students of that institution, and received their
education in it. Edmund Garvey did not resign his diploma, as asserted (qu. 909), but died a royal academician. It is not true that the Royal Academy tried to
"obstruct the British Gallery in every way." The
President, Mr. West, was consulted with other members
of the academy, by the eminent persons who formed
that institution, and rendered his willing assistance; he
was at first a member of that institution, but to avoid
the appearance of an invidious selection, artists were
afterwards excluded (qu. 980). It has been asserted
(qu. 983) that some academicians send their canvas to
the exhibition with only a head upon it, and wait to
finish it till they see what is hung beside it. It is hardly
necessary to say that this assertion is as incorrect as it
is absurd. It is not true that artists not members of
the academy have no opportunity of varnishing their
pictures. The president gives an order for that purpose
to every artist who applies before the exhibition opens
to the public, and in point of fact, many such orders are
issued. It is not true that the Royal Academy is a
monopoly, or an exclusive body, as asserted. The
honours and advantages of the academy are open to all
artists who have merit to deserve them, and who conform
to those just, necessary, and impartial conditions which

the laws of the academy prescribe for their attainment. It is not true, as asserted (qu. 750), that the laws and regulations of the Royal Academy were, from its first formation, made solely and exclusively for the interests of a private body; on the contrary, the laws and regulations of the Royal Academy were formed and have been sanctioned by the King for great public purposes, and, as his Majesty has declared, for the cultivation and improvement of the arts of painting, sculpture, and architecture, and to this great end have they been administered with undeviating zeal, integrity, and disinterestedness. It is not true, that the pictures of foreign artists are unfavourably hung in the exhibitions of the Royal Academy; on the contrary, the work of a foreign artist is often received with more favour than a work of a similar class of merit from a native artist. On one occasion in particular, the French Ambassador, the Duke de Laval Montmorency, expressed his acknowledgments to the President, Sir Martin Shee, for the liberal attention paid to a large work by Gerard, which was hung in one of the best places in the exhibition. The witness confessed he could not name an instance to support his assertion (qu. 756). It is not true, as asserted (qu. 678), that the money produced by the exhibition is in a great measure raised by the works of the artists not members of the Academy. It is not the number, but the excellence of the works exhibited which is the attraction of the public. The best exhibition can be expected to contain but few very fine works, and the largest mass of mediocrity may be considered to operate as a drawback upon the character of the exhibition. There is nothing for which the academy is so often censured by the public as for the impolicy of admitting such a quantity of indifferent material as tends to leave on the mind of the spectator an unfavourable impression of the whole display. Those artists who exhibit fine works are received into the academy, by twos and threes every year. In the course of forty years there have been but two years without one or more vacancies, and *six* have been known to occur in one year. It is not true that the members of the Royal Academy devote a larger portion of the funds to the necessities of their own body, than to those of artists not members. The gross sum expended in pensions to distressed members being 11,106*l.*, and the donations to artists not members and their families 19,249*l.* It is said that the academy has monoplised the patronage of the King and the nobility, but this is not, nor has it at any time been, the case. Some of those artists who have done great honour to the English school have been neglected by the patrons of art, and protected by the Academy; for instance, Wilson, Fuseli, Stothard; on the other hand, many who were not members have been much patronised by the public. Alderman Boydell employed Romney, R. West, M. Brown, &c. Stroehling, a foreigner, and not a member, was appointed historical painter to George IV. when he was Prince Regent. The late Sir George Beaumont and Lord de Tabley, did not limit their encouragement of art to the works of members of the academy. From its commencement to the present day it may with truth be said, that those who have enjoyed public favour possessed it in a considerable degree before they became members, and those who have not been so fortunate have received but little employment, in consequence of their becoming members. But, sir, I have no intention of going *seriatim* through all the mis-statements or the complaints regarding the Royal Academy which have been made before this Committee; some of the more important of these accusations have been refuted by Sir Martin Shee; many of them contradict each other; some are, surely, undeserving of reply; and it must be obvious, that almost all are connected with, if not founded on, personal disappointment. Looking generally at the evidence with which you have favoured me, it goes to charge the Royal Academy with inefficiency in the schools, partiality in the elections, a spirit of exclusion, a disregard of the interests of other artists, and a selfish administration of the funds. The facts

I purpose to lay before you in respect to these points will serve to place the academy in a more just light, I believe, than has been done in the evidence referred to.

2118. What is the present condition of the schools of the academy, and the terms upon which students are admitted ?— With respect to the schools of the Royal Academy, nothing can be less exclusive than the regulations relating to the admission of students. The members have not reserved to themselves the right of admitting even their own sons to schools which are wholly supported by themselves. Any one, native or foreigner, without distinction, who can produce a good drawing, and a testimonial from a respectable person of his good moral character, is equally admissible. Even the name of the individual applying is not known to the council until after he is admitted. He then remains a *probationer* for three months, during which time he is required to make a drawing in the academy, and if that be approved, that is, if it be as good as the drawing first laid before the council, he is regularly entered a student of the Royal Academy. In this manner are young artists admitted to a course of gratuitous instruction, which is to render them rivals to those who have fostered them, and perhaps ultimately to deprive their teachers of the patronage of the public, and their means of subsistence. The advantages afforded to the student in the Royal Academy are these : if *painting* be his pursuit, there are, the school of the antique, the school of the living model, and the school of painting, all of which are under the superintendence of the ablest masters in the country. The use of a good library of books on art, which is continually increasing by gifts and by purchase, a large collection of prints and some copies of the most celebrated pictures, the lectures of the professors, annual premiums for the best copies made in the painting-school, and a biennial premium for the best original historical painting. Although the privileges of a student generally continue for ten years only, upon application to the council he may be re-admitted from year to year: but if he obtain any premium in the course of the ten years, he then becomes a student for life. Any student obtaining the gold medal at the biennial distribution of prizes may become a candidate for a travelling studentship, which will further enable him to pursue his duties on the continent for three years on a pension from the academy. The student in *sculpture* has the benefit of the schools of design; an admirable collection of casts; the library, in which are engravings from all the galleries in Europe; the lectures and premiums; and, in rotation, the contingent advantage of being enabled to study on the continent for *three* years. The advantages afforded to the student in *architecture* are the schools of design, the lectures, the library, which contains all the valuable works on architecture which have been published here and on the continent, annual and biennial premiums, and the contingent advantage of the travelling studentship. The school is unfortunately deficient in architectural models, and merely because the Royal Academy has no room in which to place them. The society, notwithstanding, purchased a fine collection of architectural casts a few years since, which had belonged to Sir T. Lawrence, and presented them to the British Museum, where they are arranged in an excellent light, and are available to all the artists of the country. The students in *engraving* are in nowise distinguished from the others; the same advantages are open to all. An extensive collection of engravings from the earliest times, which is in the library, was purchased by the academy, at the price of 600 guineas, chiefly with a view to the information of this class of students. I think, then, it must appear that the Royal Academy has not been remiss in endeavouring to render their schools as efficient as circumstances have permitted.

2119. Is there a published catalogue of the prints and books belonging to the academy? — Not very recently; they are about to make another; but there is a printed catalogue up to a certain day.

2120. Is the catalogue as it stands accessible to students now ? — Yes.

2121. Are they allowed, under any circumstance, to take away books from the academy? — No ; not to take away any.

2122. Have you any statement to make to the Committee on the subject of the Royal Academy's exhibitions ? — That the rooms employed for this purpose are very unfavourable to the display of works of art is to be lamented, but it is not the fault of the academy, which has alway been striving to improve them. On the death of the late secretary, about twenty-six years since, they constructed a new exhibition-room, in the space occupied by his apartments: it is at other times used as the school of painting. The ante-room and the great room have also received every improvement that could be introduced without affecting the exterior of the building. The works of all artists, without exception, are admissible in the exhibition, under certain regulations, which are extensively circulated and may always be known. The council examines them without referring to the name of the author. All such works as are considered to have sufficient merit are immediately received, and all those which are thought too inferior are immediately rejected ; the want of merit or non-compliance with the regulations are the only grounds of exclusion. Such works as are of a more questionable character, are marked with a D. as doubtful. The arrangement, which is entrusted to a committee of the council, then begins. The received pictures are put up first, and then as many of the doubtful as the rooms will admit ; but it is impossible, till the greater part are hung up, to ascertain what number of works of such different sizes can be accommodated, and hence a necessity often occurs for excluding a work of acknowledged merit of large dimensions where smaller and doubtful works receive places which they little deserve. But the difficulties of a conscientious arrangement of the exhibition, I believe, can only be conceived by those who have made the experiment. It is hopeless, on these occasions, to satisfy all.

2123. To how many academicians is the admission or non-admission of pictures referred?—The president and council consist of nine, eight members and the president.

2124. Do the same members of the academy decide on the conditions of the first introduction and of the second; you state there is first a separation into those received and those rejected?—Those separations are made by the council; with respect to the arrangement of the pictures afterwards that is left to the committee of three or four, just as it may happen, liable to the superintendence of the council.

2124.* Does the hanging committee invariably consist of three or four members?—Generally; sometimes another is called in if expedition is necessary.

2125. What are the conditions on which exhibitors obtain the rank of an associate?—Any exhibitor may put down his name to become an associate.

2126. What is the average number of candidates for the honour?—At this time they have become very numerous; about from thirty-five to forty-five has been the average for some years past.

2127. Does the number increase?—Perhaps it does a little; not very particularly. The election of associates rests entirely with the academicians, of whom a general meeting is held at the close of the exhibition before the collection is broken up, for the purpose of particularly examining and discussing the merits of the works of those whose names have have been subscribed on the list. The election, if any be resolved on, does not take place until the first Monday in November, which gives time for a further consideration of the respective claims of the candidates; and it may be observed that it is particularly incumbent on the members to be very cautious in the election of an associate, as young artists do not always realise in the end the expectations they may have excited by one or two very promising efforts; and an associate has taken the first step towards becoming an academician. As vacancies occur, the academic body of forty is recruited from this class of members, which are chosen from the profession at large. The list of academicians elected in the last twenty-six years (consisting of thirty-three names, which I beg to read to you), will, I am convinced, require no comment, nor will anything more be necessary to show in what spirit the elections are conducted. This is a list of the members:—

ACADEMICIANS elected since 1810:

| | | |
|---|---|---|
| 1. A. W. Callcott. | 18. William Daniell. |
| 2. David Wilkie. | 19. R. R. Reinagle. |
| 3. James Ward. | 20. Jeffery Wyatville. |
| 4. Richard Westmacott. | 21. George Jones. |
| 5. Robert Smirke. | 22. W. Wilkins. |
| 6. William Theed. | 23. C. R. Leslie. |
| 7. George Dawe. | 24. W. Etty. |
| 8. Henry Raeburn. | 25. J. Constable. |
| 9. William Mulready. | 26. C. L. Eastlake. |
| 10. A. E. Chalon. | 27. E. Landseer. |
| 11. J. Jackson. | 28. H. P. Briggs. |
| 12. Francis Chantrey. | 29. G. S. Newton. |
| 13. William Hilton. | 30. C. Stanfield. |
| 14. Abraham Cooper. | 31. W. Allan. |
| 15. William Collins. | 32. J. Gibson, R. A. Ed. |
| 16. E. H. Baily. | 33. C. R. Cockerell, R. A. Ed. |
| 17. Richard Cook. | |

2128. Will you be so good as to state to the Committee the financial position of the Royal Academy, and lay before them any account of its receipts and disbursements that you have before you?—I have not with me any notes upon that particular point, but I will furnish them to the Committee, if it is required. I think upon an average the receipts of the exhibitions are about 5000*l*.

2129. What is the balance in hand held at this moment in the hands of the academy?—The academy have funded property which they have from time to time accumulated.

2130. What is the amount? — I believe about 47,000*l.*

2131. That is invested in Government funds?—Yes.

2132. In the names of trustees?—There are four trustees, three of them *ex officio*, the president, the secretary and the treasurer, and one who is elected.

2133. So that the funds of the institution progressively increase?—Twenty thousand pounds of that fund is allotted to establishing pensions to necessitous members and their widows.

2134. What is the cost to the academy of their annual festivity?—From 250*l.* to 300*l.*

2135. What are the payments made to the officers of the academy?—The president, whose situation entails upon him very considerable expenses, has no salary, nor any allowance beyond the other members. The keeper, for very arduous and important duties, receives but 160*l.* per annum, with apartments. The secretary's salary is 140*l.* per annum, with an allowance for apartments. The treasurer receives 100*l.* per annum.

2136. Is he a member of the academy?—Yes; the librarian for attending three times a week, 80*l.* per annum. I believe in Sir Martin Shee's evidence he has stated it to be 100*l.*; that is a mistake. The auditors and the inspector of works imported by any British artists for their own use, and which are in consequence allowed to pass the Custom-house duty free, have no allowance whatever. The visitors elected to serve in the painting school and in the life academy receive each one guinea for an attendance of more than two hours. The committee of arrangement have each two guineas for attending to that laborious and invidious duty the whole day. Each academician receives 5*s.* for attending a general meeting, of which there are annually from five to ten. A similar allowance is made to members attending the meetings of council; *i.e.*, the council, which consists of the president and eight members, coming in by rotation, are allowed 45s. to be divided at each meeting between the members present, which, if all attend, amounts to 5s. each.   I should have stated that the salaries of the professors are 60l. a year for delivering six lectures.

2137. Are not the office of professor and some other office sometimes accumulated in the same person ?—They have been in two instances; one is my own case.

2138. You are professor and secretary ?—Yes.

2139. Is that according to the rules ?—I conceive so.   It is not for me to defend the academy on that point; they were pleased to elect me, I believe, according to the rules.   The laws state " Pluralities are to be avoided as much as possible," which I apprehend means to say they are sometimes to be allowed.   I only knew of two instances; the other was that of Mr. Fuseli, who was professor of painting and keeper at the same time.

2140. Now, are Mr. Fuseli's case and yours the only cases in which you knew that two offices have been united in the person of the same gentleman ?—I believe formerly there was a case in which the office of librarian was given to Mr. W., who was afterwards keeper, which is in the gift of the king; but, on receiving that appointment, I believe he relinquished the first.   From what I have stated, it will appear that the greater number of the academicians derive from the funds of the academy an income of from 25s. to 50s. per annum; that of the president and council may sometimes amount to 8l. or 9l. each, if constant in their attendance throughout the year.   Instead of dividing their profits as other societies of artists do (and are quite justified in doing), the members of the Royal Academy have for above 60 years supported, without the smallest assistance from the nation, the only national school of art—a school in which all the best artists in the country have been reared, and which has given to the arts all the reputation and importance they possess.   This they have done (which in every other country is done by the government) at an expense of above 240,000l., and have distributed 30,000*l.* in charitable assistance to necessitous artists and their families. I am not aware of the existence of any other society of professional men equally disinterested and patriotic; and what I have stated will, I trust, show that it is well entitled to the gratitude of the arts and the country.

2141. Were you secretary to the academy in 1815? —Yes, I was.

2142. At that period was a communication made to the academy by the Government, on the subject of a national monument to celebrate the victory of Waterloo? —I am not perfectly clear as to that subject.

2143. Do you recollect any correspondence upon that subject?—If you think proper to ascertain that, I shall have no objection to wait upon you some other time and give you all the particulars. I am not prepared at present to say what the exact state of the case was. I know this generally, the academicians did every thing in their power, but the design appeared to have been relinquished, or else it was not left to the academy to offer any plan or any regular suggestions on the subject.

2144. Is it not in your recollection, that the academicians were invited to communicate to the Government a plan for a national monument?—It is not, indeed. I know Mr. West, the president, drew up a scheme of his own, which he supplied to the committee of taste; but I believe it was entirely left to the committee of taste.

2145. Since you have been secretary to the Royal Academy, have the laws and regulations undergone any considerable change?—There have been some improvements made, and some little alterations; there are no substantial alterations.

2146. Do you think at the present time the rules and regulations are susceptible of any important improvement?—I imagine that no society can be said to be perfect.

2147. The Committee would be glad to hear from

you any suggestion for the improvement of the laws and regulations of the society, to which they seem susceptible from your experience?—If I were aware that the academy was susceptible of any improvement on those points, I should of course lay it before the council.

2148. Do you think that the permanent number of academicians, on the whole, was a judicious arrangement?—I do not think if the number were extended there would be the same stimulus to young men to exert themselves.

2149. Must not the number of gentlemen voted to receive the honours of the Royal Academy depend very much on the number of artists, and that number fluctuating very considerably?—I conceive in a case of this kind where there are distinctions made, that unless those distinctions are applied to artists of very considerable merit they are no distinctions at all, they can have no good effect upon the art at large; and I do not think a tany time there has existed in any country above forty men of first-rate talent.

2150. What proportion of the proceeds of the exhibition are applied to the artists who are exhibitors, and not members of the Academy?—There is no division of the receipts of the exhibition between members or artists of any kind.

2151. The whole of the receipts go to the Royal Academy?—The whole of the fund goes immediately for the general purposes of the establishment, and for charities.

2152. It has been stated, are you aware of the fact, that a letter was written by the committee of taste (appointed by Lord Castlereagh) to the academy, respecting the monument of Waterloo, to which no reply was given? — No, I am persuaded that could never have been the case, but I do not remember the particulars.

2153. You mentioned the librarian having attended three days a week, does that mean that he attends three whole days?—No, three different sittings; Monday in the morning, and again in the evening, and Thursday in the evening.

2154. And publicity is given to the hours of his attendance ?—Of course each student has a copy of the laws and regulations of the Academy, and that is one of them.

2155. It was stated by Sir M. Shee that the law excluding academicians belonging to other societies has not been acted upon, though it is still existing in the regulations ?—That is so.

2156. Is there any instance in which an artist belonging to another society in London has been elected? —I believe not.

2157. Did not Mr. Stanfield resign his situation as connected with the Suffolk Street Gallery for the purpose of obtaining a Somerset House diploma ?—He offered himself as an exhibitor in the academy, became first an associate, and then an academician.

2158. In order to offer himself as a candidate, did he not consider it a necessary preliminary to dissociate himself from the society with which he had been previously connected?—It may be so.

2159. In the notice that you give to exhibitors, is it not there stated that in order to fit themselves for candidateship it is necessary they should not belong to any other society ?—I believe it does remain on the superscription of the annual list, that any artist may become a candidate who is twenty-four years of age, not an apprentice, nor a member of any other society of artists resident in London.

2160. Are the Committee to understand it is your belief that an artist belonging to another society would not, at the present moment, be considered incompetent to be elected ?—I should think it would, because I have no instance where it has been acted upon.

2161. Do you coincide with the opinions of Sir Martin Shee, that no relaxation should be made in the peculiar privileges enjoyed by the members of the academy as to retouching and varnishing of the pictures, the monopoly of the private view, the dinner and other privileges enjoyed by the academy? — If you ask me that question generally, I do not think any relaxation could be made. With respect to the first, varnishing, it is physically impossible to admit five or six hundred exhibitors for that purpose.

2162. Is it your opinion that the principle of self-election is on the whole the best, and that no reference should be made to any other constituent body? — I do not conceive it would be improved by any reference to any other. There are forty artists who may be called the *élite* of the profession. They must be as good judges of the merits of the candidates as any other persons, and they are as little likely, at least, to be partial in their judgment, because it is shown by the evidence that it is the interest of the academy to elect the best artists.

2163. Are the opinions you have been expressing the opinions of your colleagues? — I cannot pretend to say what is the opinion of my colleagues.

2164. Has this been under discussion among the members of the academy? — There may be various opinions among a body of forty men; it is impossible to say what their opinions may be.

2165. Do you think that any inconvenience has been found at the Society of British Artists and at the exhibitions of the British Gallery in allowing exhibitors to . varnish pictures before exhibition? — I do not consider them to be at all under similar circumstances or in the same position as the Royal Academy. The rooms are so much higher and the works so much more numerous, it is with difficulty that forty-five members can accomplish it; and how they would be able to do it, if they were to let in 600, I cannot conceive.

2166. But the extent (if it is well adapted to the exhibition of pictures in the Royal Academy) must be the same as in other places where pictures are exhibited, would it be more inconvenient than other places? — Not only the inconvenience would be greater, but I think it would be physically impossible to accomplish it.

2167. But how would it be accomplished elsewhere ? — Unless a much greater length of time could be afforded to it than is possible. The object of the academy is to complete the arrangement of the exhibition as quickly as possible, because during the time of exhibition and during these arrangements the schools are necessarily shut up.

2168. Still that facility is granted at other exhibitions ? — They have no schools to support, time is not so great an object to them, and their conveniences are much greater in proportion to the number of works they exhibit.

## (C.)

*Extract from the Report of the Select Committee of the House of Commons on Arts and Principles of Design, Session* 1836.

FROM the subject of Exhibitions, the Committee have naturally been led to inquire into the constitution and management of those institutions which have prevailed in Europe for the last two hundred years, under the name of ACADEMIES. Academies appear to have been originally designed to prevent or to retard the supposed decline of elevated art. Political economists have denied the advantages of such institutions, and artists themselves, of later years, have more than doubted them. It appears, on the evidence of some of the witnesses, that M. H. Vernet, the celebrated Director of the French Academy at Rome, has recommended the suppression of that establishment. It is maintained by Dr. Waagen, that what is called the academic system gives an artificial elevation to mediocrity, and that the restriction of academic rules prevents the artist from catching the feeling and spirit of the great master whom he studies; like the regulations of those literary institutions of former times which set more value on scanning the metres of the ancients, than on transfusing into the mind the thoughts and feelings of the poet. Many of the witnesses concur with Dr. Waagen in the opinion that academies ought properly to be schools only; wherein such instruction may be given as is not attainable in the *studio* of a private master. When academies go beyond this, their proper province, they degenerate into mannerism and fetter genius; and when they assume too exclusive and oligarchical a character, they damp the moral independence of the artist, and narrow the proper basis of all intellectual excellence — mental freedom.

It seems probable that the principle of free competition in art (as in commerce) will ultimately triumph over all artificial institutions. Governments may, at some future period, content themselves with holding out prizes or commissions to the different but co-equal societies of artists, and refuse the dangerous gift of pre-eminence to any. It is more than probable that our ROYAL ACADEMY is indebted for the distinguished names which adorn its annals to the necessity of competing, as a private society, with other institutions, rather than to the extraneous distinctions and privileges with which it is decorated, and, perhaps, encumbered. As it stands, it is not a public national institution, like the French Academy, since it lives by exhibition, and takes money at the door. Yet it possesses many of the privileges of a public body, without bearing the direct burthen of public responsibility.

The artists examined by the Committee frequently concur in admitting the eminence of the present and of former members of the Royal Academy; but they complain of the exclusive nature of its rules, of the limitation of its numbers, and of the principle of self-election which pervades it. Among its exclusive rules has been named one which prohibits the members of the academy from belonging to any other institution of artists in London; and another which restricts a candidate for academic honours from exhibiting beyond the walls of the academy. It is true that the inexpediency of the former of these regulations is acknowledged on the part of the academy; but it still exists, and has recently been carried into execution. The private and irresponsible nature of the proceedings of the academy; the privilege enjoyed by the academicians of exclusively consorting with the patrons of art at the annual dinner; their prerogative of retouching their own works previous to exhibition (a power denied to the other artists who exhibit), and the monopoly of the best places by the pictures of the academicians, have been adverted to by various witnesses. Of the privileges above named some have been denied to be exclusive; others have been claimed by the academy as essential to the nature of such an institution.

It is certainly to be lamented that artists so distinguished as Mr. Martin and Mr. Haydon should complain of the treatment of their works within the walls of the academy; and particularly that Mr. Martin should declare that his paintings have found that encouragement in the foreign exhibitions of France and Belgium, which they have been denied at home.

Some irregularities have been noticed in the delivery of lectures at the academy. The neglect of Architecture has been complained of by several artists *extra muros*; and the inadequacy of the instruction given in that important branch of art, is admitted by the President himself.

The exclusion of Engravers from the highest rank in the academy has often called forth the animadversions of foreign artists. In the French Academy engravers are admitted into the highest class of members. So are they in Milan, Venice, Florence, and in Rome. In England their rise is limited to the class of Associates. This mark of depreciation drove such eminent men as Woollett, Strange, and Sharpe, far from the academy. Such a distinction seems the more extraordinary, because British engraving has attained a high degree of excellence. Foreigners send pupils hither for education; and the works of British engravers are diffused and admired throughout the Continent.

The remarks of foreign critics have frequently been elicited by the unusual predominance of portraits over other works of art in our annual academic exhibitions. It appears (from the Returns appended to the Report) that fully half of the paintings annually exhibited have been portraits, which often inconsistently obtrude themselves before ideal and historical compositions. In the arrangement of a national exhibition a more appropriate classification ought surely to be adopted.

The plan annexed to the evidence of Mr. Wilkins will explain that fully one-half of the new National Gallery has been given up to the Royal Academy. Against this apportionment of the national building, a large number of artists have remonstrated; and two bodies of painters have petitioned the House of Commons on the subject. They declare their inability to compete with an institution so favoured at the public expense. It is true that the academy may be compelled to quit the National Gallery whenever public convenience requires their removal; but the great body of non-academic artists contend that a society, which possesses not only this but many other public advantages, ought to be responsible to those who contribute to their exhibitions, and whose interests they are supposed to represent. A strong feeling pervades the artists generally on this subject. They are uneasy under the ambiguous, half-public, half-private, character of the academy; and they suggest that it should either stand in the simple position of a private institution, or, if it really represents the artists of Great Britain, that it should be responsible to, and eligible by them.

THE END.

LONDON
PRINTED BY SPOTTISWOODE AND CO.
NEW-STREET SQUARE.

www.ingramcontent.com/pod-product-compliance
Lightning Source LLC
Chambersburg PA
CBHW032139110726
47902CB00003B/620